Praise for

LIBERTY STREET

"Heather Marshall's latest is dynamite. Two stories twine together with skill and suspense—a courageous young female journalist going undercover at a 1960s women's prison to uncover rumours of abuse; a dogged 1990s detective bruised from her own emotional wounds—creating a tale both timely and explosive. *Liberty Street* will linger long in the memory."
—Kate Quinn, *New York Times* bestselling author of *The Briar Club*

"*Liberty Street* confronts us with a past far closer than we'd like to admit. Heather Marshall writes with clarity and urgency about women's autonomy, reminding us that the fight for respect and choice is far from finished. A story that unsettles, ignites, and refuses to let you look away—a fierce reclaiming of women's voices once silenced."
—Ellen Keith, bestselling author of *The Dutch Orphan*

"Heather Marshall writes with such heart, precision, and power. In *Liberty Street*, she brings hidden truths and forgotten women vividly to life, weaving a story that is both beautifully told and urgently needed. Evocative, important, and gripping."
—Marissa Stapley, *New York Times* bestselling author of *Lucky*

"*Liberty Street* is the story of resistance we need right now: a brilliantly heartfelt novel of two remarkable women—separated by decades yet linked by a passion for justice—who take on patriarchal corruption. You will be on the edge of your seat as this story comes to its unforgettable conclusion."
—Maia Caron, bestselling author of *The Last Secret*

"In her latest triumph, Heather Marshall exposes Toronto's shadowed past and, with haunting grace, gives voice to the women history tried to forget. Visceral and provocative, *Liberty Street* ensures no woman is left behind."

—Karma Brown, #1 bestselling author of *Recipe for a Perfect Wife*

"*Liberty Street* is a beautiful, harrowing novel with something for every reader: mystery, action, tenderness, a righteous fury at historical injustice. Heather Marshall is a brilliant archeologist unearthing women's lost history."

—Elizabeth Renzetti, author of *What She Said*

"Utterly captivating. I found myself sneaking extra pages in whenever I could. Heather Marshall writes with urgency and passion about the injustices placed on women's lives and weaves it into a story that will latch onto your mind, with characters so real you'll want to reach through the pages to shout at them, but also to ache and cry and root for them. It's said often, and maybe too easily, but in this case I believe it to be true: this book is a triumph. Heather Marshall is a dedicated champion of women's rights, revealing the hard truths behind untold women's stories."

—Charlene Carr, author of *Hold My Girl*

Praise for
The Secret History of Audrey James

"Heather Marshall firmly establishes both her commitment to sharing women's untold stories and the intricate power of her craft. Gripping, haunting, and inspiring, *The Secret History of Audrey James* is historical fiction full of meaning and heart, and an unforgettable account of the profound impact of sacrifice and survival across generations."

—Natalie Jenner, internationally bestselling author of *Every Time We Say Goodbye*

"*The Secret History of Audrey James* is a poignant tale of friendship, the unbreakable bonds of family—both blood and chosen—and the irrefutable strength of women. The novel is full of heart, pluck, and hope, and Marshall is a writer who deeply understands what moves readers. This is storytelling at its best."

—Karma Brown, #1 bestselling author of *Recipe for a Perfect Wife*

"Heather Marshall's range is astonishing! With compassionate insight, deft characterization, and a staggering depth of historical research, *The Secret History of Audrey James* is a moving written symphony. Not only a harrowing snapshot of history but a portrait of women driven by talent and ambition striking a stark contrast against the travesties of war. Readers of Kristin Harmel and Pam Jenoff will be dazzled. As readable as it is intelligent, *The Secret History of Audrey James* is a splendour of a sophomore novel."

—Rachel McMillan, author of *The Mozart Code* and *The Liberty Scarf*

"*The Secret History of Audrey James* is a gripping read right to the end . . . a study in the enduring power of women's friendships and their resourcefulness at a time when Hitler had relegated women to 'Kinder, Küche, Kirche'—children, kitchen, and church."

—Roberta Rich, #1 bestselling author of *The Midwife of Venice* and *The Jazz Club Spy*

Praise for
Looking for Jane

"*Looking for Jane* is an emotionally charged, meticulously researched, and deftly plotted book. . . . It's a masterful debut about motherhood and choices, the things we keep, the things we lose, and the things that stay with us and change us at our core forever. . . . A searing, important, beautifully written novel about the choices we all make and where they lead us—as well as a wise and timely reminder of the difficult road women had to walk not so long ago."

—Kristin Harmel, *New York Times* bestselling author of *The Forest of Vanishing Stars*

"*Looking for Jane* is a beautifully written meditation on the lengths mothers will go to for their children as well as an eye-opening history of women. It is an ode to the doctors, nurses, and volunteers who fought for the rights of future generations to have a say over their bodies. This gracefully entwined story of three generations of women, societal mores, and mothers and daughters stole my heart."

—Janet Skeslien Charles, *New York Times* bestselling author of *The Paris Library*

"Heather Marshall shines a spotlight on the unsettling truths and heartbreaking realities faced by women of every generation. *Looking for Jane* is a compelling, courageous must-read about motherhood and choice."

—Genevieve Graham, *USA Today* and #1 bestselling author of *The Forgotten Home Child*

"Marshall's masterful novel succeeds on multiple fronts: as a poignant celebration of motherhood, and a devastating reminder of the consequences of denying women the right to choose. Fierce, beautifully written, and unforgettable."

—Fiona Davis, *New York Times* bestselling author of *The Magnolia Palace*

LIBERTY STREET

ALSO BY HEATHER MARSHALL

Looking for Jane

The Secret History of Audrey James

LIBERTY STREET

A novel

HEATHER MARSHALL

DOUBLEDAY CANADA

PUBLISHED IN 2026 BY DOUBLEDAY CANADA

Copyright © 2026 Heather Marshall Inc.
Discussion questions copyright © Penguin Random House Canada

All rights reserved. No part of this book may be reproduced, scanned, transmitted, or distributed in any form or by any electronic or mechanical means, including information storage and retrieval systems, without permission in writing from the publisher, except by a reviewer, who may quote brief passages in a review. No part of this book may be used or reproduced in any manner for the purpose of training artificial intelligence technologies or systems.

Published in the United States of America by Ballantine Books, an imprint of Random House, a division of Penguin Random House LLC, New York.

Doubleday Canada, an imprint of Penguin Random House Canada Limited,
320 Front Street West, Suite 1400,
Toronto, Ontario, M5V 3B6, Canada
penguinrandomhouse.ca

Doubleday Canada and colophon are registered trademarks of
Penguin Random House LLC.

The authorized representative in the EU for product safety and compliance is Penguin Random House Ireland, Morrison Chambers, 32 Nassau Street, Dublin, D02 YH68, Ireland, https://eu-contact.penguin.ie

This book is a work of fiction. Names, characters, places, and incidents are products of the author's imagination or are used fictitiously. Any resemblance to actual events or locales or persons, living or dead, is entirely coincidental.

Library and Archives Canada Cataloguing in Publication data is available upon request.

Original Trade Paperback ISBN 978-0-385-70051-1
Indigo Exclusive Edition ISBN 978-0-385-70412-0
Ebook ISBN 978-0-385-70052-8

Cover and text design by Kelly Hill
Cover images: (woman) Matthieu Spohn / Getty; (blue filter) Uuganbayar, (broken glass) pjhpix, (building) tomeyk, (windows) Anastasiia / Adobe Stock
Map by Andrea Nairn
Typeset by Erin Cooper

Printed in Canada

2 4 6 8 9 7 5 3 1

This one's for Mum and Dad:

Proud parents to an incorrigible feminist.

A NOTE FROM THE AUTHOR

This story takes place in an abusive prison and psychiatric setting in 1961. As such, anachronistic language and terminology are used, primarily within dialogue between characters. My intent in doing so is twofold: First, for the sake of (however regrettable) historical accuracy, and second, to demonstrate how our culture has evolved over the past several decades regarding how we conceptualize, understand, and speak about topics like mental health, prostitution, criminality, sexuality, and identity.

Mercer Women's Prison

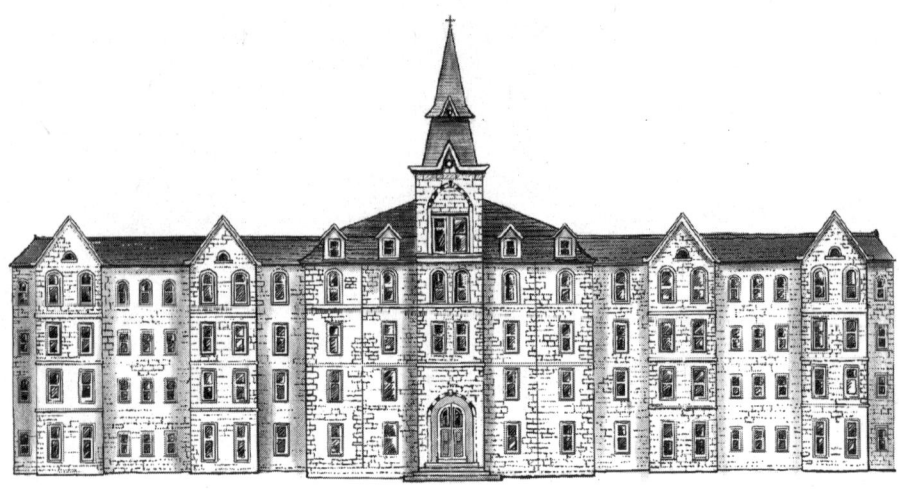

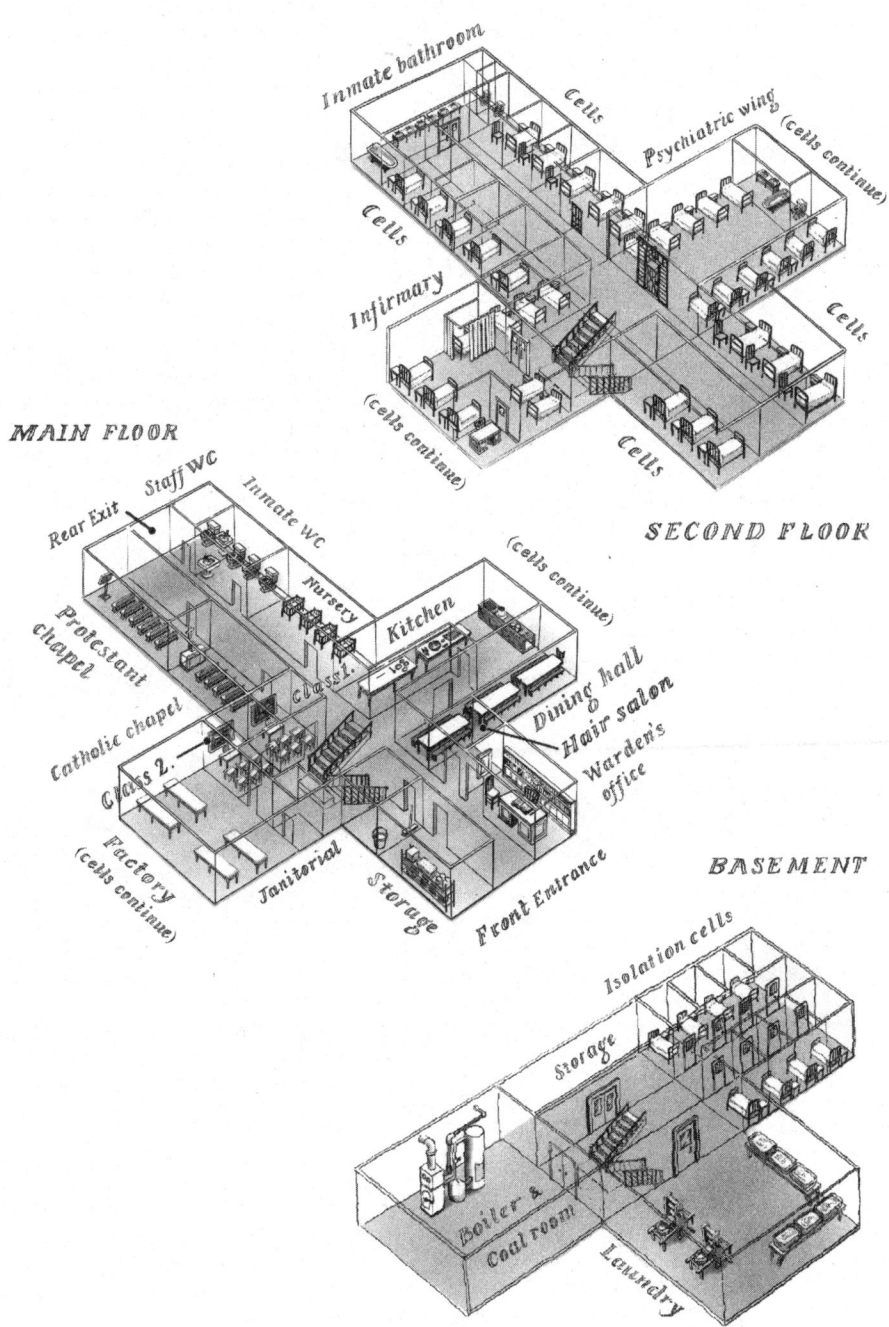

PROLOGUE

Huron County, Ontario—August, 1987

Several people had already asked her what it was like to live across the street from a cemetery.

Just three weeks prior, the woman had moved into the wartime-era home opposite the church. It had age-speckled white siding and black shutters in desperate need of a fresh coat of paint. It was dark inside, and cool, thanks to the shade of several large oak trees that dotted the lot. They towered so high that the house sometimes felt like a dwarf surrounded by giants.

It was the large front porch that first caught the woman's eye when her realtor showed her the photo. It ran the entire length of the front of the house with a wooden railing across, and it was several feet deep. It was also screened-in, which offered the opportunity for three-season enjoyment without the nuisance of mosquitoes. The pests were prevalent in the area, and sure to be drawn to the property by the ample shade provided overhead. The street itself was quiet; just a two-lane road that began at Highway 4 and stretched west all the way to the lake. Millgate was a small town, hardly more than a neighbourhood, and most of it surrounded the cemetery: a silent green core that had begun as a lone rural church cemetery but around which the town had eventually sprouted, like spring shoots encircling a tree.

It was on a muggy night in mid-August that the woman observed the curious visitor in the graveyard. She had stepped out onto the porch a little after nine in the evening to enjoy a cup of tea with her ginger tabby cat nestled in her lap. She reclined into one of the high-backed wicker chairs, releasing a sigh of relief as she felt the pressure in her bad hip sink into the cushion. The porch light was off to prevent the mosquitoes from congregating like church parishioners around the hole in the screen that needed mending. Unless she was reading, she preferred it off, anyway, as it allowed for a clearer view of the street and the cemetery beyond.

She never saw night visitors, though.

The first weekend after she moved in, she'd witnessed a burial. The mourners had filed out of the church, dignified and sombre, and made their way across the street to the gravesite. Their sweaty-browed heads inclined under black hats, overheating in the summer sun. The woman had watched discreetly as the group surrounded the grave. She saw the reverend gesticulating with one hand whilst holding a copy of the Bible in the other. Eyes were dabbed with tissue, elbows patted in sympathy.

Ashes to ashes, dust to dust.

She had seen mourners come in ones and twos as well, visiting older graves. They often arrived on Sunday afternoons, which seemed like the most popular time to remember lost loved ones at the Millgate Cemetery. It made the woman think that she should probably get around to visiting her own parents' graves from time to time. She had been remiss in that, and, as the only child, held sole responsibility for the maintenance of their gravesites.

But the odd thing about the man in the cemetery tonight—for she took it to be a man, given the size and shape of the silhouette—wasn't that he was alone, or even that he had chosen such an unorthodox hour for his vigil; it was that he wasn't standing in front of—or, for that matter, remotely nearby—a headstone. He stood before one of the largest trees in the cemetery, a good twenty feet away from the closest row of stones, the outline of his body illuminated in the weak moonlight that was just starting to shimmer through the dusk. The pale glow reflected off the leaves above his head and the grass beneath his feet, but his body seemed to absorb the light, drenching him in darkness. His head was bowed.

The woman rose and walked to the edge of the porch, so close that her nose nearly brushed the screen. She watched the man with mounting interest sprinkled with something a little more ominous that she couldn't quite identify. He knelt to the ground, brought his hand to his mouth, then pressed it against the grass before he stood and turned to leave, making his way over to the path that wound between the headstones.

He stopped abruptly when the woman's cat meowed its protest at having lost its comfortable lap. In the dead silence of the heavy night, the sound carried across the woman's lawn to the street, and the man turned. She held her breath as they faced one another. He stared, and she stared back, though she couldn't see his face clearly, and hoped he couldn't see hers.

A moment later, he turned once again and continued down the path, disappearing into the darkness. The woman's heart raced as she listened to the crunching rhythm of his retreat. Her cat's tail flicked around her ankles as she sank back into the shadows of the porch.

PART ONE

incorrigible

(Adj.: bad beyond correction
or reform)

It actually doesn't take much to be
considered a difficult woman.
That's why there are so many of us.

JANE GOODALL

CHAPTER 1

EMILY

Toronto—May, 1961

"Meeting's in ten minutes, Emily."

Emily Radcliffe nodded to her coworker Jan just as she disappeared from the doorway into the small kitchenette where Emily was preparing herself some tea in a battered, stained teacup that looked long overdue for retirement. The kitchenette in the office of *Chatelaine* magazine was stocked with the hand-me-downs of the kitchen on the floor above, which housed the men's publication and the administrative offices of their parent company, Maclean-Hunter.

Emily poured a healthy splash of milk into her tea along with a rare spoonful of sugar to jolt her senses in time for the meeting, then made her way back to the Closet to pick up her notebook and pen en route to her boss's office.

The Closet was her pet name for the space she shared with Betty, the junior editorial assistant and one of the few people in the office whom Emily outranked. Emily had never been a particularly social person, but she'd had friends in grade school. Now they, along with the girls she'd gone to university with, were almost all married, many with young children. Unable to relate to their lives very much anymore, she'd fallen out of touch with a lot of them. Emily had hoped that she might find a kindred spirit in her officemate, but she'd been sorely disappointed.

The Closet was so small and had such a damp air about it that they had both raised the suspicion that it had spent its previous life as a janitorial cupboard. Still, two years fresh from her university graduation, Emily was thrilled to have a place at the magazine at all, even if it was tinged with the smell of mildew.

As the editorial assistant, Emily was responsible for reviewing and collating the monthly letters to the editor, and had helped edit and co-write some pieces that had other journalists' names on them. That, she knew, was part of the job. But it was her dream to see her own name in the byline one day. She was ready for more.

Notebook tucked under her arm, she made her way down the long corridor toward the office of their editor-in-chief, Doris Anderson. Despite the presence of a large conference room down the hall, Doris's more intimate office served as the gathering spot for their weekly editorial meetings.

"Too much open air in the conference room," Doris had told Emily at her first meeting. "Ideas need to be able to bounce off one another. Create some friction. That's where things get exciting."

The magazine headquarters was noisy, as it always was, with the spirited cacophony of women's voices, clacking typewriters, and ringing phones. Emily hurried past the art and advertising departments—where two of her colleagues were locked in a heated debate—and the test kitchen, where the food editor created recipes using everyday ingredients, prepared with average appliances. Nothing gimmicky, nothing gourmet. Just nutritious, inexpensive recipes that could be easily prepared while children ran about underfoot, and ready for your husband's arrival home at six o'clock. As such, a distinct perk of the job was the almost constant presence of not-quite-right reject casseroles and desserts on offer for lunch and snacks to anyone who wanted them, and, on the last Friday of the month, office-wide feasts to give one final taste test to an upcoming issue's winning recipes. They were probably the best-fed women in town, and they were proud of it.

Emily's stomach growled, and she did her best to ignore the

tantalizing aroma of potato and cheese in the air as she turned the corner into Doris's office. She slid in and stood near the doorway.

The staff writers were perched on metal-backed chairs, clustered around Doris's desk like a murder of friendly crows. One of them, Virginia, looked up at Emily and nodded politely before returning to a muttered conversation with Doris herself. Doris's secretary, Clara, leaned against the windowsill that looked out onto University Avenue, her notebook at the ready. Jan, the fashion editor, was reclined in a deep-green velvet wing chair near the coffee table, slim legs crossed, clutching a cigarette over a bevelled glass ashtray.

Betty entered the room a moment later, her face a little wild.

"Sorry," she hissed. "Am I late?"

"Not yet." Emily shifted aside to make room for her. Betty was often tardy after lunchtime dates with her beau, who, she frequently told Emily, was due to propose any day now. They'd been going together just about exactly as long as Emily had been with her boyfriend, Jeremy, but Betty's very existence was tied to her boyfriend and the prospect of marriage in a way Emily's wasn't. Betty seemed intent upon winning a self-imposed race to the altar.

Emily had met Jeremy—Jem—at journalism school three years ago, after she'd graduated with her English degree from Victoria College. He was thoughtful, but ambitious and driven—just like Emily. They shared a love of adventure novels and art house films, which they frequently saw together at the Revue and then discussed over coffee afterward. She was very fond of Jem; in many ways, he was her best friend. But she was in no hurry to marry, a fact that seemed unable to penetrate Betty's heavily hairsprayed little head.

Jem would expect her to stop working if they wed; she knew that much from some of the things he'd said about his hopes for the future. He'd asked her what hers were, but something had held her back from telling him the truth: that even at twenty-four, she wasn't ready for marriage. That no, she might not want children, or at least not right away. She couldn't even bring herself to tell him she'd want to keep working after becoming his wife, because that was as outrageous as telling a man you'd fancy buying a house on the moon. She'd seen from her mother and sister how much motherhood demanded of a woman. You had to give yourself over to it completely. It seemed inherently sacrificial, especially if you wanted to do it properly. She had other things she wanted to accomplish first.

But she felt the pressure mounting, and she resented having to feel it at work as well as at home, from her mother. She hadn't explicitly told her parents that she wanted a career over marriage, though she suspected her dad already knew.

"All right," Doris said then, and silence descended over the assembled women. She leaned forward, dark, short-cropped curls framing a striking, square-shaped face above a pearl necklace. "October issue. Whad'ya got, girls?"

The content for each issue was set about five months in advance of publication. The summer she had first started, Emily found it strange to be holed up in Doris's sweltering office, fans humming like a swarm of bees as they discussed the Christmas copy for the December edition.

Today the conversation bounced around, as it always did, from writer to writer to Doris and back again like some wild tennis match as they hammered out their pitches. Maeve wanted to do a piece on the newly formed New Democratic Party, and Jan finished up with her proposal of the Christmas party-dress spread.

"Okay," Doris told them all, nodding her satisfaction. "Run with all this, and get back to me. Now, moving on: Emily!"

Emily straightened, smoothed down her shoulder-length hair. It was a light, ashy brown, the colour of a walnut.

"Here, Doris."

"Did you get a chance to read the letters in response to the battered women piece in the February issue?" Doris asked, dark brows pinched, pen clutched tightly in her hand. "I've been eager to hear the responses."

Emily sighed out the remainder of her leftover fury at those letters as all the eyes in the room turned to her. "Yes. It's about what you'd expect." She flipped a page on her clipboard and read aloud. "*I find it distasteful to read of such private matters in a ladies' magazine.* And, *It's a husband's prerogative to keep his wife in her place.*" She looked up at Doris. "But far more in support, saying we all need to be talking more openly about woman abuse, and help those who are going through it. Everyone seems to know someone."

Doris nodded. "Good. That issue has sold more than any other of the past two years, so that says something. Though *what* exactly it says is worrisome."

"Any word from upstairs?" Maeve asked, eyes narrowed. *Upstairs* was the catch-all term for the room full of executive men in the Maclean-Hunter offices on the floors above. The ones with the brand-new teacups.

Doris scoffed. "Wanted to know why the surge in sales. I told them it must have been the cover story on how to use that new PAM cooking spray for all your Easter recipes." A wry grin twisted at her mouth. Everyone laughed openly.

"They've really no clue," Virginia said, shaking her head.

"It would seem not."

"How many of these do you think we can slide through before they catch on?" Maeve asked.

Doris was smiling, a roguish grin that made Emily wonder if her boss was in this business just for the sheer fun of rebellion. "I admit I'm excited to find out. They really don't seem to care what we print as long as circulation is up, and ad revenues are consistent." She shrugged. "I don't think any of them even open the thing, and why would they? For the beauty tips? If any of their wives have caught on, they certainly haven't betrayed us yet." She paused, ran her index finger over her thumb in thoughtful circles. "I'd like to do something on Enovid, that new oral contraceptive."

"That's *bold*, Doris," Virginia said, eyebrows raised.

"I'll do it," Maeve chimed in.

"You'd have to be tricky with it," Clara said to Maeve. "We can't be seen to be disseminating information on contraception." Her voice lowered on the last word.

"We could ask Legal for their input," Jan piped up, taking a long drag on her cigarette.

Doris shook her head. "No. It's easier to ask for forgiveness than permission, remember that, girls. Besides, no one's ever been successfully prosecuted for sharing information about birth control."

"But do we want to be the first?" Clara asked.

"Of course we do," Doris said. "Do you know what that would do for our sales figures? And we can't ignore an invention that could fundamentally change women's lives."

This was why Emily loved working at *Chatelaine*, and specifically for Doris Anderson. What they did here was different. There was no other publication like this in Canada just for women, where topics of substance were tackled. It was only ever the men's publications that engaged and challenged their readers with real-world questions, debates, and investigations. No one but Doris, it seemed, thought women could handle it—or would want to. But since Emily was responsible for reviewing the letters to the editor, she knew women were eager for it. Even the ones who disagreed with the articles were at least engaging, making their voices heard. They'd send an outraged letter about the February issue, then race out to buy the new edition as soon as it hit the stands the following month.

Clara chuckled a little nervously, then glanced at the clock near the door. "Shoot, I need to get going. Sorry, Doris. Tommy's sick, and I told my sitter I'd be home early."

Doris waved her hand at the door in polite dismissal. "Off you go. I think we're done here anyway, girls." As Clara left and the others gathered their things, Doris muttered under her breath about the need for public access to child care. She was nearly forty, Emily guessed, and had a young son who was minded by a nanny while she worked.

The women dispersed in a flurry of skirts and perfume, and the noise of the office crested again outside Doris's door. But Emily hung back. She had a question for her boss that had been nagging her since she'd finished reading this batch of letters in response to the battered women piece.

"What can I do for you, Emily?" Doris asked.

Emily opened her mouth, then shut it again. She didn't typically shy away from making herself heard, but she also didn't want to be seen as impertinent, which, truth be told, she sometimes could be. But she knew Doris was always open to input from her team. From the time Emily had first joined *Chatelaine*, she'd noted the sort of maternal yet unpatronizing way in which the editor-in-chief gathered "her girls" under her wings, like some great mother swan. A soft embrace with a sharp beak. She took pride in being a mentor and teacher, and always seemed gratified when one of her fledglings learned to fly.

"Come on now," Doris said. "I didn't think any child of William Radcliffe would be shy about speaking her mind."

Emily smiled appreciatively. Her father was *the* William Radcliffe: the Second World War correspondent who had covered the Canadian troops' invasion of Sicily in 1943, losing half an arm and his vision in one eye in the dispatch. He'd left the *Star* a decade ago to write long-form articles for *Maclean's* upstairs, and had pulled more than a few tight strings to get her this job. It gave her no small sense of responsibility to perform well and prove herself capable to Doris, both to uphold her father's good name and wriggle out from beneath it.

"The battered women piece, birth control," Emily said with a flicker of hesitant daring. "If this is the direction you really want to take with the magazine, why bother with all the fluff? The decorating and fashion pieces? Why not just make it harder-hitting, like *Maclean's* is? Set us apart entirely from *Ladies' Home Journal* and the other women's mags?"

Doris eyed her. "I like the way you think, Emily, and I know you've got a lot to live up to. But we have to meet our readers where they're at."

"What do you mean?"

Doris opened her palms to the ceiling. "You know how Jan always wants to run the designer stuff in the fashion pages? All those clothes she's got stuffed on the rolling coat racks in her office?"

"Yes."

"And you know how I make her change it, almost every issue?"

Emily nodded. Doris always insisted that the fashion section of the magazine showcase styles from common department stores like Hudson's Bay, Sears, and Simpson's. She said the magazine's readership wanted advice on how to wear the main street fashions they could actually afford. They didn't want to waste their time fantasizing about a five-hundred-dollar silk dress they would never in their lives be able to lay their hands on. *They want to feel like a million bucks, not spend it*, Emily had heard her say once. *Show them how to do it on a housewife's allowance.*

"That's us meeting them where they're at," Doris continued. "The 'fluff,' as you put it, the budget and beauty tips, the decorating trends ... this is the context of these women's lives. The frame, if you will. We need to have it to draw them in to the magazine, get attached, feel as though we understand them. We need to bring value to their lives, and then hope they'll follow us, *trust* us, when we try to open their eyes to things like equal pay and birth control."

Emily tried to hide her scowl. "How do those things bring *value*, though?" She knew she was perhaps pushing too hard.

Doris clasped her hands now. "Don't take this the wrong way, Emily, but you don't quite understand these women yet. Once you have a husband and children, you will."

Emily pressed her lips together, a thin line of anger, which Doris noted.

"I apologize," Doris said, looking concerned. "I've touched a nerve?"

Emily's jaw tightened. "Yes, but it's fine. I'm sorry. Please continue."

Doris didn't press further. "Well, the pressure to *perform* as a wife and mother is enormous," she said.

Emily thought immediately of her twin sister, Eleanor, who had propped herself up in her hospital bed hours after her son was born to roll curlers into her hair as tears poured down her pale cheeks. "Harry will be coming in soon," she'd told Emily, who reluctantly handed her a can of hairspray from the bedside table as she watched her sister struggle to make herself presentable for her husband.

"And?" Emily had asked her, outraged. "You just gave birth, Ellie, he can't expect you to—"

"Except he *does*," Eleanor replied. "You don't understand, Em."

Women—married women with children, specifically—always seemed to be telling Emily she couldn't understand certain things until she was married. Emily didn't care much that other women sometimes made her feel lesser-than, but she was still tired of the insinuation.

"This magazine," Doris continued, "whether you'll believe it or not, is a lifeline for many women. It validates their lives, and for some women—the ones who are already struggling to find meaning in their efforts—these messages and tips and instructions are everything."

Emily considered her boss's words. She didn't want to relate to a woman whose biggest concern was how to lay a proper table for Sunday dinner; she wanted a more substantial life than that. More like what her father had. What Doris had. But she supposed Doris was right. If she was to do her job properly, she would have to try her best to relate to those who were different from her.

"It seems sad to me," she said finally, feeling her insides flutter with the discomfort of something bordering on anger. "A life like that."

"Perhaps it is," Doris said. "But this is how you effect change. You need to understand people before you can coax them into the tent. And we face the added challenge of trying to coax these women without their husbands noticing. Hence the vapid covers."

Emily nodded at that. They'd had an editorial meeting before the battered women piece ran to confirm how they were to manage the entire issue. It was critical, Doris had said, that a woman who might need the information be able to read it, undiscovered, with her husband in bed next to her. An abusive husband wouldn't bother monitoring what his wife was reading in a ladies' magazine. Like the women who ran it, the contents of *Chatelaine* needed to be authoritative and convincing while remaining entirely unthreatening to the status quo.

"Don't you get impatient, though?" Emily asked her. "Waiting on the change?" She swallowed, and the words tumbled out before she could stop them. "I know I do. I can't wait decades for things to get better for us." She thought of her mother's repeated hints about marriage and talk of ticking clocks, of how her father had already adopted Jem into their family as a de facto son-in-law alongside Harry, who expected his wife to always be polished and perfect. Emily's own future as Mrs. Jeremy Gordon felt frighteningly inevitable, despite the fact that she couldn't see herself in the role, couldn't see herself ever signing that name. *Emily Radcliffe* would be erased, and her hopes and dreams right along with it, all in the stroke of a pen.

"I do," Doris said. "But I have a feeling it's coming. Things aren't what they were, even a few years ago. The momentum will come, Emily. All it takes is a big enough push."

CHAPTER 2

EMILY

May, 1961

One Friday, the weather was so balmy that Emily opted to walk home from work instead of taking the streetcar. A little before five-thirty, she wandered up the moss-laced flagstone path of their family home on Borden Street.

Her nose told her that her mother had already started on dinner. Emily had always had a healthy appetite, something her mother admired. Bess Radcliffe said that feeding one's children remained one of the last vestiges of a mother's role once they were grown and, as such, the Radcliffes still hosted almost all the big holiday and Sunday night dinners, the table weighed down with enough food to feed a football team as Bess pushed third helpings on them all and sent Eleanor away with stacks of multicoloured Tupperware.

They were coming for dinner tonight, Eleanor and her family, instead of Sunday, due to some church event Eleanor was volunteering for and which Emily had managed to wriggle out of. Emily liked seeing her sister, but generally preferred to have a couple of days' rest under her belt after the workweek before being subjected to the chaos of a family dinner with eight people, including noisy children. But at least it had been a productive week at work. She'd felt even more energized since her recent conversation with Doris, and her mentor had noticed. On Monday she'd tossed Emily a more complicated bit of writing than she typically got to do. It was what Emily would have called a fluff piece before, but now she was trying her best to reframe it as necessary scaffolding for the proverbial feminist "tent" to which Doris had referred. And she did get the sense that she was being tested by the editor, who had handed her the assignment with a twitch of her maroon lip.

"All right, Emily," Doris had said, peering down at her across her little desk in the Closet. "I know you're hungry. Let's see what you come up with. On my desk by Friday, please."

Emily had hit the deadline with several hours to spare, and was pleased with herself as she sat across from Doris and watched the older woman read through her work, making notes with a red fountain pen.

"It's good," Doris had said eventually, nodding with satisfaction. "We'll tidy it up a little in copyedit, but good work, Emily. Now go enjoy your weekend. Best to your father."

Emily now hung her leather bag on the coat stand in the hall, checked her reflection in the mirror. She smoothed her flyaway hairs with some futility, then pulled off her shoes. She always felt so much more grounded in bare feet or stockings, as though she'd been floating on the balls of her feet all day, and her heels were finally getting a chance to touch down to reality. She would have worn men's loafers every day, if she were allowed.

"That you, Em?" her father called from the sitting room on the other side of the wall. Emily stepped through the doorway to find him seated at his desk. It was a rolltop from the twenties that he'd acquired cheap at an old antiques store in Kensington Market when Emily and her sister were children. She remembered the day he'd brought it in, with help from his friend Lawrence at the *Star*, who did the deliveries and had a van big enough to transport it. Back then, William's home office was in the attic of the house, away from the noise of two boisterous young girls, but the damn desk proved to be a lot heavier than it appeared and impossible to haul up the narrow staircase. And so it had stayed in the sitting room, nestled into the bay window that looked out over the small, tree-shaded yard.

William's productivity hadn't suffered, though, despite the desk's placement in the common gathering room of the house. Emily and Eleanor had played with their dolls and blocks on the rug behind him while he clacked away at the typewriter on Sunday afternoons, or during the evening, if his workday spilled into night with a deadline looming. He always preferred to bring his work home, if he could, never spending any more time at the office than he had to—a side effect, perhaps, of knowing his life should have ended on a Sicilian mountain in the summer of forty-three; that he never should have seen his wife and girls again, but by a stroke of good fortune, he did.

Emily figured his ability to tune out the noise around him while he worked was probably a souvenir of the war. He'd learned to focus, observe his surroundings, and knuckle down to write while the soldiers around him yelled to one another, talked, laughed, and cried. Bombs exploded in the distance as the dry Italian earth beneath him shuddered. What were the squeals and arguments of a pair of children compared to that? So many men had trouble sleeping in the quiet of their peaceful residential streets when they returned from the war, so accustomed they'd become to the cacophony of battle. Perhaps the same held true for productivity.

"Hey, Dad," Emily said, bending to plant a kiss on his cheek, the five-o'clock shadow prickling her lips. "What are you working on?"

She knew he missed travelling abroad to cover stories in the field, and the nature of his injuries meant he was reduced to typing with one hand, and progress was therefore slow. William Radcliffe's mind and pen were as sharp as ever, though, which had rendered him still in demand despite his physical limitations. His editor at *Maclean's* was perfectly happy to print whatever he wrote, on any timeline.

"Oh, just a snarky piece about the bank merger," he said. "It's a little too monopolistic for my liking. Mark my words, more banks will disappear and it'll be the working man who'll suffer. We need competition in lending rates."

Emily didn't know much about banking, but smiled at her father's enthusiasm as she sat down in the armchair near his desk.

"And how are you?" he asked, returning her grin. Unlike Eleanor, she'd inherited their father's smile—a little lopsided, with just one dimple on the left cheek. He always said it was a smile made for sarcasm and wit, both of which Emily had also inherited, though she didn't get to exercise them in public as much as her dad did. "Doris still treating you well?"

"Oh yes," Emily said. "She's just terrific."

"She's a bulldog in pearls," William said, and Emily chuckled. "And one hell of a fantastic mentor for you. I bet the other ladies are, too. Maeve and Virginia and the like."

Emily nodded. "It's like a whole other world over there, Dad."

"So I understand. And it's a world you enjoy, isn't it?" He was looking down at his hand now, clasped over one knee. He was a talker, her dad, but often didn't make eye contact, particularly if the content of the conversation was emotional.

"I do," Emily said. "I love being at home, of course, with family, but . . ." It was difficult for her to articulate it without telling him the bald truth, which was that within the four walls of that office on University Avenue, she felt a sense of belonging and purpose that she'd never truly experienced anywhere else before.

"I'm so very glad, Em. So very glad." He nodded solemnly. Sounds of Bess cooking dinner wafted toward them in the silence of the living room.

Emily's instincts began to tingle, and she realized her father was behaving as he did when he was about to deliver bad news. She'd seen it before. "What is it?" she asked.

He cleared his throat. "Have you thought about your future there? Do you think you want to stay?"

"Of course I want to stay," Emily said fervently. She was performing so well, she couldn't see herself getting sacked, and she was having the time of her life.

"All right," he said, then paused. "And what about later? You know, when a family is on the horizon?"

Emily felt stung. Her father had historically been her ally, had understood her in a way her mother didn't. He was so proud of her for pursuing journalism. He didn't have a son to groom into the "family business," but William had always treated her as though she were entirely capable—as capable as a man would have been. He was very fond of Jem, Emily knew, but so far—up until this moment, anyway—he'd refrained from any explicit comments about the couple's future. It left Emily feeling a little betrayed to hear him hint so heavily like this.

No one had objected to Emily pursuing a university education—in fact, it was encouraged by both her parents, and Eleanor had even politely congratulated her. But the fact that she'd had the audacity to go out and *do* anything with her hard-earned degree seemed beyond comprehension to Ellie, who had opted instead for basic secretarial training after high school and married the first man she laid eyes on at the law firm that hired her.

"Dad," Emily began, but he cut across her, which he rarely did.

"Your mother thought it would come nicer as a surprise," he said quietly, eyes darting toward the kitchen, then back to Emily, "but I don't agree. The truth is, Jem came to us last week to discuss his intentions."

It shouldn't have come as a shock, but Emily's body still reacted as though it had. Her stomach swooped like she'd missed a step and her hands clenched in her lap. For a moment, she and her father just stared at one another. She'd sensed it coming for a few months now, and couldn't ignore the fact that the suspense had felt as though she were watching her own noose being braided and tied with a knot.

"I know that's where you were headed," William said. "But . . ."

"That's where *Jem* was headed," Emily corrected him. "And Mom, and his family. But not me, Dad. I just . . ." Her knuckles were standing out white now. She flexed them, trying to relax.

"I think you have some time," her father said reassuringly. "He's saving for the ring now, but it's coming. So you're going to need to decide what your answer will be, my girl. Have you talked to him about what you want? About *Chatelaine?*"

Emily shook her head.

"You're going to need to do that. You *must* do that."

"But how can I tell him, Dad?" Emily pleaded, anger and fear and resentment all twisting together in her tone. "How can I tell him that I want more than what he can offer? That I *want* this career? That any marriage I enter into will only be a *part* of my life, and not its entirety? What man is going to want to hear that?"

William sighed heavily. "Well, I can't say that he'll *want* to hear it. But he's going to have to. And I think, if he asks for your hand and you say no . . . you have to tell him why. You've been going together long enough that he deserves an explanation."

Emily hung her head. "I know."

"Tell him what you just told me. And he'll either accept those terms, or he won't."

"And if he won't?" Emily asked, deflated. She felt tears prick at her eyes.

William shrugged. "Then he's not the man for you. Then you both move on." He looked strained, and Emily realized that he was wrestling with her situation almost as much as she was.

"But, might I suggest," he said, squinting thoughtfully, "that you speak to Doris about this?"

Emily looked up, startled. "Speak to my boss? About Jem?"

"Yes. I think you'd be interested to hear her opinion. Doris Anderson also had a rather . . . *unconventional* life trajectory, and has landed where she is. She's managed to do everything she does while also having a family. So if that's where you want to end up, go talk to the person who's done it. Just like with any other interview: get your facts straight, hear their story, then see what you take from it."

The cuckoo clock on the wall in the dining room ticked away the seconds. Emily tried to tune it out, tried to ignore the physical manifestation of the countdown that was now going to dictate her life in the coming weeks. She cleared her stuck throat. "Mom in the kitchen?" she asked, to change the subject.

"Yup," her dad said, leaning back again in his chair. "Cooking for an army."

Emily stood, brushed his shoulder affectionately and wandered through the living room into the kitchen at the back of the house. Her heart fluttered with nerves. She wished Jem wasn't coming tonight; she needed time to think.

"Hi Mom," she said, greeting Bess, who was busy at the stove, her black hair frizzing in the steam issuing from a pot.

"Hello, darling," her mother called, flashing a quick smile over her shoulder before attacking something with a whisk. "How was work?" Emily opened her mouth to answer but Bess kept talking. "Ellie will be here at six with the brood. Have you heard from Jeremy? He's still coming, isn't he? I know how he loves bourguignon. I do too, really." She chuckled.

"Yes, he's coming," Emily said, working to keep the weariness from her voice. "He called the office on my lunch break."

"Oh good! That's nice that he calls, isn't it?"

Emily half smiled, but didn't answer, which prompted her mother to glance over her shoulder again, as though to check that Emily was, indeed, in agreement. She knew Bess thought she was never enthusiastic enough about her boyfriend, whom Bess loved. They were "Jem and Em," a tidy little rhyming set.

"Your father used to come pick me up sometimes, after work, when we were courting. It was ever so lovely to know he'd been thinking about me over the day."

Bess set down the whisk and came over to Emily, patting a stray wisp of hair back and smoothing her apron as she walked. She always wore that faded red apron, even in the few hours during the day when she wasn't cooking or cleaning up after a meal. She'd worn it from breakfast through bedtime for as long as Emily could remember, and Emily wondered whether her mother had just become so used to trying to protect her clothing from the messes created by two young girls that the apron had ingrained itself as part of her wardrobe forevermore.

Emily smiled tightly at Bess, who was a couple of inches shorter than she was. Bess had been a real beauty in the height of her youth, before exuberant twins and a husband away at war had added wrinkles to her forehead and dulled the sparkle in her eyes. She was still lovely-looking, though, and was one of those people whose features shone so much brighter when they smiled. She embraced Emily.

"Is Nana coming tonight?" Emily asked when they pulled apart. Bess's parents lived in a small apartment a few blocks away, paid for in part by Emily's parents. Her papa hadn't worked since the first war left him "unsuited to employment," as Bess said, always with a pinch of her lips. Emily was fond of her nana, but hardly knew her papa at all.

"No, not tonight," Bess said. "Her asthma's too bad. But I'm planning to take her out for a nice walk on Sunday, if you'd like to join. Maybe see if the cherry blossoms are out yet in High Park. She always loves that."

Emily nodded. "What can I do to help now, then?" she asked, doing her best to shake off Jem's impending arrival. She wished that she could duck out of this dinner entirely, but that wasn't an option.

"Well, if you want to change," Bess said, "then set the table, that would be lovely. Red-wine glasses tonight, please."

Emily made her way up the narrow staircase to her bedroom at the end of the hall. She shut the door behind her, then sat down on the bed with a creak of aging springs.

Her well-loved writing desk was now where Ellie's bed used to be throughout their childhood, all the way up until the day she got married to Harry, just shy of the girls' twentieth birthday. Emily had inherited the entire room then, which at the time felt both liberating and lonely. Despite their many differences, Eleanor and Emily shared a multitude of twin commonalities and, standing up at the altar with her sister as she vowed love and obedience to her new husband, Emily couldn't help but feel a creeping sense of abandonment that had only deepened as Ellie was drawn further into marriage and motherhood. Emily felt a little left behind, but not in a way that bothered her; it was just as though Ellie had taken a one-way trip to a country Emily didn't have the least interest in. But she still missed her sister, and looked forward to the postcards.

She ran a hand over the bedspread now, still the same one from her teen years, faded and patched in several places. There were vestiges of her childhood everywhere; it wasn't a grown woman's bedroom. A pink musical jewellery box still stood atop the dresser, dusty and silent, and the children's books of their youth—*Winnie-the-Pooh*, the *Anne of Green Gables* series, and Emily's favourites, the Nancy Drew mysteries—were still stashed under the bed. Eleanor preferred the *Little House on the Prairie* books, stories of domestic adventure, while Emily craved the daring and dangerous feats of the blond teenage sleuth. She made a note to give a few of the children's stories to her nephew Charlie. Her eyes moved to the bookshelf, where the adult books were lined up: Shakespeare plays, of course, and Wilde. Jules Verne and Virginia Woolf. Lots of non-fiction, and the memoir of one of Emily's journalism heroes, Nellie Bly.

Emily sighed. A part of her wished she could have an apartment of her own. She had an income, and probably could have afforded a small studio, but it wasn't something single women did. She felt too old to live with her parents, and too young to stay with them indefinitely in a state of dependent spinsterhood. She'd read about some modern unmarried women striking out on their own. That American Marjorie Hillis had written a bestselling book about her experience as a successful "live-alone" woman.

Emily thought of her conversation with Doris, who was so confident that real change was coming for women, that all it needed was a big enough push. But what form would that "push" eventually come in, and what would be the catalyst? There must be other women out there also bursting with dissatisfaction with their lives. Surely enough of them pushing together could effect some sort of change. Someone should write a book about *that*, Emily thought.

Marriage could not be the only option for women. It simply couldn't. And her career at *Chatelaine*, as a journalist, felt like a secret passage to something more, if she had the wits to take it.

But for now, this was her home, her reality.

Twenty minutes later, freshly changed into a plaid skirt and yellow blouse, Emily had just placed the last of the dessert forks on the lace tablecloth when the doorbell rang. She glanced up at the clock on the dining room wall: it was six on the nose. Jem was always on time, a trait she appreciated in him. She thought tardiness signalled a lack of respect. There wasn't anything "fashionable" about making other people wait, as though your time were more valuable than theirs.

"I'll get it," she called, padding her way down the hall to the front door. She composed herself before opening it to find Jem standing on the stoop, looking smart, bottle of wine in hand. He was clean-shaven and smelled of earthy cologne. His infectious smile stretched ear to ear at the sight of Emily, which made her both swell with friendly affection and squirm with guilt.

"Hi Em," he said, leaning in to kiss her on the cheek. "I think the Chisholms will be here in a moment—I saw them circling for a parking space."

Emily beckoned him in, silently shocked that Eleanor and her family had arrived on time for once. With the children, they were always at least ten minutes late.

An hour later, she was grateful that they'd finally reached the dessert course, Bess's neighbourhood-famous baked Alaska. Charlie, age three, was currently trying to smear chocolate ice cream into his hair. Bess intercepted with a napkin as Eleanor bounced an impatient Jeannie on her knee, attempting to spoon her bits of rice which she was loudly resisting. The men were all on to their after-dinner Scotch as they discussed the bank merger. Emily sipped her coffee as calmly as she could with one hand. Her left was gripped in Jem's heavy palm on the table between them, and for the past five minutes he'd been gently running his thumb along her ring finger. She had no idea if it was intentional or not.

All she knew was that she wanted him to stop.

"How are things at the office?" Eleanor asked over Jeannie's continued whines as Bess rose to go refresh the coffee pot.

Emily glanced across the table at her sister. She looked buried. Buried, quite literally, beneath the wiggling child on her lap, and the weight of her married life. Though they were identical twins, Ellie's life had already aged her. For Emily, it was like looking into some mystical mirror that showed her future self, if she were to take the path that was expected of her. It was there in the puffiness around Eleanor's eyes that she couldn't quite mask with makeup; the exhaustion of sleepless nights pursued by relentlessly busy days of homemaking and childminding; in the tight roll of hair at the back of her neck that was always locked in with three layers of hairspray, as though she might be able to hold up the load of her life on that weight-bearing bun if only she could twist it tight enough. It was there in the subtle downturn of her mouth, the frown that had been present since Charlie was born and she'd silently battled "the baby blues," as their mother had called Eleanor's melancholy, whispering the term low into Emily's ear—some women's password that Emily was meant to understand, but didn't.

Emily took another sip of her coffee. "They're good," she said. "I really enjoy it. Doris just gave me a small article, so I'm working my way up to more challenging things."

Eleanor watched her through those tired eyes and nodded. "I'm glad for you, Em," she said, then glanced subtly at Jem, whose eyes were on Harry as he weighed in with an opinion at the men's end of the table. "Do you think you'll stay?" she added, quieter.

Emily opened her mouth to reply in the affirmative, thinking at first that Eleanor was referring to *Chatelaine*. But her sister's eyes flicked once more to Jem. Though she had taken a very different path, Ellie knew what Emily's career meant to her; knew that to remain at *Chatelaine*, Emily couldn't stay with Jem.

Emily licked her dry lips. *I don't know*, she mouthed.

CHAPTER 3

EMILY

June 6, 1961

A few weeks after the family dinner, Emily was seated at her desk in the Closet, poring over some revisions to a one-page piece on Thanksgiving table decor. Doris had been pleased with her previous work and was now upping the ante. This article involved Emily's first solo interviews—one with her own delighted mother, the other the eccentric proprietor of a notions store off Portland Street in the fashion district who advised her on fabric layering and the placement of glassware. Knowing Doris would want the piece to reflect *Chatelaine*'s budget-friendly approach, Emily had sought out cheap samples for the photo shoot at Honest Ed's and a few church-basement rummage sales.

THE TWO-DOLLAR THANKSGIVING TABLE:
Thrifty Decor for the Savvy Housewife

She had just finalized the title when the front desk receptionist, Constance, popped her head around the door frame.

"Do you have a minute?" she asked.

Emily looked up from her work. "Of course."

"There's a man at the desk, and he's got something . . . I'm not really sure what to do with it."

As the editorial assistant and with her "office" the closest to front reception, Emily was Constance's point of contact if Doris or Clara couldn't be reached by phone. Emily was then responsible for relaying the information to the appropriate member of staff. She didn't mind being the messenger, though, as it gave her a ready excuse to engage with Doris and the staff writers, learn a bit more about the inner workings of the magazine from whatever message she was delivering.

"What do you mean?" Emily asked, puzzled.

"I'll let him tell you," Constance said, withdrawing. With a curious twinge at the air of mystery, Emily followed her out into the small marble-floored lobby.

The man was standing, looking uncomfortable, near the reception desk. He wore a jumpsuit with the name *Ted* stitched into the breast in yellow thread, and was stooping a little, as though about to walk through a low doorway.

"May I help you?" Emily asked politely.

He nodded in her direction. "Afternoon, miss. I uh, I was sent down here by the lady upstairs," he said, pointing at the ceiling.

"From *Maclean's*?"

"Yeah. I've been around and around, see. It's just that I've come across a strange thing, and I didn't know where to go with it. The people upstairs sent me down here."

Emily's brow furrowed. "I'm afraid I don't understand."

"I'm a delivery driver, see. Groceries. To all sorts of places. Restaurants, businesses and the like. One of my drop-offs is the old prison over on King West. The ladies' prison."

Emily wasn't familiar with it. She nodded, encouraging him to continue.

"Well, I was making my drop this morning, and a ball of paper up'n falls on my head from out of the sky while I was leaning over, shifting the crates." He reached into his pocket and withdrew what looked like a crumpled note with blue lettering.

"The ladies were having their outside time," he went on. "I see them sometimes, just walking in circles or standing around in groups.

I looked up, and through the fence I see this girl running back toward the jail doors."

"Well, what did the paper say?" Emily asked. She was still flummoxed, but her curiosity was growing.

"I think it's best you read it for yourself, miss," he said, taking a step toward her and holding out the note. She took it and smoothed it out. It was written in poor penmanship with multiple spelling errors. It was also in crayon.

Emily's eyes flew across the lines, widening with shock as she read. There was no name attached.

> *Delivery man — we need help. We are starved — dirty baths — they expariment things on us, medisins that make us sick, and electrisity — Rats and lice everywhere. Food not enough, and terrible. I done nothing wrong and they still sent me here on the incorigible law. Loads of women are hear because of it, and done nothing. You put a toe out of line and you get locked up alone. No windows or exersise or nothing down there. Doctor is evil. Please tell the police!*
> *Sined,*
> *Incorigible*

"'Incorigible,'" Emily said aloud.

The elevator doors opened then and Doris stepped off. "Good day, sir," she said to Ted. "What's that?" she asked Emily as she breezed over to them, carrying the scent of coffee and something fried that was wrapped in an oily paper bag.

"Look at this, Doris." Emily handed over the letter. Doris deposited the bagged lunch onto the reception desk and took the paper. Her eyes slid across it.

"Good God," she said. "Who is this person, 'Incorigible'? Did you bring this in?" she asked Ted.

"Yes, ma'am. Fell from over the fence at the women's prison."

Doris's brow crinkled. "On King West?"

He nodded. "The Mercer Women's Prison."

"Why did you come here, sir?" Doris asked.

"Ted, ma'am. Well, it seems serious, right? So I went to the police, but they laughed it off. Wouldn't even take the note." He frowned. "So I thought someone at the news might want to see it, and I had a delivery 'round the corner anyway. The girl at the desk upstairs read it and said you're the ones what deal with ladies' stuff."

Emily could practically feel the heat burning on Doris's face beside her. It was only "ladies' stuff" because it mentioned women.

"Ted, thank you for bringing this to us. Do you mind if I keep it?" Doris asked.

"No, ma'am. As I said, police didn't give a hoot, but it seemed important. If you're happy to do something with it, that's fine by me. I've done my bit. I'll let you do yours. Have a good day, now." He turned and walked to the elevators.

Doris beckoned to Emily. "Come with me."

Emily followed her down to her office, where Doris slid her heels off, sank into her desk chair and tore open the paper takeaway bag.

"I'm ravenous," she said. "Meetings upstairs all morning. My God, those men just go *on and on* and hardly say anything at all." She took a large bite of her sandwich and handed the note back to Emily. "What do you make of this?"

Emily scanned it again. "Did you see this, about the . . . 'incorrigible law'? What is that? I've never heard of it."

Doris chewed slowly. "I don't know. But there's all kinds of strange rubbish still on the books, isn't there?" She took a swig from a cup on her desk. The drink must have gone stone cold hours ago, but she didn't flinch. "Isn't there something in the Criminal Code about 'alarming the Queen'?" Doris continued to eat, keeping her eyes on Emily. "Well," she said between mouthfuls, nodding at the note. "How do we find out what it is?"

Emily tapped a finger on the note. "Telephone a lawyer? Go to the courthouse?"

Doris nodded. "You got it. I've got a friend who's a secretary at Osgoode Hall. She knows more than half the lawyers upstairs do," she added, eyes rolling to the ceiling. Doris had friends everywhere, Emily had noticed. She was a sun around which smaller planets clustered, warming in her orbit.

Doris set the sandwich down and wiped her hands on a napkin before leaning forward and fingering through the Wheeldex beside the telephone. After a moment she withdrew a card and picked up the receiver. Emily heard it ring a few times before a woman answered. Doris made brief small talk, then straightened.

"I wonder if you could do us a favour, Helen. We have interest in something called the Incorrigible Law. Has to do with prisons, maybe. Crim—oh? Yes. Yes." Doris seized a pen from the glass cup on her desk and scribbled something down. "Confirming: 'the Female Refuges Act'? R-E-F-U-G-E-S?" She nodded and looked up at Emily again. "Do you have the text by any chance? Mmm. Okay. Thank you, Helen, you're a treasure. Best to Phil. Bye now."

She set the receiver down and slid the piece of paper over to Emily. "She says 'the Incorrigible Law' is the nickname for something called the Female Refuges Act. It legislates women's prisons, but she says it's mostly applied to vagrants and prostitutes." She raised her eyebrows.

Emily swallowed. One didn't normally hear the word "prostitute" in polite conversation. "Oh my."

"Indeed."

Feeling slightly embarrassed, though she wasn't entirely sure why, Emily dropped her eyes to the prisoner's note.

"Vagrants and . . . *prostitutes* or not," Emily said, "these are some pretty serious allegations."

She looked up again at her boss, who surveyed her. "And why doesn't it matter to you if they're prostitutes?" Doris asked casually.

"Well . . ." Emily began. She'd never had much cause to consider "women of the night," as she'd heard them called. But she thought back to the piece they'd done on battered women, the descriptions from doctors about the physical and psychological toll the violence took on women. How for most of them, it had come as a shock.

"One of the things that struck me with the battered women piece," she said, "was that those women ended up in a bad way through no fault of their own. They didn't *want* their lives to end up like that. They didn't *choose* to marry men who were violent. We hardly get much choice in whom we marry to begin with."

"And many men are adept at concealing their violent tendencies," Doris added darkly. "I'm not sure any woman really knows the man she walks back down the aisle with. The surprises tend to come afterward."

Emily's insides tightened, thinking of all she thought she knew about Jem. The more she spoke with women like Doris, who embodied the sort of future she wanted for herself, the more unappealing the idea of marriage became. It seemed astonishing to her that women didn't freely share the downsides of marriage with one another. Everyone was more focused on maintaining an image, an illusion. Like the magazine itself: a perfect glossy cover concealing the messy topics no one wanted to talk about.

"I agree with you, Emily," Doris said, rousing her. "I don't think any woman would choose a path of prostitution, either. Not as such. But we all know the system is set up against women. For many of us—the lucky ones—that just means restriction, dissatisfaction; for others, it spells total ruin and degradation." She hesitated, then took what looked like a reluctant last bite of her sandwich, as though the conversation had stolen her appetite. "This Female Refuges Act and the prisoner's note warrant a dig about." Doris sat back in her chair. "Listen, Emily. You've done some good research for other articles lately. I should like your help with the background on this one."

Emily's heart leapt. "Thank you!"

"Head up to the Legislative Library," Doris said. "See if you can locate the law. That's not to say there isn't a story here about the conditions inside the prison, regardless, but I think we need to verify the legal bit first, about how the women are getting sent there in the first place. Let me know what you find."

CHAPTER 4

EMILY

The following day, Emily headed up University Avenue, past the hospitals to the verdant lawns outside Queen's Park, her thoughts never straying far from the prisoner's letter that was now tucked into her leather bag. She was eager to get to the Legislative Library, to see the text of this Female Refuges Act, the "Incorrigible Law." She was always a fast walker, mostly because she was impatient; it was one of the reasons she didn't like waiting for people, or being late herself. But, particularly in her childhood, that impatience had occasionally manifested as impulsiveness or recklessness. She'd learned to harness it, and her tendency to do things quickly and efficiently had served her well in university, and now in her career. But in her life more broadly, patience was still a challenge for someone who wanted quick answers and fast results.

Sweaty from the brisk journey, she scaled the steps up to the front doors of the sprawling Legislature.

She had a brief exchange with the security guard, offering her credentials and requesting access to the library. He nodded her through, and she proceeded up the thickly carpeted steps to the main foyer, following the signs. She had never been in the Legislature before, and despite her feverish focus on the task at hand, she did take a moment to absorb the opulence of her surroundings. There was only one woman MPP. Not many women got to set foot inside the Legislature, unless they were a politician's secretary, or worked in the cafeteria.

Or the library.

"Hi there," Emily said, approaching the woman behind the long circulation desk, hand outstretched in greeting. The librarian was in her fifties, with short curly hair not unlike Doris's, and a neutral expression. She shook Emily's hand.

"My name's Emily Radcliffe. I'm a . . . journalist," Emily said, deciding on the spot that her training sounded far more qualified than her current job title. "For *Chatelaine* magazine." The woman nodded in interest. Most women of her age knew what *Chatelaine* was. "My editor sent me over in the hopes that you might be able to help us out. We're trying to locate a piece of legislation called the Female Refuges Act. Do you know it?"

The librarian paused, shook her head. "Not offhand, but I can find it for you. Give me a few minutes, please." She retreated to a card catalogue while Emily waited, tapping a finger against her satchel. Even on the soft leather, the sound carried in the quiet library. The librarian glanced over her shoulder, and Emily ceased her tapping.

"Sorry," she muttered. "Bad habit."

Ten minutes later, the librarian returned with a labelled file. "Here you are, then. You can use one of the reading desks over there, and just bring it back when you're finished, please."

Emily thanked her, feeling embarrassed about the impatient tapping, and hurried to a desk.

She was alone aside from one or two other young people who looked like students, probably from nearby Victoria College. She flicked on the table lamp and sat down, withdrawing her notepad and pencil from her bag.

FEMALE REFUGES ACT, 1927
ONTARIO

The Act was not long. Emily skimmed the first bit, which offered legal definitions of the terms used within. An "industrial refuge" was essentially a women's prison.

> S.2. (1) Any female between the ages of fifteen and thirty-five years, sentenced or liable to be sentenced to imprisonment in a common gaol by a judge, may be committed to an industrial refuge for an indefinite period not exceeding two years.

Emily's eyebrows raised. So they could keep a young woman in prison for *up to* two years. Who determined the length of the sentence? The judge? The prison warden?

She recorded the first section word for word, then returned to the page. "Prisoner transfers . . . parole . . ." she muttered. There was a lot of detail about logistics, as well as a clause stating an inmate had to be examined by the prison physician within three days of arrival, and every six months thereafter. So there was evidently meant to be an on-site doctor at these institutions. She glanced at the prisoner's note, which was resting beside her notebook.

Doctor is evil.

Emily tapped her pen, wondering what might be behind that particular allegation.

She turned back to the file. There were several more sections about medical care, including that prisoners could not be discharged if they were suffering from contagious or infectious disease, including venereal disease or syphilis. Emily wondered how one might contract VD in an all-women's institution. But then she remembered that this Act was meant to apply to prostitutes, who, she supposed, might well come into the prison with some sort of VD. She didn't know much about it and blushed a little at the thought, then swallowed hard. What a ghastly sort of existence that must be.

Next came the definition of who could be committed to one of these prisons:

```
S.15 (1): A person may bring before a judge any female
under the age of thirty-five years who,—
(a) is found begging . . . or receiving alms;
(b) is an habitual drunkard or by reason of other vices
is leading an idle or dissolute life.
```

Emily made a face at the vagueness of "idle life." What sorts of behaviours could be captured under such a term? Laziness? Unemployment? And could *anyone*, not just the police, bring a woman before a judge?

She thought for a moment, re-read who could be committed.

"So this isn't even for violent offenders," she said aloud. The librarian glanced over. Emily gave an apologetic wave, jotted some notes, and moved to the following sections.

And there it was, that ambiguous yet wholly incriminating title, the scarlet letter that could condemn these women to such a punitive fate. The clause referred to in the inmate's note:

```
S.17: Any parent or guardian may bring before a judge
any female under the age of twenty-five years who
proves unmanageable or incorrigible . . .
```

"Incorrigible." Emily tapped her pencil on the notepad again and stared at the text. She copied the final section and underlined the last word several times, the graphite shining dark grey on the page.

———

Ten minutes later, she was back in the brilliant sunlight of the spring afternoon, squinting as her blue eyes struggled to adjust. She wandered absently down the footpath toward College Street, ruminating on what she'd just read. The allegations from the note swirled in her mind along with a steady stream of as-yet unanswered questions.

Essentially, the Incorrigible Law allowed for women and girls under age thirty-five to be imprisoned for little more than subjective misbehaviour. But did such misbehaviour justify sentencing them to years of the sort of treatment the prisoner alleged in her note? Months-long isolation, medical experimentation, starvation, infestations?

She stopped at the corner of College and Queen's Park Crescent, staring into the middle distance, thoughts whirring.

How many people knew of this law and its impact? It had been on the books since 1927; how many women and girls had been affected by it? How many women were housed at the prison right now? What were their alleged crimes or misdemeanours? And most importantly: *Were the prisoner's allegations of abuse true?* If so, who would be culpable? The government, surely. The prison was a government institution. Emily's heart skipped. If there was any credence to the claims in the note, there was a story here. Possibly a big one.

She glanced at her watch. It wasn't lunchtime yet, so she might still catch Doris at her desk to debrief her on what she'd learned at the library. But as a small gaggle of students swarmed toward the streetcar that had screeched to a halt a few feet in front of her, a thought occurred and Emily reacted on impulse, rushing forward to join the back of the queue. This streetcar was heading west—the direction of the Mercer Women's Prison.

She rode to College and Dufferin, then transferred to a bus down to King Street. She disembarked and walked two blocks east before the dark, looming facade of the prison came into view. She slowed her pace as she approached the building, then stopped outside the gate. The lock on it was bigger than her hand.

The property was massive, took up an entire city block in all directions, and was surrounded by a tall, bare, wrought-iron fence. A gravel path led from the gate to the front doors. The building was dark-brown brick, with identical windows lined up along all four storeys. Several chimneys stood against the blue spring sky, some puffing smoke. Emily took it in, then continued along the sidewalk and around the corner.

This side of the prison was an exercise yard of some sort, though Emily couldn't see any inmates out there, and the pitiful lawn appeared to be mostly mud and little grass. She tried to absorb every detail she could with her keen reporter's eye, then walked to the southeast corner of the property and stopped beneath the street sign.

LIBERTY STREET, it declared in bold black lettering. Emily gazed up at it. She had never wondered why Liberty Village, the area she was now exploring, was so named. Was this some sort of joke? To name the area Liberty when its purpose was to incarcerate? And, as the anonymous whistleblower claimed, to incarcerate under the worst possible circumstances?

Emily went around to the back of the prison, which ran along Liberty Street. There was some kind of loading dock. This must be where the delivery driver picked up the note, Emily thought. She scanned the barred upper windows, but saw no one. She was tapping one finger against the side of her bag, considering her next move, when a back door opened, not near the loading dock but off to the side, on the southern wing of the cross-shaped building. Three women appeared: a tiny one in a loose-fitting dress and overcoat; a second with short, curly red hair and an impossibly large bust; and someone who Emily took to be a guard in uniform. They exchanged words, the guard nodded, and all three proceeded across the gravel toward the fence where Emily was standing. She stepped back, excited but unsure.

The guard eyed her suspiciously. "You here to pick up?" she barked.

Emily shook her head. "No, I was just passing," she said, offering a weak smile that was not returned.

"Well, be on your way."

Emily took a few steps to the side. The guard glared at her but said nothing as she removed a set of keys from her belt and the other two women stepped through the gate.

"Stay outta trouble, Jones," the guard drawled.

The red-headed woman laughed deeply. "Oh, yeah. You know me. See ya again in a few weeks, Grimes. If I'm lucky."

The guard shook her head, locked the gate again and retreated without a backward glance.

"Who the hell are you?" the large-busted woman demanded of Emily. The small one's eyes flicked from Emily to the other woman and back again.

"My name is Emily Radcliffe, I'm a journalist," she said, extending a hand.

The woman didn't take it. "June Jones. But they call me Mama."

Emily glanced at the smaller woman, who did not introduce herself, and seemed to shrink behind June.

"This is Lila. She's not much for talking," June said. "Now why are you down here, reporter?"

"Did you just get out?" Emily deflected.

"Obviously."

"How long were you in?"

"Couple of months. Is this an interview?" June asked.

"I'd like it to be, yes," Emily said with a lurch of excitement. "Is it as bad as they say in there?"

June squinted. "How bad do 'they' say it is? And who's 'they'?"

Emily licked her lips. Journalists didn't talk about their sources—even anonymous ones. "How did you get that bruise?" she asked instead, gesturing to a greenish spot on the woman's cheekbone.

June twisted her large lips, then shook her head. "I just got out, reporter. They'll round me up again soon anyway, sure as death and taxes, but I don't want to give them any reason to bring me back sooner. I got a business to run."

Her eyes flicked to the smaller woman, and Emily suddenly understood. "You . . . are you a—a madam?" she asked, recalling the term at the last moment. "Is that why you're here?"

"'Course it is," June said. "Police have to pretend to be shutting down the same brothels they patronize, now don't they? Wouldn't happen to have a cigarette, would you?"

Emily shook her head. "No, I'm sorry."

"Right. Well, goodbye, reporter lady," June said, turning to leave and beckoning the tiny Lila, who followed in her wake.

"Wait!" Emily said, darting after them as they headed east toward the village. "You won't talk to me at all? Can I buy you lunch? Cigarettes?"

June stopped short and regarded Emily with exasperation. "My time's valuable, and the goddamn state keeps robbing me by putting me in that place," she said. "I'm a businesswoman. I don't have time to talk to you."

"I want to do a story on the prison," Emily said, trying to keep the desperation from her voice. "The conditions inside. There's a story there, isn't there?"

June sighed, nodded. "Yeah. There's a *story* all right." Excitement flared again in Emily's stomach. "But no one ever gives a shit when we tell 'em," June continued. "Told the police a dozen times. They know. Everyone knows. They call it the 'House of Horrors,' for Christ's sake."

Doctor is evil . . .

"What kind of horrors?" Emily nudged as her memory scanned the prisoner's note. June's mouth puckered again. Emily knew she had to offer her something, hook her trust somehow. "I heard from someone—I can't say who—but they're alleging the conditions are atrocious: vermin, not enough to eat, abuse. Can you speak about any of that?"

"'Course I can speak about it, kid, speak til I'm blue in the face, but it won't make any difference, that's what I'm telling you. Everyone knows what it's like in there, but it's not going to change."

"The public doesn't know," Emily said, mind scrambling for a way to seize this interview, to convince June Jones to tell her everything she knew.

"Because they don't want 'em to," June snapped, and Emily saw an unexpected shimmer of tears in her eyes. "You want to know what it's like in there, eh? Go get yourself thrown in. Lord knows it's easy enough to do with that goddamn law. Although maybe not for a high-class lady like you," she said, looking Emily up and down and scowling. "I bet *you* lot have a whole other set o' rules than the ones the likes of us gotta live by. Let's go, Lila."

"Wait—please!"

But June stalked away, the small girl trailing her mother hen. Emily took a step forward but knew enough not to follow. She was not going to get any more information out of June Jones.

"Damn it," she cursed, tapping her bag again. Her heart pounded as she watched June and Lila grow smaller in the distance. She loved that feeling of adrenaline, like when she had too much wine at dinner, or rode the roller coaster at the CNE. It coursed through her now like electricity, exciting and energizing and a little frightening.

But she wanted more of it. More of it in this job, more of it in her own life, more of that intoxicating rush that reminded her she was alive. Men were allowed to have it—it was encouraged. Military men, adventurers, police officers—even male journalists like her dad, and pilots. There weren't many women celebrated for chasing danger, though one was her hero Nellie Bly, for a record-breaking trip around the world.

Emily's busy mind skipped ahead, writing her future. She now had the details of the Incorrigible Law and this account from June Jones to take back to Doris. Could she convince her boss to let her try to scoop this story? If she could somehow break this . . . well, an exposé like that could solidify her career and establish her as a journalist independent from her father's name. Doris might promote her, and that could be the beginning of something big.

How to go about it, though? She clenched her fist to stop herself tapping again and began to pace the sidewalk instead. Movement always helped to grease the gears of her mind.

She couldn't very well camp out by the prison gates waiting for inmates to be released at random. So how to get in touch with them?

Suddenly, Emily was rooted to the spot, the skin on her arms tingling as a thought hit her like an electric jolt.

Nellie Bly was famous for her record-breaking trip around the world in seventy-two days, yes—but also for her work as a journalist. She'd gone undercover at the insane asylum at Blackwell's Island in New York in 1887 to break the story of the deplorable conditions there.

Maybe June Jones was right. Maybe the easiest way to get this scoop, to uncover the true story behind the prisoner's note, was to get into the Mercer herself. It didn't sound as though the warden would welcome a journalist in for a tour of the place, so it would have to be a secret. She'd have to get herself declared "incorrigible" as a way to get inside.

She knew she had the guts to do it. She was William Radcliffe's daughter, after all, and had inherited the sense of daring—though her mother would call it recklessness—that had made him such a successful correspondent. He never shied away from leaping into the fray, getting as close to the story and its subjects as possible. Emily wanted to be on the ground, get her boots into the proverbial mud like her father had. Be a *real* reporter.

She turned back to face the building, dark and imposing and sinister as a bad omen. In some way she couldn't quite explain, the opportunity felt familiar, as though Emily had been waiting for it her whole life.

And it, in turn, had been waiting for Emily.

CHAPTER 5

RACHEL

Huron County, Ontario—May 27, 1996

No one has seen seventeen-year-old Stacy Cooper in a year.

It was a warm spring day just like this one—the anniversary of her disappearance—that Stacy vanished without a trace. The blond had attended an after-hours cheerleading practice in the back field of the high school, but never made it home to her parents' house in Grand Bend, which is a thirty-seven-minute drive from Rachel Mackenzie's office at the Ontario Provincial Police detachment in Clinton.

It seems almost impossible that they should get this phone call today, of all days. Too coincidental. But it's folly to jump to conclusions or fall for superstitions in this line of work. Rachel isn't paid to think fanciful thoughts about the missing and murdered and maltreated. Her job as a detective is to assess the facts, which are all tacked on a corkboard on the wall of her windowless office; a confused constellation of witness and suspect photos, dates, location pins and minutiae connected by black and red threads—some weaker than others.

The lead detective on the case, Gary Green, who is also her supervisor, doesn't like that she continues to pursue it. They arrested the girl's father a few months after she disappeared, and he'll be on trial for her murder next fall. As far as Green is concerned, it's a done deal. Except for the fact that, as Rachel frequently reminds him, they still haven't located Stacy Cooper's body, and there was seemingly no motive for her father to kill her. By all accounts, they had a good relationship. Strained at times, like that of all parents and teens, but nothing out of the ordinary. Yet Green seemed to just *know* it was John Cooper from the day he and Stacy's mother reported their daughter missing—which is bad police work, plain and simple. Rachel's told him that, too, more times than she can count and certainly more than are good for her career.

So when their office got the call today from a rattled staff member at the tiny Millgate Cemetery who claimed there was an unidentified body buried in their graveyard that maybe-sorta looked female, the detachment exploded into a chaotic uproar, and Rachel and Green leapt into their cars.

They're now careening down the two-lane highway toward Millgate, a town of about a thousand people just southwest of Clinton.

Red lights flash on the car in front of Rachel's squad, and she hits her brakes, then dips out into the oncoming lane, craning her neck to see what the slowdown is. Though she knows exactly what it'll be this time of year, in farm country. Sure enough, the enormous outline of a planter comes into view three car-lengths in front of her, crawling along at thirty clicks, its green and yellow arms extended out like some giant Tolkienian arachnid, kicking up a haze of beige dust from the gravel shoulder. She ducks out again to check for oncoming traffic, but she can't get a long enough break to flick on her siren and overtake this glacially paced country parade. She taps the steering wheel and sighs, accepting the momentary delay and the extra time it gives her to consider what this alleged discovery might mean.

It's the anniversary of Stacy Cooper's disappearance, and so her name is in the air today—quite literally: it's on the radio. Everyone is thinking about her, wondering, and guessing guessing guessing. It's the most sensational case the community has seen since Rachel's own family gave them plenty to talk about a decade ago. Everyone's got a theory. Everyone's got an opinion.

What was it that happened, a year ago today, to push John Cooper to murder and dispose of his daughter in the depths of Lake Huron, the newspaper said this morning, *where the remains of over a hundred doomed ships languish in the rocky darkness, the lake bed their final resting place?*

Oh, please, thought Rachel. Detective Green had gathered the best sonar and technicians from across North America to search the lake last summer because he was "absolutely sure" they would find Stacy's body there.

They didn't.

Who are these people who claim to have seen Stacy since her disappearance? Can they be believed? a radio DJ asked the airwaves.

Possibly.

Is she working the streets of London, prostituting for drugs only an hour down the road?

Also possible.

Did she run away? With whom? Her boyfriend, they say . . .

Well, her friends said *maybe*. But then why did she leave one hundred dollars, untouched, on top of her dresser? Wouldn't a runaway take the cash?

Was she murdered?

Green says yes. Rachel's eyes flick to her rear-view mirror and she sees him in his squad car behind her, his mouth a sour knot.

Well, of course she was, her father's in prison for it, isn't he? The police must have had enough to charge him on.

They didn't. They really didn't.

Rachel half expects this call at the cemetery to be some kind of prank or obvious misunderstanding that any rational human could explain easily—an oddly shaped series of white sedimentary rocks, or frail animal bones—though a small part of her hopes it's the remains of Stacy Cooper, and that her body might provide more evidence than the thin layer of dubious crumbs Green used to nail her father for murder. But another part of Rachel hopes it's not the girl, that she's still alive somewhere. Though there are some options for her whereabouts that are arguably worse than death.

Rachel still isn't convinced John Cooper did it, not by a stretch. But the lack of evidence and answers is driving her up the wall. She's the one who still gets the calls from Stacy's tormented mother, Tamara, who has lost her only child to God knows what fate, and her husband to what might well turn out to be a bogus prison sentence. Tamara doesn't believe he did it. And if the police service doesn't close this off, if they don't deliver some kind of real justice based on actual evidence, Rachel fears they might find Tamara Cooper's own body in the lake someday soon. And who could blame her?

"Finally," Rachel mutters as the planter makes a turn onto a side road and the line of cars picks up speed again, like a faucet freed of a stubborn clog. Millgate is a tiny town, just a handful of shops and houses clustered around the old Millgate Methodist Church and its adjoining cemetery. It's all one neighbourhood, fifteen minutes from the lake, but without the waterfront price tag. Rachel knows it well.

She pulls into the laneway leading to the church, then parks the car near the cemetery office as Green pulls in right beside her. After taking a moment to prepare herself for this visit, she pastes a neutral expression on her face, hops out of the car and grabs her kit from the trunk, heart fluttering.

"Do you think it's her?" she asks Green.

He clears his throat, doesn't answer. Rachel wants to push him to, to make him acknowledge that it *could* be; that maybe he's wrong and Stacy Cooper isn't at the bottom of Lake Huron after all. But he says nothing, because in Rachel's experience, men are allowed to just say nothing when they're wrong. Women are always forced to apologize, defend themselves.

They make their way toward the far end of the cemetery where a woman and two men are standing beside a mini excavator at the base of a towering maple tree. Rachel recognizes the woman, an old classmate named Julie Jamieson—now Randolph. Rachel runs into everyone she went to school with who stuck around the county—not that there's very many of them. Most moved to Windsor, London, or Toronto as soon as they got the chance after high school or university. She knew Julie worked at Millgate Methodist, but had forgotten until now; Rachel's always keen to avoid the place. But she liked Julie well enough. They had homeroom together and both played flute in the high school band. Rachel remembered her as an anxious type, so she can only imagine what this morning's discovery has done to her.

"Oh, Rachel—Detective Mackenzie, sorry," Julie stammers when she sees her. "I thought it might be you coming, and I'm so glad it is."

Rachel nods at her. "Hey, Julie."

The men with Julie are Reverend Holland Jr., who took over the ministry from his prick of a father a few years ago, and a young man Rachel doesn't recognize but who she suspects was the person who called in the discovery. He'd said his name was Jake, and that he was the contract gravedigger. He's built like most landscapers are—muscly and sturdy. He has smooth hands with long fingers and absolutely filthy fingernails. But Rachel is an avid gardener and is used to that, doesn't judge him for it. It's nothing a good nail brush won't solve, and that's more than can be said for most of life's messes.

"So what have you got for us?" Green asks.

Reverend Holland sighs audibly and steps forward just as the other man opens his mouth to speak.

"One at a time," Green says. He looks at Jake. "Mr. . . . ?"

"Easton. Jake Easton."

"You're the one that found the body?"

Rachel's eyes dart to the open hole beside the mini excavator, but she can't see much from where she's standing.

"Yes."

"Go ahead."

"Well, I was just going to dig the hole, same as I always do."

"Always do?"

"I'm on contract for landscaping, but I also dig the graves. Doesn't happen often, really. Not 'round here."

"Okay."

"And I hit something, so of course I stopped. But it was already a bit late. You'll see what I mean. I hit some kind of casket. But the body, well . . ." He trails off with an expression of distaste. "I kind of panicked, to be honest, and I don't get shook easily."

"This plot wasn't taken yet," Julie pipes up, her voice meek. "There shouldn't be a body there, that's the problem. We don't know who it is."

"And Julie, are you *quite sure* this plot wasn't already taken when the Richards family selected it?" Reverend Holland asks.

"I already told you," Julie says. "I know this cemetery like my own backyard. There isn't supposed to be a body in this plot. I'm positive."

"Well, let's see it," Green says, gesturing to the hole several feet away.

They walk over to the excavation, Rachel and Green pulling blue rubber gloves out of their pockets as they go. When they reach the edge, they kneel. The late spring breeze lifts Rachel's dark-brown bangs. The rest of her hair is tied back in a tight bun.

She takes in the sight and her heart falls.

"Not her," Green mutters beside her.

"No. Not her."

From the size of the skull and what they can see of the torso, combined with the narrow jawline, the remains are likely female. But they're just bones. This body has been here for decades. It's not Stacy Cooper.

"Shit," Rachel curses.

"Yeah. My guess is administrative error," Green says with a glance back in Julie's direction. "Seems a bit scattered, jumpy. Probably not the most organized."

Rachel gives him a sidelong scowl. She hates when people question whether women are good at their jobs. She herself had more than enough of that from Bloody Mary when she was a child. It was only ever her grandmother Dora, pausing over her blue-patterned Bicycle playing cards, who would praise Rachel for her successes.

Good game, little one. Your turn to deal.

"Except this body has clearly been here longer than Julie's been running the cemetery office," Rachel notes. She wants to snarl it at him, but keeps her tone calm.

"Bad record-keeping in the past, then, and not organized now. Think about it, Mackenzie: what are the odds that an unidentified body in a cemetery *isn't* just an error?"

"Well, maybe, but isn't that presumption also why it might be a perfect place to dispose of a body? Because the perp thought we *would* assume it's an error?"

He shrugs. "But it's in a casket."

"Well, I don't—"

"You can take lead on this one, Mackenzie."

"What? Why?" Rachel says, heated. "Can't you give it to Garrison? I'm still on the Cooper case."

And I don't want to be here any longer than I have to.

"Except the Cooper case is solved," Green says, anger threading his tone like coarse twine. "John Cooper—"

"I don't want to do this with you, Gary, I really don't," Rachel interrupts. "But we still don't have a body, there're still too many unanswered questions."

"*Enough*," he snaps, and Rachel swallows as she sees Reverend Holland glance over out of the corner of her eye.

"Sir," she begins again, feeling her face grow warm and silently cursing it.

"It's done, Mackenzie. Let it go, for God's sake. We'll find Stacy Cooper's body in the lake eventually. Give that poor woman some peace."

Rachel's mouth falls open but she catches herself, presses her lips together and raises her chin. She's *trying* to give Tamara Cooper some peace by solving the fucking case, by giving her real information as to what actually happened to her daughter.

"Look," Green says, with an exasperated sigh that makes Rachel know he's hit the limit of how much so-called insubordination he'll tolerate from her today. How much *truth*, more like. "You say there's still too many questions in the Cooper case, and there are. I'll give you that. But that's true about any case," he continues. "This is your job, Mackenzie. Drop the Cooper case. You're on this one now."

Rachel clenches her fist around her pen. "Yes, sir."

"Start with the cemetery records. If we can tie this off as a mistake, I'd prefer it."

Rachel bites her tongue so hard she worries she might taste blood. It's his "preference" for how he wants his cases to turn out that makes him so difficult to work with. You don't start with a conclusion and work your way backward.

"And tell *them*," he adds, nodding darkly at Julie, Jake, and the reverend, "not to go spouting off about this to anyone. *Especially* today. Last thing we need is the news finding out a woman's body's been discovered."

Rachel nods. She doesn't want Tamara Cooper to hear about this, either. She's had enough visits and phone calls with Stacy's grief-stricken mother. Each one weighs more than the one before it, and this news might just about break her.

"Not sure what to do about that, though," Rachel says, indicating the street along the only side of the cemetery that isn't walled in with tall hedges, encasing it like a secret garden. There are people out on the street in front of six of the ten houses, all watching curiously, drawing their own conclusions. "As soon as they see us cordon it off as a crime scene, it's game over."

Yellow tape around the trees, snapping in the wind.

She clears her throat, shakes the image away. Of all the horrendous things she witnessed that night nearly ten years ago, she's not sure why the yellow tape has stuck with her.

"Well," Green says with an impatient bite, "we can't do anything about that but try to tell them it's nothing. I'll go talk to 'em. You go into the office and get started on those records. I'll go back to HQ and send Stevens and Fisher over to help you. And if that secretary"—he frowns in Julie's direction—"can't gather all the records because they aren't organized, then I think we know what happened here, don't we?"

"Sure, sir," Rachel says. She can't say any more without getting in shit.

He smiles, smug. "I think this is good. It'll finally get you off the Cooper case. It's time you had another body." He heads off in the direction of the onlookers, ready to give them a telling-off that will only spark more rumour and speculation.

Rachel watches him go, breathing deep to try to lessen the clenching sensation in her chest. She isn't sure she'll ever "get off" the Stacy Cooper case. Not until her body is found and they can deliver some real answers to the girl's poor mother.

Rachel walks back over to the open hole in the earth, kneels and looks down on the remains of a person. There isn't a whole lot to see—most of the skeleton is encased in the battered remains of a cheap, splintered casket. She'll get a better look when the Ident team comes in to exhume it. She'll take notes and pictures, collate the questions that need to be answered.

And that's when it really hits her: she's been so tied up in the Cooper case, but this person here in the Millgate Cemetery is someone else's unsolved case, their loss. The tragedy they need answers to if they can ever hope to move on. There could be some other Tamara Cooper out there waiting for the truth.

Rachel sighs heavily, and stands.

If there's one thing she hates, it's an unanswered question.

CHAPTER 6

EMILY

Early June, 1961

After her conversation with June Jones, Emily stood on the sidewalk beneath the Liberty Street sign for a solid three minutes, mind and heart still racing, before turning and walking north to catch the streetcar on Queen. Her journey was a distracted trance filled with a cascade of questions and thoughts about the Incorrigible Law, the Mercer prison, and how she would propose her plan to Doris.

She hopped off outside Osgoode Hall after nearly missing her stop, then made her way up to Dundas, weaving through the throngs of commuters, clamorous students, and newspaper kiosks. Two new subway lines were under construction to add to the existing Yonge line, with a new station being built right next to her office building. Most of her officemates couldn't wait for the new lines to open, but not Emily. She preferred the streetcars and her own feet. More time for staring out foggy windows and working through her thoughts as the city whizzed past in a blur of colour and human activity.

She walked the final block up University until she reached the big intersection at Dundas. She stared up at the Maclean-Hunter building, waiting for the light to turn green. It was the same building her father worked in when he wasn't at the rolltop desk at home.

Emily had known she wanted to write like he did from the time she was young. Working in a glamorous building like that, right downtown in the thick of it all, had been her dream when other girls her age—including her sister—were interested only in dolls and barrettes.

She crossed the street and walked toward the building, stopping outside the doors to check her watch. It was nearly noon, but she might still catch Doris before she left for lunch.

Emily tucked a stray strand of hair behind her ear, then wrenched the glass door open and stepped into the echoing lobby. She jammed the small black button on the brass plate beside the elevator and the doors opened. As the car rose to the fourth floor, Emily's finger tapped her bag like rapid Morse code.

The elevator bell dinged and the doors slid open. As Emily stepped off, she saw Doris standing near the reception desk, shrugging on her coat.

"Doris!" Emily yelped, hurrying over.

Doris's eyes had shadows beneath them and despite her impressive height, her shoulders were a little stooped. She was clearly already eager for the weekend. But at the sight of Emily, her eyebrows shot upward, and she stepped back a pace.

"Well, don't you look like a woman with a story," she said as she took in Emily's bright eyes and breathlessness.

Emily nodded fervently. "Yes, ma'am."

Doris smirked. "Come on, darlin'. I was headed out for lunch, but uh . . . let's see what we can scrounge from the kitchen, and you can tell me all about it."

Back in Doris's office, Emily sat down across from her boss at the coffee table. She held a glass of brandy poured with enthusiasm from the bottle in Doris's desk drawer in one hand, a plate of slightly too-salty quiche that they'd swiped from the test kitchen in the other. The rest of the office was silent, with almost everyone else gone for lunch or eating quietly at their desks, and the lack of voices, typewriters, and phones added a sense of gravitas to the impending conversation.

"All right," Doris said. "Shoot."

Emily took a deep breath. "Okay, so first of all, I read the Female Refuges Act at the Legislative Library. It's not long, but the scope is huge, Doris. It's practically a carte blanche to punish women and teenagers for subjective misbehaviour."

"How so?" Doris took a bite of quiche.

Emily set hers down and flipped a page of her notebook. "Anyone—*anyone*—can bring a woman under age thirty-five before a judge if they think she's 'unmanageable or incorrigible.'"

Doris chuckled darkly. "Indeed. So, failure to abide by societal rules dictating the lives of women. Continue."

"Well, exactly," Emily said. "And they can be incarcerated for up to two years. Without ever committing any real crime."

She handed the notes across the table to her boss, then shoved a large forkful of quiche into her mouth. She didn't even care that it was too salty. Brainpower and adrenaline always fuelled her appetite.

Doris leaned back in the large green wing chair, legs crossed at the ankles above her chunky black heels, eyes on Emily's notes.

"Goodness," she said finally. "That's a fair bit to go on. Well done."

Emily flushed a little. "Thank you."

Doris took a long swig of her drink, and Emily copied her. She wasn't used to the potency of the liquor—she only ever had wine at Sunday dinner. The brandy burned her throat, but she didn't let on. She was sitting in her boss's office, just the two of them, discussing what Emily desperately hoped would be her first-ever scoop. She was at the grown-up table now, and it was time to ditch the Shirley Temples.

She waited until Doris set the notes down again before launching back in.

"So after I got all that, I went to see the prison," she said.

Doris nodded slowly, mouth twitching with amused approval. "Naturally. And?"

"Obviously I couldn't go in. But two women were being released. One was named June Jones. She's a madam, actually." She waited for Doris to react, but she didn't. "She told me the police have to pretend to be shutting down the brothels while, she claims, they patronize them on the side."

"I would not be at all surprised." Doris sighed. "What else did she tell you? Did you get a proper interview?"

"I tried. She got a bit emotional, but she wouldn't do it. She did say, though," Emily steeled herself for her pitch, "that it's easy to get sent to the Mercer under this law, and that maybe I should try to get myself committed to find out what it's like."

She chewed her lip and watched Doris, unblinking. "Maybe I should do that."

"Oh, Emily," Doris said, shaking her head. "You have no idea what you're suggesting. Let's back up a moment." She ran a thumb up and down her glass, eyes narrowed on Emily, whose gut clenched, but she didn't want to back down.

"Doris, there are women in that prison because of a hugely unjust law!" Emily argued. "A law that every woman under thirty-five is subject to, and we didn't even know it existed. The general public must not know, either. Our *readers* don't know, and I think it's important that they do." She heaved a breath. "You've said this sort of thing yourself," she pressed, keenly aware that she might be overstepping. "When women are under attack from any quarter, it matters to all women. Unmarried women should still care about the inequities of divorce, you said. Women who want children should still care about access to birth control. Women who would never dream of being sent to prison need to care about this, because clearly it *is* too easy for them—for us all—to be incarcerated. This law allows for it within ludicrously broad parameters." She swallowed hard, fighting the heat in her cheeks. "It matters. I think this matters. *I want this story.* Please."

Doris's dark brows popped, reluctantly impressed. She leaned forward and tossed Emily's notes onto the coffee table with a swish. "Well, you've got clout. But this is higher stakes than I think you realize. With respect, you have lived a sheltered life, Emily. And I don't mean that as an insult; it is simply a fact."

Emily nodded tightly. "You're right," she admitted. "But Doris, if I don't take on some risk, really get out there, how will I gain experience? How will I get out from under that shelter?"

Doris gestured her acknowledgment. "Fair. But you saw that prisoner's note, and this Jones woman told you herself: the conditions in there could be ghastly."

"I know."

Noises were beginning to filter in from the hallway now. Lunch hour was nearly over.

"What would you suggest we do next?" Doris asked her. "You came in here looking like you had a plan."

Emily had thought this through on the streetcar.

"Well, we've validated the existence of this law. Next, I think we need to contact the prison, see if we can get some kind of statement on the claims. Although I don't imagine they're going to admit to anything. They may not even talk to us. And I do worry a bit that us digging around might come back on the inmates."

Doris watched her thoughtfully. "Well, if these claims are indeed true, I'm not sure what more the administration could do to make these women's lives a misery. But I take your point. We would need to be careful not to tip our hand."

"So . . ." Emily began with a swoop of nerves. "Are you saying I can—?"

"I am absolutely *not* saying that," Doris said firmly, and Emily felt herself deflate. "But . . ." She shook her head, clearly considering something. "Let's get the writers in here. We need to bat this around a little."

Twenty minutes later, they were back in Doris's office with a pot of tea and Virginia, Maeve, and Sonya all clustered around them. Doris shut the door, which she rarely did. The staff writers looked curiously at Emily. Assistants didn't often have one-on-one meetings with the editor.

"All right, girls," Doris said, sitting back down and leaning forward to pour herself a cup. "I'd like your input on a matter of some delicacy."

"Did one of the men upstairs make an advance on her?" Sonya asked, indicating Emily.

"Uh, no," Emily said quickly, taken aback. "Nothing like that."

"Only it wouldn't be the first time," Sonya replied darkly.

"Emily has a scoop," Doris said, taking a careful sip of tea. Emily seized a cup and saucer for herself, too, mostly to give her fingers something to do other than tap on the sofa beside her.

"A scoop, eh?" Maeve asked, smiling at Emily, impressed. "Well done, junior."

"Thank you," Emily said. "It sort of came to us here at the office, though. I only chased it down."

"Don't sell yourself short, dear," Virginia said firmly. She was dressed in a smart cream blouse and matching skirt, her dark hair swept up. "Always take credit when it's yours. If you leave it on the table, a man's just going to come along and pick it up for himself."

Emily cracked a smile, then looked at Doris, who launched into the summary of how they were tipped off by the "incorrigible" inmate at the Mercer Women's Prison, Emily's findings, and her proposal to try to get inside.

When she'd finished, all three of the staff writers sat in silence for a few moments. Then Maeve whistled.

"Gosh," she breathed. "And this is allegedly happening just down in Liberty Village?"

"Yes," Emily said. "But the legislation applies to any woman under age thirty-five. So—"

"Practically everyone in this office, aside from me," Doris said.

A beat of silence again as the reality sank in.

"I think Emily's right," Sonya said finally. "I think we need to get someone in there."

"And I don't necessarily disagree," Doris said, setting her cup down and crossing her legs with an air of business. "But Emily is still very junior."

"I know I am," Emily admitted, as everyone looked at her. "But you also know how much I want this. I want what you all have."

"Mm. But what I have is a career I love and children I also love who I can't leave for weeks or months on end for an investigation," Sonya said. "I can't do this, and I can't ask my mother to help for that long. I'm sorry, Doris."

Doris nodded. "Maeve? Virginia?"

Maeve shook her head regretfully. "I wish I had the flexibility, but I can't. With the kids, you know how it is."

Virginia exhaled in a huff. "Except if any of our husbands were taken away for work for weeks or months, it wouldn't even be a conversation, now would it?"

"True, but I also wouldn't want to leave my children for that long," Sonya said. "I'd miss them sorely."

Emily watched them all in turn, these women she looked up to. The fact that they were married, working mothers was unusual enough, particularly for middle-class women. But the truth was that all the husbands of the women at *Chatelaine* must have had some level of understanding or appreciation for their wives' jobs. She couldn't see how you could do it otherwise. A familiar sensation tickled at her throat as she thought of Jem. He was not one of those men, and she wondered how these women had found *those* sorts of men, or convinced them to accept their careers. At any rate, supportive as their husbands might be, it was the children that now held them back from career freedom. That much was clear.

Maeve chuckled heartily. "What I would have given to have this kind of scoop land in my lap when I was first coming up. I understand why you want it, Emily. I really do. It's a dream."

"Well," Doris said, with a heavy air, "my concern is that it will, in fact, turn out to be quite the nightmare."

They were all silent, eyes darting between teacups and Emily, who ignored the nerves in her gut. She was either going to do it, or she wasn't. There was no sense being nervous.

"So none of the three of you can take this," Doris said. "And Emily . . ." She pinched her maroon lips, the same colour that now lingered on the rim of the teacup.

"I want to do it," Emily said as firmly as she dared.

"She may be junior," Maeve said, shifting in her seat, "but it looks like she's the only one who *can* do it, Doris."

Doris still looked unconvinced.

"Then should we abandon the infiltration attempt altogether?" Sonya suggested. "We could just run the story about this Incorrigible Law. There's enough meat on those bones already, isn't there?"

"Yes, but the conditions inside that place where the women are being held at the behest of such a tenuous law, being subjected to all sorts of horrors because of it—"

"That's the real scoop," Virginia finished.

Silence again. They all knew that was true, and Emily was hesitant now to say anything that might create a wedge for further resistance from Doris. She still hoped her boss might consent.

"Is there any other way to do this?" Virginia pressed. "I don't know... see if some contact inside the prison might sneak Emily in for a quick glance? Some disgruntled employee, a guard or some such?"

"We have no contact except for this anonymous note-writer," Doris said.

"And what happens if she goes in and gets found out?" Virginia mused.

"Better to ask for forgiveness than permission," Maeve quoted, winking at Doris, who offered a reluctant smirk.

"And by then, we'd have the story," Emily said. "How could Legal complain about that, if it's big news? The Mercer prison won't want a headline announcing they're trying to sue us for breaking a story about how they've abused their inmates for the past seventy years."

Doris let out a grunt. "Well, you've got me there."

"And maybe I wouldn't have to be gone more than, say, a month," Emily offered. "We don't know yet how the sentencing works under this Act. If someone brought me to a judge, saying I was incorrigible, maybe they could, I don't know... request a short sentence, just enough to straighten me out."

"Perhaps," Doris said, "But as you say, we have no idea. And that's a wild card I don't particularly want to gamble on."

"Well . . ." Emily sat forward now and cast around for another argument to convince her boss. "Nellie Bly got her scoop at Blackwell's Island in two weeks." She shrugged. As a woman journalist, Doris knew who Bly was, of course.

"And perhaps it is time for a revival of the 'girl stunt reporters,'" Doris said. "Though I admit, I don't ever like to put my own girls in harm's way. There's enough harm to be had out there without your job adding to it." She paused. "But let's say I agree, Emily . . . how would we get you admitted?"

"I've thought about that, too," Emily said. "And I think I could ask my dad. I think he'd help. It says here a parent can bring their daughter before a judge. He could say I'm 'unmanageable.' I am, in a way," she added with a self-conscious grin that Maeve returned with interest.

"I can see how much this means to you," Doris said. "And I know you want to prove yourself. I understand, we've all been there. But this is one hell of a way to get your feet wet."

"I know. But I think I'm ready. I want to do it."

Doris ran her tongue over her teeth, twitched her head almost in resignation as the other three women watched on. Emily tried not to get too excited about the air of agreement that seemed to have settled over them all.

"You've got your father's grit, that's for sure," Doris said. "All right. I need to get some things done before the weekend. But on Monday, I say we at least call the prison and see if we can swindle any info out of anyone there before we commit to this." She stood, studying Emily. "That fire in your belly is freshly kindled from what you learned today. I know how that is. But let it cool a little over the weekend, and see if the spark is still there come Monday, okay?"

CHAPTER 7

EMILY

Early June, 1961

The Monday after the meeting in Doris's office with the staff writers, Emily glanced at the clock above the door of the Closet, as she had every half-hour since she arrived.

10:52.

Doris had meetings in the early morning, but had left a memo for Emily to come to her office at eleven and they would discuss "the Mercer matter." Emily had spent most of the weekend and that morning making discreet phone calls and reviewing her notes on the Female Refuges Act to figure out exactly what steps they would need to take—*if* Doris approved it—to get her before a judge.

With a little flutter of excitement, she collected her notes and stood to go fetch herself a fresh cup of tea before the meeting. She'd gone just two steps when Betty swept through the door.

"Betty!" Emily said, a little exasperated. "Where have you been? I wondered if you were ill."

"No-oooo!" Betty sang playfully. A grin split across her face and she held her left hand up, wiggling a finger with a sparkling diamond ring. Her nails matched her pale-pink trench coat. "Stuart proposed on Saturday night, at the Silver Rail! I'm engaged, Emily! *Finally!*"

"Oh!" Emily forced an expression of cheer onto her face, chose her next words carefully. "Well, this is just what you wanted, isn't it? Congratulations, Betty."

"We were up late last night celebrating with our families. Lots of champagne," Betty said, "So I'm a teensy bit tardy, I know." Emily raised an eyebrow. She was over two hours late. "But I figured, special circumstances and all . . ."

Betty shed her coat and sat down, grin wilting to a pouty frown at the sight of her overflowing in-tray.

"So when's the big day?" Emily asked, struggling to feign enthusiasm.

"Well," Betty said, her tone shifting to businesslike, "Mother wants us to wait an entire *year* because she thinks a spring wedding is chic. But Stuart doesn't want to wait that long. And you can understand why—he's waited long enough." She winked. "So I think we might aim for September."

"Oh wow, three months," Emily said, backing toward the door. If she didn't extract herself from this unwelcome conversation soon, she'd miss the opportunity to get her tea before the meeting with Doris. Also, the encroaching panic might win.

"Yes," Betty said happily. "So I have to let Doris know today that I'll be leaving."

Emily tried to resist the retort, but it came out anyway. "Why do you have to leave just because you're getting married?"

Betty looked at Emily as though she'd lost her senses. "I can't *work* once I'm married," she said, scowling. "I'll be raising a family soon. And besides, Stuart wouldn't stand the shame of having a working wife. Jem wouldn't either, would he?"

Emily's fists clenched at her sides. She needed to get out of there. "Well, it certainly won't be the same without you," she offered.

Betty leaned back in her chair. "It won't be long for you, then, will it? You're what, mid-twenties? Not getting any younger, really. You could be next. And then maybe they could turn this place back into a proper closet," she added, nose crinkling at the windowless walls. "It wouldn't take much."

Emily was rooted to the spot, blinking.

You could be next. Not getting any younger. The spinster's refrain, an insult wrapped in the clever silkiness of well-intentioned optimism.

"And if you're on your way out, too, you needn't take your work so *seriously*, Emily," Betty continued, relentless. "Do you really want to be like these women here?" She dropped her voice, cocked her head toward the open door. "Spending all your time at the office, missing out on family life? I wonder what their husbands must think of it all."

Emily exhaled her outrage in a cough of disgust. She was genuinely surprised by Betty's words. As much as Emily had found her silly and stupid over the past year they'd been coworkers, they'd never had a real argument. Betty hadn't cared enough about any of her work to dig her three-inch heels in on anything, but clearly the engagement had caused her to jettison all pretense to collegiality. She had one foot out the door now, and was thrilled about it.

"They *do* have families and family lives," Emily said. "They just have other ambitions and dreams, too. Other things they think are important. And so do I," she added with a snap of defiance. "There's nothing wrong with that."

Betty's face clouded over. "If you say so," she said icily, taking in Emily's plain navy linen skirt. Bare face and low heels. "But you're burning precious time here in this working-girl prison. You do know that, don't you?"

Emily looked away from her, glancing at the clock again. She'd missed out on her damn tea now. "I have to go," she said. "I have a meeting with Doris in three minutes to discuss my continued path to spinsterhood. Excuse me."

She left the Closet and stomped down the hall to the kitchenette. There was no time to boil the kettle, but she snatched a glass and gulped down some cold tap water to help settle her nerves. She needed to forget about Betty, Eleanor, her mother, and Jem and focus on this monumental thing she was about to discuss with Doris: the scoop that could make her career as a journalist, which, despite what others might suggest, was the thing she wanted most in the world right now.

Emily approached Doris's office and rapped smartly on the door frame to announce herself. The editor looked up from her work, dark eyes piercing Emily from behind black horn-rimmed reading glasses.

"Emily, come in," she said, standing. Emily sat down in the same spot on the couch where she had last Friday with the staff writers, notes resting on her thighs. She tapped them rapidly with her index finger as Doris took a seat opposite in the green armchair.

"You seem flustered, Emily," she said. "Are you having second thoughts about this? I wouldn't blame you in the least."

"No, no it's not that. It's uh . . ." She didn't want to speak ill of her coworker to their boss, but was having trouble holding it in. "It's Betty, actually. She got engaged over the weekend and we got into an odd argument about it."

"Ah. So she'll be leaving, then. That one was only a matter of time. I'm not surprised."

Emily shrugged the tension from her neck. She hesitated, but then remembered her father's suggestion that she speak to Doris about her situation with Jem.

"Can I ask how you do it all?" she burst out in desperation. "Marriage? Children? Work?"

"Oh, well, that's a question and a half," Doris said, scratching a spot on her forehead. "I think part of it is just raw determination. Stubbornness, or whatever title you want to slap on it. I always wanted children, but I wanted a career, too. A real one. And by the time I met my husband and we got down to having a family, I was so entrenched here that I simply couldn't stomach giving it all up. I had my first child at thirty-seven, and . . . well . . ." She shrugged, paused. "I'm pregnant again now, in fact."

"*Really?*" Emily gaped, then caught herself. "I'm sorry, that's just—"

"I know, I am positively *ancient*, as everyone from my family to the delivery nurses delighted in telling me last time. I can't wait to hear what they have to say about a forty-year-old giving birth. The way they act, I might as well be a grandmother. But this career took time to establish, and I didn't even marry David until I was thirty-six, so . . ." She smiled thinly.

Emily took a breath, encouraged but daunted, too. "My father told me the man I'm going with is about to propose," she confided.

Doris watched her. "And?"

"And I'm terrified," Emily said, her voice cracking on a humourless laugh.

"Why is that?"

Emily angrily fought back the tears that pricked her eyes. She wasn't a crier. "Because I'm not ready. Because there's still a lot I want to do, specifically here, with my career. And I can't see how marriage and babies fit into that."

Doris nodded knowingly. "Well, it doesn't necessarily have to be one or the other, but it sure isn't easy. I never quite feel like I'm exactly where I should be. At work, I worry I should have stayed with my son longer before finding a nanny. At home, I have work on my mind—and on my bedside table—because it never really ends. To some extent, you have to just accept that everything is going to be chaos, and do the best you can. But you've got to have the right man beside you, willing to let you do it." She paused. "So, if I may: Do you think your beau is that kind of man? Or no?"

Emily's throat was tight. Jem was *not* that kind of man. He was amusing and friendly but firm in his traditional beliefs. He would not be willing to let her keep working.

"I shall let you mull that one over," Doris said, spotting Emily's dismay and sparing her from having to answer. "But we aren't here to only discuss Betty and babies. The Mercer: What are your thoughts after the weekend?"

Emily shoved rumination of Jem aside. "I gave it a lot of thought, Doris. Honestly I did. And I spent this morning sorting out the process for being deemed 'incorrigible.' It seems my father could bring me down to the courthouse and tell them he wants me brought before the judge for whatever fabricated reason. Unruliness, maybe. Staying out after curfew, refusing authority or some such. If the judge will see us, I'll just act surly and 'unmanageable,' like it says in the Act. And then I suppose we'll find out whether June Jones is right, and if it is actually that easy to get locked up at the Mercer."

Doris sighed deeply. "And you are prepared for that, if it comes to it? The allegations in that inmate's note make it quite clear what sort of horrid conditions you could be facing."

"I know," Emily said. "But as I said on Friday, if it's that bad, it should be obvious fairly quickly, right? I won't need long to talk to some inmates, witness—or experience"—she shifted a little in her seat—"the treatment from prison staff." She thought of her father, of the year and a half he spent on the front lines and in the mountains of Italy, the hunger and physical discomfort, recording the horrendous things humans were capable of doing to one another in the name of righteousness. He saw it through. And so could she. "The trouble is, according to the Act, it looks like the minimum sentence is three months."

Doris removed her glasses and massaged the bridge of her nose.

"I know. I know," Emily said quickly. "I was hoping maybe my dad could just request my release or something, but it doesn't seem as simple as that. But I've thought of almost nothing else all weekend, and I think I can handle it, Doris." She swallowed the little bead of doubt that pinched her throat.

Doris put her glasses back on and watched Emily for a long, drawn-out moment. "I don't doubt you, Emily. But I do think we should call the Mercer first. Let's see what we can learn from the outside."

"All right. When?" Emily asked.

"Now." Doris stood, and Emily followed her to the desk, watching as she hauled the phone book out of a drawer and slammed it down. "It's got to have a phone number," she said. The thin paper of the book crackled as she turned page after page. "There. There it is." She landed her index finger with a soft thud. Emily's insides clenched with excitement and apprehension.

"Are you going to call, or should I?" she asked.

Doris surveyed her for a moment, clearly calculating. "I will. This call could potentially send up a red flag. If you do end up going in there, I don't want to risk anyone recognizing your voice. Mine's much deeper. All right. Here we go." Doris glanced back and forth at the number as the rotary whirred seven times. She waited, eyes on the desk in front of her. They flashed up to Emily.

"Yes, good morning, ma'am. I wonder if the warden might be available, please." Doris held Emily's eager gaze as the woman responded. "Well, when will she be in? . . . ah . . . yes . . . all right. No. Well, I wonder then if *you* can comment on some allegations of sub-par living conditions at your institution. I have heard . . . I . . . yes . . . no . . ." It wasn't going well, but Doris seemed unfazed. "Well, if the warden . . . excuse me? I don't see how my name is—" She made a regretful face. "Yes, I work for a magazine," she said eventually. If they asked outright, she couldn't lie. "Hello? Ma'am?" She shook her head and set the receiver back down.

"She hung up?" Emily asked, biting her lip.

"She hung up."

"So what does that say?"

Doris licked her lips, and Emily saw that despite her cool demeanour, pink patches had risen in her cheeks, and there was a shine in her eyes that Emily recognized. She'd seen it before, when Doris proposed the battered women article last fall. "I've been at this a long time, and my instinct says there's something here."

Emily nodded. Doris gestured for her notes, and she handed them over. Her boss re-read the legislation, eyes narrowing, and then the inmate's note once again. She shook her head.

"We don't have any other way to validate this, Doris," Emily said.

Doris pressed her tongue into the side of her cheek. "No. I spent a while on the weekend sorting through options, but there aren't many. That madam you talked to said women have tried to report the conditions to police, correct?"

"Yes. But who's going to listen to a bunch of prostitutes and delinquents?" Emily asked boldly.

"Exactly."

There was a beat of silence between them as Doris sat down in her oversized executive chair. Emily decided that now was her moment.

"I want to do this, Doris." She took a seat across the desk in a chair that was usually occupied by one of the staff writers—the women with windows in their offices and their own names in the byline.

"I know you do. I would, too, to tell you the truth. In another season of my life, before marriage and children, I might have." A ghost of a smile haunted Doris's dark lips. "If it's as bad as we think it is, this is an enormous scoop: abuse of power, abuse of *women*—and right on the heels of our other exposé—government culpability, and probably corruption somewhere along the line. From a journalism perspective, it's a deep scoop. And from a women's issues perspective, well . . . it's critical." She stared at Emily for several long moments, then seemed to come to a decision. "You'll need to be as careful as you can be." Emily's heart surged. "Do not put yourself in harm's way for the sake of this story, Emily. Get in, get what you need, then lie low until your release."

With a rush, Emily nodded. "Yes, ma'am."

"But you're going to need your father's help with this. Speak to him tonight. Let me know what he says, and we'll go from there." She paused. "I'm still not entirely comfortable with it, but you seem determined, it's a great story, and you're a bit uniquely positioned to be able to do it."

Emily swelled with excitement and pride and a touch of nerves. "Thank you, Doris."

A car horn blared from four floors below on University Avenue, where traffic hummed through a cloud of grey exhaust all hours of the day. Phones rang in the offices down the hall, as they did in hundreds of other offices and homes around the city. They were everyday sounds that carried on no matter what was happening. A light blanket of normalcy shrouding the darkness in every corner of every neighbourhood. Emily wondered what might be happening to the inmates at the Mercer prison right at that very moment.

No one knew.

But if Emily could pull this off, she would make sure they did.

CHAPTER 8

RACHEL

Huron County, Ontario—May, 1996

After their rookies Stevens and Fisher arrive at the Millgate Cemetery, Green heads back to HQ. Rachel assigns Fisher to guard the body and interview Jake Easton for a full statement, then brings Stevens with her to the cemetery office. Fisher is a young kid, fresh out of the academy, and isn't too pleased with being told what to do by a woman detective. But he's a misogynist with a revolting sense of humour who could use a little menial work to knock his ego down a few pegs.

Stevens, on the other hand, is the nephew of Green's predecessor and Rachel's mentor, Tom Stevens, and she hasn't quite gotten the measure of him yet. He's been shadowing her for the past few weeks, but he's been quiet, watching her closely. He's the complete opposite of Fisher, and Rachel hopes he's got what it takes. Some kids want to be cops because their parents or other family members were, but the reality of the work hits with a hard landing and they end up quitting, or pivoting to security services. As glamorous as being a detective might appear from the outside, a huge chunk of police work involves waiting around for something to happen, or poring over documents searching for a needle in a haystack. Especially in a rural detachment.

Julie went back to the office a few minutes ago, so Rachel knocks, waits until the door opens.

"Hey, Julie." Rachel scales the small steps. "This is Stevens, my rookie. He's going to assist with the records search."

"Oh, uh, hi," Julie says, her face turning pink as she holds the door open for them. "Just uh . . ." She's clearly flustered at having her little space invaded. But Rachel knows that most people get that way around cops, and it usually indicates innocence. It's the complacency or defensiveness you've got to watch out for.

The cemetery office is hardly bigger than a toll booth, but with less air circulation. It certainly isn't any larger than the covered porch of her late grandmother's house on Lake Huron—now Rachel's home—where they'd played Go Fish on summer afternoons. Rachel would munch arrowroot cookies, watching the lines that formed around Dora's mouth when she was deliberating her next move.

"It's a bit tight," Julie says, "but maybe just wait there a sec, and I'll pull the files. They're back here." She gestures to what Rachel assumes is a storage closet, beside which stands Reverend Holland.

"Hello, detectives." He offers Rachel an uncomfortable smile that she doesn't return, though Stevens does. "I'll help you," the reverend tells Julie.

As they get to work, Rachel studies the office. It's like the temporary trailers that home builders set up on the muddy fields of future developments to welcome new buyers. Those people sell the dream of a bright future to new families; their employees help homeowners select paint colour and floor tiles as they picture their lives in a brand-new home on an undersized and barren lot. But she supposes Julie helps buyers pick out their "forever home," too, in a way, as they envision spending eternity resting in this spot. And in some ways, it's a better deal than a new home. You don't have to worry about noisy neighbours, and you even get free landscaping thrown into the deal.

Rachel rolls her shoulders back, a little uncomfortable. Her grandparents and some other family members are buried here, but she only visits the graves twice a year: once on the anniversary of her grandmother Dora's death, and again on Christmas Eve. Otherwise, she prefers to avoid it.

After a few minutes of continued muttering and effort, Julie and Reverend Holland shove six cardboard banker boxes across the thin carpet. Rachel and Stevens kneel down next to them.

"They go back to about halfway through the 1800s," Julie says. "We don't have anything before that. The cemetery itself was established along with the church in, what?" She looks to the reverend.

"In 1832," he says, with a proud nod of his narrow head.

Rachel will need to get another good look at the body, but from what she saw, its state of decomposition likely means it's more recent than 1832.

"All right. Let's get started, then," she says. "We'll each take two boxes and go from there." She pushes the nearest two to Stevens. She takes another two, as does Julie, who glances at Reverend Holland.

"I can assist," he says, brow furrowing.

"No, we've got it in hand, Reverend," Rachel says forcefully. "I'm sure you have things to do. Some sermon to prepare."

He stares down at her, and she doesn't like the height differential. She stands.

"Rachel . . ." he begins, protest thick in his tone.

"Detective Mackenzie," she corrects him. "If we have any questions, we know where to find you."

His lips purse, but he retreats down the short hallway leading to the main building and his own office at the back of the church. Rachel can feel Stevens's curious eyes on her.

Julie swallows, her throat twitching beneath the mousy brown hair that lands at her jawline in a bob. "I really don't think we're going to find anything," she says, her tone aiming for offhand. "I understand why we have to do this first, but when I started here, I went through and double-checked the records from my predecessor. I'm sure I would have caught this if there had been a record-keeping error."

Rachel likes Julie, and doesn't want her to have messed up, primarily because she can already tell Reverend Holland might be an ass about it. She remembers Julie's meticulous nature from high school, how she underlined titles with red pen and a ruler, was never late to class. Never broke the rules.

A lot like Rachel, really. But the fact remains they have a body in a graveyard, and despite her argument with Green, Rachel reluctantly acknowledges that human error is a reasonable hypothesis here, the Occam's razor. Millgate is a tiny hamlet of a town with a nearly non-existent crime rate. The only crimes reported here in the last five years were some minor B and E's—mostly of vacant cottage properties in the off-season and, once, a neighbourly spat over a property line that ended in some bloodied lips, one broken rib and a giant embarrassment hangover for both parties.

"And you could be right," Rachel concedes. "Is that the plot map?" she adds, nodding at the wall behind Julie's little desk.

"Yes. Here, I'll show you where the woman is," she says, before Rachel even asks.

"We don't know it's a woman yet," Rachel corrects her as they walk over, followed by Stevens. She's pretty sure it *is* a female body, but this is exactly how rumours get started, ripping through gossip-starved small towns like fire through dry August grass.

"Sorry, I mean the body. Here." Julie indicates the location. "Plot 135. Close to that big maple. The Richards family chose it specifically."

"Do you know why?" Rachel asks.

"They said he was a 'larger than life' man. Big, like the tree."

That could be true. Or not. "I'll speak with them," Rachel tells her. "I'll need their contact information."

"Sure. I have to call them today anyway," Julie says a little nervously. "We can't use it as the site now, and the funeral's on Saturday."

Rachel frowns, feeling a little sorry for her. "Call them in, and we'll talk to them together," she says. "If they take issue with it, you can blame the police service. But I'm sure there are loads of other nice plots available."

"There are. All the ones around it, see? Available plots have a green sticker." Julie points to the map, and Rachel leans in closer. The plots are laid out in an imperfect grid, some varying in shape but all about the same overall size. The maple tree is surrounded by several other numbers, all with green stickers. Her eyes rove over the map, drawn to Dora and Walter's graves.

"When did these start being numbered, Julie?"

"Ohh"—her eyes grow large—"as far back as the records go. These"—she circles the central area of the cemetery—"were labelled from one to about a hundred before my predecessor arrived, and he laid out the rest of the cemetery, all the way up to about two hundred gravesites."

"How many people do you have buried here?"

"Ninety-four, plus twenty-one in the children's cemetery. That's it there." She points to a small area on the western side of the property.

"I didn't know there was a children's cemetery here," Stevens pipes up, grimacing.

"Yeah," Julie tells him. "Fortunately, we haven't had a burial there in decades, as far as I know. Thank God for vaccines and modern medicine, right? I can show you if you like, Detectives."

Rachel shakes her head fervently. "No, I'm not concerned about that. There's no way that's a child's skeleton, so *not* a misplaced burial from those records. And you can call me Rachel, Julie."

Deep breath.

"All right." Julie smiles and they return to the small area on the carpeted floor, which issues hollow thuds as they kneel and sit, shifting the boxes around.

"And what exactly are we looking for?" Stevens asks, opening the lid of the box nearest him, sending a puff of dust into the air that dances in a ray of light from the large window. Rachel raises her chin at him, and finally, when he registers the heat of her eyes, he meets them a little sheepishly.

"What do you think?" she asks. She watches him with a neutral expression despite the storm brewing in her chest.

"I guess, uh, any references to plot 135?"

"That's right. We need to check whether there's a record for that plot that didn't make it onto the map somehow. Some way we can ID that body, confirm whether it's supposed to be here, or accounted for in any way. So let's get digging."

She glances at Julie, whose face is still pink. She's nervous about this, doesn't want to bear responsibility for this incident. No one likes to wear a mistake, but especially not an organized introvert like Julie. Rachel understands that.

"You two go ahead and get started. I just need to, uh, excuse me." Rachel stands and walks to the tiny washroom to her right, shuts the door behind her.

A ferocious panic attack has been building since they arrived, and she needs to succumb to it in private before it overtakes her in front of the others. Though the claustrophobia of this bathroom does nothing to help. It's about four feet square, like an airplane washroom, and reeks of that slimy pink institutional hand soap elementary schools use.

But Rachel clutches the edge of the miniature sink and leans over it, finding her own brown eyes in the mirror. She doesn't have time for this. And yet, is she surprised?

She closes her eyes and tries to regulate her breaths, pacing them to the countdown in her head.

Breathe in . . . 10 . . . breathe out. Breathe in . . . 9 . . . breathe out. Breathe in . . . 8 . . .

Of all the places an unknown body could turn up, it just had to be the Millgate Cemetery.

―――

JULY, 1975

During the longest stretch of time Rachel could remember her mother, Mary, returning home for, she came with Rachel and her grandmother to church every Sunday. Dora was a gentle and loving caregiver whose only rules were related to safety or righteousness.

Call when you get someplace.
Don't walk alone at night.
Never take the Lord's name in vain.
Church every Sunday, barring illness or death.

There wasn't much Dora seemed capable of making Mary do if she didn't want to, but going to church seemed almost voluntary for her. It was only in her adulthood that Rachel finally understood that perhaps her mercurial mother was reaching into the earth in search of her own roots during those visits, grasping at whatever might have helped her to steady herself after the latest bad boyfriend, job loss, or arrest for some petty crime for which someone else was—of course and invariably—entirely to blame. Mary was, by both Dora's account and Rachel's own experience, incapable of accepting responsibility for herself no matter the circumstances, opting instead to defend even the most egregious of her own decisions with dismissive obstinacy while she holed herself up in her childhood bedroom with Gordon Lightfoot on the turntable.

One warm Sunday morning in late June, the summer Rachel was eight, she found herself pressed thigh to thigh between her mother and grandmother on a hard pew at Millgate Methodist Church. On her right, Dora smelled of lily-of-the-valley perfume layered over Ivory soap. On her left, incense and cigarettes clung to Mary's old blue blouse with the lacy trim, pulled from the back of her closet and ironed by Dora the night before. Rachel shifted uncomfortably in her own buttercream polka-dot dress as sweat trickled down her back. She looked up at the old ceiling fan in the centre of the church as Reverend Holland droned on. It was churning slower than a merry-go-round, cutting through the humidity with all the efficacy of a spoon into a frozen watermelon.

Finally, a last round of prayers were said, heads were bowed, the organ played and the overheated flock was freed out into the breeze of the pasture.

The Methodist church was the nucleus of the little town of Millgate, and only a ten- or fifteen-minute drive from their house in Bayfield. Dora had attended the church with Rachel's grandfather Walter from the time they were married, and his family's rear ends had polished those pews for at least two generations before that. He was buried on the west side of the cemetery, and Rachel sighed with relief as she exited the church, feet turned in the direction of his headstone.

They visited his gravesite every Sunday after the service. When they finished, Dora always took a short walk around the cemetery on her own, saying she needed to clear her head of grief in the fresh air. Rachel was happy to wait for her in the car, sneaking Werther's candies from the glovebox. She sometimes felt guilty about not staying longer at her grandfather's stone, but she hated the way her grandmother lingered over it with a determined vehemence, as though she might bring him back to life if only she could grieve hard enough, pray hard enough. She also found it eerie that the stone listed her grandmother's name, too, ready and waiting for her, like some macabre passport poised for a date stamp upon entry.

DOROTHEA "DORA" MACKENZIE
Wife and mother
1925 –

Cemeteries gave Rachel the creeps; all those dead and rotting bodies beneath their feet. And the fact that there was a children's section . . . she didn't even know what to make of that. She'd only ever heard about old people dying. Her grandmother had told her to stay away from the children's area, and Rachel didn't need telling twice.

Rachel's stomach grumbled its protest now as she fantasized about the turkey sandwiches and lemonade that awaited them at home. She fanned herself, shading her eyes from the sun as her grandmother said a silent prayer beside her. Mary hung back ten feet from the headstone as though worried the ground might cave right in beneath her. Her eyes stayed on her feet as sweat beaded above her lips, which were painted with a slick of Revlon—the Cherries in the Snow shade of raspberry pink she'd swiped from Harper's Drugstore when she thought Rachel wasn't looking. She seemed even less interested in her father's grave than Rachel was, which wasn't new. Aside from rage and contempt, Rachel had rarely seen her mother express any sort of emotion. Certainly not grief, or true sadness.

"Superstitious," Dora had once called Mary with a curt shake of the head, which led Rachel to understand that superstition must be some foolish thing, because Dora said Mary was always doing and thinking foolish things, always looking for explanations in wild and unlikely places.

One time, a couple of years before, Mary had come home at the Civic Holiday long weekend and taken Rachel to a fair up in Goderich. They'd had one ride on the Ferris wheel before Mary pressed a paper cone of cotton candy into Rachel's surprised and delighted hand and told her to wait outside a lamp-lit tent while she ducked behind a curtain to speak to a lady who could predict her future. She'd emerged ten minutes later in a state of euphoria, shoved the last bit of Rachel's cotton candy into her own mouth and knelt to face her daughter.

Everything's going to be okay now, she'd said, her tongue stained pink as a rose petal. *And I'm going to stick around this time, I promise.*

Two days later, she was gone again.

But now she was back. *Maybe to stay this time*, she said, and Rachel couldn't decide whether that was a good thing or not.

"Amen," Dora said now after finishing her prayer.

"Amen," Rachel parroted, not having thought two words about the man buried there. She'd never met her grandfather, who died before Rachel was born. To her, he existed only in the aging photographs in brass frames on the living room walls and the fireplace mantel, and in the occasional story her grandmother spun over Sunday dinner or a game of cards on the back porch. He'd drunk himself to death, Mary had told her, but Dora always maintained he'd had some sort of cardiovascular defect.

"It was his heart that killed him," she said.

Rachel looked up from his headstone to see the minister, Reverend Holland, striding toward them down the nearest path. He raised a slim hand in greeting. He was built like a grasshopper, all long limbs and big eyes in a narrow skull. His black pulpit robe must have cooked him like a Dutch oven in this heat. A white stole embroidered with gold crosses fluttered in the welcome midday breeze.

"I thought I saw you, Miss Mackenzie," he said, voice projecting to Mary over the headstones, just as it did over the heads of his parishioners in the tiny church. "It has been a while since you've joined us."

CHAPTER 9
EMILY

Early June, 1961

Needing more time to think about Doris's approval of the Mercer scoop, Emily decided to walk home from work again instead of taking the streetcar. The gears of her mind were turning in a way she'd never experienced. A fuse had been lit in her gut, and she didn't know what to do other than let the flame burn to its natural combustion.

Because she knew her parents well, she'd decided she would try speaking to her father first, to see whether he'd agree to help her get declared "incorrigible" without Bess's influence or immediate rejection of Emily's proposal. If he said yes, then they could talk to her mother, which Emily knew would be a deeply unpleasant conversation.

When dinner was finished, Bess declined Emily's offer to help with the dishes, which brought a wave of relief as Emily seized her chance and stepped out onto the back porch to sit with her dad. He always nursed a cigarillo and glass of Scotch out there in the evening; rain or shine or the frigid depths of January.

Emily took the rocking chair across from him and let out a sigh just as he exhaled a plume of smoke. They both chuckled.

"You were quiet at dinner. Something's got your tail," William said. "What's it look like?"

Emily scuffed her foot absent-mindedly on the patio. "You know me well, Dad."

"I do, my girl."

She considered how to open the conversation. They had never before discussed what Emily might call the *real* content of *Chatelaine*. She would need to begin there, in order to explain the rest.

"Do you ever read *Chatelaine*?" she asked him.

A smile twitched around his lips as he drew again on the cigarillo. "Mhm."

"So you've seen—"

"Mhm."

Emily snorted out a laugh as her dad's dimply smile widened.

"Why do you think I tried so hard to get you a job *there* instead of one of the papers?" he asked. "Doris Anderson knows what she's about. She knows why the magazine appeals, including the weightier topics that impact women's day-to-day lives as much as their need for decorating tips. No disrespect meant to your recent piece," he said, mouth twitching again. "But I don't think you will always have to write articles about recipes and the like. The ladies' stuff."

Emily's shoulders relaxed. This might go all right after all.

"Doris also doesn't suffer fools," William added, "and doesn't shy away from challenging authority. A lot like you. Hence the politically charged articles she slips in between the cosmetic ads."

"And no one upstairs has caught on?"

Her father shook his head. "I hate to say it, but Maclean-Hunter doesn't give a hoot about *Chatelaine* as long as it keeps them in the black."

Emily nodded. "That's what Doris says, too." She took a deep breath, thinking for a moment about the "ladies' stuff," about Doris's evident frustration when Ted the delivery driver innocently reported that *Maclean's* had sent him downstairs to *Chatelaine* simply because the content of the note referenced women, and was therefore relegated to some tacit second tier of journalism.

"Well," she began, "what you were just saying, about me probably not having to write the fluff forever?" She withdrew the prisoner's letter from the pocket of her skirt, passed it to her father. "This found its way to me at the office."

He scanned the crumpled paper, which had become softer now from so many hands on it. Emily herself had read it at least a dozen times. She watched him, as she often did when he worked, to see the analysis in his blue eyes. Curls of smoke wafted upward from the cigarillo in the brown-glass ashtray beside him, disappearing like a spectre into the warm spring air.

"Well," he said, finishing. "That's quite something, Em." He looked up at her, eyes twinkling. "So I assume you're showing me this for a reason."

She told him everything then, from what she'd learned at the Legislative Library to her exchange with June Jones, and the conversations they'd had in Doris's office. She braced herself for the proposal, then plowed on.

"Having a woman incarcerated there appears to be more a matter of opinion than any real reflection of her wrongdoing. So, we'd like to see if it's really as simple as it seems."

"Well," he began, head tilting from side to side as he mulled it over, "if there's credence to it, it is a great story. And I'm sure Doris is right, if the abuse is as bad as the allegations, and it's government-run, that's headline news, and in a women's mag to boot. Even the men upstairs would be impressed by that. So what's the plan?"

Emily's insides jolted with excitement. "The only thing we can think of is to get in there somehow. Get a writer inside to witness it for herself. And, well . . . we're talking about that writer being me."

He paused, tapped the cigarillo on the ashtray. "Undercover, you mean? Inside the Mercer prison?"

"Yes."

A long pause. "And Doris is asking *you* to do this? Why?"

"Because the other writers can't take the time away from their families," Emily told him. "But I want to do it, and I'm the only one who can."

He pulled on his little cigar once again, brow furrowed in concern. The sound of dishes clattering and Bess humming drifted out the screen door behind them. The scent of lilacs wafted from the back of the yard.

"Mm. So how would you go about it?"

"Well, I would need your help," Emily said, "to have me deemed 'incorrigible.' A parent can bring their daughter before the judge. You could make up some story about how you and Mom are at the end of your wits with me, and need them to sort me out."

She smiled at her little joke, tried to get him to soften, but this time he didn't return the grin.

"Jeez, Em," he said. He crossed one leg over the other. "You want me to help you get sent to prison?"

The heat rose in her neck. She had to convince him, or there was no hope for it. "I want you to help me scoop a story *about* a prison that could solidify my career, Dad. And hopefully make a difference while I'm at it."

He exhaled smoke again, meeting her eyes now, but said nothing.

Emily sat forward. "Dad, having your name got me into *Chatelaine*, but I want more than what an editorial assistant gets to do. I want to be a *real reporter* like you were. Like you *are*. You know that's what I've wanted since I was a child."

He did let out a breathy chuckle then, holding her gaze. "I know. I've still got those stacks of family newsletters you used to produce, remember? They're in my desk drawer. Reports on the neighbours' comings and goings, reviews of your mother's new recipes. The argumentative column you wrote for three months straight when you were campaigning for a cat."

Emily watched the emotion of the memory wash over his features, and it made her strangely sad then, to think of that ten-year-old girl clacking away at her dad's typewriter and filling notebook after notebook with diary entries, short stories, even poetry, all of which were still stashed under her bed along with the children's books. That girl had wanted to emulate her father, her dreams bigger and more out of reach than she could even comprehend. Emily didn't know now if the Nancy Drew stories she'd read were, at the end of the day, a liberating escape or a fallacy that tricked her young mind into believing that girls could ever be seen as just as clever and brave and capable as boys. Because she knew now, as a grown woman, that the stories she'd read of women leading adventurous lives were a fantasy, not a mirror. There were only a handful who had managed to forge such paths for themselves. If Nancy's story had continued all the way to adulthood, what would have happened? Would it have ended in her capitulating to marriage and babies and burying forever her sense of curiosity, her thirst for adventure and justice? That would have been the end of Nancy's life as she knew it, and Emily couldn't let it be hers. Knowing Jem was going to propose soon, the Mercer opportunity now felt imperative, as though it was both the long-term ticket to the life she wanted, and an escape hatch from the current situation with Jem.

"Dad," she continued. "If I can secure a scoop like this at *Chatelaine*, I'll probably get promoted, or I could take that clout elsewhere—the *Star*, or *Globe*. But I'm a woman. They won't even look at me if I don't have some serious stories to my name, even if it is Radcliffe. You know that. *This is my chance.*"

Her dad nodded slowly. "I'm sorry, Em. I'm sorry it's different for you. Life would be much easier for so many girls if they'd just been born boys. I'm not sure why it matters so much, eh." He paused. "But, if I'm honest, it does. Somehow it does. If you were my son I'd be telling you to do it, that your girl would wait for you, that this *is* a great opportunity. But I'm having trouble. I'm sorry. This seems so dangerous. This note . . ." He handed it back to her.

Emily's heart sank. "So . . . is that a no?"

He shook his head. "No. It's not a no. But I do have questions. What about Jem, for a start? You'd be gone for, what . . . three months, you said?"

Emily swallowed. "I know. That would be the end of us. But the truth is, I don't see that as a bad thing, Dad." She'd considered this, too. "Instead of outright refusing him, with this plan, we can both save face a little by hanging the reason for our split on this investigation, on the time I would need to take away from my loved ones."

Her father shook his head.

"Jem will move on," she said. She knew she would miss him as a friend, but that was all. "There are plenty of girls like Ellie who want that traditional sort of life. But you and I both know I don't want what Ellie has. I want a career. *This* career."

Her father watched her, still looking skeptical, and now also a little sad.

"And maybe someday I'll find a man who . . ." She faltered. She loathed the word *allow*. "A man who will *accept* who I am and that I need to work, to use my mind like this, to not be tied down. Maybe." She shrugged. "But if I don't, I need an income anyway. I can't live with you and Mom for the rest of my life. You just said yourself, if I were a man, you wouldn't hesitate on this. After all your support, would you really stand in my way on what could be my big break? *Please* help me, Dad." Emily hated the feeling in her belly, that bitter guilt, as though she were trying to wrestle something from her father's grip. But in a way, she was. He held the key to the door to the life she longed for. The one that felt as though it fit properly over all her rough edges.

He was quiet for a long while. The sounds from the kitchen had ceased, and dusk was falling across the yard now. He cleared his throat. "As a journalist, I respect the hell out of the idea, Em. But as your father, I'm struggling. It feels unnatural to have my own daughter committed to a prison. But when I really think about it, the truth is I'd be *that* proud of you, if you broke this story and helped shine light onto that sort of injustice."

"Really?"

"'Course I would! You've been champing at the bit for a worthwhile story since you were yea high," he said, gesturing a foot off the ground. "And if it works," he added, "it actually really *could* be the break for your career. You're not wrong about that." He sighed a little regretfully. "But you're sure this is what you want? The job, splitting with Jem? The risk? Because there wouldn't be much option to turn back once the thing's been decided."

Emily swallowed the swelling sensation in her throat, as though she'd bitten off too much. Perhaps she had. But perhaps she wanted to. "Yes. I'm sure."

"And you don't think a judge will know who we are?" he asked.

Emily thought for a moment. Her father's name was big in the publishing and news industries in the city, but how far his notoriety reached beyond that was questionable. She told him as much. "And no judge will know who *I* am," she said. "I'm just a woman."

He stubbed out his forgotten cigarillo. "All right, then. I'll help you get in there, if I can."

A surge of emotion gripped Emily and she leaned across, wrapping her father in a hug. His arm came around her as her smooth cheek rubbed against his stubbled one.

"Aw, thanks, sweetheart. You're my favourite incorrigible daughter."

Emily breathed a chuckle and wiped a tear from her eye as they pulled apart.

"But now," her father said heavily, "I'm afraid we still have to convince your mother."

CHAPTER 10

EMILY

Later that night after the conversation with her father, Emily was holed up in her bedroom, staring down at her cornflower-blue patterned quilt and pinching her chin in concentration. Her essential belongings were splayed out across the bed like archeological findings as she debated what to eventually bring with her to the Mercer. It couldn't be much, and she had to assume most, if not all of it, would be taken from her upon arrival. But it also felt strange to go down to the courthouse entirely empty-handed. Surely even within their fiction of a father trying to knock some sense into his unruly adult daughter, the "accused" would at least have her handbag with her: some lipstick, a pen, cash. Emily had no idea what sorts of writing implements might be allowed within the prison, but she figured she would have to commit most of her findings to memory, anyway, as she couldn't risk her notes being found. She needed to get this story discreetly, fly under the radar of the guards and administration as she silently observed, then pour it all out onto the page after her release.

Two hours ago, she and her dad had sat in the living room with her mother and explained the story, the plan for Emily's investigation. Bess was very still as Emily recounted all the details—leaving out some of the finer points of the inmate's note. But, predictably, the conversation had rapidly dissolved into an argument.

"I can't see how either Doris or *you*," Bess had fired at William, "could possibly be comfortable with this!" Her hands were clenched atop the apron draped over her thighs.

"Because they believe in me, Mom. They think I can handle it, and so do I," Emily exclaimed.

"It really is her big break, Bess," William had said, shooting their daughter a sympathetic look that was neither smile nor frown. "And she won't be gone too long. It's a fantastic adventure, really—"

"An adventure?" Bess said, glaring at them both and leaning forward on the couch. "It's a *prison*, for God's sake! You're going off to try to prove that this horrendous treatment of those women is happening, Emily. Which means you will be subjected to it yourself! Or at the very least, *witness* these atrocities."

William had met her eyes then, and his tone was direct, yet gentle. "That's what I did, too, Bess. Bore witness and was subjected to it. All to report on something important."

"*Yes*," Bess said, with a look of incredulity, "and look at what it did to you, darling. Look what it took from you."

Emily swallowed. She was so used to seeing her father's shirtsleeve tied in a knot just below the elbow that she sometimes forgot about his injury. The whole family had adjusted to it. Bess knotted his ties every morning and pre-cut his meat at suppertime.

"And this is not a *war*, you two," she said, clearly making an effort not to scoff. "These are criminals in a penal institution. It's not *that* important."

"Except it is, Mom," Emily said. "The entire point is that this law applies to every young woman and girl in this country. We can be tossed in prison for next to *nothing*. And if it's as easy as we think it is, Dad getting a judge to sentence me there is part of the story, part of the scandal—that it *is* so easy. And that sort of legal vulnerability should matter to every woman. Including you."

"And what about Jeremy?!" Bess demanded, hands in the air. "Are you just to throw him over to go live in a prison? For goodness' sake, he's about to—" She stopped, looking regretful, and Emily suddenly felt sorry for her.

"I know he's going to propose, Mom," she admitted softly, letting her off the hook.

Bess didn't ask how she knew, but glared at William as though he were responsible for the whole mess.

"This isn't Dad's fault," Emily said. "I knew it was coming anyway."

"And you aren't at all excited?" Bess asked, exasperated.

Emily looked at her with a heavy heart, shook her head. "No, Mom. I don't want to marry Jem."

Bess's mouth hung open for a long moment before she turned away, tears in her eyes. Emily had hoped she could do this with her mother's blessing, but she didn't need her permission. Still, she felt sick about making her mother feel so rotten.

The conversation had gone around in increasingly exhausting circles for another half-hour until Bess eventually stormed off.

"She'll come around," her father had said, nodding from his seat in the large, worn leather armchair. "It's a mother's job to worry for her children. I understand that. But I'm not as worried. I know you can handle it." He watched her intently for a moment. "Are you afraid?"

Emily thought of what her mother had said, the damage wrought on her father's body in pursuit of the truth. She knew she would be okay; that she could even cope with a limited dose of the treatment alleged in the prisoner's letter, knowing it would be so temporary. But she couldn't deny that the prospect of it all made her apprehensive. She nodded. "A little."

"I think about the women in the war sometimes," he said. "The nurses especially. They were as gritty as the men, just in skirts instead of trousers. Carrying bandages instead of guns. Courage and fear were both written on their faces, too, just like the men. So often they coexist, don't they, those things? I suppose because courage only exists *because* of fear. It grows out of, and despite fear."

The sound of distant kitchen clatter had filled the silence that followed. Emily knew she would need to go talk to her mother again. She couldn't leave like this.

"I know you're aching to prove yourself, Em, and now's the time to do the really dangerous stuff, before you have a family," her dad said. "And I don't mean that as pressure," he clarified. "I mean it as encouragement, and, frankly, as advice. The war didn't come to me; I had to go because we all had to go. But I was terrified I wasn't going to make it home. It broke my heart to know my girls were all waiting, that I might never see you again. It would have been a lot easier if it had just been myself that I had to be concerned for, that's all I mean."

He'd risen then, planted a kiss on her hair as he headed for the kitchen. "I'll see what I can do to soothe her."

Emily had gone up to her bedroom, where she now plucked her toothbrush and toothpaste out of the array on her bedspread, stuffing them into her small purse. It was a smart look for ladies to carry the clutch style, but Emily preferred a loop handle, which allowed her to hang the bag on her arm and free up both hands to hold her notebook and pen. She went to her dresser and pulled out a pair of underwear and a brassiere, tucked them into the bottom of the handbag. She supposed it might be odd when her bag was searched, as it almost certainly would be at the prison, but she had no idea what clothing or sundries would be allowed or provided, and it felt unprepared to set out on any sort of overnight trip without a fresh change of underthings. She also grabbed three pens from the cup on her desk. She felt naked without one.

She had just stood to go take a bath when her mother appeared in the doorway.

"May I come in?"

Emily nodded, a little unsure of what to expect, but glad that they were speaking again. She sat back down on the bed. Her mother joined her, and for a beat they just took each other in.

"Your father came to talk to me," Bess said. "And he . . . reminded me of a few things I may have forgotten." Emily watched her, waiting, stomach swirling a little. She loved and respected her mother very much. She didn't want to upset her, but knew she had to do this assignment regardless of how Bess felt about it.

"Before I met your father," her mother continued, "I worked on the line at the Princess Pat hairnet factory."

Emily nodded. She knew that.

"You know your grandparents aren't wealthy," Bess said with a little dismissive twitch of the head, "and I had to contribute. When my father came back from the first war, he couldn't work. He had some physical injuries, yes, but mentally, well . . ." She pressed her lips together—in sympathy or judgment, Emily couldn't tell. "I was born right before the war broke out, and as you know, my parents never had any other children—I think for the same reasons he couldn't work. He was just a shell of what he'd been before. So I was terrified, when the second war started, that your father would come home that broken, too. Or not at all. I feared I would end up in the same fix my mother had. Thank God it wasn't as bad as that for us. At any rate, your nana held things together on her own as long as she could so that I could get some education, but I had to leave school at thirteen to go work."

Emily listened with waning interest, wondering where this was headed. She knew all this.

"She worked in the Royal York laundry for nearly thirty years, working her fingers raw. She used to come home with burns on her hands, blisters from grazing those big copper cauldrons she boiled the sheets in."

Emily had seen the scars, but a person didn't ask for details about such things. "I never knew that's what the marks were from," she said quietly.

Her mother nodded. "Yes. I could have easily gotten a job alongside her, but she wanted better for me. So she got me the job at Princess Pat through a woman in Rosedale whose laundry she took in on the side, for extra money. The woman's husband owned the place. He was a decent man, and he kept an eye on me. It didn't pay as much as the Royal York, which was why my mother stayed there all those years. It was the most money she could make with so few skills, and no education. Aside from, well . . ." Her nostrils flared. "The point is, she didn't want me coming home with burns, or to be harassed by the laundry supervisor, who was a lecher. With the things he said to her, and did to other laundresses . . ." She shook her head. "They should have poisoned his tea with bleach, that's all I'll say."

"Mom!" Emily gaped. She hadn't known her nana had put up with all that at her job.

"What I am trying to say," Bess pressed on, "is that she wanted better for me than she'd ever had. She didn't want my life to be as difficult as hers had been. And when I met your father that day at the cinema, well . . . we loved each other, he made a good wage, and I thought, 'Excellent, I can stop working and give my own children a more stable childhood than I ever had. And if I have girls, they won't have to work. They can have an education if they wish, stay in school longer than I did, maybe even attend university'"—she nodded at Emily, her spine straightening with pride. "Then they can marry well, and be taken care of."

Emily sighed. She understood better now why Bess had been pushing her so hard toward Jem, and marriage. The campaign had deeper roots, was more well-intentioned than she'd given her mother credit for. "Mom—"

"I wanted your and Eleanor's lives to be easier than mine, *better* than mine," Bess said emphatically. "It's what every good mother wants, really, if she's worth her salt. No one wants their child to suffer. So when I hear about you willingly walking into a *prison*, to be hurt, or shamed, or . . ." She trailed off, eyes shining. "But your father reminded me that we gave you greater opportunities than I or your grandmother had so that you could have *choices*. Because it's always a lack of options that hangs women, in the end. But in making these choices: to delay marriage, and work in the man's world where things are still so limited for us . . . I can't help but feel as though you're deliberately taking the difficult road when you don't have to." She searched Emily's blue eyes as though looking for an answer. "But you are who you are, my dear, and I love you still. Lord knows I may not always understand you, but I love you, and I don't want you to get hurt."

Emily tried to see things from her mother's perspective. Her concerns were all reasonable, really. The most daring thing Emily had ever done before now was enrolling as the only woman in her year in journalism school.

Emily had expected that upon graduation, she would be lucky to scrape a part-time junior position at one of the big newspapers or men's magazines, knowing she would have to work twice as hard as her male classmates to succeed in the industry. She was luckier than she'd even realized when she landed the job at *Chatelaine*: to be working at a publication that was *by* women, *for* women, and in a woman-dominated office, made Emily feel like she'd won a prize. There were no other professional offices headed by a woman. That only happened in underpaid service work, where women drudged like her grandmother had in hotel laundries, starching businessmen's shirts and boiling their soiled sheets clean—or, she thought with an uncomfortable start, in brothels like June Jones's, where women laboured in ghastly conditions night and day, solely for the pleasure of men. There were no woman-led law firms, banks, radio stations. They simply didn't exist. *Chatelaine* was it.

"Thanks, Mom. But I need to do this, and it won't be for long. And then"—she smiled—"my options will expand. Maybe I'll get a promotion and a raise, things that will open even *more* doors."

Her mother observed her, looking strained. "And what about poor Jeremy? Does he truly not factor in at all?"

Emily kept her gaze, though she felt a flush rise, unbidden. "It's not that he doesn't factor in," she said with a shrug. "It's nothing to do with *him*, really. I like Jem very much. But it's any man, it's marriage. I'm just not ready." She swallowed hard, but pressed on, finally voicing the thing she'd been too afraid to tell her mother for five years. "I don't want it. At least, not yet—but maybe never. I don't know." She paused. "I have an opportunity here, and I need to take it. For my own sake, and for yours, I think, and Nana's, too. I'm the first university-educated woman in our family. I think I can be the first professional one, too. The first published one. Don't you think that opportunity is worth the risk?"

As Emily took in the soft lines around her mother's eyes, she saw both concern and understanding. She wondered what her mother was seeing as she scanned her face. Her own nervousness was reflected, certainly.

Bess exhaled in a sigh weighed down with the relentless conflict of motherhood. "I suppose it is," she said. "And I have to trust that you know what you're doing."

Emily nodded. "I do."

CHAPTER 11

RACHEL

Bayfield, Ontario—May, 1996

Gravel crunches beneath the wheels of Rachel's blue Toyota as she pulls into her driveway and turns off the ignition. She drops her shoulders from where they've been hitched up, as though trying to become one with her earlobes. She's just worked an unexpected fifteen-hour day, and she's exhausted.

The records search in the Millgate office turned up a big fat nothing. They'd combed the boxes for hours before Rachel was comfortable declaring that there was no administrative error to explain the presence of the body. Julie hadn't messed up, and Rachel's glad for her. But it now means that the case is very much active. Fisher interviewed and then dismissed the landscaper, standing guard over the body before he was relieved by another officer to keep watch during the night shift. Green's threats to the owners of the surrounding houses had held out for a while, but when it was declared a crime scene, the yellow tape went up. The police presence continued, squad cars piling up in the parking lot as the neighbours looked on with macabre excitement. One of them, of course, immediately told Green she'd seen a suspicious-looking man in that part of the cemetery a decade ago. They'll take her statement for the sake of procedure, but this sort of thing happens all the time: you always get some random "witness" who likes to think they have the Golden Tip that'll blow a case wide open and render them a hero.

Rachel's had twenty-six of those in the Cooper case alone, and none have come to anything.

Once Rachel had confirmed the lack of record for the body in the cemetery office, she'd phoned Green, who contacted the Ident team down in London to come assist with identifying the remains before the forensic archeologists removed them to the lab in Toronto. Rachel spent the entire afternoon supervising as they took photos of the remains and casket from every conceivable angle and collected soil samples from the grave and surrounding area. Rachel always finds evidence collection a tedious but exciting process, knowing every phial and photo will—hopefully—get them one step closer to solving the case.

Around seven-thirty, the evidence had finally been loaded onto the truck headed for the Toronto lab, at which point Rachel drove back to HQ, sweaty and hungry. She'd returned her squad car and then headed home, deliberately avoiding her desk to retain ignorance of whether the voicemail light was flashing on her phone. She didn't want to hear from Tamara Cooper, but knew she probably would at some point soon. Tamara would want to hear from Rachel's own lips that the body wasn't Stacy's and Rachel would have to tell her so, which would deliver both a crushing blow and overwhelming relief to the girl's wretched mother. What a multiheaded Hydra information could be.

She takes a deep breath now and exits the car into the gathering dusk, taking a moment to survey her gardens before she goes into the house, a two-storey yellow-brick beauty that sits up on the cliff overlooking Lake Huron.

Rachel has lived here as long as she can remember, aside from the year she turned seven, when Mary had moved them to Etobicoke for six months, chasing some man who said he loved her but drank as though wishing for an early death. Simon, Rachel thought his name was, but it didn't really matter. All the men blur together in her mind now, all versions of the same kind: unemployed and manipulative and angry, except when they wanted to charm, and that always frightened Rachel more than the rage did, because you never knew when the spell would be broken, along with a couple of her mother's fingers or ribs. The only name Rachel was ever interested in was her own father's, though her mother didn't know who he was.

It was a party. We were drunk. How should I know his name?

When Children's Aid finally intervened and Rachel's grandmother had taken official custody of her, she'd moved back to Bayfield, where attendance at school was a requirement and they ate healthy meals off a clean table at regular times. As much as she had dreamed of her grandmother's house during those lonely, frightening nights in Etobicoke, it had taken Rachel a while to settle in again, to acclimatize to the comfortable rhythm of routine and predictability.

She stoops to get a full whiff of her bubblegum-pink Hermione peonies, which are coming into bloom and can be smelled from as far away as the road when the wind blows in from the lake. She'd planted these with her grandmother on her eleventh birthday, when Dora gifted her the yard at the front of the house so that she could grow the flowers she was always asking to plant, the roses and marigolds and sunflowers she admired in the books borrowed from the little library over on Main Street. Dora didn't fuss much with flowers. Her specialty was herbs and vegetables. Her raised beds still fill most of the backyard, from the porch almost out to the wrought-iron fence on the edge of the cliff, where the rocks and weeds cascade down the slope to the lake. Rachel tends to them regularly.

Peonies, for a happy life, Dora had told her when they first planted the young bush. *Or at least something close to it.*

Rachel breathes in the citrusy perfume of the peonies, and tears prick at her eyes. The charm for a happy life her grandmother had tried to wield in planting the peonies had mostly come true in the years Dora had been alive, and Rachel knows that it wasn't the peonies themselves, but the woman who planted them that had worked magic in ensuring Rachel's relative happiness.

She moves now to inspect the climbing roses. Still buds, but they should be in bloom soon, if this sunny streak continues. The breed that creeps up and down the cedar arbour is the fiery-red Impatient rose she'd planted at sixteen, which she'd thought—in the throes of self-importance and sexual frustration—had so accurately captured the feeling of the age. She still loves them, but her adult preferences lean toward the more subdued hues, the white rose of York with its soft-pink edges, the buttery-yellow Charlottes.

When Rachel went away for a while after her grandmother's death, she'd found the most successful rehabilitation came in the form of her daily garden therapy. She didn't wear gloves, preferring to use her own fingers to dig into the damp soil as she planted seeds for tomatoes, beans, marigolds, and glorious yellow sunflowers in the institution's garden beds. When her anxiety attacks were at their peak, nothing calmed her down like gardening. The rhythm of it kept her hands busy and stilled their fidgeting as she drilled down into the dirt, filled it with seeds, and covered them with nurturing soil. She pulled weeds and imagined each individual stem as a problem or intrusive thought that she was able to physically yank out at its root and discard. But the best part, over the longer term, was the satisfaction of the process, of seeing the bright green shoots just breaking through the surface of the soil, then growing over weeks or months into a full multicoloured flower garden, or all the ingredients required for a crisp salad.

The seeds are buried in darkness, her therapist at Pineview, Lynn, had told her. *But then they break through into the light.*

In short: The act of gardening was nothing more or less than the act of hope.

You don't see the flower on the same day you plant the seed, Lynn had reminded Rachel on some of the hardest days of her stay. Lynn was big on mantras, but Rachel has enfolded that one into her life ever since, because it helps her to look forward and not back. She can't let herself get pulled down into the darkness again.

The sound of a car on the street behind her causes her to turn. A black SUV has stopped in front of the house. A middle-aged woman in the passenger seat points as a man leans over from the driver's side. The woman says something to him, but when they notice Rachel, her finger drops to her lap. She gives Rachel a fleeting, embarrassed look as they speed away.

As if her day could have been any more tiring, now there's been a Gawker. It's what Rachel's called all the people who have performed this same nosy ritual over the years. They want to see where it all happened, the events they'd read about in the local and national papers. Rachel's reframe would like to believe that they slow down to marvel at the sprawling garden beds, the verdure of the yard that Rachel takes such pride in.

But she doubts it. In her experience, every time you try to assume the best of people, they almost always disappoint.

Doing her best to shake it off, Rachel walks around to the back porch and unlocks the kitchen door. The house is cool, though a little dark, even in the summer months, thanks to the shade of the large oaks and maples overhead and the screened windows on the west side of the house that welcome in the breeze off the lake. Dora always said air conditioning was for shopping malls and grocery stores and not for a person's home. She believed heat made a person feel alive, and couldn't understand why people who spent at least six months of the year in a deep freeze that burned their cheeks were so swift to cool things down once the summer sun finally made its reappearance.

The house was indeed so comfortable that the lack of AC hadn't ever bothered Rachel, save on two scorching nights—one when she was ten, the other when she was seventeen—where the very air felt bogged down with sweat and fire. On those occasions, she and Dora had retreated out onto the back porch and slept in the chaise longues beneath the stars as a chorus of crickets and the rhythmic rush of the waves lulled them to sleep.

It's a Victorian house, built just after the turn of the century when the kitchen, not the room that housed the television, was the heartbeat of the home. Cream-coloured cabinets line the walls on three sides, with a large maple prep table in the centre, the same wood used for the countertops. Burnished copper pots hang from a rack on the ceiling and glint in the light of the sunset framed in the large windows at the back of the house, overlooking the lake.

As she drops her purse on the kitchen prep table, her eyes fall on yesterday's pile of mail. She flips through the bank statements, bills, and flyers, and finally, a letter with a familiar return address. Without opening it, she scoops it up with the flyers and dumps the lot in the recycling bin by the back door.

The Gawkers—and now the letter—haven't helped Rachel's anxiety, and she knows she'll need something to calm her nerves tonight, or she'll have no hope of a decent sleep before what's sure to be another marathon shift tomorrow. She pauses for a moment, then makes her way toward a pocket door to the right of the stove, which opens onto the small, narrow scullery. She flicks on the light, illuminating the rows of pantry staples: bags of flour, canned beans, crackers, and two dozen large Mason jars full of dried herbs. The deep, floor-to-ceiling shelves along one side combined with Dora's small stature had required the installation of a library ladder to allow her to reach the top. Rachel pushes it gently aside with a light rumble and pulls out the herbs she needs: valerian, chamomile, passionflower, and spearmint. She turns around and sets them down with a *clink* on the small counter beside the sink, reaching for Dora's mortar and pestle. Her mind wanders, as it sometimes does when she's in the scullery, back to one of her mother's visits years ago. Her grandmother had ground up other herbs for Mary that time. *For her nerves*, she'd told Rachel. But the pennyroyal and black cohosh she'd crushed on that occasion weren't meant for anxious thoughts and racing hearts, Rachel knows now.

The herbs had always been Dora's specialty. Tea, specifically. She believed there wasn't much the right tisane couldn't cure.

OCTOBER, 1977

Mary had arrived on the doorstep just after midnight, the favoured hour of anyone wishing to move about unnoticed. When Rachel woke up on Saturday morning, she stumbled downstairs to find her mother seated at the kitchen table, thin fingers curled around a mug. Her hair was different than the last time she'd dropped in, at least a year ago. It was longer now, falling nearly past her armpits in dark, loose waves that looked in need of a brush. Her eyelids were heavy, lined in some kind of kohl the colour of trouble.

"Hey," she said to Rachel, who had stopped short at the sight of her. Rachel's eyes flicked to Dora, who had just turned around from the sink and was bringing a plate of waffles to the table. She always made them when Mary showed up, because Rachel had once loved them. Dora thought it helped comfort her for the upcoming inevitable stress of Mary's visit, but the gesture had long ago coiled back in on itself like a foolish snake. Rachel couldn't stand them now.

Her grandmother nodded at her, nudging a response.

"Hi," Rachel said.

"You've gotten bigger."

"Yeah."

Rachel took the empty seat beside her mother and forked a couple of waffles onto her plate, drowning them in maple syrup. She ate as quickly as she could, sparing curious glances at Mary as she and Dora made conversation that went mostly over Rachel's head.

"Can I be excused?" she asked Dora when she'd finished.

"Yes. Go rinse your plate and then you can watch cartoons in the living room if you like. There's a good girl."

Rachel did as she was told, then made a beeline for the television set to turn on *Looney Tunes*. She watched it for a while, but at the sound of raised voices, crept around the corner and stood in the shadows.

"Are you pregnant again?" Dora asked.

Mary was silent but for the sound of her foot tapping against the metal stool on which she was seated. Rachel's breath caught. She knew that word, "pregnant." Her grandmother used it when she talked about the rabbits that liked to nest beneath the rhubarb bushes. Her mother was having a baby. She might have a brother or sister.

"How far along are you?"

"About a month, I think."

"You think?" Dora asked darkly.

"Yeah. Maybe two," Mary said.

"Who is the father this time? Do you know?"

"Ron Lister."

"And he is . . . ?"

Mary paused. "A friend of a friend."

Silence again.

"What's the postal code for your most recent address, Mary?" Dora asked.

Mary scoffed. "What—?"

"You cannot raise a child hopping from couch to couch and bed to bed. Children need stability, and—"

"So because I can't remember my fucking postal code, that makes me an unfit mother?"

"No," Dora said, her tone rising, then dropping again to almost a whisper. "And don't you dare swear at me in my own house, child. Your *erratic behaviour* is what makes you an unfit mother. Your taste in men. Your constant lies and manipulation make you an unfit caregiver for Rachel or any other child."

"Mama, stop—"

"Why you don't take steps to prevent yourself from falling pregnant in the first place is beyond my comprehension. You're just one crisis after another. Do you think you could manage to be responsible *one day* out of your life? Ever?"

Mary was quiet for a while. "I could get settled, though, before this one comes. Get my own place. I could—"

"It may not even come," Dora said. "You lost the last one."

"But if it sticks—"

"If it sticks, you would be wise to get rid of it."

"I don't want to get rid of it. Maybe it's what I need, Mama. Maybe it could set me straight."

"Like Rachel set you straight? Or the one before her?" Dora's tone was ice now, and Rachel froze at the mention of her name. She thought of the other girls in her class, the ones whose mothers dropped them off in the morning and picked them up in the afternoon with promises of freshly baked cookies waiting at home. She never heard those mothers use swear words. They turned up for school concerts and track meets and cheered on their kids. They were like a whole different breed of mother to Rachel, so disparate from her own experience that she couldn't even compare them. They were like daisies and roses; one simple and pure and bright, the other thorny and particular and quick to wilt. She wished her mother could just be like the others, wondered why she wasn't. But her grandmother had just said it was all Rachel's fault, and she felt something wither inside.

"I could take her with me this time," Mary said, and Rachel's heart began to race.

No. Please no!

"She could help with the baby—"

"Don't be ridiculous," Dora snapped. "She *is* a baby, Mary. She's still a child, not a nanny! And you know you are not allowed to take her anywhere."

"But what if you said it was all right?"

"I will never do such a thing. For Christ's sake, listen to yourself."

Rachel blanched. She'd never heard her grandmother take the Lord's name in vain before. And the thought of having to leave with her mother terrified her. The first time Mary had left, Dora said, Rachel was three. She came back again, a couple of years later, and stayed for nine months, until Rachel started preschool. And then she was gone again. She'd never moved back in in any real sense, and Dora always referred to the time Mary did spend there as "visits." Some were longer, a few months here and there, and some were shorter. But it always ended in arguments, slammed doors and bitterness.

Mary didn't stay long this time, either. Only a few weeks. She didn't even stay for Christmas. She slept a lot of the time, mostly during the day. She seemed to prefer the dark. Her exchanges with Rachel were limited and awkward, Mary only paying her daughter any attention when she had nothing else to do. When she did, it was as though her mind were darting around from thought to thought, as unsettled and transitory as a hummingbird.

The night before her mother slammed the screen door behind her with a clap and sped off down the street in her rusting white Falcon, Rachel had woken up to the sound of sobbing from the bathroom on the other side of the wall. She lay awake for several minutes, wondering what to do. She knew the cries were Mary's, not Dora's. She had never seen Dora cry, not even when her eighteen-year-old cat Gracie had died the previous spring.

Pushing back the covers, she crept from her bed out into the dim hallway. A strip of yellow light illuminated the crack beneath the bathroom door. She hesitated, then knocked quietly. The door opened a second later and there was her mother, kneeling on the white-and-black-tiled floor, which was smeared with blood. Rachel recoiled. It was all over her legs and hands, and the light from the bathroom shone on the dark tracks down the hall from Mary's bedroom, too.

Rachel gasped. "What happened? Are you okay?"

Mary's face crumpled as she swiped at the blood with a bath towel. She shook her head.

Rachel knew something about periods. She'd read the library's copy of *Are You There God? It's Me, Margaret*. A swooping fear overtook her as she wondered whether this was what it would look like when her time finally came.

"Come here," Mary said, reaching her blood-streaked hands out to her daughter. Rachel didn't want to, but she stepped over and Mary wrapped her arms tightly around her. Rachel stiffened. Her mother had never hugged her before. Not that she could recall, anyway.

After a moment, Mary let go, sniffling and breathing hard. "Oh," she said, looking at Rachel. "You've got blood on you."

"What happened?" Rachel asked again. "Is it your period?"

Her mother looked at her with swollen eyes. "Something like that. The baby's gone. We need to clean up."

"I should get Gran," Rachel said.

She turned to leave, but Mary reached over and shut the door, boxing Rachel inside. She was truly frightened now.

Mary shoved the shower curtain aside with a swish and turned on the water, then took Rachel's hand and led her over. "Get in."

"But my pyjamas—"

"Just get in, we'll clean them. We need to be clean."

Rachel didn't like it, but she stepped into the tub, squinting a little under the heavy spray of hot water. Mary climbed in after her and pulled the curtain closed, leaving a bloody print behind on the fabric. She put her head under the water and shut her eyes against the stream. Rachel stood in front of her, water ricocheting uncomfortably into her eyes off her mother's body as she watched pink trails of blood course down the drain. After a moment, Mary knelt down to her eye level.

"That witch did this, you know," she said, nodding knowingly. "She's always trying to punish me. You remember this, Rachel."

Rachel would indeed remember it. And Mary wouldn't turn up again for another three years.

CHAPTER 12

EMILY

Toronto—June 19, 1961

"How are you doing, my girl?" William muttered beside Emily on the wooden bench outside the courtroom.

She took a deep breath, tried to quell the nervousness that was swirling in her stomach like a flock of starlings. She tapped the edge of the bench in time to the clock on the wall across from them, which told her they'd already been waiting three hours to see a judge.

"Wishing I'd eaten a bigger lunch, for a start," she said, trying to lighten the mood. Her dad let out a reluctant chuckle.

They'd had lunch as a family at home, in relative silence as each of them contemplated the day, weeks, and months ahead. Afterward, Emily had picked up her handbag and said goodbye to her tearful mother at the door.

"I'll write, if I'm allowed," she'd said, embracing Bess tightly and breathing in the smells of Aqua Net and sugar. "I just won't be able to be very direct. You'll have to read between the lines."

"William Radcliffe?" a deep voice called now, and Emily and her father looked up. A bailiff stood outside a set of double doors twenty feet away. "You're next."

"Well," William said quietly. "Put on your best-actress-award face, my girl. Here we go."

Emily stood, whispered "I love you, Dad," and followed him, deliberately lagging and fixing an irritable expression onto her face, mouth pursed in what she hoped would be evident obstinacy.

The courtroom was small but grand, with shining dark walnut wood floors that matched the high bench on which sat a large and passive-faced judge. He wore flowing black robes that hardly contrasted against the wood-panelled wall behind him, creating the rather disconcerting illusion that his head was floating in mid-air. Emily had never been in a courtroom before.

The bailiff rattled off the judge's name and credentials.

"Come forward," the judge drawled, hardly looking up from a sheet of paper in front of him. The bailiff ushered Emily and her father into place near a desk that, she thought, would have typically been reserved for the accused in a criminal trial. Though the women taken before a judge under the Female Refuges Act had committed no crime, they were apparently still treated as though they had from the outset.

"My docket here says that your daughter, Miss Emily Carolyn Radcliffe, aged twenty-four, has been brought here today for reasons of incorrigibility, is that correct?"

Her father cleared his throat, and Emily's gut twinged as the reality of what they were about to learn hit home. This was the moment they would discover just how easy it was to be incarcerated under the FRA, and whether she would, in fact, be going to prison for three months.

"That is correct, your honour," William said, shifting his feet.

"State your case," the judge said, making a note.

He still hadn't even looked up. He could not have appeared less interested in her as a person. Was this the same judge who did all the sentencing under this Act? She hoped there were more. It could not all be down to one man.

"It's uh, it's my daughter, you see." They had briefly rehearsed what William would say, but they had deliberately decided not to oversell it. Part of the question here was whether it truly was so easy to be sentenced to jail time under this Act for subjective misbehaviour. Emily didn't want her father to *convince* the judge; she wanted to see whether it would be a fair fight at all.

"She's old enough to be married now but has no interest," William said, and Emily squirmed a little, thinking of her last conversation with Jem. He'd been heartbroken. And, understandably, angry. But he'd also shouted and made her feel small and ridiculous for taking the path she wanted, and she didn't think she could ever forgive him for that.

"She's at home with her mother and me," her father continued, "but she stays out until all hours with no regard for curfew, or propriety at all. No respect for authority, your honour."

The judge nodded, finally looking up at them. His eyes raked Emily up and down once, utterly dispassionately, as though simply confirming that yes, she was a woman. His attention returned to her father.

"And you feel she is in need of reform?"

William hesitated only a beat, and in it, Emily sensed his reluctance to say that she needed fixing. She loved him for it, and her heart swelled. "Yes, your honour."

"Very well, then," the judge said, gaze returning again to his docket. "I hereby sentence you"—he referred to his notes—"Emily Carolyn Radcliffe, to no less than six months in an industrial refuge. You will be transferred to the Mercer Women's Prison forthwith."

Six months?

Emily's mouth opened, but her father beat her to it.

"Six months, your honour?" he asked. "I had thought maybe perhaps a shorter stay. I cannot imagine it would take more than—"

"Sir, are you questioning the authority of the Bench?" the judge demanded.

William cleared his throat. "No, your honour, it's only—"

"You have told me that she requires reform. Six months is the standard sentence for cases of this type. Little of value can be accomplished in less time. My decision stands. She will be released back into your custody on the nineteenth of December."

He then actually waved them out of his courtroom as though keen to be rid of them. William met Emily's eyes, her own unpleasant surprise and fear reflected in his. This was a sham, hardly better than a kangaroo court.

She followed behind the bailiff and her father, cursing as her heart raced. She knew her father could be relied upon to tell Doris of the change in plan, but her mother would be beside herself, and angry with William, no doubt. And Emily . . . she hadn't bargained for this long a sentence, and felt a little nauseous. But she took a few deep, steadying breaths and willed herself to keep her head.

When they reached the large foyer, the bailiff told them to wait while he retrieved the paperwork "and a woman," he said rather cryptically. Emily puzzled for a moment, then recalled a section of the Female Refuges Act that declared prisoners were to be taken by a female bailiff to the industrial refuges. What was the concern? That the accused women were so scandalously out of control that the male bailiffs might be wantonly seduced? Emily refrained from rolling her eyes. This whole thing was so painfully obsolete.

"Emily," her dad said under his breath after the bailiff had gone. "There must be something we can do, this—"

"No, Dad," Emily said, her mouth dry. "I can do this." Nellie Bly's words came back to her, a line from her article when she began to question her own ability.

Did I think I had the courage to go through such an ordeal as the mission would demand? Could I assume the characteristics of insanity to such a degree that I could pass the doctors, live for a week among the insane without the authorities there finding out? I said I could, and I would.

"It's fine," she said. "I can do it."

He shook his head, then reached forward and pulled her into a tight hug with his single arm. She breathed in his aftershave and blinked hard. "Will you tell Doris what's happened, please?" she whispered, and he nodded. "I'll write as soon as I can, I promise. Tell Mom I love her. It's going to be okay. Doris told me not to get into any trouble, and I won't. I'm just there to observe. It'll be okay."

She wasn't entirely sure why she kept saying it was going to be all right. Perhaps if she said it enough, they might both believe it.

"It's an adventure. Keep thinking of it that way," her father advised. "That helped me in the field. It's an adventure and you're there to tell the story. Just tell the story, Em."

She thought back on her last conversation with Doris, two days before, when the details of the plan were finalized.

"This is a great scoop, and an important one. But get in, get the story, and get out," her boss had told her, actually holding Emily by the shoulders with her large hands, locking eyes with her. "Observe, but do not deliberately put yourself in harm's way, or I shall chain you to your desk for the rest of your career. I mean that, Emily. Watch, listen, learn, and take notes, not risks."

"I'll be careful, I promise," she told her dad now. "I love you."

They quickly pulled apart as the bailiff returned with a stern-looking woman in uniform who beckoned to Emily.

"Come on this way. I've called ahead. They'll have finished supper over there by the time we arrive, so let's get on with it. I don't want to be out all night."

Emily was ushered forward, clutching her bag tightly. She glanced over her shoulder to see her father standing alone in the hall, his eyes conflicted, but also full of pride. He offered a tight smile.

Good luck! he mouthed.

She faced front again, swallowed hard on the irritating lump in her throat, and set her feet toward the next step in her career, the great leap into the rest of her life.

CHAPTER 13

EMILY

The Mercer Women's Prison, Toronto—June, 1961

The drive to the prison took less time than Emily had imagined, and, sitting in the back seat of the bailiff's car, she was filled with a mix of emotions. Never in her life had she done anything so audacious, and she was surprised by the exhilaration it wrought. But there was also nervousness, and fear. Shock, too, at how easy it had been for two men to arrange the incarceration of a woman who wasn't a minor and had committed no crime. She was also in disbelief that she would be in the Mercer for twice as long as she'd bargained for. But she couldn't dwell on that. She did her best to focus on the thrill of this chase, the adventure that awaited her. The thing was done now; there was little point in regret.

I said I could, and I would.

The bailiff pulled up at the curb outside the prison on King Street, and she was ordered out of the car. It was after six o'clock now, and the early-summer sun was beginning to lower in the sky to the west, cooling the air. Emily had worn an outfit appropriate for court: a brown tweed skirt and cream button-up blouse with an olive-green cardigan—both of which the wind now cut through. As she waited for further instructions, she looked up at the prison, thinking how it hadn't been long since she'd wandered around its perimeter and spoken with June Jones.

"This way, come on. Front door," the bailiff said, hustling. She sounded bored, as though she had done this three times already this week.

Emily gathered herself, and focused. If this woman *did* in fact do this often, she might have good information to offer. "How many girls have you dropped off in the past month?" Emily asked as the bailiff unlocked the gate and they made their way down the gravel path.

The bailiff looked sideways at her and scowled. "What an odd question," she said, not answering it. Emily didn't press for more. She couldn't risk drawing suspicion before she'd even set foot in the place.

They were nearing the doors now, and Emily looked up at the sign above them, carved in capital letters in aged stone: MERCER WOMEN'S PRISON.

A surge of adrenaline hit her then. *She was walking into a prison*, something she'd never dreamed would ever happen in her middle-class, law-abiding life. And for a fleeting moment her nerves threatened to choke out her determination. Maybe this was too dangerous, or even mad. Maybe she couldn't, or shouldn't do it. What if she was risking herself, and there wasn't even a story here?

But she knew in her heart that there was.

The bailiff rang a doorbell that Emily couldn't hear inside, and a moment later, a female guard clad in a pressed white uniform and cap answered the door and greeted the bailiff by name, confirming Emily's suspicion that there was some regularity to these proceedings.

"Radcliffe, Emily Carolyn," the bailiff droned.

The matron waved them through. "Warden Barrow is expecting you. You're late."

Emily didn't have much time to take in the foyer before she was shunted to an open door on the right. She saw *Warden's Office* stencilled on it as she passed through, then stood awkwardly, hands clasped in front of her.

The office was surprisingly homey, with shining wood floors. Dark-blue curtains hung from the large windows, which Emily noticed were not barred, though she was sure she'd seen bars on the other windows from the outside. But this boded well; perhaps the place was not the concrete block she'd been envisioning.

There was a woman seated at the desk who must be the warden. Emily reckoned she was about the same age as her own mother, somewhere in her late forties. She wore a deep rose-coloured lipstick but no eye makeup, which was counter to the current trend.

The warden and the bailiff hardly exchanged a dozen words between them as Emily waited. The bailiff thrust some paperwork at the warden, who signed something. The bailiff handed her a file and departed without a word to Emily, passing the guard who had greeted them.

"Sit down," the warden instructed. Emily sat in the chair across from her and peered over the warden's shoulder out the window. She could just make out the traffic in the distance at the corner of Fraser and King, and the dark-brown brick and arched glass windows of the Toronto Carpet Factory, the prison's closest neighbour to the west. She looked back at Warden Barrow and waited.

"Emily Radcliffe," Warden Barrow finally said in the tone of a strict schoolteacher, scanning the file in front of her. "I understand you are here by means of the FRA, is that correct?"

"Yes." Emily looked at the brown file on the warden's desk, aching with curiosity to know how the court record had characterized her. She looked up at the warden, took in her brownish-red hair swept back in a roll. She was a curvy woman with wide shoulders, but her expression was as flat as a prairie desert.

"Our rules at the Mercer are simple," Warden Barrow clipped. "Adhere to your schedule, obey the matrons, and don't stir up trouble. Wait out your time until your release, and do not do anything to get sent back here. And if you step out of line, Miss Radcliffe, there will be consequences."

Emily opened her mouth to ask what sort of consequences the warden referred to, but Barrow plowed on. "Your file tells me you harbour a certain disregard for rules. I hope your time at the Mercer will serve to remedy this unfortunate blight on your character." She fixed

Emily with a sharp look. "I expect better of you than what I see here, Miss Radcliffe. And you should expect better of yourself, too."

She thrust a sheet of paper at Emily.

```
7:00   Wake and breakfast
7:45   Prayer time
8:15   Laundry duty
10:30  Exercise
11:30  Lesson—typing
12:30  Dinner
13:30  Lesson—domestics
14:30  Cleaning duty OR factory
16:00  Meal prep'n duty
18:00  Supper
19:00  Recreation
21:00  To cell
22:00  Lights out

Note: RADCLIFFE, Emily C. — Block D, Cell 216 to
bathe WEDNESDAYS / 20:05 / 2nd floor prisoner WC

Note: Wed-Thur no cleaning duty / report instead to
factory
```

"Follow your schedule to the letter," Warden Barrow said. "Listen for the bell and don't be tardy, or there will be consequences."

"Yes, and what exactly—"

"And exercise hour takes place indoors now," the warden continued, ignoring Emily. "You may walk around at your leisure."

Emily paused. "Isn't there an exercise yard?"

The warden vented her irritation in a dramatic sigh. "Normally yes, but outdoor privileges are on suspension. Some inmates chose to abuse that privilege by trying to interact with . . . at any rate, until further notice, you may exercise indoors."

The hair on Emily's arms stood up. Had the inmate who passed the note to Ted the delivery driver caused outdoor time to be suspended? Or, rather, had Doris's phone call referencing it?

"Now," the warden continued, "you've arrived well after supper, and I'm meant to be gone already." She said it with a huff, as though it were entirely Emily's fault. "I'll have a matron try to scrounge something from the kitchen. They will bring it up to your cell. Now, go with Matron White. I don't expect to see you back in my office until your release date. Behave yourself." She raked her eyes over Emily and then snapped her fingers. "Your handbag."

Emily wasn't surprised by this, but passed it over reluctantly.

"I brought a toothbrush, underwear," she said. "Do—"

"They will be provided for you."

Emily watched her bag disappear into a drawer. Clutching her schedule, she rose and followed Matron White, who was waiting at the door, from the office.

They made their way out into the small foyer, off which Emily spotted three more doors, all shut. They were labelled "Storage," "Salon," and "Janitorial."

Salon?

She knew from studying the outside of the prison that it was laid out in a cross shape, and she was led now to the centre junction and over to two staircases—one leading up, the other down. She followed the tall and broad-hipped guard—matron, they apparently called them—up to the second floor, and then down one of the four corridors that led off it. It was lined with cells, their barred doors open. They were small, and dim inside. She glimpsed narrow beds low to the ground, all tidily made with the same grey blanket. Her throat tightened. It was quiet here, but Emily could hear loud women's voices on the floor above.

"It's the recreation hour right now," Matron White answered her silent question. "The women are mostly upstairs in the rec room. You'll see it tomorrow, I suppose, as they're due to return to their cells soon." She suddenly stopped. "You're here."

Emily looked at the plaque outside the cell—216. She swallowed and stepped over the threshold. The matron shut the door behind her, locked it. Her heart pounded harder.

"I might return with some baked beans and bread, if I have time," she said, and left.

Emily took a deep breath and observed her new living space—if one could call it that.

A bed was shoved into one corner but still took up most of the floor, even though it was narrower than the one she had at home. It was already made, and on the bed was a small pile of items, which Emily pawed through: a nightdress and day dress with an apron and shoes. A toothbrush and a tin of toothpowder rested on top, along with a supply of cloth sanitary pads and a belt. *I suppose the hairpins I'm wearing now will have to last six months*, Emily thought wryly. She noted a metal chamber pot on the concrete floor with a roll of toilet paper that felt more like butcher's paper to the touch, thick and rough.

A tap stuck out from the wall a couple of feet up from the floor. She assumed it was for drinking water when the inmates were stuck in their cells each night for hours on end, but Emily didn't see a cup. Did they have to use their hands? There was also no drain, so any dripping water would pool until it dried naturally. There was no desk or table, and nothing on the brick walls except a bare light bulb, high up near the ceiling. No rug. Nothing, Emily realized, that an inmate could use as a weapon against herself or the staff. There was, at least, natural light. Hers and the cells she could see across the hall each had a small window, high up and barred. She stepped around the perimeter of the room to estimate the size. It was about seven feet wide by eight feet long. She'd used water closets bigger than this.

Emily gingerly sat down on the bed, taking it all in. She'd rarely slept in a room that wasn't hers; her parents couldn't afford to travel much beyond day trips to the beach or to see a play at the new theatres in

Stratford when the girls were young. She'd never been to a sleep-away camp, or stayed in a hotel.

Doris had described her as sheltered, inexperienced. And it hit her then, not with the creeping realization that slinks its way over your shoulders, but with the force of a slap to the face, that she would not retain those labels for much longer. For better or worse, they would be shed like outgrown skin, and she wasn't entirely sure what she would find underneath. But once more, Nellie Bly's words came back to her. Taunting. Galvanizing.

I said I could, and I would.

CHAPTER 14

EMILY

The Mercer Women's Prison, Toronto—June 20, 1961
Day 1 (182 to go)

Emily woke at 7 a.m. to a clanging bell assaulting her eardrums. *Listen for the bell,* Warden Barrow had said. A person would have to be dead to miss it.

She sat upright on the stiff, creaking mattress and massaged the stiffness in her neck with a wince. She stood up to stretch her hands overhead, and her stomach fluttered. She'd been more nervous than she cared to admit the moment her cell door slammed shut for the first time the night before. After gagging down the cold baked beans and stale bread Matron White had resentfully brought her, Emily had spent an hour staring at the ceiling, listening to the other inmates noisily returning to their cells before finally dozing off into a fitful sleep.

But now she was—mostly—excited. The conditions hadn't been too much of a shock. She'd suspected it would all look and feel, well . . . like a prison. And it did. But there was a novelty about it, a sort of immersive rush, as though she were in costume on a detailed film set, or had been dropped into the pages of *The Count of Monte Cristo.*

She smirked in a little self-satisfied way as the first lines of her eventual exposé floated to mind, echoing Nellie Bly's style:

Chapter One: A Delicate Mission.

It was on the 6th of June that I first became aware of the goings-on at the Mercer Women's Prison on King West...

But she pushed the composition aside in her mind and tried to focus. Emily shed her linen nightgown—which must have begun its life white, but was now greyish from an unknowable number of bleaching cycles—and exchanged it for the loose brown dress that was the inmates' uniform, with a white apron tied overtop. The dress was wildly oversized for her frame and came right down to her ankles, but once she tied the apron around her waist, it cinched the whole thing in. She pulled on the white stockings and slid her feet into her new black shoes, thinking of how Jan the fashion editor would review this antiquated attire. Pinning her hair up, Emily waited for her cell to be unlocked, listening to the rhythm of jangling keys and the creaks of aged hinges as the cells down the hall were unlocked. A minute later, a matron different from the one who had locked her in last night came to the door and released her. Emily considered the method.

> The cell doors must all be opened individually, rather than by a unified mechanism, which is most assuredly a dreadful fire hazard.

She stepped out into the hall, where her fellow inmates were lined up, each woman standing in front of her open cell door. She waited a few more minutes as the matrons released the women from the cells to her right, using the time to take in her surroundings.

There were about twenty women that she could count in her cellblock alone—the southern wing of the second floor. They were all dressed identically, down to the same black shoes. Emily studied their feet. Most of the shoes were worn and scuffed, though a couple in her line of sight were still shiny like her own—the newer inmates. She would try to speak to the women with the older-looking shoes. They would have witnessed more, might have more stories and information to share.

There was a smell of cooked eggs in the air, which was itself a bit damp, making for an earthy sort of atmosphere.

"Roll call!" one of the matrons shouted from twenty feet down the hall. Emily ducked her head a little to get a better view of Matron White, her hair tucked under a cap. She began to shout out inmates' names, which Emily quickly realized were not in alphabetical order but rather by order of their cell geography. Finally, it was Emily's turn.

"Radcliffe!"

"Yes!" Emily called back, echoing her fellow inmates.

"Cook!"

"Yeah," the woman behind her answered, and the matron moved on down the line. "You're new today?" her neighbour added in a quieter tone.

Emily turned around, nodded. "I'm Emily," she whispered.

"Lizzie." The woman was tall, with striking black hair and dark eyes. She didn't smile at Emily, but nor did she appear mean. "Chamber pots are next," Lizzie hissed. "We get to carry our own shit to the toilets. And get your toothbrush, too."

Emily's mouth fell open, but she composed herself a moment later just as, sure enough, the matron barked for them all to retrieve their pots. Emily seized her toothbrush and powder, and the pot, though hers was empty. She hadn't emptied her bladder and was desperate to. But she'd assumed they would have an opportunity to use the toilet in the morning. Surely the metal pot was only in case of a midnight emergency?

Nevertheless, when her name was called, she hastened down the long hallway to the washroom, carrying the pot aloft, passing other inmates on their way back.

The entire washroom—including the tile floor and walls—was white but aged, the door dented and the paint scratched, revealing the rusted metal beneath. There were no mirrors, and only one large copper bathtub out in the open. Emily bolted into one of the doorless stalls. The ceramic on the toilet tank was chipped. With a deep breath, she set her pot down on the floor and hiked up her voluminous skirt, squatted over the seat to relieve herself. Two other inmates came in with their pots as Emily finished wiping with the crunchy paper. They eyed Emily with curiosity through the open stall as they walked into the ones on either side. She was treated to the sounds and smells of their pots being emptied into the toilets before she picked up her own and made for the trough-like metal sink to wash her hands.

She exhaled deeply as she rinsed them, cheeks burning a little from having urinated in plain view like that. But she thought of the article, thought of Nellie Bly, thought of all she would write about this first day's experience once she had the chance. If she could leverage it into the story of her career, every humiliation and discomfort would turn out to be a good thing. Through her shock and distaste, she vowed to welcome it in the name of the article.

Once everyone had completed their business and was back in line, the inmates began to move, herding in single file toward the staircase at the matron's instruction. Emily had tried to catch a bit of detail about the layout of the place the night before, as she was being taken to her cell, but was able to get her bearings better in the morning light. When she reached the staircase now she glanced around, taking in the other three long hallways. The one to the north looked a lot like hers, with cells lined up on both sides, the barred doors spaced less than ten feet apart. The walls were large bricks painted over in a thin whitewash, and most of the dim light seemed to come from the little windows inside the cells, but there were overhead lights as well, bare bulbs that were currently off.

A large side-by-side staircase led both up and down, and was situated in one corner of the crux where the four hallways met at the centre of the building. Following the short inmate in front of her, Emily glanced back and noticed that the cellblock to the west was gated. Down the hall to the east was another series of cells and a wide-open door at the very end, where sunlight poured in. Above it, a sign proclaimed INFIRMARY.

"Keep your eyes in front, if you know what's good for you," Lizzie muttered behind her. Emily quickly complied.

The women were herded downward, their footfalls thundering in the stairwell. Her cellblock was on the second floor, but the staircase leading up meant there must be a third, and she was sure she'd seen four stories from the outside. Just how many women were housed here? What was the capacity? It had to be at least a hundred.

On the main floor, Emily smelled food: the eggs she'd caught a whiff of upstairs, and something burning. She followed the rest of the women to a set of open doors she'd only briefly noted on her way upstairs the night before. It was the dining hall, a long, rectangular room with large barred windows on the north side facing King Street. Several round tables with battered wooden chairs were set around the room, with a handful of inmates already seated. The rest lined up at a buffet table along the far wall. Emily shuffled forward with the queue, glancing around surreptitiously as she waited. The women now dispersed from the quiet file they'd tramped downstairs in and became more talkative, some reuniting warmly with evident friends from other cellblocks. She saw several women watching her, and she imagined there must be a certain amount of curiosity about new inmates. She wondered again how often they were admitted.

When she reached the front, an inmate wearing a hairnet and gloves thrust a metal tray at her. Emily's nose wrinkled at the small portions of oatmeal, meat, a piece of dry toast and what looked like a quarter cup of scrambled egg. She crafted the sentences for her article in her mind:

> A grossly inadequate breakfast was provided on my first morning. I awaited dinner and supper with hungry anticipation to learn whether this pitiful meal was anomalous or standard to the institution.

She hadn't received any instruction on where to sit, so she held her tray and looked around at the tables, uncomfortably reminded of her secondary school days when she and Eleanor had lunch at different times. Emily had never been in the popular crowd, though nor was she bullied or undermined. She was just sort of invisible, except to a couple of the girlfriends she'd now fallen out of touch with. That was one thing about having a twin: people often thought you didn't have any use or desire for friends; that all your social needs were inherently met by your doppelgänger. The few friends she had made eventually admitted they'd felt intimidated to penetrate the eerie barrier of twindom in the effort to forge a friendship with either Radcliffe girl. And so she was out of practice in an exercise that had never come very naturally to her to begin with: making friends, however temporary—or useful—they might be.

She would need to get to know some of the inmates so that she could learn the histories and experiences that would form the background of her piece. *Who* exactly were these women? What lives had they lived before their incarceration at the Mercer, and how had it impacted them?

She took a deep breath and studied the tables. Most were now full of chatting inmates tucking hungrily into their meagre breakfasts. Off to the side of the hall near the kitchen door, she spied a table whose sole occupant was a slim woman with brown hair, who appeared to be somewhere in her thirties. Emily strode over.

"Hello," she said. "I'm Emily. Do you mind if I sit here?"

The woman looked up from a piece of toast. She had dark circles beneath her blue eyes, but the eyes themselves were gentle, and pleasantly set off by her uniform, which was the colour of a clear June sky. On her way downstairs, Emily had only spotted two other inmates wearing blue rather than brown, and had assumed that they were simply old uniforms, or maybe new ones being phased in. The blue, at least, was some spot of colour in this depressingly monochromatic establishment.

After a moment, the woman nodded her consent, a hint of a smile tugging at her hollow cheeks. But she didn't introduce herself, so Emily prompted her. "What's your name?"

"Annie," she said, looking surprised to be asked. "Annie Little."

"Pleasure to meet you," Emily said, then looked down at her breakfast. She'd been given a spoon but no fork, and the dullest table knife she'd ever seen. The edge of the spoon was probably sharper. She scooped up some oatmeal, which was tasteless and stone-cold to the point of making her gag, but she forged on, recalling the claims from the "Incorrigible" note—that there was never enough to eat at the Mercer. The meat languishing sadly beside the bowl of oatmeal was a greyish piece of beef hardly bigger than a tin of mints.

They ate in silence for a moment as Emily scanned the noisy room again, eyes on the other inmates as the thought occurred to her that the mysterious author of the note might be sitting at the very next table. She wondered whether she would be able to suss her out over the course of this project. But she was pulled from her thoughts when Annie spoke, her voice soft and gentle.

"Would you mind cutting my beef into smaller bits?" she asked. "I'm not allowed a knife."

Emily paused, struggling to chew a piece of toast with no butter. "Oh, yes of course." She was surprised; the dull knife could hardly be considered a weapon. She made to hand it over, but Annie shook her head, glancing at the open double doors, where matrons were standing watch on either side.

"I'm not allowed it. You'll get into trouble."

Emily hesitated, swallowed the dry lump of bread.

"Why aren't you allowed?" she asked.

Annie took a deep breath. "Some inmates just aren't. But I'm not going to hurt anyone."

Emily ran her tongue over her teeth, eyed the dull knife again. She slid a finger over the blade. "I don't think you could even if you wanted to," she said, trying to smile.

Annie's eyes grew wide, and she let out a breathy laugh, then clapped a hand to her mouth, eyes darting to the matrons.

Emily watched her with a mixture of pity and amusement. "Are jokes not allowed here, either?" she asked with a smirk.

Annie lowered her hand, shook her head. "You know, I'm not sure they are . . ."

Emily smiled, then passed the knife to Annie. They both glanced again at the matrons, who appeared not to have seen the exchange.

"Thank you," Annie said, quickly breaking up the meat.

"You're welcome." Emily sipped her tea now. Predictably, it was tepid and weak, but she was thirsty. She thought of what her mother would have to say about this pitiful breakfast.

The chatter of voices swelled, and Emily noticed most people by now had empty plates. She glanced up at the clock over the doorway, recalled her schedule. Breakfast was nearly over, so she turned her attention to what information she might be able to glean from Annie Little in the next few minutes.

"Is breakfast always this bad?" she asked.

Annie scoffed. "Yes. Been the same for fifteen years. Hardly any fruit. Some vegetables, just what they grow in the prison garden. Tinned green beans, and tinned tomatoes, too, sometimes. *Sometimes*."

Emily stared, mouth agape. "You've been here for *fifteen years*?"

Annie nodded.

"But . . ." Emily thought fast. She didn't want to sound as though she had swallowed the Female Refuges Act. "I didn't think they could keep us more than, what, a couple of years? Usually less, right? I'm here for six months."

Annie watched her. "I think that's how it works, yes. But my case is different. I'm not here for being incorrigible."

Before Emily could ask more, the same ear-splitting bell that had woken them that morning sounded from somewhere outside the dining hall doors.

"Thanks for the help," Annie said. She placed the knife back on Emily's empty plate and walked off without another word.

CHAPTER 15

RACHEL

Clinton, Ontario—June, 1996

"Rachel?"

A week after the Jane Doe in the Millgate Cemetery was sent to Toronto for forensic analysis, Crystal, the secretary at the police headquarters, appears in Rachel's doorway.

"Yes?" Rachel sits back in her chair, tamping down her frustration.

Crystal is Green's daughter, working at HQ for the summer before she starts university in the fall. Rachel would like to think Crystal's just being friendly by using her first name, but no one calls any of the male detectives by their first names. They're always Detective So-And-So, delivered with respect and something bordering on reverence. But Rachel isn't about to correct her on how to address a detective; this girl is her boss's daughter. Crystal could practically take a shit on Rachel's desk if she wanted to, and Rachel couldn't say a damn thing about it.

She looks at Crystal with some dread. The last time she'd appeared in Rachel's doorway, the day after the discovery, she'd announced Tamara Cooper was waiting for her in the lobby. Tamara had sobbed as Rachel explained that the body was not, in fact, Stacy's. There was still some minor buzzing from a couple of reporters in the county eager for more information, but Rachel had put them off, telling them it was now an active investigation and there would be no further comment on the matter.

"There's someone named Sawyer on the phone for you," Crystal says now. "From something called . . . CFF, I think?"

Rachel blinks, then the penny drops. "CF*S*?"

"Maybe. What's that?"

"The Centre of Forensic Sciences." *You should know this.*

"Oh!" Crystal laughs. "Yeah. I guess! Sounds right."

She floats away and Rachel takes a moment to breathe before she reaches for the phone.

"This is Mackenzie."

"Hi, Detective Mackenzie," a deep female voice says. "It's Sawyer."

"Hey Sawyer." She's a forensic archeologist Rachel has worked with before. She's efficient and thorough.

"Got your body here, Jane Doe from the cemetery?"

"Yeah. Weird one."

"Agreed. Got a bit of info though. Do you have a minute?"

"Absolutely." Rachel agitates the mouse to wake up her IBM, and the screen comes alive with a tiny *plink* sound. She opens the word processor and pins the phone between her ear and shoulder. "Go ahead."

"Okay, I'll fax you the full docs for your records, but the summary is that the body is definitely female, height approximately five foot five, age between twenty and forty years, dating from the early 1960s."

"Sixties? Huh. Okay."

"Yeah. The skeleton is mostly intact, but she's missing two teeth. I assume they would have been found in the initial excavation if they were elsewhere in the grave, so I think she must have already had fewer teeth to begin with when she died. Could be a genetic defect, but most likely just lost at some point during her lifetime."

The keyboard clacks too loudly as Rachel takes notes, so she gives up in favour of a pen and paper.

"As for the casket," Sawyer continues, "aside from the damage from the initial discovery—they said a gravedigger found it, hit it by accident?"

"Yup."

"Well, aside from the hole and splintering from that, it's in decent shape. Moisture levels in the area must not have been too bad. But it's very basic, just a pine box, no lining or anything. It's from around the same time, early sixties."

"Excellent, thanks. Anything else?" Rachel jots it all down.

"There's a small brass plate, like a plaque, that was found in the soil and debris removed from the area. It has traces of adhesive on the back, and we found the same traces on the side of the casket, so it was affixed at some point. I imagine it'll be helpful; looks like the name of the company that made it."

Rachel lets out a little breath of relief. It's a place to start. "What does the plaque say?"

"Cartwright-Cambridge Co., Toronto. Very legible."

Rachel asks for the exact spelling, makes a note. "Got it."

"Also," Sawyer says, "you're going to love this: There are numbers stamped on the side of the casket, like a serial number. They're faded, but still legible."

Excellent, Rachel thinks. "Go ahead, Sawyer."

"MWP0326-P. That's Mike-Whiskey-Papa-zero-three-two-six-dash-Papa."

Rachel pauses, looking at the letters and numbers she's just written down. "That seems . . . institutional, somehow, doesn't it? Official? I've never seen that on a casket before." Her mind is already whirring.

"I agree," Sawyer says. "The casket has been processed into evidence here if you want to come see it in more detail, but the photos of the plaque and serial number are on their way to you."

"Thanks, Sawyer. And any idea on cause of death?"

"Can't tell yet, honestly. Nothing obvious. But I'll fax over my report with all the nitty gritty. Let me know if you have any questions after you've reviewed it."

They sign off, and Rachel slumps a little in her chair, eyes narrowed at her notes. She can't make sense of all this. Not yet. But she will.

She turns to face the corkboard behind her desk, which is a third full of details from the Stacy Cooper case. She wonders briefly if it's time to take it down, but it's the girl's face staring at her every day that stokes the flames of her burning need to solve it. Because once a victim's face disappears from view, it's too easy to let it go. And Rachel can't let it go. Not yet. She'll just set up a second board for Jane Doe right beside Stacy's.

She makes her way toward the break room for a coffee to fuel her upcoming brainstorm, stopping first at the fax machine where a stack of papers wait for her in the tray. She picks them up, confirms they're the documents Sawyer was sending over. It's always a rush, starting to tack up evidence, but she's usually at it for a couple of hours before she emerges with a list of questions and next steps. This time is a bit different; she already knows she'll have to locate this Cartwright-Cambridge company and work from there, but she wants to see the casket again in person, for a closer look. She'll head into Toronto tomorrow. But for now, coffee.

Stevens is the only other person in the break room when she enters.

"Hey Mackenzie," he says, not looking up as he stirs a revolting amount of sweetener into his drink.

"Hey," she replies, setting the CFS documents down on the counter beside her and retrieving a mug from the cupboard.

He glances over at the top sheet. "That from the cemetery Jane Doe?"

"Yeah, just came in." She pours herself a cup of coffee and recaps Sawyer's summary as they both stand by the sink, sipping. "It dates from the sixties, and there's a good lead from the casket, a company name. They might have records."

Stevens nods slowly, taking in the update. "All right. Well, let me know if you need any backup with it."

She studies him for a moment. He's in his early twenties, a little nondescript-looking with brown hair and eyes, pale skin. A buzz cut his uncle probably recommended.

"You interested in a detective track, Stevens?" she asks, lifting the mug to her lips.

He nods. "Yeah. You know my uncle is—"

"Tom Stevens."

He watches her, and in that moment she knows that her name has definitely come up at Stevens family dinners. She shouldn't be surprised. And she isn't angry. Not really. Tom Stevens was Rachel's boss and mentor until he retired two years ago and Green took over as chief. It's been a while since she's seen Tom, but even having lunch with him would be seen as some kind of insubordination by Green, like she'd be somehow undermining his authority by daring to have a Reuben and coffee with her former chief. He's already suspicious that Tom and Rachel's relationship wasn't above board. He's been making sidelong, sexist comments for years about her "working under" Tom and being his favourite for unknown, suspicious reasons. He couldn't just call her Tom Stevens's protege.

Fucking asshole.

The younger Stevens glances now at the open break-room door, then back to Rachel. He has something discreet to say.

"Come to my office," she prompts. He nods gratefully and follows her. She shuts the door behind them, ignoring the raised eyebrow from Crystal at the reception desk twenty feet away.

"My uncle said I should shadow you," Stevens tells her. "Instead of . . . well . . ."

Green. Neither of them needs to say it.

"He says you're the best," Stevens continues, "and that I should just watch what you do."

Rachel smiles with a bittersweet pang in her gut. She misses Tom Stevens, and his opinion still means a lot to her.

"All right," she says. "If you want, you can come to CFS with me. I'm heading out first thing tomorrow."

"Ah, I can't," Stevens says regretfully. "Sorry. Green's got me on patrol with Garrison. But I'll check in with you when you're back."

"Sounds good." Rachel nods to him to signal the end of the conversation. She needs to look over these docs before tomorrow. But Stevens stays put, running a hand over the guest chair in front of her desk as he examines the corkboards on the wall behind her, stalling.

"Out with it, Stevens," she says, not unkindly. "I've got work to do."

"Can I ask you something?"

"Sure."

"How do you do murders? Investigate them, I mean," he quickly adds, stuttering. "Doesn't it . . . I don't know. I'll be honest, I've wondered since my uncle told me about you."

Rachel's nervous system gives an unpleasant lurch.

"With respect," Stevens continues, his face reddening. "It seems strange that you're a detective, after . . . you know."

Rachel clears her throat. "What did your uncle tell you?"

He looks a little sheepish, shrugs. "Just your name, and like I said, that I should shadow you. But then I realized I knew your name from—"

"Yeah, got it," Rachel says, unable to soften the barbs in her voice. "Also, we don't know if the Jane Doe is a murder yet. *Or* Stacy Cooper, despite what Green says. So watch your presumptions."

He drops his gaze, clearly embarrassed. As he should be. But at the same time, she can't entirely blame him for his curiosity. She's used to the infamy, the judgment.

That's what happens to a family when a daughter pushes her own mother off a cliff.

BAYFIELD, ONTARIO—JULY, 1981

"Who was that woman with you at Two Scoops last Saturday?" Kimberly asked, squinting at Rachel in the baking overhead sun. They were down at the beach along with two other girls from their class, Lori and Tammy.

Rachel had gotten a part-time summer job scooping ice cream for four bucks an hour. She left each shift smelling like vanilla and sweat and had more pocket money than she'd ever been given by Dora for doing chores around the house. But Dora hadn't objected in the least, saying it was never too early to learn the value of a dollar and hard, honest work.

She'd been a nurse when she was younger, but hadn't worked as long as Rachel had lived with her. Rachel supposed there must be income from her grandfather Walter's war pension and life insurance that allowed Dora to keep the house and buy groceries.

But Mary had dropped in during her shift on Saturday night. Rachel was scrubbing hot fudge off the counter that opened onto the Main Street sidewalk when Mary appeared in the window, shocking Rachel so much that her mouth fell open. She stared at her mother and waited, a series of questions racing through her mind as the cash register dinged and shut with a crash behind her.

With a couple of exceptions, Mary always came back to Bayfield during the summer months, and Rachel wondered whether it was something about the heat that drove her home, longing for the cool darkness of the old house and the breeze that blew in over the cliff edge from the peacock-blue lake beyond. It was serene enough to calm almost anyone—even a cyclone like her mother.

"Hey there," Mary had said with a half-smile. "Dora said I'd find you here."

"She told you to come?" Rachel asked, her incredulity tinged with a sense of betrayal.

Mary had swallowed, and in the neon lights above their heads, Rachel spied dark spots, bruises, along one side of her mother's face and beneath her eye. Some teenage boys a bit older than Rachel laughed raucously at a picnic table to the right, something about someone's dick. "No. But I asked where you were, and she said you got a job."

Mary had waited another fifteen minutes for the store to close up for the night, then walked with Rachel back to the house as crickets and spring peepers filled the humid evening air with their song. Rachel could hardly believe Mary had been willing to wait for her shift to end. She couldn't seem to live in one place for very long, let alone stand still for any length of time. Rachel longed to ask what had happened to her face, but she was a little afraid of her, too, and the fear was silencing.

Since Mary had been home, she hadn't done much besides lurk around the house drinking Cokes and smoking, and going to Millgate Methodist nearly every day. She was always talking about a conversation she'd just had with Reverend Holland, who Rachel thought must be one of the dullest people on the planet.

So Rachel didn't know, now, how to answer Kimberly's question. She didn't know Kim had even spotted her and Mary together, but she wasn't really surprised. It was a small town. Everyone knew Rachel lived with her grandmother because her mother was—as she'd heard Tammy's mom whisper once when the girls were twelve—"unfit." She'd looked up the word in the dictionary that time, and found it to be true.

Rachel was too embarrassed by Mary to want her around in any way. She seemed crazy sometimes, or at least what Rachel assumed a crazy person must be like, with emotional outbursts and mood swings that could range from despair to elation to rage in the course of an hour. It wasn't normal. There weren't many crazy people in their small town, as far as Rachel knew. Which made it even worse to be the daughter of one. Every time Mary came back, all it did was remind Rachel that she wasn't truly like her girlfriends, and never could be. Because of Mary. Of all that she was and all that she wasn't.

She never forgot that night in the shower with the blood, Mary's whispered oath that Dora was a witch. But normal people didn't believe in witches, didn't accuse their own mothers of being one. She knew Tammy had never been pulled into a shower with her naked mother to wash off more blood than she'd ever seen before. Rachel had her period now, and it didn't look anything like that. She still had no idea what had happened that night. All Dora had said, as she scrubbed the blood from between the bathroom tiles with baking soda and an old toothbrush after the screen door slammed the next day, was that Mary was sick.

She's always sick, little one.

And now, at fourteen, Rachel still didn't know how to articulate the questions to get the answers she was looking for. She didn't know anyone else who had a crazy mother. No one—other than Dora—could possibly understand.

"Yeah, that was my mom," she said to Kim, waving away the question as though Mary's return were of no consequence. It was, and it wasn't, really. It was always disruptive, but also short-lived. Mary would probably be gone by Labour Day, if not next week. "She lives in Toronto but comes back to visit sometimes," Rachel said, repeating the script she'd come up with years ago to deflect the conversation should the topic of her mother ever arise. Like how she'd told her girlfriends her dad was dead. Because they'd never know otherwise. It's not as though the man who'd drunkenly screwed her mother in the bathroom of some coke dealer's house in Scarborough was about to show up on Dora's doorstep in Bayfield. She was safe with that lie. Death was an honourable absence, an inarguable excuse.

Mary had only lived in downtown Toronto once, as far as Rachel knew, but it sounded glamorous, and maybe Kimberly might even believe Mary was doing something cool or interesting in the big city; that she was too busy with her "modern woman" job to be a parent. In reality, Mary had lived everywhere from Windsor to Toronto and up to Owen Sound, always moving on to follow a man or because "things got dull there" or "there was too much heat," as Rachel heard Mary tell her grandmother once. But she would always retreat back to the lake, like a tide rushing in and out with the pull of the moon. Fickle, yet somehow predictable.

"But isn't she like . . ." Lori began, trailing off with a look that was both mischievous and apologetic. "My mom said she's kind of a mess, isn't she? They were in the same grade. But your mom dropped out of high school in, like, grade ten or something?"

Rachel swallowed. She knew that grade ten was the first time her mother had run away from home, after some big fight. Dora had told her that much. Mary'd had to be dragged back home by the Goderich police.

"Yeah. She's a bit of a spaz. But like, in an artist sort of way, you know? She's a free spirit. She does her own thing." Rachel did her best to conjure the ghost of some leftover hippie, to cast her mother as a mysterious, intriguingly romantic soul that simply preferred movement to stagnation.

She hoped Lori and Tammy wouldn't guess that Mary was actually just unemployable, unhinged, unfocused. "Free spirit" was a gentler label for the harsh reality.

The girls watched Rachel for a moment, and she crafted her expression into one of polite disinterest, hoping the sunburn that had begun to tingle on her skin would suffice to mask the redness rising in her cheeks. She took a large swig of her warm Coke.

Suddenly, Lori gasped and they all looked up. "Check it out," she said, biting her lip. "Eric Tomlin. With Mike and Julie Jamieson." They watched the trio trudge onto the beach, swimsuit-clad with neon-patterned towels slung over their shoulders. Rachel had always had a bit of a crush on Eric Tomlin, but knew she never stood a chance. He was tall and lean and likeable and looked like he was pulled straight from the sand-crusted pages of the *Seventeen* magazine she had open on her striped beach towel.

It wasn't that she thought she wasn't good enough for him. It was more that the whole idea of a boyfriend still frightened her a little. It was *boyfriends* that always seemed to have gotten her mother into trouble.

Lori stood and waved over Mike, Julie, and Eric, who joined them a moment later. After a half-hour of chatter, the boys decided to go for a swim, and the girls followed, Lori whining about not wanting to get her hair wet as Julie stopped to slather on some Coppertone. Rachel, who tended to follow the crowd so that she'd blend in as much as possible, adjusted her bikini and strode out into the water, trailing the other girls.

She exhaled as the coolness of the water crept up her legs, to her knees, her thighs. She gasped as it hit her hips, heard the other girls scream—playfully, flirtatiously—then lowered her hands and swept them through the water, enjoying the resistance against her palms. The others laughed and shouted and splashed as Lori and Kim convinced the boys to let them sit on their shoulders. The sun beat down, and suddenly Rachel wanted to be beneath the water. She waded out a little farther until the sand dropped off steeper and she was submerged up to her chin. She pressed the balls of her feet into the bottom to cast off, breast-stroking out into the lake, which felt warmer now. She ducked her head under and the water coursed through her hair and over her skin. She rose then, sucked in a deep breath and squinted into the sunlight as she treaded, getting her bearings. She'd gone out farther than usual, but that was all right. She was a strong swimmer.

Lake Huron was so vast you couldn't even see the other side. If you didn't know any better, you'd think it was an ocean. But she could still see her friends, who didn't seem to have noticed she'd disappeared. She breathed heavily, enjoying the feeling of being alive that swimming in the lake always brought—the awareness of her body, her limbs and skin, the sun reflecting back up at her from the surface of the shimmering water.

She looked down the beach and up onto the bluffs in the distance, searching for her house. She found it, and her tread faltered as she spotted Mary.

Her mother was sitting on the cliff's edge, feet dangling down just above the mess of weeds and shrubs that populated the bluff. It was truly high up, Rachel realized with a start. It looked different from the water, and the height surprised her. Her grandmother had always told her to stay away from the edge, not go within five feet of it. Just for a moment, she worried for Mary.

And then something inside Rachel erupted, and all the disappointment and confusion and shame she'd felt over the years reared up, sore and angry, with tears in its black eyes.

"Jump," she whispered into the wind, half hoping the sound would carry up onto the cliffs and into her mother's ears.

But those ears had never heard Rachel's pleas before. Not when she was a baby screaming in her crib to be fed and held and loved.

Not when she was ten and begging Mary to tell her where all the blood came from.

Not ever.

Not once.

"Please, Mom," she said. "*Just jump.*"

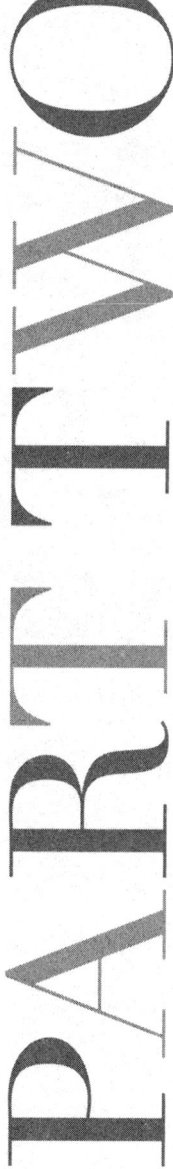

PART TWO

incurable

(Adj.: that which cannot be cured or remedied)

I am not free while any woman is unfree, even when her shackles are very different from my own.

AUDRE LORDE

CHAPTER 16
EMILY

June 21, 1961
Day 2 (181 to go)

"Now lie back, put your feet in the stirrups, and stay still."

Emily swallowed and complied with the prison physician, Dr. Eris Stone. She was a short woman in every respect: her stature, hair, tone, nails, temper. She was clipped and efficient to the point of being disconcerting, and wore a white coat over a black dress. Her hair was black, and her eyes were dark in a pale face. She was as colourless as the prison itself.

The smell of bleach from the sheet beneath Emily filled her nostrils as she stared up at the ceiling, hands clenched together on her abdomen. Through her trepidation about the medical exam, she thought of her grandmother, how she smelled of bleach until the day she finally stopped working at the Royal York laundry. Emily had always wondered whether the years of exposure to all the chemicals were responsible for the asthma and lung troubles that now plagued her nana.

Emily gasped and her focus was jerked back to the present as something cold and hard pressed up against her vagina.

"What is that?" she demanded, alarmed. She'd never been with a man. No one had ever touched her in such an intimate, sensitive place.

"The genital exam," Dr. Stone said.

"But what is that—"

"Do not speak, Radcliffe," the doctor snapped. "It will only make the procedure more difficult for me. Stay still, or I shall be forced to employ the restraints."

Emily clenched her teeth, eyes falling on the leather strap near her wrist. There was one on each side. Then she gasped as pain shot through her privates, a sort of pain she'd never experienced, not even during her worst periods. There was a metallic sound akin to screws being tightened. She strained her neck to try to see, but her view was blocked by the white sheet tenting her knees, which began to shake.

"Inmate, I said *keep still*," Dr. Stone growled. Emily set her head back down, willing herself not to cry out. *Why is this necessary?* she wondered frantically. Her alleged crime had nothing to do with her body. Why was a genital exam required at all?

The doctor continued poking around, jabbing at her and stretching her skin to the point that Emily feared injury. Blinking back tears drawn from the pain and indignity, she held her breath and did her best to focus on the ceiling until, mercifully, it was over.

"Get dressed and return to your duties," Dr. Stone said. "I'll see you again in a month." She gathered the metal tools and rolled them away on a cart toward the sink.

"Why?" Emily demanded.

"Routine exam." Dr. Stone disappeared into her office at the back of the infirmary.

Emily sat up, breath coming in shallow spurts. She slid off the table and shuffled to the hook on the wall where she'd been told to hang her uniform. She tore off the hospital gown and threw it to the floor, then dressed hastily, desperate to get the hell out of there.

In the corridor outside, she pressed her back against the brick wall, mind reeling as the ache between her legs persisted. She took a deep breath, then, driven by a trickling sensation, scooted around the corner to the inmates' washroom. She sat down on the toilet and lifted her skirt to check her underwear, which was heavily spotted with blood. Her entire body went cold.

What did she do to me?

But there was no time to dwell on it; she was due downstairs for cleaning duty. She directed her attention instead to making a mental list of all the details of the infirmary and the horrendous experience. But she stopped short then, horrified at the prospect of sharing with the world the invasive and degrading thing Dr. Stone had just done, the thing she didn't even have a word for. It hadn't fully occurred to her that things might happen *to her* at the Mercer that she wouldn't necessarily want repeated or shared. She'd thought mostly of the things she would witness being done to the other inmates.

She exhaled in a little puff, recalling what she'd told herself the day before: She must try to welcome each event for the sake of the article. Perhaps there was a way she could report on this to simply *suggest* the more personal details. She would speak with Doris about it. But right now, she was already late for duty. She wadded up some crunchy toilet paper for a makeshift sanitary pad and left the washroom, encountering few other inmates on her way.

As Emily headed for her cleaning shift down on the main floor, the prison throbbed with sounds of institutionalized life, much like a school. A constant hum of female conversation was peppered with barked instructions and admonitions from matrons. Doors slammed and creaked, the telephone rang in the warden's office near the main entry.

Emily wound her way down the echoing staircase and crossed the X-junction of the main hall to the kitchen doors. A handful of inmates was already there and looked up at her when she entered.

"Emily Radcliffe," she said to the matron on duty. "I was called to the infirmary, but I'm meant to be here now."

The matron was hardly older than Emily herself, but her features were strained and tired. Her blond hair was pulled back in a bun and her apron was stained in front.

"Emily Radcliffe?" she said, sparing Emily half a glance before consulting a clipboard. "You're new. First time on shift?"

"No. I cleaned yesterday, but it was in the basement."

"Ah, you been promoted already?" one of the other inmates asked, smirking. Emily detected a slight Irish accent. She was just a girl, really, hardly older than sixteen. She was a tiny little thing with strawberry-blond hair, bony with a sharply defined chin and high cheekbones, like one of the fairies in *A Midsummer Night's Dream*.

"Enough, Eliza," the Matron reprimanded wearily, as though this wasn't the first time she'd heard the complaint.

"What? The basement's the worst!"

The matron rolled her eyes. "Right," she told Emily. "You can do the floors with Eliza. Grab a mop and get to it. Soap flakes are in the store cupboard in the corner. Fill up your bucket in the kitchen sink and dump it in the toilet down the hall when you're done."

Emily nodded and seized the required materials, then she and Eliza moved to the attached dining hall while the three remaining inmates stayed in the kitchen to clean. She glanced at Eliza, whose wide hazel eyes stared back at her, and she offered a tentative hello. They walked to the sink to fill up their buckets.

"I'm Emily."

"Yeah, yer new, eh."

"Yes."

"I seen ya talkin' to one of the Blues at breakfast yesterday. Wasn't that you? With Crazy Annie?"

Emily looked up from her bucket. "The Blues?"

"Yeah. Crazy Annie and the others. All the lunatics hafta wear blue dresses, so they're easy to see."

"Oh," Emily said, taking note. She paused. "How many of those inmates are there?"

They turned off the taps and made their way back to where they'd started.

"Dunno," Eliza said. "They're all behind that gate on the second floor. Where's yer cell?" She dipped her mop into the steaming, sudsy water. "I'm on the third. Matrons' quarters are on the fourth."

"Second floor," Emily said. "The south corridor. I did wonder about the gate."

"Yeah. They 'ave their own bathroom 'n everything 'cause most o' them are violent whacks. But some o' them are allowed out with the rest of us. Like that Annie woman."

"What do you know about her?" Emily asked, kneeling to wring the mop with her hands. The warm water coursed up her forearms, wetting her pushed-back sleeves. She set the mop back down on the floor and wiped her gritty hands on her apron.

"Well, I heard she killed 'er own baby. Total loony."

Emily's hands stilled. "Are you serious?"

"That's what they say. Tried to kill 'er man, too."

"But . . . why is she here, then? Why isn't she in Kingston?" Violent criminals were sent to the maximum-security penitentiary there.

Eliza shrugged. "Search me. Word gets 'round here, though. So, if I was you I'd stay clear of 'er. She screams in 'er sleep, too, we can hear it even up on the third floor. Good luck gettin' a decent rest. They usually hafta sedate 'er when that happens."

"Ah. Yes. Thanks," Emily said, shooting her a half-smile. The Mercer wasn't meant to be a prison for violent offenders. It was allegedly a reform institution. But Emily had to admit that so far, she hadn't observed much in the way of reform. The place was one giant holding cell powered by its inmates' labour. Over a hundred women waiting out their months- or years-long sentences for petty offences. Emily considered Eliza's claim, piecing it together with what Annie Little had told her directly at breakfast the day before. Prison terms at the Mercer were limited to two years under the FRA, except under very extreme circumstances.

"So what are ya in for?" Eliza asked.

Emily cleared her throat. She had a spiel planned, the details as generic as possible. "My parents thought I was too unruly. Unmanageable. I think they did it just to frighten me into behaving the way they want me to."

Eliza scoffed, laughed. "'S it working?"

Emily shrugged. "I'm in for six months. But I think once I'm out, I'm leaving my parents." She scrubbed hard at a sticky spot on the floor and swallowed, realizing that what she said was inadvertently the truth. She'd mused about it before coming to the Mercer, but now that she was out of her parents' house—for better or worse—the idea of living apart from them felt more possible than it had before. "I mean... women have more options than we used to. I don't think you have to be a spinster to have an independent life." She caught herself. She'd gotten too personal. "So uh." She cast around for a useful change of subject, and saw an opportunity to wheedle some information. "Do you know why we aren't allowed outside for exercise hour? Warden Barrow said some inmates had misbehaved, but—"

"Oh, yeah," Eliza said, eyes widening. "They think somebody musta contacted somebody on the outside, told 'em what's goin' on 'ere." She nodded knowingly and dipped her mop back into the bucket. "The mail gets checked before it goes out, so anything bad anybody says isn't gettin' out—remember that when ye write yer letters. I'm not sure how else they coulda done it except during yard hour. But I heard from Pearl Wilson that she heard Barrow's secretary talkin' about some reporter lady that called askin' questions."

Emily's stomach flipped with guilt. "Can ya believe that?" Eliza went on. "Don't know why a reporter would care, though," she said with a dismissive shrug. "Nobody ever has."

Emily paused, chose her words with care. "But really," she said in a low tone, "it's awful in here, isn't it? The food alone, my goodness. If you can call it food. Do you know if this place ever gets inspected?"

"Oh, it does," Eliza said, chuckling. "Once a year or somethin'. But Warden Barrow oughtta be a stage director, she's so good at puttin' on that show. It's scheduled, so she has lotsa time to plan it."

Emily supposed she shouldn't be surprised. There was no way a place like this could have gone on undetected as long as it had without some kind of cover-up, or corruption. But she would need to see some of it for herself if she was going to name names. She squinted at Eliza.

"How have you learned all this?"

"Hey, ya keep yer head down and stay friendly, ya hear stuff."

Eliza was right, of course. Staying friendly and keeping her head down was precisely how a person could overhear important things. But what Emily needed to do was *witness* them. "Can I ask why you're here?" she inquired.

"Ah," Eliza said, shaking her head at the floor. "Well, home's a wreck. Da's a drunk, Mam's his punchin' bag. Six kids, never enough food. Electrical gets cut off all the time, we get evicted. An' when Mam's had enough, Da beats on us kids."

Emily grimaced. "Good Lord."

"I'm the youngest," Eliza went on, eyes still on the floor as she worked. "All but two of me brothers already up and left, nobody finishes school. Mam won't do nothin' about it, so I get meself tossed in here on purpose." She looked at Emily, whose mop had stilled. "Hey, 's three meals a day. Me own bed. Some clothes, heat 'n electricity. 'S better here than home. And no men tryna get at me, like on the street. After they turf me outta here I just steal and let meself get caught til they send me back."

Emily was unsure how to respond.

"And no beatings here unless you step outta line," Eliza continued. "So s'long as I keep me head down, it's fine. Once I'm grown up like you I'll skip town. Try to get a job. I'll know enough about cleaning and laundry, anyway. I can do somethin' for meself. I seen what it cost me mam, needing Da for money. Hell, I'm not doin' that."

Emily processed all Eliza had said. "I'm very sorry," she said, and meant it. No child should have to live like that.

"Ah, hell, some's got it worse, right? I can't gripe."

Emily didn't know what do other than nod understandingly. But her ears had pricked. She waited a moment before speaking again.

"So there's no beatings unless we step out of line?" she asked quietly.

"Yeah. If you really piss 'em off, they'll beat ya with leather straps in the basement. The doctor supervises it. I guess to make sure no one gets hurt too bad, but me, I think she likes it. She's right twisted, that one. Soul's as black as that hair o' hers."

After her encounter with Dr. Stone that morning, Emily had no doubt that Eliza was right.

CHAPTER 17

RACHEL

Toronto—June, 1996

Rachel knocks back the last of the cold drive-through coffee she stopped for in Kitchener as she merges onto the Gardiner Expressway, headed for Grosvenor Street right downtown where the Centre of Forensic Sciences office is located. She left Bayfield at dawn to try to avoid some of the worst of the rush hour traffic into the city, with marginal success.

After the CFS, she has an appointment at Cartwright-Cambridge Co.'s offices and warehouse just north of the Junction. She'd contacted a colleague at the Toronto office of the OPP yesterday afternoon, asking him to check the local Yellow Pages. Fortunately, the coffin maker is still in business, so Rachel called and spoke with the owner, the son of the man who established the company in 1956. He's expecting her around midday.

She finds some overpriced parking just off Bay Street and heads through the financial district up Grosvenor to one of a cluster of government buildings surrounding Queen's Park.

Once she's through the security checkpoint, she's led into a large tiled lobby, where Sawyer is waiting for her in a crisp grey skirt and white lab coat, her dark hair clipped short like Winona Ryder's in *Reality Bites*. She offers Rachel her hand and a brief smile.

"Nice to see you, Mackenzie. I hope the traffic wasn't too bad."

"Oh, it was."

Sawyer chuckles, and Rachel feels a silly little swell of pride. A chuckle from Sawyer is a belly laugh from anyone else. "Come on this way."

As Sawyer leads Rachel to an elevator bank, they make brief small talk that echoes in the dark but expansive foyer. They descend to the basement levels, and after another security check outside the evidence-bay doors in the windowless corridor, Sawyer hands her a pair of gloves, keys in a passcode, and guides them to Jane Doe's locker.

Rachel has only ever seen smaller evidence bins and storage, nothing bigger than the size of a high school locker. This feels a bit like stepping into the giant walk-in refrigerator they had at Two Scoops, only slightly warmer and without droplets of fudge and squashed strawberries stuck to the floor. It's temperature- and humidity-controlled down here, and silent as a library. Sawyer ushers Rachel through the door, and a motion-sensor light flickers to life overhead.

"It's a drying cabinet," Sawyer says. "I didn't want to contribute any more to the rot it had already been subjected to. Although as I said on the phone, I've seen worse, for the age of it. Go ahead."

Rachel pulls her file and notebook out of her bag and squats down as Sawyer hangs back. The photos Sawyer sent her were good, but she always needs to see her evidence in person. Feel it, smell it. Get to know it.

The casket is laid out on a table in the centre of the small room. Rachel pores over it, squinting closely at the stamped serial number, then asks to see the smaller items: some remnants of fabric and the brass plaque. Sawyer takes her out of the walk-in cabinet to the outer room, where she fetches two plastic bags from a storage wall similar to a library's card catalogue. She lays them out for Rachel on a stainless-steel table beneath a harsh overhead light, then picks up the bag with the fabric, hands it to Rachel.

"They're tiny," she says. "I'm not sure how far it'll get you. It's just blue dyed cotton, nothing fancy or distinctive."

She waits silently until Rachel hands the bag back to her. There really isn't much to see. Sawyer passes over the brass plaque. "Did you get a lead on that?" she asks.

"Yes, actually," Rachel says. "It's definitely a coffin maker, and they're still in business, up in the Junction. I'm headed there next." She looks down at the plate in her hand, runs her gloved finger over the raised letters. Cartwright-Cambridge Co. is probably where she'll find her next breadcrumb, or possibly even the whole sandwich, if they happen to have a name on record for the Jane Doe in the casket.

After finishing up with Sawyer at the CFS, Rachel heads north toward the Junction. The Cartwright-Cambridge Co. warehouse is at the end of Old Stock Yards Road, backing onto the railroad tracks. She parks near the loading dock and pulls her navy blazer from where it's hanging above the back passenger seat. It's too hot for it, but she shrugs it on anyway, covering up her white sleeveless blouse, then pulls her long brown hair up into a tight bun. She's had enough experience interviewing men to know that she can't look too appealing, and needs to up the ante on the professionalism. Green, on the other hand, can wear whatever the fuck he wants to an interview.

She slings her bag over her shoulder and heads toward the metal door labelled "Office" as a freight train chugs loudly along the tracks to her left, covered in graffiti. She's had plenty of self-defence training, knows how to handle herself. She even has a firearm. But solo calls to these sorts of secluded locations that are all but soundproofed to the outside world still make the hairs stand up on the back of her neck. Because it's all part of the invisible cage women find themselves in, every day of their lives. Sometimes you can even see it, if you look closely. Women like Rachel who venture into booby-trapped fields that have been the exclusive domain of men often bear the telltale signs. You can see the deep purple and blue marks in their eyes, the bruises that come from throwing themselves against the bars of that cage, looking for the secret latch that they just *know* must be there. Sometimes those women even manage to find a key, thinking they might dare to make a run for it. But the Cage was designed by men. It has a glass ceiling and is full of false doors and tricky locks designed to exhaust women into submission.

Outside the building, Rachel clears her throat, buttons her blazer to the top before yanking on the thick metal door handle. Bells jingle overhead as she enters. The room is dimmer and cooler than outside. It looks like the reception area of an autobody shop, with a couple of folding chairs, an unmanned desk, and a drip coffee maker in the corner. Rachel sees a bell on the desk and taps it, noting the series of filing cabinets against the wall behind.

Thirty seconds later, a man emerges from a door off the main room, which must lead farther into the factory. He stops short.

"Mr. Cambridge? Detective Rachel Mackenzie, OPP," she says. "We spoke on the phone."

"Detective?" he asks, grinning. "You're not, uh, what I expected."

Her nostrils flare instinctively. She can't count the number of times she's had comments about a "lady detective" and that she wasn't what someone expected. She's dealt with a hundred guys like Mitch Cambridge before. It's infuriating, but nothing new.

"Mr. Cambridge, I'm tracing a coffin for the purposes of trying to identify the remains found inside it. A plaque with your company name," she says, withdrawing the photo of the casket from her file and holding it out to him, "was found in the soil surrounding the coffin in question."

He examines the photo. "Yeah, these were our most basic coffins," he says, "the ones the government ordered for the prisons, and that old loony bin on Queen. Just a pine box. That was back in my dad's day. Nowadays, even the most basic one isn't this cheap. But that's government for ya."

"I wonder"—she pulls out the photo of the serial number now—"if you can help me understand what *this* means."

He takes it from her, letting his fingers linger on hers in the handoff. He squints at the image.

"Mmm . . . yeah. We stamped these sort of serial numbers on the ones we provided to the government places."

"And what do the letters mean?"

He shrugs. "As I say, this was my dad's stuff. But I think the different places were coded. Don't know what 'MWP' is. Might be in the old records, though."

"I'm going to need to see those."

Mitch Cambridge looks up at her, eyes glinting now with interest as he takes in her features. It's the look a guy might give her in a bar after midnight and too many shots of Smirnoff. At once flirtatious and undeniably predatory.

"It might take a while," he says. "How about I find 'em, and then give you a call once I've got 'em? Or you could come back for 'em. I could take you out for dinner, or drinks. Make a night of it."

"I'll wait," Rachel says pointedly, accenting her insistence with a smug grin.

He runs his tongue along the inside of his teeth, nostrils flaring like a tiger who's been outrun by his prey. How quickly lust mutates into rage in the face of rejection. "It's gonna be a while," he snaps.

"You have an hour. But I doubt very much you'll need that long."

Rachel tucks the photos back into her file and strides to the coffee maker, pours herself a drink. She stands by the door and sips it, face impassive, though inside she's raging and humiliated.

He stomps back to the filing cabinets and finds everything she needs in thirteen minutes.

"Here," he says, thrusting some sheets at her and not making eye contact, "that's a list of the government places my dad made caskets for in the fifties to seventies, until they cancelled the contract."

No surprise there, if your dad was anything like you, Rachel thinks. She accepts the stack of paper and hands him her dirty coffee cup. He takes it automatically, looking confused. Then he scowls.

"I don't know who was buried in what casket though," he snaps. "We don't have that. We just provided the coffins to order. Is that it?" He's resolutely staring at a spot beside her head.

She nods. "Yes. If I need anything else, I'll be in touch."

She turns and leaves without another word, knowing he's waiting until the door closes before uttering something revolting or sexist about her. But there's nothing she can do about that.

She heads back to the car as another train rattles by, takes off her blazer, cranks down the driver's side window to tempt in a breeze and spreads the documents over the passenger seat. She studies them, squinting in the summer light, quickly locating the information she needs.

Cartwright-Cambridge Co. provided coffins to a dozen different government institutions over the course of two decades. The codes are easy to identify: among them are "OH": the Ontario Hospital—formerly called the Toronto Asylum for the Insane—over on Queen; "DJ," that'll be the Don Jail in the east end; and "KP," for the max-security Kingston Penitentiary.

And then she finds it, the answer to the "MWP" serial code, at the top of the first invoice from when the contract began in 1959:

Mercer Women's Prison
1155 King Street W., Toronto

DECEMBER, 1982

Mary came back again at Christmas when Rachel was fifteen. Unusually, she'd called ahead, and it had been Rachel who'd answered the phone.

"Hey, so can you tell Dora I'm going to be coming for Christmas?" Mary had said, sounding for all the world as though she and Rachel had weekly phone calls and she was merely updating her on a recent development. She was in St. Catharines, she'd said, and she'd gotten some time off from her job at Zellers in the mall. She'd arrive on the twenty-third, and head back on Christmas night in time for her Boxing Day shift the next morning.

"Well, that's promising," Dora had said when Rachel walked into the kitchen to relay the news. "She hasn't had a job since she was your age."

"Where did she work?" Rachel asked as she took a seat at the kitchen table.

Dora was chopping apples she'd stored in the cool crawl space back in the fall, to be boiled down for her homemade applesauce. She always made it chunky, with an overload of cinnamon and a pinch of cardamom. It was one of Rachel's favourite things to eat, especially spooned over the vanilla ice cream she brought home from Two Scoops. It had become a Christmas tradition.

"She babysat," Dora said, furiously chopping for another moment before scraping the apple chunks off the wooden cutting board into a large copper pot. "Anyway, as always, her coming does throw a bit of a wrench into things. We can stretch dinner to three, and maybe you could pull out her stocking? It won't be in the usual bin because, well . . . it's probably up in the attic." She sighed. "I don't have anything for it, so it'll have to just be chocolate from the grocery store."

Rachel had seen, over the years, the toll it took on Dora every time Mary dropped back into their lives, however temporarily. When she was younger, Rachel was more ambivalent about Mary's visits, at once fearful of her mother and curious about who she was. It was an intrigue that had never been satisfied, because her mother was unknowable. But the older she got, the more Rachel resented the impact her transience had on Dora, who was her true mother in every way that mattered.

"Sure, Gran," Rachel said, then hesitated over the question she'd circled around a dozen times, like a boat caught in a whirlpool. Dora glanced back, then put a lid on the pot with a *clank* and came over to sit across from her. She could always tell when Rachel had something to say. It had been that way her whole life. All it took was a sidelong look from Rachel, and Dora knew. She never pushed, though; she'd just sit and wait.

Rachel held eyes with Dora, who was fifty-seven now, with ample wrinkles and loosening skin around her jawline. Her chin-length hair was entirely grey, curled every night with teal and pink foam rollers and set in the morning with a liberal application of Pantene Firm Hold. Rachel knew the smell of hairspray would forever bring her back to her grandmother's house, to the wooden-framed antique mirror on the vanity in her bedroom at the end of the hall where Rachel would sit on the swivel stool, playing with the rollers in the morning light as Dora removed them and passed them into her granddaughter's little hands one by one.

"Why is she like this?" Rachel asked now, heart hammering. "What the hell's wrong with her?"

Dora kept Rachel's gaze. "I don't know that there's really a word for it, little one," she said. "There *is* something wrong with her, but I don't know what. She's been like this nearly her entire life, since she was at least your age." She looked away from Rachel, just for a moment, her eyes landing on the photo of her late husband, his military portrait in pride of place above the fireplace mantel in the living room. "Maybe longer, I don't know. She had a terrible time after you were born."

Rachel felt cold, her memory tugging her back to that conversation between her grandmother and mother that she'd overheard years before, when Dora had all but said it was Rachel's fault that Mary was so messed up.

"Some women go a bit . . . funny, after they have a baby. For a while anyway. But Mary was already . . ." Dora paused, turned back to her granddaughter, and her tone was harsher now. "She's selfish and irresponsible and impulsive, and as changeable as the damn weather. And I don't know that there's any fixing a person like that."

"So is she crazy?" Rachel pressed, frustrated and imploring, but also fearful of a confirmation. "Is she, I don't know . . . Has she seen a doctor, or a shrink or something?"

Dora sighed deeply and shrugged her small shoulders. "Perhaps. I think so. And no, she hasn't seen a doctor. Not that I know of."

"But if she's like that, will I be like that, too?" Rachel asked, finally voicing her greatest fear.

Dora reached out a hand, covering Rachel's, whose nails were painted a Hard Candy sparkly black, just like her friends'.

"Well, *that* I can answer with more conviction, and the answer is no, little one. I don't think you'll be like her," Dora said.

The pot on the stove hissed in the silence of the kitchen.

"How do you know?" Rachel's voice was a miserable mumble.

"Because you're very different from your mother. You've had different experiences, and made far better choices." Her nostrils flared on a deep breath that she quickly huffed out, as though trying to be rid of it. "Your mother is sick. You *aren't* sick, Rachel. You're just as a teenage girl ought to be. And half the battle in life is knowing what you *don't* want to be like. Figuring out what you *do* want to be will come easily from there."

She patted Rachel's hand and stood up to stir the pot.

After taking a moment to collect herself, Rachel headed out of the kitchen and up the stairs onto the creaking landing, then around the corner to the attic access at the end of the hall, where she stood on a desk chair borrowed from her bedroom to lower the folding stairs.

It had been one of her favourite rooms to play in during the winter as a child, full of old trunks of clothes to dress up in, and treasures from bygone times that were only otherwise glimpsed in history books: wooden dolls with creepy painted-on faces, brass compasses, boxes of old cardboard-backed photographs. A gramophone. It was as though that attic had remained sheltered from the aggressive, pushy hands of time, left to collect dust and reluctantly entertain visits from Rachel every once in a while. But now that she was mostly grown, those visits were limited to when she was dispatched by Dora to fetch something.

It only took a few minutes to find the boxes. They were beneath a white sheet covered in a thick layer of dust, a representation of all the Christmases Mary had been absent, all the years her stocking was left undisturbed.

Rachel lifted the folded flaps to find the stockings right on top. Her mother's was a fine-gauge knit in dark red with a capital "M" sewn on in a cream-coloured fabric. But there were two others beneath it: one larger, forest green, with a scrolling "W" intricately embroidered with gold thread; and another smaller one in the same colour, with another gold "W" above a red-and-white train engine. It looked like a child's stocking, not unlike the one Dora had made for Rachel when she was a baby, and which currently hung from a nail on the stair banister. Hers was the same size, only made of red knitted yarn like Mary's, with a cream "R" on it. She wrinkled her nose, seeing how similar hers was to her mother's. But she was quickly distracted from her distaste by curiosity about the others. Why had her grandfather Walter seemingly had two stockings?

When she got back downstairs, the kitchen was filled with the warm aroma of apples and cinnamon, which normally would have made Rachel's mouth water, but she was too sidetracked to be enticed.

"Hey Gran," she said, laying the three stockings out in front of Dora on the kitchen table, a patchwork blanket of green and scarlet. "I found Mary's—Mom's—old stocking. But . . . I was wondering . . . are these both Grandad's?"

Rachel's eyes moved from the large and small stockings embroidered with the letter "W" up to Dora's face, which had blanched.

"Gran?" she asked, concerned. "What's wrong?"

But Dora was shaking her head, lips pulled back over a trembling smile. She blinked fast, eyes bright.

"Nothing, of course. And yes, the uh . . . the small one was from when your grandfather was a boy. His—his mother made it, I think."

Rachel looked back down at the identical gold stitching on the two green stockings, made of the same fabric as hers and Mary's, and even Dora's own. And then she looked up at Dora as an uncomfortable, unfamiliar sensation trickled through her body.

Her grandmother was lying.

To the best of Rachel's knowledge, Dora had never lied to her before. But she did it now, not a half-hour after she'd reassured Rachel that she wouldn't turn out like her mother. Was she lying about that, too?

"Well," Dora said, stacking the "W" stockings one on top of the other, not looking at them. "Go put these back in the box and hang up your mother's with ours on the banister. There's a good girl."

There's a good girl.

It was the phrase Dora had always used when she was trying to hustle Rachel along. Because Rachel *was* a good girl, and she knew it. She liked to be good, liked to obey her grandmother, follow the rules and fit in.

Go get your shoes on.

It's ten o'clock, off to bed with you.

Your mother and I need to have a grown-up conversation. There's a good girl . . .

And it was that, more than anything else, that made Rachel wonder why her grandmother was lying. Why now? Why this? And what did it mean?

She made her way back up to the attic and the old Christmas box. She set the "W" stockings back in and watched them disappear into the darkness as she closed the flaps, packed away and hidden from sight once more. The buried evidence of something Rachel couldn't yet understand or make sense of.

There's a good girl.

CHAPTER 18

EMILY

Mercer Women's Prison, Toronto—July, 1961
Day 15 (168 to go)

Emily stood at the large basin sink in the prison laundry, which was located in the basement, scrubbing at her hands and forearms with a harsh yellow soap to clean off the chemical residue.

Every morning as she worked in the laundry after breakfast and prayer time, her skin becoming more cracked and dry by the day, Emily thought of her nana. She wondered how similar their experiences were. For how different could a laundry have been in an upscale hotel? It required the same sort of labour, the same conditions, chemicals, and muscles. Sheets and towels, clothes and rags were boiled and scrubbed and wrung out to dry.

But slowly, she was acclimating.

She had already lost weight from her average-sized frame, as she was doing more manual labour than ever before, and eating less. She would have committed a crime worthy of her sentence to have a roast beef sandwich on rye from her favourite deli on Gerrard, the one that threw in those really excellent kosher pickles on the side at no extra charge. She had dark circles under her eyes from poor sleep, though that had slowly begun to improve. The hard springs poking into her back from the old mattress in her cell combined with the stress of her situation had made sleep difficult in the first few days. But being kept so busy with such physical exertion, plus the lack of food, meant she fell into bed most nights too exhausted to even notice the discomfort. And between the conditions and what she'd learned of a few of her fellow inmates, she was steadily gathering the ingredients for the story, setting them side by side in her mind as she mapped out the article.

Every day, Emily ate supper with Eliza and a couple of inmates she was now friendly with. There was Gertrude, a twenty-year-old lesbian who'd been caught in bed with another girl six months before, and whose case file was allegedly stamped with a "D" for "deviant." She'd met Gertrude in their mind-numbing "typing" class, which was devoid of any typing whatsoever. Gertrude was tall, smart, and boldly sarcastic in a way Emily envied, and she'd liked her immediately. Then there was her cell neighbour Lizzie, who had five children by three different fathers.

"They locked me up to keep me away from men," she told Emily, dark eyes shadowed beneath thin black brows. "Can't go having any more kids, they say, or they'll take the rest of 'em, too." She was four months into a two-year sentence at the Mercer; her children had been separated and sent to live with each of their fathers for the duration. "Judge gave me the option of being sterilized or coming here." Emily had never heard of a woman having that many children by different fathers, but she reminded herself that she was here to observe, not judge. Lizzie was obviously intelligent, patient, and unwaveringly kind—particularly to a woman named Peggy, whose cell was across from Lizzie and Emily's. She was a slight, mousy young woman who didn't talk much. Lizzie said Peggy had been routinely beaten by her husband and was in such a state of hysterics when the police arrived to sort out the most recent disturbance that *she* was arrested instead of him.

"If it isn't one prison, it's just another, or another," Lizzie had told Emily one morning, downing the last of her watery tea. "It's all just a bunch of bullshit, isn't it?"

Emily had made furious mental notes of these women's stories, which she planned to include in the article, substituting their names for false ones. She had never in her life felt more fortunate for her position. She had agency and options and family support. They didn't.

The alarm that indicated a shift change went off beside the laundry room door, shattering the quiet. Emily set down the soap, rinsed then dried her hands on the already damp and slightly musty hand towel hanging on a rusted nail by the basin. She made her way up to the main floor for "exercise" hour, which mostly consisted of the inmates milling around the centre hall, gossiping. From her usual spot, pressed against the wall near the staircase, Emily utilized this time as an opportunity to quietly observe her fellow inmates and the supervising staff. But she wondered how much longer these indoor break times could go on.

> Surely, I thought, there must be some regulation which guaranteed the prisoners a certain amount of fresh air and exercise about the yard each day? But no. It seemed that we were all sentenced not only to restrictions on our general bodily liberty, but on our lungs and souls as well. The only glimpses afforded of the summer sky were the slivers of view we snatched through the cold bars of our cell windows.

It was another piece of the story she would need to research and confirm once she was out. She was growing desperate to go for a walk, even just around the prison yard. She felt caged. She was so used to walking all around Toronto, usually preferring it to other transport. She was not one of those women who could remain cloistered inside with domestic pursuits all day. It was enough to drive her mad.

After the stand-about hour, the bell blared and Emily filed into Classroom 2, in the east corridor near the factory. This was, allegedly, the typing class. But upon her first visit to the classroom, Emily had been appalled to learn that there was no instructor, just two old, dusty typewriters in the corner, not nearly enough for the twenty or so inmates scheduled for the class. All they did was chat and argue as their stomachs growled for dinner. It was ludicrous. The women referred to the time as a "lesson" purely in jest as they sat draped over the mismatched chairs, loudly gossiping; others napped, their heads resting on folded arms. The prison had begun to heat up as they moved further into July, and the room was stuffy. Several girls were fanning themselves ineffectually.

They weren't monitored during this time; it was simply a place to stick groups of inmates on a rotation where they couldn't possibly get up to any mischief—and of course, it was a way for the warden to tell the government inspectors that typing class was on the daily schedule.

The young woman beside Emily today was visibly pregnant. Emily had seen her during mealtimes, and they shared a shift in the factory, too. There were plenty of pregnant women at the Mercer, almost all of whom, Emily had learned, had been sent there *because* they were pregnant. There was even a nursery on-site, just around the corner from where they currently sat.

The girl was slumped back a little in the small wooden school chair, fingers entwined on top of her belly, her face drawn, as though she were suppressing a complaint. Emily recalled her sister's two pregnancies, how she'd feigned nonchalance in front of Harry but had nearly broken down in tears one night when she was expecting Charlie. Emily had wandered into the kitchen after Sunday dinner to fetch the tea tray and caught the end of Eleanor's conversation with Bess.

"Feels like I'm sleeping on tree roots, no matter how many pillows I use," Eleanor was saying. "I've hardly had any sleep for weeks. I know I'm supposed to love this, but I can't wait for it to be over, Mom." Her voice cracked, and Bess embraced her as Emily ducked back out into the living room.

Emily thought of the atrociously lumpy mattress in her cell, doubted whether this woman's was any better. But it occurred to her it might be good to know whether anything was different for the pregnant women at the Mercer. She leaned over and smiled at the girl. "Hi. I'm Emily."

The girl glanced up from her belly, eyes dull. "Hi," she said. "Vera. You're new here, eh?"

Emily nodded. "A few weeks. You?"

Vera sighed and wiped some sweat from her forehead. "I've been here about six months now. I'm due in a couple of months. Then I get out sometime after that, I suppose. I don't know the details, really. My parents fixed it."

Emily's brow furrowed. "I'm sorry."

Vera shook her head and looked down again, scratched at a spot on her upper lip. "My boyfriend is Chinese. My parents didn't like that very much, even before I got pregnant. Neither did the judge. My dad reported me to the police, and now here I am."

Emily had thought that by now her surprise at these inmates' experiences and origins might have lessened, but hearing about how so many of them had come to be incarcerated for the most subjective moral and pseudo-legal reasons still astonished her. Though it was a good thing, really. Hopefully that meant *Chatelaine*'s readers would be astonished, too—and outraged.

"My mother's written a couple of times," Vera said, "but she just talks around the fact that I'm expecting. Talks about the family business and getting me married off when I get out, the dresses she bought on sale. She doesn't ask about the baby. Not ever." She ran a hand over her belly again.

Emily hesitated on her next question. "And what happens after? When the baby's born?"

Vera swallowed. "It will go to the nursery for a month until I finish my sentence, and then I'm not sure. My mother keeps talking as though there won't be a baby with me when I get out." Emily glimpsed a tear forming in the corner of her eye, quickly blinked into non-existence. "I—"

"Why are you talking to *her*, Vera?" a loud voice demanded from the front of the room. Emily's eyes snapped to the speaker, a tall, broad-shouldered young woman about Emily's age with a pile of blond curls on the crown of her head. "She's friends with Crazy Annie. Probably crazy herself, too. Aren't you?"

Emily was taken aback by the woman's bluntness, and it took her a moment to recover. No one in her world spoke to each other like some of these women did.

"Do you suppose you could be a little kinder?" Emily suggested, working to keep the condescension from her tone. "I've done nothing to offend you. Has Annie?"

The woman scoffed. Her face was red with the heat. "Listen to how you talk, too. Better than the rest of us, eh?" she chided, a little smirk playing around her thin lips. "Daddy send you here 'cause you swallowed something else along with your dictionary?"

A couple of girls on either side of her guffawed, and Emily's face burned. Though she didn't fully understand the comment, she knew she'd been insulted.

"Oh lay off her, Thelma," Gertrude piped up from the row behind Emily. "Just because your *own* daddy—"

"SHUT UP!" the belligerent woman shouted, and now she and Gertrude were both on their feet as several other women jeered and hissed. Never in her life had Emily drawn ire for doing absolutely nothing, but these women seemed to delight in tearing one another down. Girls began to scramble away from the angry pair, who were in each other's faces now. Vera and Emily stood and backed away between the desks. Thelma's eyes were bulging, but Gertrude wore an expression of taunting nonchalance.

"Get out of my face, bitch," she told Thelma, giving her a shove. Thelma responded with a punch to Gertrude's shoulder, and in a blink, the two were wrestling each other on the floor.

"Stop! Stop it!" Emily shouted, but she was the only one who thought they should. Most of the other girls were cheering and hooting and had picked a champion they were now egging on.

Emily liked Gertrude, and didn't want her injured for her sake over a foolish comment. It wasn't worth it. She lunged forward and seized Gertrude's shoulders, attempting to pull her off Thelma. She vaguely registered more shouting from near the door, and suddenly her own arms were pinned behind her. She whipped her head around and was faced with Matron White. Two other matrons were wrenching Gertrude and Thelma apart. The other inmates had gone quiet now.

"Get off her this instant, Rains!" Matron Smith bellowed at Gertrude, who finally complied.

"She just wants an excuse to touch girls!" Thelma shot at her, wiping a dribble of blood from her lip. Her wild curls were a mess, and there were angry tears in her eyes.

Gertrude laughed, which only infuriated Thelma even more. She tried to take another swing, but the matron intercepted.

"To your cells, all three of you! No dinner!" White screamed right next to Emily's ear. She blinked as her eardrum protested. Her heart was racing. She'd never been in a fight before and hadn't meant to be in one now. Ladies didn't get into fights. But still, there was something about the adrenaline she felt now that was undeniably appealing. She looked at Thelma and Gertrude and wondered if their inexplicable antagonism and quick fuses weren't born of a need to simply feel *something* in this desolate place.

"Go!" Matron White shouted. "And consider yourselves lucky you're not headed to the hole. The rest of you: to dinner. No dawdling!"

Thelma left first, followed by a swaggering Gertrude who appeared utterly unfazed by the encounter, smoothing her dishevelled hair down as she made her away across the main hall to the stairs. Emily trailed behind her. Thelma stomped up the stairs, casting nasty looks over her shoulder at Gertrude and Emily, who ignored her.

"Thanks, Gertrude," Emily said quietly as they reached the second floor. It was even hotter up here. "But you didn't have to do that. She's not worth losing dinner over."

"Ah, I can't stand her," Gertrude said with a huff. "She needs to be put in her place every so often. Looks like a poodle with that stupid hair, and needs training like one, too. Yapping all over the place. Wish we could just put a muzzle on her. See you later, Em."

Gertrude continued up to the third-floor cells, and Emily made her way to her own, suppressing a smile despite the fact that she was already sorely regretting having to miss dinner. Her stomach ached, even for the horrid stew or whatever scraps that would be on offer that day.

She'd be ready to faint by suppertime, especially after all the exertion of cleaning duty in between. She'd always been a sharp person, blessed with a good memory and a quick mind; it didn't take her long to get a joke or do sums in her head. But she'd noticed over the last two weeks that her brain was not as sharp as it used to be—and she was certain malnutrition was a factor. How could a person think straight on a diet of runny eggs, fatty meat, and bland starches?

A thought suddenly came to her: Would she be able to remember the details of her experience six months from now, when it came time to write the article? She hadn't planned to take notes for fear of them being found, but the matrons hadn't done any kind of cell search since she'd arrived. She didn't want to forget certain details, and had trusted her mind to recall them, but she wondered now if it would be riskier to *not* write them down.

She lay down on the concrete floor of her cell, seeking cool. The midday light was weak in her window now. It faced west, so she got the most light toward the end of the day, which was not particularly helpful when trying to fall asleep, especially at this time of year.

If she were to take notes, she might be able to hide them beneath the mattress. Though that seemed like the first place the matrons would look if her cell ever was searched. Emily chewed on her lip and looked up at the ceiling. There was paper in the warden's office for writing letters home, along with a jar of crayons—no pens or pencils, which must be considered too sharp. But you could only get the paper when the warden was *in* her office. Would she even notice if Emily took paper but didn't come back to submit a letter every time? She wasn't sure. Warden Barrow rarely left her office; in fact, Matron White, the head matron, seemed to run the place more than the warden, in practice. Emily's stomach grumbled at the smells of dinner that wafted up to her floor. She forced her mind to wander, trying to ignore it, eyes sliding a little out of focus. They landed on the chamber pot on the floor, the tap above it. Then on the roll of crunchy toilet paper.

She rose from the bed and walked over, sounds from the dining hall drifting gently up the stairs. She crouched down, picked up the roll of paper and unfurled it into her hand. She massaged it between her thumb and index finger. It was off-white, and really not much thinner than wrapping or butcher's paper. She could write on it, certainly. And no one would be checking how much toilet paper she was using. Inmates had access to new rolls from a basket in the washroom, and could bring a new roll back with them in the morning after the Chamber Pot Parade, as Emily had come to call it.

But even if she were to take notes on the toilet paper, the question still remained: where to hide it? There were no floorboards in her cell, nothing on the walls to conceal something behind. She tore a length of paper and experimented with it, folding it as small as she could and then coiling it tightly, though gently, as though she were rolling a cigarette. She tried again, with a longer length, wrapping it around the outside of the first. It hardly grew in girth. That was good. But still, where to hide it? She shook her head, already feeling the effects of her inadvertent fast, and tried to think.

Her eyes fell to the water tap in front of her. It was an inch and a half wide at the mouth, and curved a little where it protruded from the wall—about six inches. With a surge of excitement, Emily inserted the little roll into the pipe. It was dry in there; she hadn't used the faucet in a couple of days, and it was deeper than it appeared on the outside.

She smiled, wiping her sweaty brow. This could work.

CHAPTER 19

EMILY

July, 1961
Day 17 (166 to go)

I was pleased about the hiding place I had procured for the toilet paper notes upon which I was recording the details of my incarceration. Time would tell whether I was in fact able to keep it a secret, but for the moment, at least, I was calmed somewhat by the assurance that I had a reliable backup record if, months later, my memory failed me. As I could no longer use the tap for water during the night, I resolved to have my evening drink in the inmate washroom before returning to my cell at lights out.

Two days after Emily had decided how and where to take her notes, she finished recording the entry with a sharpened crayon she'd swiped from the warden's office the day before. The morning bell clanged out in the corridor, and she vowed to try to do a little writing early in the morning every few days, or when there had been a development or observation that called for it. She rolled it up as tightly as she could and fed it back into the tap on the wall.

She'd given a lot of thought to her mission the night before, now that she was a little more settled into life at the Mercer. She was used to her routine now—unpleasant as it might be—and had been recording her observations about the matrons, her fellow inmates, the physical prison and its conditions. She missed her parents, her sister, and even Jem, a little. She missed hot baths and privacy and her mother's cooking. And God, she missed the office. But she was coping well with the immersion so far, approaching it all from a place of curiosity in the hope that it might feel like more of an adventure than a misery.

Emily had several questions that she needed answers for, but currently, her biggest fascination was with Annie Little, and how she had come to be incarcerated at the Mercer for the past fifteen years when the maximum sentence was meant to be two. That seemed like a monstrous abuse of the Female Refuges Act, and Emily needed to learn more.

As she waited outside her cell for the Chamber Pot Parade, Emily's thoughts were interrupted by the sound of whistles from the psychiatric wing. She'd noticed that the matrons had whistles tied to a string on the belts of their dresses—not unlike old-fashioned housekeeper's chatelaines—which were used to call for assistance in the event an inmate became unmanageable. Emily had heard them used twice since she'd been in the Mercer, both times in the psych wing. A drawn-out shriek echoed down the hall.

"Enough, Rose. Quiet now!" Emily heard. A muffled shriek again, then silence.

After she'd been to the bathroom, Emily got back in line in front of Lizzie as the inmates made their daily stampede downstairs to the dining hall for breakfast. But as she stepped onto the main floor, Emily was suddenly shoved into the brick wall. Looking up in alarm, she saw Thelma, who sneered before turning her back on Emily.

"She's such a shit," Lizzie said beside her. "Are you okay?"

Emily's shoulder hurt where it had hit the brick. "What's her problem? I haven't done anything to her." Inmates swirled around them as they stood still, like rocks in a stream. Emily wasn't easily intimidated, but this situation with Thelma unsettled her. She hadn't come here to make enemies, and having someone intent on antagonizing her would be a waste of valuable energy.

"She's just a creep," Lizzie assured her. "She's picking on you because you're new and you're nice. She thinks she can bully you. My advice is don't let her."

"But why is she such a creep?"

Lizzie shrugged. "Some people are just bad, Radcliffe. Come on, let's get breakfast before Eliza eats it all."

Trying to shake off what had just happened, Emily turned with Lizzie into the dining hall, determined to focus on her objective and get more information out of Annie Little. She sidled next to Eliza and they made their way through the cafeteria line. When she spotted Annie alone at her usual table, Emily decided now was her moment. "I'm going to sit with Annie," she said.

"Why?" Eliza demanded, gaping at her. "Yer crazier than she is if ya keep doin' that! Yer gonna get in trouble, Emily. It's no joke, associatin' with the Blues."

"I'll catch up with you later," Emily said as Eliza walked off, shaking her head.

As Emily approached Annie, who looked as alone as a lost dog, she noticed two other women in blue, both seated together near the doors. A dark-haired matron loitered nearby.

Emily sat down.

"It's back bacon," she said, nodding at Annie's plate. The fatty meat had been set aside as Annie ate her eggs with a spoon. "Thought you might need it cut. Is there a reason they can't do that for you in the kitchen?" It seemed like the easiest and most reasonable thing to pre-cut a woman's meal if she wasn't allowed a knife.

Annie stared at her a moment, swallowed her egg with a passive expression. Her skin was so pale, from lack of sunlight or nutrition or both. But Emily tried not to see through her. "No one has ever offered," Annie said. "And I can't ask."

Psychiatric inmates are denied basic eating utensils (or assistance with same) and ostracized in the dining hall, relegated to isolation among their fellows even when they are considered safe enough to fraternise with the general prison population.

Emily frowned. "Well, here," she said, proffering the knife. She didn't glance over at the security matrons, but they would either see this or they wouldn't, would discipline her or not. She couldn't very well sit there and do nothing while Annie tried to eat her bacon with her hands, like some animal. There wasn't much dignity in this place, and surely the inmates— even the Blues—were entitled to *some*. And besides, Annie had information Emily needed.

Annie's chest rose and fell on a deep breath before she accepted the knife. "Why are you being so friendly?" she asked quietly. "You know what the blue means, don't you?"

Emily nodded. "But you don't seem insane to me. Why are you here?"

Annie sighed again and cut the pork, glanced up briefly from beneath her dark lashes to check that the matrons weren't watching. Emily remained focused on Annie, tried to ignore her own increased heart rate. Her interviewee handed back the knife.

"No, I'm not insane," Annie said, taking a bite of her meat, chewing slowly. She swallowed, eyes still on her plate. "I haven't been insane—not really, anyway—for fourteen and a half years."

Only Emily's need for sustenance kept her eating now. Her appetite had vanished, but she knew she would be hungry well before dinner if she didn't finish this measly breakfast. She forced down a spoonful of over-salted, lukewarm egg and waited for Annie to say more. It looked like she was deliberating. Emily offered a small smile to nudge her. It worked.

"What have you heard about me?" Annie asked, a bitter smirk tickling her lips.

Emily decided on the truth. It seemed unfair to lie to her. "I heard you killed your child," she said gently. "But something tells me there's more to the story than that, if it's true at all."

Annie blinked rapidly. "That rumour's gone around since I got here, I think." She paused. The chatter in the room swelled, which always meant everyone was nearly finished eating; it was good cover for a secretive conversation. "I didn't kill my child," she said, finally making eye contact with Emily. "But after Gregory was born, I did go insane. It's blurry, especially now, after all this time, and the medications and shock treatments." Emily's ears pricked. "I sometimes wonder how much of what I remember is real," Annie said. "Good and bad." Another deep breath. "I think I thought there was some sort of ghost or demon or something that was trying to hurt me. And somehow that idea got mixed up with my baby's cries, like he was a demon screaming. Or something." She shook her head. "I remember lunging at my husband, but I don't remember hurting my child. I really don't think I did, but my husband got me committed. I haven't told anyone this in years," she added, looking nervous.

Emily's throat swelled with pity. "Why not?"

"No one asks. Word gets around to the new inmates and they all stay away. Why didn't you?" She looked skeptical. "I'm sure your friend over there must have said something." She nodded in Eliza's direction.

"You're observant," Emily said with a half-smile.

"Yes. That happens when you're invisible. People see right through you, but in turn, you begin to see them more clearly."

Emily waited again. She knew how to interview—leave an empty space, and someone who's already willing to talk will always fill the silence.

"I was here on an indefinite sentence, because they called me a lunatic. 'Puerperal insanity,' they said. Something about new mothers going mad after their babies are born. Sort of like hysteria, I think. But after a few months here, I felt back to normal. Well . . . as normal as I could be in a prison." Her eyes slid a little out of focus, and Emily saw the past fifteen years of Annie's incarceration slide across them like a dark cloud. "And then I was just left with sadness. But I'm not insane."

Emily watched her with a piercing ache in her heart. "I believe you, Annie," she said, her own voice barely audible over the clamour of the dining hall. "So why do you think you're still here? I don't understand."

Annie didn't hesitate, and her voice was stronger now. "I'm here because *she* thinks I'm still insane. Dr. Stone. Because I raged at them, once I was back to myself, to let me out. I wanted to be with my husband and child. The law says she needs to sign off on my release, but she won't. She tries me on some new drug every few months. But I'm not going to hurt anyone. I have nightmares sometimes, but they torture me alone, no one else. And that's more than my husband can say, let me tell you. My son was conceived after John came back from the war, in forty-four. He used to thrash and scream in his sleep like I do. Seeing things, you know. Reliving them in his nightmares."

Emily opened and shut her mouth. "But couldn't your husband ask for—"

"He stopped writing ten years ago, without a word. I can only suspect he moved on to someone else. Men can divorce their wives if they're insane." She offered a pained smile, then was silent for a long moment.

"At least the girls who come here pregnant get to have their babies with them." Annie flicked her chin to the left, and Emily followed her gaze to Vera, who was sitting with another pregnant girl. "For a while at least. That's more than I ever got. I never go within twenty feet of the nursery. I can't bear it."

The bell rang, and Emily jumped, so invested she'd been in Annie's tale. They both stood.

"Thank you for telling me this," Emily said.

Annie nodded. "I appreciate your kindness. Maybe tomorrow you can tell me your story, how you got here. We've all got one."

Emily warmed at the idea that Annie was looking forward to speaking with her again. They parted ways, Annie disappearing back up to the second floor.

As other inmates swarmed around her, Emily gravitated toward the nursery down the hall, in the south corridor across from the chapels. She hadn't taken much notice of it before. The doors were always shut against the noise of the main floor. She peered in through the small glass window in the centre of the door; it was dim in there, the curtains over the large windows half shut to block out some of the sunlight so the babies could sleep. Emily could see two lines of wooden cradles, twenty or so in all, though fewer than half appeared full. Two mothers were seated in armchairs, nursing in the soft light. One looked up at Emily, hollow-eyed with a single tear track bisecting her cheek, a stream through a dark wood. Emily saw a flash of Eleanor in the woman's face, glimpsed the torment in her eyes before two strong hands gripped Emily's upper arms and hauled her away from the window.

CHAPTER 20

RACHEL

Bayfield—February, 1984

Rachel was sitting at the kitchen table with her homework spread out when she heard the key in the lock. Her eyes slid off her lined workbook, where she was making notes for her English essay, a biography of Virginia Woolf. She hadn't been assigned the book, but was irresistibly drawn to it after hearing about Woolf's obsession with her dead mother, how her writing and personal letters were littered with mentions of their relationship.

She has haunted me, Woolf had said.

Rachel was taking a moment to let her thoughts percolate as she stared out the big kitchen windows at the frozen lake. This time of year, the beach looked like a miniature mountain range, the sand and ice forming into peaks that were regularly covered in snow. The sand hardly moved when stepped on, and the water was frozen as far out as Rachel could see from their vantage point on the cliff.

At the sound of the key in the rarely used front door, she roused herself from her stare and turned, curious. Dora had been out earlier, fetching some groceries, but Rachel thought she'd already returned. Realization dawned on her then and she stood, apprehension buzzing in her veins as a figure emerged from the dark hallway.

"Mom?"

"Hey," Mary said, walking into the kitchen. It was late afternoon, and the grey-filtered light from outside mixed with the golden glow of the lamp over the table, casting Mary's skin a pale yellow. Rachel was reminded of lemon curd: bland to look at, but sharp on the tongue.

"What are you doing here?" Rachel asked, taking a tentative step toward her.

"I'm just . . ." Mary's voice was high-pitched and wavering as she teetered on the edge of tears. She looked at Rachel, then lowered herself to the floor and began to sob. Rachel watched her for a moment as Mary hugged her own shoulders like she was trying to stop herself from breaking apart, rocking back and forth on her knees as her cries began to crest.

"I—are you okay?" Rachel asked, knowing she most certainly wasn't. Mary lunged for her then, sudden and ferocious. Rachel cried out in fear as Mary pulled her into a tight hug and held on, tears drenching her sweater. Rachel could feel Mary shaking, heart pounding hard in her chest as her breaths came sharp and shallow.

"I don't—want to—be like this!" Mary's words stuttered with her sobs and she held tighter to Rachel. It was starting to hurt.

"Gran!" Rachel shouted desperately to wherever Dora was in the house. "Gran, come quick!"

Rachel felt helpless, but nevertheless patted her mother's back softly. This *was* sickness, she knew. Her mother was ill and needed help. But at the same time, she knew what would happen next. This sort of meltdown could only mean disruption and drama and chaos. Rachel didn't think she had ever pitied her mother more than she did in this moment, but she also hated her for the storm she would bring down upon Rachel and Dora until her whims blew her away from them again.

Dora hurried into the room, and relief flooded Rachel. Mary let out a little cry and released herself, flung her body instead into Dora's waiting arms.

"Mama," Mary moaned, as Dora rocked her like an inconsolable child. She met eyes with Rachel over Mary's head. *What happened?*

Rachel shrugged.

"Mama . . ."

And so Rachel stood by, watched as a mother and daughter loved and despised one another, resented and depended on each other in the same desperate breath. No matter the distance between them, the love and dependence somehow always won out. In her times of crisis, all Mary wanted was for her mother to hold her and tell her it was going to be okay.

And Rachel watched it all from afar, knowing she would never in her life feel the same.

Three days later, all they'd been able to get Mary to eat was a few bowls of tomato soup and a single sleeve of saltine crackers. She sipped on tepid water from a green Depression glass that Dora said was her favourite from childhood. She slept fifteen hours a day and stared at her bedroom wall or the television the rest of the time, leaving her bed only to use the toilet.

All they'd been able to get out of her was that something had happened with the guy she'd been seeing, and that she'd had thoughts of suicide for the past two weeks—egged on, she claimed, by images from her dreams.

New year.

New boyfriend.

New failure.

New crisis.

So often, Mary came back to the lake in the heat of summer, but this time, she'd come to hibernate. To overwinter like the perennials in Dora's sprawling gardens, shrouded in protective burlap as they lay dormant beneath the frost and snow, their hearts filled with raw longing for spring.

"She needs help," Rachel said to Dora on the fourth night as she stood watching her grandmother grind chamomile and spearmint for a calming tea.

"That's what I'm trying to do, little one," Dora said, brow furrowed as she worked away with the pestle.

"No, Gran, I mean . . ." Rachel hesitated, not wanting to offend. "I mean *real* help, like professional help. She needs a doctor. There's something wrong."

"Of course there's something wrong," Dora said, shaking her head. "There always has been."

"No, but Gran, this is . . ." Rachel's eyes were wide and imploring. "I'm really worried about her." As she said it, she realized it was true, and was overcome with a confusing sense of achievement. It was often so difficult to understand or forgive Mary, but seeing her in such a vulnerable state was eye-opening. Her mother was, in many ways, the oblivious author of her own misfortunes. But how much of her poor judgment was dictated—or at least influenced—by her mental illness? Seeing her now, reduced to a childlike shell of a person who could barely feed herself, Rachel wondered how anyone could make the right choices from such a place of helplessness. It was all so complicated, but Rachel was doing her best to untangle it. All she knew was that she had never felt sorrier for her mother than she did now.

"I'm concerned, too," Dora muttered, tapping the side of the mortar with a *clink* to empty the herb blend into a jar. "I've never seen her quite like this." She met Rachel's eyes now. "She keeps asking for Reverend Holland. I suppose they made quite a connection the last time she was here."

Rachel remembered a couple of summers ago, when her mother had spent most of her visit alternating between painting her nails and meeting with the reverend. She'd seemed better that time, though, and Rachel wondered if perhaps the minister *had* had some positive impact on her. She knew Mary was always looking for answers anywhere she could find them. Rachel recalled with disdain the fortune-tellers, the televangelists and mediums Mary had touted over the years. Was the reverend really any better?

At Dora's invitation, he arrived that evening, and sat with Mary for an hour as though she were on her deathbed. In a way, she sort of was: She'd given up all hope for her life and the images and voices had taken over any rational thought she possessed. She cried constantly.

Rachel stood outside her mother's bedroom door, just out of sight, and eavesdropped. The reverend spoke of finding strength from God and from within.

"I want to be better, Reverend. I do." Mary sobbed, blew her nose loudly.

"You have not had an easy life, Mary," the reverend reassured her. "God has tested you with trials others have not been challenged with. It is a lot to bear."

"And my mother, she just . . . she'll never understand. She and Rachel hate me. I know they do. All they do is—"

"Your family does not hate you, Mary," he interrupted gently. "You must—"

"But I hear the words," she whispered.

"They tell you this?"

Silence. "No. In my head, I hear it. I hear that they hate me." She paused. "Are they right? Do I need help?"

A pause. "No, I do not think you need any help that God cannot provide."

Rachel had had enough. Fuming, she stepped into the room, and they both looked up at her in surprise.

"Rachel," the reverend began, "I—"

"She doesn't need *God*," Rachel snapped. "She needs a *doctor*. Medication."

Mary's face was blotchy and wet, her nose running.

"When someone is sick, you call a doctor," Rachel pressed, her mouth dry. She'd never spoken to an adult like this before, but had to say it.

Reverend Holland looked at her with something close to pity, and Rachel felt a squirm of defeat.

"Yes. But there are also chapels in hospitals, aren't there?" he said.

Rachel gnashed her teeth.

"They trust the care of doctors," Reverend Holland said. "But still they pray."

That night, Rachel stayed up late to catch up on her homework. It had been almost impossible to focus, with everything going on. At midnight she stumbled, exhausted, into the bathroom. She always wished the house had more than one shower, because ever since that night with Mary years ago, she hated using this one. Every single time, she'd fight to shake off the lingering images of Mary, hands outstretched like Lady Macbeth, uttering accusations of witchcraft that could have gotten a woman hanged by the neck once upon a time.

The house was quiet now. Mary had finally stopped crying an hour ago and found her way into sleep. Rachel had finished her research, and could go to sleep now herself.

She sat on the toilet beside the shower, ran her eyes over the grid of grey grout between the tiles, a little moldy in places, thinking of Woolf's words about her own mother.

Rachel never lingered in the shower like some teenagers did. She'd lather and rinse as fast as possible, fighting against the memories of water ricocheting off her mother's body into her face.

Blood, so much blood, in the cracks between the tiles.

The madness in her swollen eyes that seemed never to fully fade.

She has haunted me.

TORONTO—JUNE, 1996

MWP. The Mercer Women's Prison.

Rachel has no idea what that place is. The old Toronto psych hospital and the Kingston Penitentiary, she knows; they're both still in operation. But she's never heard of the Mercer Women's Prison.

Her stomach growls. It's lunchtime. She locks the files in the trunk of her car and drives around the corner beneath the railroad tracks, pulling into a street parking space on Dundas. She gets out and locates a hot dog cart a block over. Then, hungrily chomping in the shade of a tattoo shop, considers her next move.

She needs to locate this prison. If it's right in the city, she can go there next, before she heads back up to Huron County.

She scarfs the rest of the street dog, washes it down with a Pepsi, then scans the sidewalks along the sunny stretch of Dundas West for a phone booth. She heads for a heavily graffitied one three blocks down. Her HQ doesn't have cellular phones yet, though there's been buzz about the Toronto Police Service testing out that new Motorola one in their squads. Knowing Green, it'll probably be at least a decade before he's willing to advocate for funding to have them. Until then, they all have to use pay phones. Rachel should probably just bite the bullet and get her own car phone in the meantime.

When she reaches the booth, she realizes that the phone book that's meant to be hanging from a cord has been ripped out. Only shreds of the spine remain on the metal coil, like a fish skeleton picked clean. She walks another three blocks to the next booth, which does still have its book intact. She balances it on one raised knee, flipping through the government pages in search of the Mercer Women's Prison, but doesn't find it. She rummages in her pocket for the change from her lunch, presses a quarter in with a *clink* to call a colleague in the Toronto OPP office.

"Hey, Chapman. It's Mackenzie, from Clinton." She recaps the morning's discoveries quickly. "I haven't heard of this Mercer Women's Prison; can't see it in the phone book I've got here. Know anything about it?"

"Women's prison?" he asks.

"Yeah."

"Hmm. I didn't think there was one here. Just Vanier in Brampton, and Kingston obviously. And uh . . ."

Rachel clears her throat. "Grand River. Yeah, I'm aware—"

"Mackenzie—," Chapman begins, tone thick with apology.

"I'm actually wondering if the Mercer is defunct," she says, plowing on. "The case dates from the sixties, so it could be."

"Yeah, sure, uh . . . Hang on a sec, I'll ask Deb in our finance office.

She's been around for decades. Don't think she's ever going to retire. Too stubborn. But she might know."

Rachel smiles despite herself. "Thanks, Chapman."

She takes in the street as standard-issue tinny elevator music crackles through the line. It's always a bit strange when she's in plain clothes, which is more often now that she's a detective. People act differently around cops—for better or worse—when they see the uniform. Which is, in large part, the point of wearing one. But when she looks like a civilian, she can observe with a little more ease, so long as no one notices the firearm on her hip holster beneath the blazer.

Some teens from the school down the street are still roaming during their lunch hour, pushing one another and laughing on the sidewalk. Rachel looks at her watch. They aren't truant yet, but will be in about six minutes. A man wearing an apron emerges from the Chinese restaurant twenty metres away, dumps a couple of garbage bags at the curb between the newspaper box and the telephone pole. A curious pigeon lands on the garbage, then takes off again as a streetcar rattles past. Rachel misses the city sometimes. She came here a lot more as a teenager than she does now.

The music on the phone stops. "Mackenzie?"

"Here, Chapman."

"All right, apparently the Mercer Women's Prison was in Liberty Village until the sixties sometime, Deb says. But the building is gone. It was where the Allan Lamport Stadium is now."

"Huh. Okay. Thanks, Chapman."

She signs off and steps away from the booth, thinking. There's no point going to the site, really, if the building's been razed—at least not yet. What she needs are prisoner records.

And for that, she needs a librarian.

Rachel moves her car to a parking lot near Dundas West Station, where she boards the subway, heading to College Station and the Ontario archives. It's been ages since she's taken the Toronto subway, and she takes a moment to enjoy the memories it conjures, of summer visits to the city with Kimberly or Lori to see concerts at the Forum down at the waterfront. The outdoor concert space drew in their rebellious teen selves with its revolving round stage surrounded by screaming, singing, drunken fans and a haze of pot smoke. She was appalled when they demolished it two years ago. The last concert she'd seen there was Radiohead, at Edgefest in 1993, with her friend Steve. They'd originally met at Pineview and dated on and off after they left, which was at best a mistake and at worst scraped against the outline of the rules. They stayed friends for a while, mostly because—aside from Tom Stevens—he was one of the few people Rachel could relate to. But she hasn't heard from him since he relapsed last year.

She exits the station now and walks the rest of the way. Inside the archives building, she identifies herself to the receptionist, whose blond eyebrows lift with intrigue. She leads Rachel back into an office area and asks her to wait.

Rachel's never been here before, and isn't entirely sure what to expect, but she holds her files in her resting hand, the manila folder pressed against her firearm. She takes a deep breath of the air that smells like carpet cleaner and freshly photocopied paper, feeling eager. If these archives can produce the prisoner register for the Mercer from the 1950s and '60s, that should be enough to take back to headquarters and start whittling down the list of possible identities for her Jane Doe. She needs to know who died there during that window.

Another woman arrives within minutes, sweeping over the threshold of her small office in a cloud of purposefulness and Elizabeth Arden Red Door.

"Good afternoon, Detective . . . ?"

"Mackenzie. Rachel Mackenzie." Rachel extends a hand, which the woman shakes firmly.

"I'm Lydia Jacek, Director of Archives. I understand you're looking for some prisoner records."

"Yes," Rachel says. "It's part of an investigation into a Jane Doe found up in Huron County." She recaps the Mercer prison info. "It's defunct, but I wondered if any of the records might still be extant."

The director is already nodding fervently. "Absolutely. I'll do what I can."

Rachel withdraws from her folder the sheet from Cartwright-Cambridge Co. with the Mercer Women's Prison's information. She passes it into Lydia's hands, the nails trimmed short but impeccably well-manicured. It bodes well—she values attention to detail.

"There's the spelling, and the address, if that helps," Rachel says. "It was in Liberty Village."

Lydia nods again. "Excellent. I'll see what we can do. Normally we would need some time to pull this information, a day or two." She glances at the clock on the wall. "But I can get two staff on it right now, and we'll do our best. It may take a while, though, I'm sorry."

"I'll wait," Rachel says with a smile, thinking fondly of saying the same thing to Mitch Jackass Cambridge under very different circumstances a little over an hour ago. "Thank you, Ms. Jacek."

"Lydia, please."

"Lydia." Rachel smiles. "I don't mind waiting. There's a lot of that in my line of work. Just show me where I can find the coffee, and I'll be fine."

"Ha!" Lydia smiles indulgently and gestures for Rachel to follow.

She waits back in Lydia's office after securing some fresh coffee in a ceramic mug with a faded image of a blue cat sitting atop a stack of multicoloured books. Rachel's always a bit fascinated by the mugs she gets offered in her day-to-day while waiting for information. She wonders what the mugs say about the people. Snarky quips. *Best Grandpa Ever.* Shakespeare quotes. Snoopy and Woodstock. Such-and-Such University crests. But it's the nondescript ones without any identifying characteristics that always make her the most suspicious, as though the person supplying the coffee is self-conscious, reluctant to give her anything to analyze. She finishes the drink and then sneaks a couple of the Werther's candies from the dish on Lydia's desk.

Nearly two hours later, she's memorized the details of the director's degrees on the wall and established theories for all four of the stains on the carpet when Lydia finally reappears.

"We've got them, Detective. I'm sorry it took so long. Back this way, please."

"Don't apologize, I appreciate your help on such short notice." Rachel follows her through a different part of the office where study rooms are situated along one wall. Lydia approaches one labelled "3" and holds open the door. Rachel enters to find a series of documents spread out on a large conference-style table, a set of white gloves resting beside them.

"If I could ask you to put on the gloves, please. It's protocol."

Rachel nods. "Not a problem," she says, pulling them on and noting how strange and luxurious the cotton feels on her fingers compared to the rubbery blue ones she's used to. It's like stepping out of high heels and into slippers.

"Here," Lydia says, pointing, "we've got the register from the prison for the years 1950 through 1960, then 1960 to 1962. They end there, so let's hope that's the year it closed. I've also pulled some of the other records we had in relation: the prisoner punishment register—"

"Oof." Rachel grimaces.

"Yes, I know. I've also got here the inmate medical records, and various others referencing the Mercer Women's Prison. I wasn't sure what else might be helpful."

"This is excellent, thank you."

"Well," Lydia says, exhaling a quick breath of a laugh. "I'm glad we could get it in time. If there's anything else you need, just let me know. We technically close at five to the public, but I'll stay through until you're done, detective."

"And is there any way to get copies of these documents?" Rachel asks.

"Most of them should be okay to copy. Just me know."

"Thank you so much."

Lydia closes the door with a polite nod. Rachel takes a focusing breath and leans over the table.

She ends up staying overnight at a hotel nearby, returning to the archives the next morning to finish reviewing the documents. Had she kept going the day before, she and Lydia would have been there well past midnight. Despite the fact that Rachel is eager to get home, there's no huge rush. She always has a go bag packed in her car for times like this, anyway: extra underwear, socks, deodorant, toothbrush and toothpaste, her antidepressants.

She finishes around ten-thirty, bids Lydia goodbye and heads back to her car with a fresh stack of copies folded neatly into her folio. She takes a sip of the last cold bit of her hotel takeout coffee and shakes her head. Mercer was a truly horrific place. No wonder they shut it down and razed the whole thing for a soccer stadium.

Rachel's spent plenty of time in prisons, knows the standards and laws and how things work—or are supposed to work. What she's seen here, even for the sixties, is beyond the pale. The treatment of the psychiatric patients, particularly. She pauses, then crumples up the paper cup with undue force.

She hadn't had much interest in seeing the site of the prison when she'd learned from Chapman that it no longer existed, but after reading all of this, her fingers are itching to steer over to Liberty Village before she leaves the city.

She looks down at her notes now, at the list of five inmates she isolated from the hundreds registered at the Mercer throughout the '50s and '60s; the names that will form the bulk of her work over the next several weeks. Though she has no idea how any one of them would have ended up in the Millgate Cemetery, two hundred kilometres from Liberty Village.

Three of these women died at the prison between 1958 and 1962.

Another two are mysteriously unaccounted for, with no death or discharge dates at all.

And one of them, she's sure, is her Jane Doe.

CHAPTER 21

EMILY

July, 1961
Day 37 (146 to go)

Emily clutched the wet rag against her mouth and nose, eyes shut tight. The fumes from the gasoline were overwhelming, and she was terrified it would splash into her eyes and blind her.

"Just hold still," the prison hairdresser, Maria, said. "A few more minutes." Emily could hear the disgust in her voice as she brushed more of the cold chemical onto Emily's scalp and strands as though she were applying Miss Clairol. It dripped down Emily's neck into the towel tied around her shoulders as the hairdresser tugged at the hair around Emily's right ear.

Maria was a fourth-generation Italian woman about Emily's age, whose aspiring career in acting had spiralled into high-end prostitution. Three months ago, she was caught with a politician of some importance—she refused to say who—at the Windsor Arms Hotel. She was arrested and sent to the Mercer for a year. He didn't even lose his job.

Maria had dark eyes, a rosebud mouth worthy of the screen and a sharp tongue that might very well have impeded her professional success.

"You're lucky you only have to do this once," she said darkly. "I'll be doing it a hundred and twenty bloody times." She herself hadn't been infected yet, and wore a prophylactic plastic cap over her own spectacular head of dark locks. "My sentence'll be up by the time I finish murdering all these damn cooties. And God help my sense of smell. Burned half to hell already, I'm sure."

The lice outbreak had spread through the Mercer faster than the fire at the turn of the century that destroyed most of the city's core. The mites hopped from head to head over the course of two weeks, infesting nearly everyone except the prisoners currently in isolation cells in the basement.

> I am certain those lonesome souls sequestered in the claustrophobic bowels of the damp basement had never before had cause to celebrate their punitive seclusion.

"All right, there you are." Maria fixed a pink plastic shower cap onto Emily's head with a grunt. "Go sit over there and watch the clock. It needs to sit for an hour, and then we'll wash it out with water hot enough to cook a lobster."

"Thanks," Emily muttered, revolted. She stood and made her way over to the line of chairs against the wall as another inmate took her place in the salon chair. She noted the time on the clock opposite: 1:16 p.m. At least this was getting her out of her domestics lesson and a decent chunk of her cleaning shift. Three other women, including Eliza and Peggy, were seated already. Eliza appeared to be napping, her shower-capped head resting on the wall behind her, and Peggy was crying silently, tears absorbing into the cloth she held over her nose. Emily didn't know the third woman, who was staring vacantly at the floor.

Emily ran her tongue over her teeth, swearing she could actually taste the gasoline fumes wafting from her head. The windows were barred in the hair salon, but the matrons had thrown up the casements in an attempt to filter the air. She held the cloth to her mouth again, repelled by the situation she found herself in, had *put* herself in for the sake of the story. By God . . . the medical exam had been awful enough, the food a disgrace. If she was also going to scorch her scalp and its resident vermin, she sure as hell was going to get this story and see her name in that goddamn byline. That image was the talisman that kept her going, counting down the days to the end of her sentence and the beginning of her career.

"I've done this three times now," Eliza said, not even opening her eyes. "Ev'ry time I been inside, there's some sorta vermin. Nits. Bedbugs. Even had a rat in me cell once. In the winter. Burrowed into me mattress tryna keep warm."

Maria scoffed, and Emily could only stare, incredulous. "And you still say this place is better than your home, Eliza?"

Eliza didn't open her eyes, but nodded. "Yes ma'am."

Emily sat beside Eliza, imagining, with no small measure of discomfort, the horrid realities of a home that rendered life at the Mercer preferable. Eliza appeared to doze off again, her head nodding, impervious to the fumes that choked her fellow inmates.

A little over twenty minutes later, a commotion in the hallway around Warden Barrow's office next door caught Emily's attention. The salon door was open onto the hall for ventilation, and she had a clear view from her seat.

A group of young women Emily didn't recognize—many of them only teenagers—was clustered together, shuffling around awkwardly with suitcases. Nearly every girl displayed a rounded, pregnant belly. Emily stared, uncomprehending. Their expressions were fearful, and several of them spoke to one another, commenting on the fumes. A voice Emily didn't recognize called instructions to them to file down the corridor and wait. She strained her ears, finally isolating the warden's smooth voice in the clamour, just out of sight. Glancing at Maria, who was busy now dousing another inmate's scalp like an arsonist intent on burning the place to the ground, Emily stood and wandered closer to the door, taking several long strides under the pretence of stretching her stiff legs.

"They are spread out over the second and third floors, wherever we've found room for them," Warden Barrow was saying. "It was good luck that we aren't currently at capacity. Here's the chart. Matron Smith and Matron White can assist the girls with finding their cells—*rooms*. Are you staying here to get them processed and settled, Sister?"

"Well, yes, I think so," a soft voice said. "But then we need to be getting back."

"Yes," Warden Barrow said, voice dripping with contempt. "I imagine there's plenty to sort out over there with the police."

"Yes. And the parish as well."

"And the inmate who escaped, what of her? She isn't in this batch, is she?"

"No, no," the woman replied firmly. "We do not know where she is."

"Just as well, I should think. Though she deserves her comeuppance for that ghastly attack. And the paper said an inmate was found dead, Sister?"

A pause. "Yes. But by her own hand, God rest her soul."

"Mm. Well. Fortunately we have better security here for the staff than you have at St. Agnes's. The fourth-floor staff quarters are secured for just this sort of reason. These girls are always better off in cells than running wild in dormitories. Give them an inch and they take a mile, every time." Barrow *tsk*ed. "Now . . . get them lined up against that wall there and we'll process them through my office. I was told there would be eighteen, is that right?"

"Correct."

"Any of them due to give birth imminently?"

"Two or three, in the next month or so. I'm sorry, but may I ask what that odour is?"

The warden let out a dramatic sigh. "A lice outbreak. We have it under control."

There was a clipping of heels and Emily stepped back from the door just as the warden appeared there. Their eyes met.

"What are you doing, Radcliffe?" Barrow snapped. "Get away from the door. Go sit until your hour is up." She grasped the doorknob and yanked it shut with a snap.

"Oh, this tastes like summer, doesn't it?" Emily said, popping one of the five local strawberries on her plate into her mouth and biting down, revelling in the explosion of tangy juice. The strawberries were the first fresh fruit—aside from bruised apples—that Emily had seen since her arrival at the Mercer. The girls on dinner prep duty had reported to anyone who would listen that the fruit had been delivered by the uncle of one of the inmates. He had a farm just outside the city, near Brampton. Emily was already dreaming of the autumn harvest she loved, the corn, squash, parsnips, and the pumpkin tarts her mother made every Thanksgiving. She would miss it this year, but she knew Bess would put up preserves and freeze the pies for Christmas.

As the weeks wore on, Emily felt a greater sense of accomplishment at the information she'd collected so far. The gasoline treatment, as horrendous as it had been, seemed to have had some effect on the lice infestation, though Emily's scalp still burned in some places where she was sure the skin was permanently damaged. Once she was out, she would visit her family physician and have him take a look. But what she wouldn't give now for a jar of Pond's Cold Cream to soothe it.

Annie hesitated, a plump berry between her small fingers. "It does taste like summer," she said, as half a sad smile pulled at her lips. "They've always been my favourite. There were loads of strawberry fields outside the town I grew up in. We had them in my backyard as a child, too. I'd eat them as soon as they ripened on the bush, before the rabbits got them. It used to drive my mother mad. She loved canning jellies, but she never canned a thing from that strawberry patch." She chuckled. "She had to go to one of the market stalls on the edge of town. I'd help her in the kitchen," she added. "It was my job to sit and watch the jars, make sure the lids all went *pop* when the seals formed. And she'd let me lick the mixing spoon while I waited."

Emily always sat with Annie Little now at breakfast, then Eliza, Lizzie, Peggy, and Gertrude at dinner and supper, when Annie sat with another psychiatric inmate who was hesitant about other company. Emily felt the matrons keeping a closer eye on her lately, surely wondering why she had chosen to befriend one of the Blues. But so far they'd said nothing. And Annie, it turned out, was a calm and interesting conversationalist now that Emily had gotten her talking.

"No one ever asks me questions," she'd told Emily, "except medically related ones. I haven't had a real conversation with anyone in years. Talking to you has made me feel a bit like myself again. *Alive*."

She came from a small town, was married at twenty and moved to Toronto when her husband got a job at an architectural firm. He'd gone to Trinity College and always wanted to return to the city, so they did. Thinking Annie was settled, her parents had moved to Ottawa when her father was elected to the House of Commons in 1945. He'd been re-elected four times since.

"It sounds like you had a good relationship with your mother," Emily ventured as she shovelled toast into her mouth. She didn't want to hurt Annie, but couldn't help asking the next obvious question. "Do they write?"

Annie fixed her with an expression that was both sad and wry. "No. My mother used to, but having a lunatic daughter isn't good for my father's professional reputation, now is it? If anyone found out, he'd be ruined."

Emily ceased eating, then exhaled heavily, thinking how lucky she was to have the father she did. She pictured the mischievous smirk on William's face the night she'd told him about this mission, and how he had fought to support her. She thought of how, as dusk had settled on their backyard and cigar smoke curled over his head like a question mark, he asked her how she was going to get this story. Not whether she *could*; how she *would*. He had an inherent belief in her abilities, and the thought nearly brought tears to her eyes right there in the dining hall. Oh, how she missed him. She'd sent one letter so far, in coded language, telling her parents she was all right. She would send another this week, but would need to leave out the lice infestation or it would never get delivered.

"Have they ever met your son?" Emily asked.

Annie inclined her head. "Mother has, yes. Not Father, I don't think."

Emily was becoming enraged by Annie's continued incarceration, and was already determined to try to advocate for her release—somehow—at the end of her own sentence, even before the article was published, if she could. Although, if the article had the impact Emily hoped for, it might be enough to at least trigger some sort of official investigation, which might then lead to Annie's release regardless. Emily had tried and failed to imagine what it would be like to meet your fifteen-year-old child whom you hadn't seen since birth. Equal parts terrifying and elating, surely. Annie didn't talk about the future much, though, and Emily understood why.

Strawberries consumed, Emily shook some salt and pepper onto her scrambled egg now in a desperate attempt to coax some flavour out of it.

"It feels a bit different in here now, doesn't it?" she said to Annie, raising her voice over the chatter. The dining hall was notably louder with the addition of the eighteen girls from the shuttered maternity home, who tended to cluster together at a couple of the large round tables. It must have come as quite a shock, Emily supposed, to find themselves in a prison, but word had spread as fast as the lice that the other maternity homes in the city were full. Theirs had shut, the sedulous rumour mill reported, because one of the residents had stabbed their headmistress and hanged herself in the foyer. Apparently the girls were all openly talking about it; one of them had even seen the body. However, with no access to a newspaper, there was no way for Emily to verify the story. Still, it seemed likely that it was all true, since the home had shut down suddenly, leaving the expectant girls with nowhere to go. Only the four nearest their due dates had been removed to the few vacancies available at the other maternity homes around the city. The rest were relegated to the Mercer.

Emily wondered why some girls pregnant out of wedlock were sent to more comfortable maternity homes to begin with, while others, like Vera, were consigned immediately to prison. Based on the scope of the Female Refuges Act, it might simply have been a matter of how angry and vengeful their parents had become at news of the pregnancy. Some families reported it to the police as an "incorrigible" offence, while others clamped down on it with a morality-driven vise as they shipped their girls off in secrecy, determined to smother the misdeed with a blanket of discretion.

"Yes," Annie said now, eyes on the new inmates. "We've been this full before, but not for a while. I like it better when there's more people, though. The Blues don't stick out quite so much in the crowd." She chewed her lower lip. "It used to bother me, seeing the expectant girls. But I had to get used to it if I wanted to be let out of the psych ward for mealtimes."

Emily nodded sympathetically. "I imagine it's incredibly difficult, Annie. I'm sorry."

Annie shrugged. "The medicines help—some of them, anyway. But some of the experimental drugs Dr. Stone's tried me on have made me feel more insane than I did when I came in. Others dull the pain. And I guess that's the point. Dull us into submission." Her face twisted in frustration as she tried to cut some beef with the edge of her fork. "Speaking of dull . . ."

"Here," Emily said, handing over her knife. Emily glanced up at the table of new girls only to find Matron White staring back at her, green eyes piercing Emily's like a cold syringe.

Annie followed her gaze. "Did she see you give me that?"

Emily nodded. "Yes. Don't worry about it. Just stay calm." She swallowed the hot little flicker of foreboding. "Can I ask why you keep taking the medications?" She did her best to appear nonchalant, though she could still feel the matron's eyes on her. "If you say you don't feel unstable anymore, why are you still on them?"

Annie took a slow sip of her lukewarm tea. They were never served drinks any warmer than body temperature. "Because," she said to her plate, pushing some mushy beans around, "I can't very well say no, can I?"

Emily nearly pressed her as to why not, then thought better of it. She recalled Dr. Stone's tray full of silver instruments, the cupboards of drugs and the restraints she'd spotted on the hospital bed. If an inmate refused to comply, the staff had the means to force it. And the psych cells and washroom were gated off with controlled entry and exit.

"So Stone tries different drugs on you?" Emily asked.

Annie nodded.

"Why you?"

Annie sighed, glanced up at Matron White, who was no longer watching them, sharp eyes on the new girls instead.

"Well, that's the biggest question of my life. *Why me*, indeed."

Emily was quiet a moment, silently composing lines for her article, heart fluttering with mild triumph. Annie was corroborating the claims of experimentation in the Incorrigible note.

"I guess I'm definitely one of the calmer psychiatric inmates," Annie mused. "I'm afraid of some of the others, honestly. Though I think most of them wouldn't be as bad as they are if they weren't stuck in this place."

"Are they drugged as well?"

"Yes. Sedatives mostly. And nearly all of us have electroshock therapy. It helps some more than others."

"Does it help you?"

Annie shrugged. "Not especially. Afterward my whole body aches. Sometimes I'm sick. It makes me terribly tired, and more sensitive, I think." She pauses. "And then when I get emotional, they call me crazy." She raises her eyebrows at the irony.

Emily's insides contorted in anger and grief on her friend's behalf. "And this is still happening today all because *fifteen* years ago, you had a bout of psychosis? And you've felt mentally healthy ever since?"

Annie simply looked at her in confirmation. Emily swore under her breath as the bell clanged outside the dining hall. They rose with the swell of chatter and movement, then made their way upstairs to the second floor. Annie always had to return to the psychiatric wing after meals, and Emily wanted to use the toilet before she hurried back downstairs for chapel.

The two women pulled over at the locked psych wing gates, Emily lingering for a moment as Annie flagged Matron Carnegie on the other side. Carnegie was a small, round sort of woman with a plain but kind face. She had pale brows that rarely furrowed in anger and disdain like so many of the other matrons' did. She was fairly new to the psychiatric wing, Annie said, and perhaps that accounted for her kindness and compassion.

Just as Matron Carnegie unlocked the gate, a woman about her size but thin as a child and with dirty hair came racing up behind her, eyes wild, lips pulled back in a sort of snarl, like a lion baring its teeth. Emily screamed just as Annie cried, "Rose, no!"

The matron turned in alarm as the madwoman launched herself at the gate and gave it a violent rattle. Her eyes were on Emily. "Get away from Annie!" She shrieked. "Get away! Go away! She's not yours!"

"Rose—!" Annie protested as Carnegie seized the wild woman and shouted for assistance. Emily backed away several paces, horrified. Two more matrons came rushing down the hall and all three struggled to subdue the insane woman. After a moment of struggle she was dragged away, raving, and eventually her growls dissipated as the solid door of her cell shut behind them.

"Who was that?" Emily gasped, heart flinging itself against her collarbone.

Annie entered the psych wing and shut the gates behind her before responding. "Her name is Rose," she said. "She's a friend of mine. Sort of. At least, I think *I'm* the only friend she's got."

"I don't wonder!"

"Don't," Annie implored, and Emily was surprised into silence. "She's not as insane as she seems. She—" She glanced over her shoulder, but the psych hall was now deserted. "Everyone says she murdered her husband in cold blood. Stabbed him in the back."

Emily blanched. "Did she?"

"Well . . . yes. But he'd beaten her senseless for years before that, she says. The night she killed him, they'd had a terrible fight, and she was all bloodied. He had a knife, and told her if she didn't get him first, he was going to kill her. She says he handed it to her, like a dare, almost. Then he turned his back, so she lunged for him."

Emily's hand came to her mouth.

"She told the court it was in defence, said that after years of him treating her like that, she fully believed he was serious, that he was going to kill her later that night." She shrugged. "Apparently, they thought she must have been insane because when the police came to arrest her, she attacked them. Nearly bit off one of their ears, I overheard once, because she couldn't stand to have another man touch her that night. And I suppose that must have looked insane, mustn't it?"

Emily thought of Peggy, of her similar experience. She'd been in such a state of hysterics when the police arrived that they'd arrested her instead of her husband. Perhaps she, too, couldn't stand to be touched by any man after all her husband had done to her.

Emily nodded slowly. "I wonder," she mused, "how things might go differently for women if we were allowed to become police officers. A woman would have understood. She wouldn't have seemed like another threat, at least."

Annie's brows raised. "Goodness . . . women police officers. That's quite a thought." She exhaled. "At any rate, I am sorry about that. I think Rose is just jealous I have another friend." She blushed, eyes sweeping Emily's face as though nervous she might disagree with the word.

"Oh," Emily said. She smiled, then stopped, feeling somehow guilty for expressing pleasure when Rose was evidently so distraught about it. "I can understand that." And she did, but also hoped Rose wouldn't come at her like that ever, ever again.

"I'll talk to her, Emily," Annie said. "But I should go, as should you. I don't want you in trouble for being tardy." She gave a little wave, then turned and walked back down the hall, disappearing beyond her open cell door.

Emily turned reluctantly, heading downstairs for the chapel, her mind fixated on how in the name of God Annie had been incarcerated for the past fifteen years.

CHAPTER 22

EMILY

Late July, 1961
Day 43 (140 to go)

A little over a month after Emily's first visit to Dr. Stone's office, she was once again called to the infirmary. She'd known this was coming—Dr. Stone had said the exams were "routine"—but still found herself dragging her feet up to the second-floor corridor, nauseous after a breakfast of runny eggs that did nothing to quell her nerves about the appointment.

There was a lineup of five other girls ahead of her and, frowning, Emily took her place at the back of the queue. She leaned against the whitewashed brick wall and pressed her weight into it in an attempt to ease the ache in her back. Her exhaustion drove her to sleep each night, but the mattress was still atrocious. Movement helped, and at least there was no shortage of that at the Mercer, worked off their feet as they were.

Emily was just beginning to wonder how long she was going to have to wait to see Dr. Stone when a wail sounded from the psychiatric ward down the hall. All six of the women's heads turned, though there was nothing to see.

"Stop it! I don't want it! *I said I don't want it!*" the voice shrieked, and Emily's stomach jolted. It sounded like Annie. A matron responded gently with something Emily didn't catch, and Annie began to moan and cry. Emily was next to tears just listening to it.

"It's just one of the Blues," a woman in line said. "That Crazy Annie, who killed her kid. Don't know why they don't just keep her drugged."

Emily opened her mouth to retort, but at that moment Dr. Stone's office door opened and the rude woman was admitted. The girl who had just emerged was hugging herself, clearly upset. Her eyes were bright, nose red. She was in Emily's domestics class.

"Are you all right?" Emily asked her as she passed.

The girl looked up. "I don't know what she did," she said, eyes watering now. "I don't feel right. Down there." She flushed as her gaze flashed down to her legs. "I don't . . . I don't know." She shuffled off and around the corner as Emily's trepidation increased.

Annie's crying had subsided, and Emily hoped she would see her at dinner, find out what happened. She'd seemed fine at breakfast.

The wait for her turn with the doctor felt both painfully slow and too short. Each of the girls ahead of her came out of the office looking shaken, and Emily caught herself tapping the wall in anxiety. Even the rude woman who had disparaged Annie kept her eyes downcast as she passed, hurrying around the corner and out of sight.

Emily's heart hammered as the door opened and the nurse beckoned her in with a stiff hand.

"Clothes off, gown on, up on the table," she said dispassionately. Emily's legs felt as though they belonged to someone else, but she summoned all the courage she could, and complied. As she climbed up, she spotted a red hair on the sheet at the head of the table.

It did not belong to me, nor the patient who had vacated the infirmary before me. I plucked it off and tossed it to the floor with a grimace. Evidently, the sheets were not changed between patients, which caused me no small amount of disquiet. Were the doctor's tools sanitized before and after procedures, or was that process similarly unsanitary?

Dr. Stone emerged a moment later from the office at the back of the infirmary. Remembering her first pelvic exam, just the sight of the woman sent Emily's pulse racing. She struggled to calm it.

"Lay back, Radcliffe," Dr. Stone said, sitting down on the short stool and rolling it over toward Emily's feet with a rattle. Emily did as she was told, fighting every instinct she had to kick the doctor in the face and run for it.

"What's the exam for today?" she asked instead, as politely as possible.

"These are routine exams to ensure the health and well-being of the prison population," Dr. Stone declared in a deadpan voice.

> It was a rehearsed line, a politician's lie, regurgitated so often that it had lost all trace of believability or meaning. I still did not understand why the pelvic exams were routine, but the moment before my genitals were at the mercy of this doctor was not the time to question the procedure. But how I would come to wish that I had, in fact, protested.

Emily took a deep breath and pressed her feet down into the stirrups, tensing the muscles in her legs to keep her knees from snapping shut. She stared up at the ceiling, willing her heart rate down as she clutched the edges of the bed.

Without warning, Dr. Stone began poking around. Emily bit down hard to avoiding demanding what, exactly, the doctor was looking for, or doing. Other than occasional trips to her family doctor for a cough that persisted, a tetanus shot, or remedy for an earache, Emily had had very little experience with medical professionals. She'd heard her mother talk about how she'd been treated at the hospital when she gave birth to a stillborn at seven months, a couple of years before Emily and Eleanor arrived. The day after she laboured her dead child into the world, she'd been sitting up in her hospital bed, staring blankly at her own feet with swollen eyes when the resident and a gaggle of medical students that resembled a hockey team came through her ward on their rounds.

"That one aborted," the resident had said, throwing a thumb in Bess's direction before moving on to the next bed. They'd never even let her hold the baby, didn't tell her what had gone wrong. *It was a boy*, was all they'd said. *Don't fret so, Mrs. Radcliffe. You're young, you'll have more.*

She'd made Emily's father drive her to a different hospital when she gave birth to Emily and Eleanor, but was still separated from her babies, where they were poked and prodded in the nursery by a similar group of medical students while she waited anxiously on the other side of the window, unable to hold her own children until the men had finished with them.

Without warning, a stinging sensation tore through Emily's vulva. "Ouch!"

"You're done, Radcliffe," Dr. Stone said as, to Emily's horror, she set a syringe down on the metal tray beside the bed.

"What was that?" Emily demanded, feeling the blood drain from her face.

Doctor is evil...

"I said you're done. Get dressed." Dr. Stone stood and walked back into her office without another word. Emily sat up and shot a look at the nurse standing by the door.

"What was that? What was in that syringe?" The nurse didn't respond, wouldn't look at her. "What was it?!" Emily shouted.

But the nurse was already rolling the tray away and opening the infirmary door for the next patient.

Two weeks later, Emily felt the sores.

———

"Good Christ," Emily swore, closing her eyes against the burning pain and itching. She was lying on her bed, staring at the ceiling with her legs spread open for some relief. It was noisy in the corridor, as it always was in the evening around this time, when the inmates had completed their work and were granted a bit of free time before lights out.

The previous day was Wednesday—her weekly bath night—and she'd been awkwardly semi-crouched beside the old copper tub, wiping herself dry, when she paused. A wave of cold came over her, though the bathroom was damp and stuffy from the bath and the summer heat. She fingered the bumps between her legs. There were at least six of them that she could feel, and as she let out a shaking breath, they began to burn, whether from the coal tar soap or the abrasion of the towel, she didn't know. But she was certain that whatever these wart-like lesions were, they were the result of the injection by Dr. Stone. Had the syringe been contaminated with something? Was she having some sort of allergic reaction?

"Hey," she heard from her cell doorway now, and turned to see Lizzie leaning casually against the frame, long dark hair falling over her shoulder.

Emily cleared her throat and sat up, wincing as she shifted her weight onto her bum, squashing the bumps. Tears threatened.

"Do you want to come play crib—what's wrong?" Lizzie asked, suddenly concerned.

Emily met her friend's eyes, unsure what to say.

"What is it?" Lizzie asked again, coming to sit beside her on the bed with a creaking of springs. Someone shouted out in the hallway, laughed.

"I . . ." Emily began. She knew Lizzie was a mother, and probably knew more about women's bodies than she did, but one didn't speak about such things. Then a shooting pain forced the words out.

"There's something on my . . . my nethers. Bumps or something." Her face burned with mortification. "They hurt, and itch. I don't know what it is. It just started yesterday, and it's getting worse."

Lizzie made a face. "Sounds like VD, Em."

Emily stared. "VD?"

"You gotta go see Dr. Stone to get it treated."

A sickening swoop struck Emily as a memory crashed over her.

Venereal disease.

The Female Refuges Act . . .

"I can't leave until it's gone." She was panicking, recalling the clause about inmate releases being delayed if they had VD. She'd wondered briefly how it would spread in a women's-only prison, but hadn't given it a second thought. How naive she'd been. "They can keep me here!" Her voice rose with her dread, cresting together like high tide. "By law, they can!"

Lizzie frowned. "I heard somethin' about that. Some girl a few years ago said she got it off the tools in the infirmary, said she'd never been with anybody. Sounded a bit made-up to me, but the warden told her she couldn't leave until Dr. Stone cleared her. I guess they claim we can contaminate the public or some shit," Lizzie said, rolling her eyes.

"But I think I got it from Dr. Stone, too," Emily hissed, fighting the tears. "She injected me with something a couple of weeks ago, wouldn't tell me what it was." Her cheeks burned to discuss such things, though Lizzie seemed at ease. "I've never—you know—been with a man, either. I didn't come in with this."

"Have you been with a woman? 'Cause you can get it—"

"What? No," Emily said. "No one. Not . . . like that. But does it go away on its own?" Fear bubbled in her throat.

"I don't think so. Dr. Stone's got something for it, though. Couple other girls have it, sounds like it's spreading."

"How does it spread? Off the toilet seats or something?" She was seized with a new fear of going to the washroom, or having to clean one. They weren't even given rubber gloves for cleaning duty.

Lizzie gave her a pitying sort of look. "Maybe. But mostly from, you know, touching. Sex. There's lots of girls here like Gertrude. Maybe it's going around. But anyway . . . if you want to get out of here at the end of your sentence, you gotta go back to Dr. Stone, and hope you get rid of it fast."

———

"Annie," Emily said, sliding gingerly into a seat at her friend's otherwise empty table in the noisy dining hall the following day at breakfast. Annie looked up from her meal and smiled. There were bags under her eyes, and she seemed more slouched than usual. "Are you all right?" Emily asked.

Annie shrugged. "Same as always, I guess." She studied Emily. "Though I reckon I feel about as good as you look."

Emily had been up half the night. Several things had combined to render sleep next to impossible: the burning in her groin, the thought that she could be trapped in the Mercer for some indefinite period if she didn't recover from the VD, her rage at Dr. Stone—both about her own condition and what Annie had confirmed were renewed electroshock therapies.

Emily hesitated, then spoke quietly as chatter and the clinking of plates and glasses swirled around them. "You told me once that Dr. Stone experiments on you with different medications, is that right?"

Annie exhaled heavily, nodded. "Yes. Some of them work. They sometimes help me feel better, truly. Other times . . . not as much." She hesitated then, eyeing Emily shrewdly. "I appreciate your concern, Emily, really I do. But can I ask why you care so much? It's not as though there's anything you or I can do to stop it."

Emily opened her mouth, then closed it. She was on the verge of telling Annie who she was and why—precisely—she was so interested in the actions of Dr. Stone and all the goings-on at the Mercer. But she held her tongue for now. She and Annie had grown closer. They were friends, and she believed Annie could be trusted. But she still worried about tipping her hand too soon. It wouldn't do for word to get out who she really was before she'd had a chance to gather the whole story. She probably owed it to Annie to tell her the truth, but this wasn't the right moment.

"I just think maybe she's done some kind of experiment on me, too, that's all," Emily said, hedging. "So I'd like to know if it's just me, or if any of the other girls have had the same thing happen."

Annie watched her, musing, then nodded. "Well, you can always try to talk to the other girls. They usually want to share, want to talk about themselves. Because everyone feels they're in here unjustly," she said, smirking without humour. "If you ask them if they've been wronged, I'm sure they'll—"

She was cut off as a tall woman wearing a blue dress that seemed too small for her plunked herself down at their table. Emily and Annie looked up in surprise. This was a first. Usually everyone avoided Annie.

"Um, hi, Bernie," Annie said now, offering the other inmate a small smile. She was watching her curiously, though, as was Emily.

"Sorry to break up your little party," the woman said, "but since those pregnant girls came, there's not as much room to sit anymore." Emily recognized Bernie as one of the other Blues she would occasionally see at a table by the door, closely monitored by Matron White. Bernie had a plain but not unattractive face with long eyelashes, and hair buzzed short like a boy's. Emily had never seen a woman with hair that short, not even on the twenties film starlets.

"That's all right," she said, shifting her mental track away from her and Annie's conversation. She was curious to speak to another of the psych inmates—at least, one who seemed safe enough to engage with, unlike the violent Rose. She thought of what Annie had just told her, about the inmates all generally being willing to talk about the injustices that had landed them in the Mercer to begin with.

"I'm Emily," she said, reaching out a hand. The woman squinted at her a little skeptically, as though Emily were trying to trick her. But Emily kept her hand extended, and eventually Bernie shook it.

"Huh. Hi. What are you in for, Emily?" Bernie asked, tucking into her meal with gusto.

"Oh, you know," Emily said, raising a humourless eyebrow. "The usual. My parents thought me incorrigible, wanted to straighten me out."

"Mm," Bernie said, nodding, mouth full. "Is that the usual?"

Emily shrugged. "For some, yes. How about you?"

"Emily—" Annie began quietly, but Bernie held up a hand like a stop sign. "'S okay, Annie," she said. She swallowed, then spoke to her plate, not meeting Emily's eyes. "The trouble is, I'm a man. So they all think I'm a lunatic."

Emily stared at Bernie, uncomprehending. "I'm sorry? I—"

"There's nothing wrong with my mind. I was just born with the wrong body," Bernie said simply. "I've known that since I was eleven. I can't tell you what happened, but I got the wrong body. I haven't done anything wrong except tell my sister I thought God made a mistake. Now I'm here. So I get a prison within a prison. Isn't that nice?"

Emily was speechless, unsure what to make of what she'd heard, or how to respond. Annie gave her a sidelong look and a small shrug. Bernie finished eating a few minutes later and stood suddenly. "See you around," she said, and stalked off without another word.

Emily tried to gather her thoughts. "She doesn't seem insane," she said quietly to Annie, who shook her head.

"No. I don't think she is, either. She's pleasant and chatty with the matrons, but she maintains she's a man in a woman's body, so I think by their definition she's insane. Delusional, they've called her. But . . . I don't know. It doesn't make much sense to me, but I suppose a lot of people's lives don't make much sense to others, do they?"

Emily chewed this over for a moment, considering all she knew of Annie and the other women, of Bernie. "I've been thinking a lot about that," she mused, watching Bernie's back as she exited the dining hall. "With you, and now with Bernie. They seem to be able to call women insane just for *saying things* that *sound* insane, even when there's no evidence of insane or violent behaviour, like there is with Rose. That seems wrong somehow, don't you think?"

Annie nodded. "Yes. It is wrong. But there isn't much we can do about it, is there?"

Emily watched Annie finish the last of her food, wondering when she should tell her new friend who she really was, but the bell rang a couple of minutes later, and Emily bid Annie goodbye.

As she made for the chapel before her domestics lesson, a thought occurred to her.

"I need the infirmary," she announced to Matron Smith at the dining hall door, massaging her forehead. "I have a dreadful headache."

The matron waved her away with a lazy hand. "Go. Then straight on to your duties when you're finished, Radcliffe. No mucking about."

"Yes ma'am."

Emily went up to the second floor and pulled up short in the corridor outside the infirmary. There was already a queue of four other women lined up along the wall outside. There never used to be queues. They turned at Emily's approach, and she took in the pained expressions on their faces. Two of them were standing with their feet wide apart, a most unladylike stance that would earn them at best a verbal lashing from a matron, or a shot to the back of the leg with a stick.

Emily took her place at the end of the line and waited, considering. The girl in front of her kept shifting her feet, and looked close to tears. She was a little younger than Emily, heavy-set with dark hair pulled up into a bun. Emily thought her name might be Jessica.

"I think we might be here for the same reason," Emily ventured quietly, then introduced herself. "Is yours burning?"

The girl's face reddened, but she looked relieved. "And itching!" she hissed. "The bumps . . ." She trailed off, aghast. "And I don't even know how I got it! The lice was better than this!"

"Me too," Emily said, not bothering to keep her voice down. "What about you?" She directed the question at the other two women in line, who both nodded.

"Do you think Stone'll just douse our fannies in gasoline, too?" the woman at the front joked.

Emily glanced at the closed infirmary door. "Did this start for all of you after you saw Dr. Stone last time? Did she, uh . . ." She swallowed. "Did she inject you with anything? Use a needle down there?"

They all nodded, and Emily's sense of foreboding increased, but it was laced with anger, and curiosity, and a sense that this story was about to go deeper than she'd imagined. These girls—and who knew how many more—had all been deliberately infected by a doctor who was supposed to be healing them.

Why?

CHAPTER 23

RACHEL

Summer, 1985

As was often the case in the summer, Mary was back, and without much explanation beyond "I felt like a visit."

She had a new boyfriend, some guy named Roger who owned his own contracting business in Kitchener, where she was now living in a brand-new townhouse with trendy white-tile countertops in the kitchen, black appliances and even a microwave.

"None of this old wood," she'd told Dora and Rachel with a dismissive wave around their beloved kitchen.

Dora had asked how she afforded the rent on a place like that, working an hourly wage at Tim Hortons, but, fast as a whip, Mary had already moved on to talking about *Back to the Future*, which she and Rachel had just gone to see at the Starlite Drive-In. She also seemed able to continue to pay the rent on that house even though she was taking the summer off work to be in Bayfield. That hadn't even occurred to Rachel until she overheard her grandmother pressing her mother about it later.

Since Rachel's graduation from high school, she'd spent most of her time slinging ice cream at Two Scoops on Main Street, as she always did, and—uncharacteristically—spending time with her mother. Mary hadn't been to visit in a year and a half, not since the two months she'd spent wintering on the couch and in her childhood bed, depressed and unhinged. There was, Rachel had to admit, a marked improvement in her since then.

She had more weight on her frame, and the dark circles that had entrenched themselves beneath her eyes had faded in the toasty tan she spent her days accruing, lounging on the chaise in the backyard with a cigarette in one hand and a lukewarm Coke in the other. But mentally she seemed better, too. She was less scattered and erratic, didn't drive as though she had a death wish for herself and everyone else on the road. She slept a normal number of hours, and at night instead of in the day. Dora thought she might be on, as she put it, "proper medication," and Rachel wondered what might be possible in their relationship if only she would fucking stay on it.

Rachel was going to study science at the University of Windsor in the fall. She'd done well in science in school, liking the cut-and-dry nature of science and math: that something was right or it was wrong. It was or it wasn't. She couldn't stand her mandatory English and History classes, where she had to argue for something on one side or another. It was exhausting. Rachel wanted facts, not opinions. There was always an answer to something, you just had to dig deep enough until you found it.

"The first person in the family to go to university," Dora had said, beaming, when Rachel ran into the kitchen back in February, dancing on the spot holding the acceptance letter aloft. "I'm so proud of you. This is a tremendous accomplishment, my not-so-little one."

When Mary had heard the news upon her sudden reappearance in June, she'd given Rachel a look that Rachel still couldn't quite decipher—some mix of anger and pleasure, perhaps a latent sense of motherly pride attempting to scratch its way to the surface of her bitterness. But she hadn't congratulated her daughter. "You'll like Windsor," was all she said, reaching into the fridge for another Coke. "Good party town, if you know where to go. I can tell you the best places."

It was a Tuesday afternoon now, and Dora was out at her weekly quilting circle. It was a group of twelve women who had met at the community centre with their needles and thread and gossip every Tuesday since 1971. It was one of the few routine things Dora did solely for herself.

Mary and Rachel had just returned from Grand Bend, where Mary liked to go to the beach. It was only a twenty-minute drive south, but more populated than the Bayfield beaches, and Mary said she liked the mood better, didn't have to run into as many people she knew from high school. Rachel could relate to that. She didn't want to run into anyone *she* knew from high school, either, when she was with Mary. There was still just too much to explain, and she had few answers, no defence for her mother's choices.

Rachel took some chicken out of the freezer in preparation for dinner that night while her mother pulled two glasses out of the dishwasher, leaving the rest in there without unloading it. Rachel glanced at her. It felt strange to admonish her own mother, tell her to contribute, but she was always cutting corners and avoiding doing her share of the housework. It was starting to irritate Rachel, who had been taught to clean up after herself from the time she could manage a dustpan and reach the knobs on the washing machine. Dora had been on Mary about getting a local job, but she hadn't yet.

Mary stepped in behind Rachel and opened the freezer again, releasing another cloud of fog that cooled Rachel's legs rather pleasantly. Her mother twisted the ice cube tray with a satisfying crack and plucked a few out, dropping them into the glasses and filling them to the brim with pop.

"Backyard?" her mother asked, handing her one.

"Sure."

Rachel followed her through the screen door, which slammed with a clap behind them as they made their way down the porch stairs. Rachel loved just sitting back here, reading a thriller as she listened to the leaves sigh overhead, her nostrils filled with the scent of Dora's lavender and mint.

She made her way toward her favourite Muskoka chair, but her mother beckoned her, walking toward the cliff edge.

"Come sit with me."

She sat down and patted the ground beside her, right there on the edge of the bluffs where Rachel had seen her sit so often before—including that time when she was out swimming in the lake—dangling her legs off the side.

Rachel's stomach swooped. "Gran doesn't let me—"

"Oh Jesus Christ, Rachel," her mother said with an aggravated sigh. "She doesn't *own* you. Come sit. Live a little."

Rachel hesitated, glanced back at the house, at the deep covered porch and butter-yellow screen-door frame, the bedroom windows along the back, their heavy curtains pulled shut to ward off the summer heat that accumulated like thick fog as soon as the sun crossed over its midpoint to the west. The house always had such an empty air about it when Dora was out, as though it shut down in the absence of its mistress.

Rachel turned away from it, guilt tingling in her extremities, then settled near her mother on the rough carpet of dry grass and weeds. It itched the backs of her thighs, uncomfortable and nagging. She slowly extended her legs out and let her ankles and calves rest over the edge, planting her hands firmly on either side of her for stability. She was a good foot back from where her mother was, though, perched with her thin butt flirting six inches from the face of death.

Rachel adjusted her sunglasses in the glare of the afternoon. The breeze blew in from the water, fluttering her hair. She watched her mother from her vantage point a little behind. At the roots, her mom's natural brown hair had more streaks of red in it than Rachel's dark locks did, but the rest was growing out a brassy shade of gold highlights. She often had some sort of lightening in her hair, depending on which mood had struck when she walked into the drugstore and reached for the box. Sometimes the dye came with a side of bleach. She was always fighting against the dark parts of herself. Sometimes more successfully than others.

"You're an adult, you're allowed to do what you want, Rachel," she said. "You don't have to stay here with her anymore, or play by her rules."

"Well, I'm not staying here, I'm going to school in Windsor. You know that. But also—" Rachel looked back at the wooden arbour, the green rose leaves beginning to climb their way up. They'd been in full yellow bloom a week ago. She'd planted them herself, the previous year. Their roots had taken hold. "I don't really want to leave. Not permanently. I like it here, well enough, until I find somewhere I like better. I don't know yet. Windsor is three hours away, though. I can drive home on weekends and stuff."

"Well, what if we lived together? I could get a job there."

Rachel was silent for a moment, shocked at the suggestion. "What about your boyfriend?" she finally managed, perplexed.

Her mother shifted where she sat, raked her fingers through the grass beside her.

"He's nothing. I can break it off with him. You're more important."

She bit down on the inside of her cheek, the one Rachel could see. Her mother wasn't making eye contact with her. She was lying, Rachel realized. There was no boyfriend. She exhaled deeply, sighing out her frustration, her anger at being lied to by Mary—yet again.

"Since when?"

Silence.

"What about your house?" Rachel pressed.

Mary shrugged.

Rachel waited, searching for the real reason why her mother was proposing this.

"I'm really trying here, Rachel," Mary said finally. "Things have kept us apart for so long, and I'd like to be more a part of your life."

Rachel was savvy enough to note how her mother externalized the blame, as she always did. Everything that went wrong was someone else's fault.

Things have kept us apart.

"*Things* haven't kept us apart, Mom," Rachel said. "*You* have."

"Your grandmother isn't the saint you think she is," Mary spat back.

"What do you mean?"

"She poisoned me to end a pregnancy. Did you know that?"

Rachel's breath suspended.

"That time in the shower," Mary said, her voice a gleaming dagger, intent on harm. "You must remember that. I told her I was pregnant and she gave me some shit in a tea she said would calm me down and I miscarried the next day. I know she did it."

Rachel swallowed hard. "She may not be a saint," she said, angry at herself when her voice cracked, tripping on the sudden understanding of her grandmother's complexities. "But at least she's taken care of me, been there for me, which is more than you can say for yourself." Her blood felt like it was on fire. In the face of all of Mary's many misdeeds and broken promises, her addictions and madness, Rachel had never accused her mother of anything before. She was frightened, but proud of her own courage, like she'd just jumped off a high diving board.

"She didn't pull me into a bloody shower with her and call *you* a witch," she continued. "She didn't drag me out to live in Etobicoke. I slept on a couch and *didn't go to school*. You were drunk or high or off fucking Simon half the time. I ate *Twinkies* for breakfast, if I had one at all. Child Services took me away from you for good reason. So don't criticize Gran for giving me a home and doing what you wouldn't. My relationship with her is clearly very different than her relationship with you, and I won't apologize for that."

She already knew that later she would need to sit with the knowledge that she might have had a sibling. That, if what Mary claimed was true, Dora had intervened to abort the pregnancy. She knew by then that there were indeed things her grandmother hadn't told her, but surely everyone was entitled to a couple of secrets. And perhaps her grandmother had a good reason for keeping that one from her.

"Right," Mary said, scowling, "because she's the perfect parent. She's just never wanted me to have any happiness since . . ." She dragged on the forgotten cigarette in her hand, burned mostly down to the filter. Rachel looked at Mary's nails, painted the same abalone blue as Rachel's. They'd sat out on the back porch three nights ago, flipping through magazines and drinking Dora's iced tea as they painted each other's nails.

"This is nice," Mary had said, wiggling her fingers in the air and smiling, which she rarely did unless she wanted something from someone. "We match. Like sisters or something."

Rachel had smiled then, but with a mixture of pleasure and hesitancy. She was drawn to her mother's attention—she'd had more of it this summer than she'd ever experienced in her entire life—but she also didn't want to be anything like her, even if it was just a matching manicure.

Now, in the heat of their argument, she knew she'd been a fool to think she and Mary had truly gotten anywhere with their relationship that summer, that two months of trips to the drive-in and painting each other's nails the same colour could possibly make up for eighteen years of abandonment.

She looked at her mother's back, a little sunburned above the line of her black spaghetti-strap tank top. Then a thought flashed through her mind, unbidden and intrusive as a lightning bolt.

Just one push, and she'd be gone.

And she saw herself do it in her mind's eye, heard the quick rustle of the grass and weeds as Mary's body disappeared over the cliff edge.

Rachel's breath came hard and fast with fearful shame. She shook her head to dispel the image in her mind, recoiled farther away from Mary.

"Anyway," Mary said, finishing the cigarette and flicking the butt into Dora's herb garden to land among the lavender. Rachel jolted her mind back to the moment. "I don't want to talk about the past, Rachel. I just won't. I've gotten my shit together and I want to move forward with you and have a future."

Mary really didn't get it, and Rachel didn't know whether it was deliberate ignorance, or that whatever was wrong with Mary made it impossible for her to see the damage she inflicted on others.

"Except all we have is the past," Rachel said icily. "If you won't talk about that, won't explain why you've—"

"You know what?" Mary barked. "Never mind. I'm done here. I'm done." She threw up her hands, swung her legs around and stood, leaving Rachel alone facing the lake, the serenity of it taunting her as her insides boiled with bitterness. After so many years, with countless disappointments and devastations added to her quiver of life experience, she was still unable to believe how quickly and easily her mother was willing to give up on her.

CHAPTER 24

EMILY

August, 1961
Day 55 (128 to go)

Emily closed her eyes against the incessant burning between her legs. She shifted in the old rickety school chair she was perched on in Classroom 2 during their so-called typing hour. She slid her bum farther down the seat, which she wished to God had a chair pad. She could hardly get comfortable sitting anymore, especially the day after a treatment.

She'd gone to Dr. Stone's office yesterday morning for the second time in as many weeks, held back her sobs as the doctor lanced the warts, then sprayed them with something from an aerosol can. Emily had watched carefully, trying to get a look at the label, which was small, with minuscule type, but couldn't see much. The good news was that the warts had felt a little better after a few days, in between treatments. They still burned, but didn't itch quite as much.

Emily had never experienced anything like this. Of course, she'd never experienced anything like this entire assignment. It seemed mad that she was doing it, and even more mad that things like this and lice and bathing once a week were now a regular part of her existence. How foreign it all was to her. It seemed impossible that beyond these walls there were a million and a half people who bathed regularly, who slept on proper mattresses and saw their families and didn't have vermin living on their bodies. But then, that wasn't exactly true, was it? That comfort may have existed for many people, but meeting these women at the Mercer had opened Emily's eyes to the realities of others. Women who came from broken homes and poverty, who were ill in the mind or body. She could see now how those things limited a person's opportunities, dictated the direction of her life as they forced her down paths that were rockier, darker and more dangerous than the ones Emily had been allowed to traverse. She thought of June Jones's accusation on the sidewalk back in the spring: *I bet you lot have a whole other set o' rules than the ones the likes of us gotta live by.*

She looked around at her fellow inmates now, the ones she knew, like Vera and Gertrude. Vera would leave here eventually, perhaps with her baby, perhaps not. Maybe, if she behaved as they wanted her to, she might stand a chance of keeping it. But what about after? What about the future for any of these women? Would they end up in June Jones's brothel? On the street? Tied to a bad man out of economic necessity? Lizzie's words continued to echo in her head, and she knew they would appear in the article.

If it isn't one prison, it's just another . . .

Emily had to bide her time now until the treatment cleared the infection, which she hoped would be before the end of her sentence in December. She had no idea how long this type of thing usually persisted. She knew she had enough now for a solid story, but by the judge's order, there was no way she would be released until her sentence was completed. But she found, in the meantime, she could hardly sit by and watch blandly as this alleged "reform institution" provided no actual reform or benefit to its residents. No skills training beyond mopping floors, laundry, and bad sewing. This classroom may as well have been a cardboard prop for the benefit of the board of governors, and nothing more.

The burning in her groin came then in an almighty wave, and she stood up instinctively to ease the pressure. Twenty-odd sets of eyes in all colours turned and looked at her, waiting, as though she had something to say.

Perhaps she did.

Emily swallowed, walked toward the blackboard, and turned to face them.

"Does anyone want to *actually* learn how to type?" she asked, an impatient bite to her voice. "I don't know about you, but I'm sick of just sitting here doing nothing." Everyone stared. "Because I know how to type. I can teach you, if you want. It's an important skill. If you know how to type, when you get out of here, you might have a chance at a secretarial job. It can take you a lot of places."

A couple of the women were frowning, though they looked interested. Others were smirking, as though Emily were a joke. And maybe she was. Who knew. But she couldn't just sit here anymore.

"It's um, I'll start with the keyboard," she said, casting around for a piece of chalk. She found a small chunk on the floor beneath the blackboard. There was no eraser.

"The keys are arranged based on how frequently we're going to use them, for the most part. Also, so that letters we often use one after another are spread out a little across the keyboard, so we avoid our fingers getting tied up. Here."

She sketched out the keys on the blackboard.

"*Kwerty?*" someone piped up. Emily turned.

"What's your name?" she asked the inmate.

"Betty."

Emily smiled wryly. "I know a Betty. I'm sure you'll be a better typist than she is. And yes, the top left row starts with Q, and we do actually call it the QWERTY keyboard. All the letters are there, plus punctuation."

"What's punc—punctulation?" Betty asked. Emily hesitated, surprised, then a little embarrassed at herself. She was going to need to cover off the basics here. She couldn't assume these girls knew them.

"Uh, here," she said, drawing a period, comma, colon, and question mark on the blackboard. "These symbols are punctuation. I'm sure you've seen them. We use them in writing, and typing, to convey certain information about the way the sentence is being said. A period means a sentence has ended, a comma is a brief pause, et cetera."

A girl in the front row frowned. A couple of others were snickering.

"You use a lot of big words for a Mercer girl," one of them said.

Emily shrugged. "I read a lot of books."

"And those always get used when somebody writes?" another inmate piped up, pointing at the blackboard. She was sitting at the back of the room.

"A lot of the time, yes," Emily said. She hadn't intended to get into a basic English lesson. She examined the group; so many were young, not much older than Eliza, and Emily wondered then whether Eliza was literate. She knew she herself had had more opportunity than other women to stay in school, but it was a shock that so many clearly didn't have even a basic education. She swallowed hard as an uncomfortable realization settled on her. This was actually what most women's lives were like. She was privileged to know how to write and read and type. She never would have considered literacy a privilege. Until now.

"Why are you bothering with this?" Thelma drawled. She was slouched down low in her chair.

Emily fought to keep her contempt in check. "I just think . . ." She felt the entire group's gaze on her now, penetrating and curious. Judgmental. "I mean, aren't you all just bored to death?" she exploded. "Don't you want to at least spend this hour doing something interesting? So much of what we do here is utter *nonsense*. Cleaning floors that were cleaned by another shift fifteen minutes before, scrubbing each other's clothes until our hands bleed on them and we have to start all over." Her voice rose in anger. She thought of her grandmother again, and the words tumbled out. "My nana worked in a laundry for decades, working her body to the bone, and she could hardly spell her own name. I got to . . . uh . . ." She caught herself before she spilled about being university educated. "I got to finish high school, and learn how to type, because she wanted more for her daughter, and my mom wanted even more for me. So all I'm saying is it's okay to want something more, to *work* for something more. Women's opportunities are so limited, and I think it's important to find them and grab them and try to *make something of them* any time you get the chance." She was breathing hard. "So if you want to leave this damn place knowing how to type, with a real skill, I'm willing to teach you. That's all I'm saying."

She glanced at Thelma, who rolled her eyes dramatically and sank even lower. Everyone else was quiet for a moment, and then several people nodded. Others still looked skeptical, or amused. Emily cleared her throat.

"We're going to need paper," she said. "So you can all—or anyone who wants to learn—have one of these 'keyboards' to practice on. There are only two actual typewriters," she said, glaring at the dusty old Remingtons on top of a cupboard in the corner. No one had bothered to cover them, and who knew if the ink ribbons were fresh. But paper would suffice for now.

She managed to find a few sheets along with some crayons in the store cupboard. She tore the sheets in half so they would have enough, then distributed them, instructing each girl to copy the chart on the blackboard. She had spent so much time in classrooms her whole life, and it felt odd, though not unpleasant, to be on the teaching end now. But she was galvanized. She had enough for her article, and it vexed her that she couldn't go home, hole up in her bedroom and hammer it out. She had to wait, she had to get healthy, and then she would blow the lid off this godforsaken place. In the meantime, maybe she could effect some kind of positive change in these women's lives.

At the end of the class, Emily gathered the sheets and stuffed them, face down, into the back of the store cupboard until next time.

> Based on my experiences to date of both the ineptitude and punitive disposition of the Mercer prison's administrative staff, I felt compelled to conceal from the warden and matrons that the women were now actually learning the skill they were ostensibly meant to be acquiring during the unsupervised typing class hour. Only time would tell what their reaction would be if they were to find out about the clandestine education occurring right under their noses.

"Ow!" Emily gasped as a bead of blood bloomed on her index finger. She set down the offending needle and winced.

"Here, I'll do it," Gertrude said, leaning over to help with the sewing machine. They were on factory duty on a scorching afternoon at the end of August, baking in the sun that poured through the barred windows. It was a large open room, a little bigger than the dining hall, with rectangular tables set with outdated and mismatched sewing machines. The Mercer used the women's labour to produce bedsheets; piles upon piles of plain white cotton sheets, which were shipped to hospitals across the province, as well as to the national military bases.

"Thanks," Emily said, sucking on the blood until it slowed. She watched Gertrude fit the new needle into the machine in a flash, as effortless and automatic as tying her shoes. "How do you know so much about sewing machines?"

Gertrude didn't look up, just returned to her own work, threaded a bobbin. "My mom's a seamstress," she said. "I pretty much learned how to use one of these before I could even talk. Certainly before I could read. Small hands are useful. Why should they hold a book when they could be working instead?"

Emily thought uncomfortably of her own childhood, spent surrounded by as many books as she could devour. She'd helped with household chores, of course, but not so that her mother could pay the bills.

"Anyway," Gert said, "it's a *skill*, at least." She looked over at Emily and smiled shrewdly. "Speaking of skills, you gave quite the speech in typing class a couple of weeks ago. I'm still thinking about it." Emily swallowed, nodded. "Don't worry," Gert muttered. She didn't need to drop her voice, though. The room was a cacophony of whirring machines, and they wouldn't be overheard. "I like your style, Em. I won't rat you out. Besides, I'm not sure how you could get in trouble just for teaching us what we were supposed to be learning, but that's not how this place works. God, I can't wait to be out of here. Five more months."

"What are you going to do after?" Emily asked, returning to her work with the fresh needle.

Gertrude kept her eyes on her seam, and Emily noticed she never blinked when she worked. Her seams were straighter than a ruler. "Not sure. I guess I have to go back home, for a while at least. Figure out where I'm gonna go. I'll need some work, though. I can't stay at home anymore. And if I want any chance of seeing Susie again . . ." She bit her lip. "I don't even know if she'll be waiting for me. She says she will be, in her letters. But they come less often now."

Emily knew Gertrude was in the Mercer because she was homosexual, and Gert didn't deny or dodge the reality. But Emily was still adjusting to the blatant way she talked about it. She'd heard mutterings, though, about these sorts of things; her mother speaking in low tones to her father about two neighbour women who spent rather a lot of time together. But it was always whispered about, never openly stated.

"But I think—" Gertrude was interrupted by a hoot from the table next to them.

"Hey, Mama!"

Emily looked up. The two girls there had ceased their work and thrown their hands up in greeting at a woman who had just walked through the door with a matron at her side.

Emily took in the buxom silhouette and fiery orange hair of June Jones.

Her insides plummeted, and she watched as June nodded her recognition to the two girls, one heavily pencilled eyebrow raised haughtily. She was escorted to a table at the back as Emily, Gertrude, and the rest of the women looked on. The room had gone conspicuously silent as the sewing machines paused.

"Settle down, back to work," the supervisory matron droned lazily from her desk at the front. The machines started up again, and eventually conversation swelled.

Emily's mouth was dry as paper. She recalled now, with a sickening sense of ineptness, how Matron Grimes had jeered at June Jones that she didn't want to see her again too soon; that Jones herself had cursed the fact that she was in and out of the Mercer so often it was impacting her "business." June Jones knew Emily was a reporter. But the possibility of the madam being sent back while Emily was still there had never even occurred to her. Although, she thought, it hadn't occurred to Doris either. And Doris usually thought of everything.

What would Doris tell her to do now? What would her own father advise? Surely, they were both used to managing professional curveballs. She might be able to find a way to ask him, coded, as her occasional letters home—and her parents' letters back—always were. But what would happen if Jones blew her cover, and her identity and objective were discovered? Could she *actually* be arrested then?

Jones was walking smoothly up the aisle now toward the supervisor's desk. Emily had never seen anyone move like June did. Most women took small steps, impeded by skirts, inflexible fabrics, high heels, and persistent finishing school habits. But June Jones swaggered as a man would, moved slowly and deliberately with her large body as though trying to take up as much space as possible. It was so unfamiliar it was intimidating, but also somehow admirable.

The supervisor looked up at Jones and sighed. "Back so soon?"

Jones nodded as Emily watched her through her eyelashes, pretending to pick out a loose stitch. "You know me. Can't get enough of this place."

"Well, you seem to leave here every time with a few new girls under your wing. Can't be all bad for business."

Jones twisted her mouth and glared at the matron, shot half a glance over her shoulder at the assembled women.

"Tick off the wrong cop again?" the matron asked.

Jones shook her head. "Naw. Politician this time. Didn't like that one of my girls wouldn't agree to get beat as part of the date. She punched 'im in the cock and ran for it, and lo and behold, suddenly my liquor licence expired a month earlier than it should have. Now I'm back in on a six-month, the pricks."

Beside Emily, Gert's eyebrows had nearly disappeared into her hairline and her lips were pressed in an appreciative smile.

"Welcome home, then," the matron muttered. "Here's your materials. You know what to do. Get to work."

Jones took her stack of white cotton and began walking back to her spot. As she passed in front of Emily's workstation, she looked down. Emily cursed silently and tried to duck her head toward her machine before realizing the ludicrousness of the effort. She would run into June Jones elsewhere: the dining hall, the recreation room, the bathroom. Her best bet would be to look innocent and detached. Hopefully the months of confinement, her longer hair and the equalizing nature of the uniform might save her from recognition.

With a surge of apprehension, she met the madam's eyes and gave a half-smile of greeting. Jones took her in, face impassive.

"You new?" she asked.

Emily tried to wet her lips, but couldn't. "Yeah."

Jones's eyes lingered on her another moment, then she walked away back down the aisle with her fabric. Emily rolled her shoulders and reset her machine. She was behind on the day's quota; she needed to focus and catch up.

"Sizing you up for a new job, I think," Gert muttered beside her, shooting her a sly look.

Emily forced a chuckle as her insides clenched. "Yeah. Maybe."

CHAPTER 25

EMILY

Mid-September, 1961
Day 85 (98 to go)

On a bright Wednesday morning in late summer, Emily scaled the steps to the second floor after breakfast for her weekly wart treatment in the infirmary.

There was always a queue in the corridor outside now. Emily overheard girls complain about various ailments, from menstrual cramps to migraines and constipation, which, given the fact that she hadn't seen a piece of fruit on her plate since July, was unsurprising. She always loaded her plate as much as she was allowed with the revolting canned string beans offered three times a week, for the sole purpose of keeping things moving. She longed for her mother's Sunday dinners, her warm roasts and casseroles, her fresh fruit pies. She would even take an aspic at this point if it freed her tastebuds from the bland, unbuttered potatoes and grey scraps of meat that constituted most of their meals at the Mercer.

> As I approached the infirmary that day, I noted that the queue was longer than it had yet been. Although some coughs and colds were clearly beginning to circulate as we entered the autumn, I could not help but wonder how many other women had been infected with the same disease I had, and were now in need of treatment.

She slowed as she spotted June Jones at the end of the line. Despite being clad in the exact same uniform as everyone else, Jones's silhouette and flaming hair rendered her unmistakable, even from a distance. Emily had known she would run into the madam from time to time, and reminded herself that her best bet was still to face Jones unabashed, to give the impression she had nothing to hide, and hope the woman didn't recognize her. If she did, there would be little point in denying it, or playing the fool. She would simply have to try to leverage it to her advantage, show Jones what she stood to gain by keeping Emily's secret.

The other women in line peered at Emily as she approached. She smiled vaguely at them and leaned against the wall a few feet behind Jones, who spared a half-glance over her shoulder.

They waited in frustrated silence as each girl was called into the office in turn. A half-hour later, the door shut behind the woman in front of June Jones, leaving just the madam and Emily in the corridor. Jones spun around immediately. A smirk played at her mouth, but her eyes were hard and unblinking.

"Hey there, reporter lady."

Emily's insides went frigid, but she tried to keep her head. "I thought you hadn't recognized me," she said. "In the factory."

"I never forget a face. Especially not a soft one like yours, all innocence and surprise. The real Mercer girls are hard. You stick out. I'm not stupid, honey."

"I know that."

"Do you?"

Emily's mind grasped for a solution. She knew June Jones couldn't be tricked or sweet-talked. She cut to the chase.

"You've been in and out of here a lot," she said, lowering her voice and meeting June's gaze square-on. Emily wasn't easily intimidated, but something about this woman's presence disarmed her. "You must know things," she continued, "know the prison." She paused, then pressed on. "*Help me*. I'm trying to blow this story wide open, and that will benefit you. If you can stay out of here in future, your business—"

"Don't you talk to me about my business," June snapped. "You've never walked a day in my shoes, so don't pretend to understand me. You're just here playing at life to prove a point to someone, right?"

Emily felt a flush creeping up her neck. It was hotter than Hades inside now; the place had spent three months heating up in the scorching sun and humidity. She was sweating through her dress.

"And you still have no idea how this works, do you?" June continued. "Haven't you been paying any attention?" She stepped toward Emily, who fought the urge to back away. "It's all down in that goddamn law: if they say we have VD, they can keep us as long as they want. If they say we're crazy, they can keep us as long as they want. They have all the power here, honey, and no one on the outside gives a plug nickel about us. No one is going to stop them. Women are dispensable, and criminals and whores and lunatics even more so. The only reason this place is here is to keep everybody else's streets nice and pretty. No one wants to see us. No one wants the likes of us to even exist. They'd rather we were locked up til we died. *Wake up, kid.*" Her nostrils were flared, eyes flashing. She was angry, and that was something. Emily knew that feelings could always be manipulated with carefully chosen words. Find the right tool, and you could pick the lock.

"But I told you before, they *should* know about this," Emily argued. "They *should* care. I'm trying to make them care. I—"

June exhaled and dragged one foot along the ground, like an angry bull. "Then you go ahead, but I'm not helping you. I'm in good with Stone and Barrow. Why would I risk that for some reporter who claims she can fix all this?" She laughed, a harsh exhale. "It's a bigger risk for me to help you than it is for me to keep my head down and wait til my sentence is up. This system got set up long before either of us was born. You think you can tear all that down in a day with some fancy words?"

Emily swallowed. She'd been in here for three months now. She'd been infected, practically starved and worked to the bone, but she'd done it all for the story, to gather the "fancy words" June was now dismissing as useless. She felt flustered, and didn't like it. "I don't know," she said sharply. "But I have to try."

"Why?"

Sounds from downstairs echoed up the nearby stairwell as the two women faced each other. Emily struggled to sort out her thoughts. This story could make her career, plain and simple. But there was something else growing in her mind now, too. She'd felt it when she began teaching the typing lessons, some anger-driven sense that she might be able to make a difference. That, given her position, she might even have a responsibility to.

"Let me tell you something, kid," June went on before Emily could speak. "A smart woman doesn't argue over the rules of someone else's game. Don't whine and complain. Learn how to play, how to cheat, and every once in a while, you get to win. That's been women's lot since the beginning of time. There ain't no changing it, and the sooner you get that through your head, the better off you'll be. Trust me."

Emily watched her with mingled intrigue and offence. Her bluntness, evident protectiveness of her "girls," and accurate—however brutal—understanding of the world reminded her of Doris. She wondered what June Jones could have made of her life under other circumstances.

"Trust you?" Emily shot back. "Well that depends. Are you going to tell the warden who I am?"

June surveyed Emily, from her dirty hair down to her scuffed prison-issue Mary Janes. Her eyes narrowed. "I'll stay quiet until it's better for me not to. I always like to have an ace up my sleeve," she said. "You better just hope my hand doesn't get bad enough for me to use it."

Emily exhaled her cautious relief. "Thank you." Then she pivoted. "So what are you seeing Dr. Stone for? Because I think there's something going on, I think she's infecting—"

The door opened and the most recent patient came out. Her face was blotchy, eyes wet. June stepped forward as the nurse beckoned her in, then glanced back at Emily.

"I'm here to play the game," she said.

Half an hour later, the nurse shut the infirmary door behind Emily, who made her way over to the exam table on the right-hand side of the large room. Two beds were occupied today; one by a woman who was clearly nursing some sort of stomach ailment. She was propped up in bed clutching a tin bucket, and Emily caught a whiff of vomit as she passed. The other woman lay prone with her eyes closed, a cloth pressed to her forehead. It was Peggy, who was plagued with migraines. Lizzie had told Emily she wondered if Peggy had suffered some sort of brain damage from the many blows rained upon her head by her abusive husband, and wished him an early and painful death. Emily didn't disturb her to say hello.

Ducking behind the privacy partition that separated the exam table from the rest of the room, she imagined how unpleasant it must be for the women taken to bed in the infirmary to be forced to listen to pelvic exams all day.

Emily was about to undress when she spotted the rolling cart containing the doctor's tools, and this time, the aerosol can, which was usually brought in when Emily was already up on the table. With a rush, she swiped the can off the cart and examined it.

```
                    Trichlorovir
      Trichloroacetic acid - trial preparation
```

"Radcliffe!" The voice shocked Emily into nearly dropping the can, which she hastily put back on the cart with a betraying clatter. She forced her face into neutrality and began to undress.

Dr. Stone stepped slowly forward, dark eyes glittering in that eerily pale face.

"Do not touch the materials, *ever*. They are none of your concern."

"Yes, Dr. Stone," Emily answered mechanically.

The doctor took a seat and Emily was about to climb up onto the table, but hesitated. The sheet was damp in a patch down near the end, from the previous patient's exam.

"Is this a fresh sheet?" she asked.

Dr. Stone looked up at her, slowly. She paused in pulling on her examination gloves. "Excuse me?"

"There's a mark on the sheet," Emily said, pointing. Her nerves jangled, but she pressed on anyway, spying an opportunity to see how the doctor would react. Also, she was angry. "That doesn't seem very sanitary. Especially when so many girls are dealing with disease."

Stone stared at Emily as though she'd just asked to have her shoes licked clean by the doctor. "The sheet is changed at intervals adequate enough to maintain the health of the inmates," she said, once again sounding as though she were regurgitating an instruction manual.

"It's *clearly* dirty," Emily said. "It's wet. Look. Last time there was a hair on it."

But Dr. Stone did not look. Her eyes remained locked on Emily.

"Up on the table, Radcliffe," she said softly, "or there will be consequences, I assure you."

One of the patients in the beds behind the privacy screen cleared her throat. Emily didn't want to break eye contact first, but did anyway. Reluctantly, she shifted her body up onto the table, ensuring her gown was pulled down far enough to cover the wet spot on the sheet.

The doctor pulled the cart over and reached for the can and scalpel. She treated the warts as Emily stared at the mottled, water-damaged ceiling. There was a spiderweb in the upper corner of the room that she'd taken to monitoring, to see how long it would be before someone noticed and took a broom to it. She held her breath as she heard the metallic click of that horrible tool, the pressure and pinch as it was inserted. She tried to take her focus off the pain, wondered how often the infirmary got cleaned. And by whom? It occurred to her that she'd never been set to cleaning duty here. She would need to ask the other girls.

And then, without warning, there was a jab of something deep in her belly and everything from her ribs to her knees felt as though it were on fire from the inside out. She writhed, sobbing as tears spilled down her temples.

"What are you doing?!" she cried, feet pressing hard into the stirrups. Her legs were trembling. "Stop it! Stop it!" But Dr. Stone didn't stop.

Emily didn't know how much longer it went on. Maybe seconds, maybe minutes.

When it finally ceased, she was disoriented, aching and terrified. She felt a violent tug between her legs as the tool was removed. Relief only barely tempered the lingering shock.

"I hear you've been taking it upon yourself to teach other inmates how to *type*," Dr. Stone said, standing up from her stool. "You will quit doing so immediately. The only lessons these women are capable of learning are simple and painful. They are like animals." She leaned in now, her face inches from Emily, who wished she weren't lying down. "And despite your delusions, Radcliffe, you are no different. Do not think for a moment that you are in control here. *We* are in control."

Emily nodded, swallowing hard.

"I've just taught you a little of what childbirth feels like," Stone went on quietly. "Labour pain, from a dilated cervix. Just like this. Keep that in mind, should you ever take it into your head to pollute the population with your deficient offspring. This is what it will feel like. Hopefully worse." Her eyes lingered on Emily's. "Perhaps this will make you think twice about procreating, and about your little typing class. I do not want to hear of you doing it again. Your next exam with me will reflect your behaviour in the interim."

She stood and disappeared to the other side of the privacy screen. Emily released her breath as a sob crept up her throat. She blinked hard at the ceiling as the word floated on her vision, the word that would be a headline all its own in the middle of her article.

TORTURE

The following Wednesday, Emily was sitting at breakfast with Annie. As always, Gertrude, Lizzie, Peggy, Eliza, and a couple of other women were at another table together off near the doors. Emily had told them that

Annie's true nature wasn't what rumour and malice had chalked it up to be, but the other women hadn't taken up her invitation to sit with them. Despite her assurances, there was still a stigma attached to the Blues, even the few like Annie who were permitted to engage with the broader prison population. *It's like they think insanity is contagious*, Emily thought.

Annie, though, had been doing better lately. She'd confided to Emily that her depression often became more acute as her son Gregory's birthday approached each year. It was coming up in a couple of weeks, but this year, she'd said, she felt stronger, better able to face it.

"Are you all right?" she asked Emily now, abandoning her lighthearted report of her chat with Matron Carnegie about the matron's recent misadventure with a mouse at the bottom of her wardrobe.

"No, actually, I'm not, Annie," Emily said.

"What is it?"

Emily had spent the past several days unable to think about much besides Eris Stone and her experience in the infirmary. The excruciating pain had faded almost instantly after Stone removed the tools, but her abhorrence of Stone's decision to torture her, to "teach her a lesson," was lingering like a malady. She still couldn't quite believe it had happened. That it had confirmed, once again, one of the Incorrigible note's allegations. Perhaps the biggest one: that the doctor was, in fact, evil.

"Something happened with Stone, in the infirmary," she began in a low tone.

"What was it?"

TORTURE

Emily closed her eyes for a moment, then opened them into Annie's concerned face. "I saw a side of her that was uh . . . truly disturbing. Before, she was mean and dismissive. But this time she hurt me. Very deliberately. As though she were enjoying it," Emily finished. Her legs pressed together and she began to tap her thigh. "I've never seen anything like that."

She looked to her friend, wondering if Annie had.

"Dr. Stone is no one to trifle with," Annie said seriously. "I'm afraid of her half the time, even when I think she might be trying to help me. There's a darkness in her that's just . . ." She swallowed, eyes wide.

"I know that now," Emily began, "*Really*, I do. But I need to understand her. I think she infected me with something, too. I need to know why."

"She's a horrid woman. I don't know if there is any explanation."

"Well I *need* one," Emily snapped as the pain from her warts surged. "I'm sorry," she added, quieter. "I'm not feeling well and . . ."

Annie reached out, her hand warm on Emily's arm. Emily looked into Annie's eyes, and in that moment of true connection, she felt close to tears.

"Why do you care so much?" Annie asked. "She's not worth understanding. Can't you just wait out your sentence, then put her behind you? This is just how it is here, Emily. There's no fixing it."

Emily looked into Annie's big blue eyes. She was sure they had once been soft, but had been hardened by all that was done to her by her husband, by this prison. Emily longed to explain who she really was, what she was trying to do. After all, Annie had entrusted Emily with her own deep secrets. Perhaps it was time.

Emily glanced around the room, making sure no one was watching them, but the inmates at the other tables were focused on their food and conversations, the matrons monitoring the room in a half-hearted way. Still, she shifted her chair a little closer to Annie, and leaned forward.

"We're friends, right?" she asked.

Annie nodded, smiled. "Yes."

"And I can trust you?"

Her smile faltered a little then, replaced with a shadow of concern. "Yes. Of course."

Emily took a deep breath. "I'm a journalist," she whispered. "For a magazine. I'm here to expose the story of how the inmates are treated."

Annie's mouth fell open. "*What?*"

"I know," Emily said, keeping her voice quiet. "I know. But I'm still me. I'm still your friend. I just wasn't sent here for the reason I told you before."

"You're here *voluntarily*?" Annie breathed. "But this is so dangerous, Emily!"

Emily nodded. "Yes. But I'll be out in December, and then I'll write this story. I'll tell people what happened to you, if you'll let me. They need to know the truth of how women are treated here."

"Who does?" Anne asked, confused.

"The public! The government that funds this place—*barely*," she added.

Annie's mouth opened and shut again as she tried to absorb the revelation. "But . . . no one cares about us. Not even our families," she said, eyes watering. "We're a bunch of lunatics and criminals and . . . *prostitutes*." She whispered the last word, eyes darting around the room. They fell on June, then shifted back to Emily.

"I'm going to make them care," Emily stressed.

"So . . ." Annie stuttered. "How does this work?"

Relief flooded Emily. Annie knew, and was on her side. She glanced at the clock above the door. They didn't have long, but she might have enough time to enlist her help.

"I'm just here to observe, really. I'm taking note of what I see, what the women and girls tell me about how they ended up here, and what they've experienced. And I'm experiencing it myself, first-hand," she added. "I need to talk to the other girls, try to get a bit more detail about their visits to Stone, how they ended up infected with whatever this is. And I want to know how and why *you're* still here, Annie," she said emphatically. "You seem perfectly sane to me. Can't you try to get a clean bill of health from Stone, and get released?"

Annie's eyes welled with tears, and Emily felt the keen sting of guilt in her chest. Her friend shook her head.

"I never stay well for long enough," Annie said, her voice brittle, bitter. "And Stone says I would need to be stable for *months* before she'd talk about discharging me."

"And do your relapses happen on their own, or because Stone's put you on some new medication?"

Annie blinked hard, but kept eye contact. She was silent, but Emily knew the answer. So much of what was wrong with the Mercer prison traced back to Eris Stone; the evidence was piling up at her door.

The bell rang its shrill cry. A deafening scrape of chairs and chatter erupted as the women all stood to move on to the next activity in their pointless, gruelling schedules.

"I'll see you later, Emily," Annie muttered. "Please be careful with what you're doing. I beg you."

Later in the afternoon, Emily was on cleaning duty. They were in the basement today, with assignments for cleaning out the laundry room, boiler room, dank hallways, and the vacant isolation cells. Emily had only ever seen one or two prisoners in there; as far as she had gathered, women in the general population were usually only sent to isolation for violent infractions. Even the Blues were only separated from the psych ward when their behaviour became impossible for the psych matrons to handle with restraints and sedatives. Annie had told Emily she'd been down there just twice. Once during her second month, and the other five years ago when she was on a medication she said gave her horrific thoughts and paranoia, and caused her to physically lash out at the matrons.

"I never want to be sent there again," she'd said, eyes hollow. "The rats come out at night. They nest in the boiler room."

As she descended the stairs and felt the temperature drop about five degrees, Emily ruminated, as she so often did, on Annie's predicament. She had trouble picturing a man who could so swiftly commit his wife—mother to his newborn child—to a psychiatric institution, then leave her there to rot without a backward glance, long after the acute condition had righted itself. It enraged her that the system was set up so that despicable man could commit Annie so easily, and only Dr. Stone could secure her release. Annie had absolutely no control over her present or her future. She was a true prisoner in every sense of the word—of this place, of her own mind, of her former husband. Her body and mind and child all belonged to those who had wronged her. She had nothing that was actually her own.

"You're late, Radcliffe." Matron Smith's high-pitched voice roused Emily from her cloud of rage, and she looked up to see her standing next to the doorway to the laundry room with a mop and bucket, along with Eliza and the other inmates on their shift.

"I'm sorry, Matron Smith," Emily said, hanging her head in sombre, affected apology.

"For your tardiness, you can have the boiler room with Eliza."

Emily clenched her teeth as Eliza glared at her. She took the proffered bucket and headed into the laundry room to fill it in the sink. Eliza followed her as the other two women were dispatched to sweep out the isolation cells and hallway.

"Sorry," Emily muttered under the roar of the water filling the metal bucket. "I'm a bit distracted. Annie—"

"I can't believe you're still havin' breakfast with that Blue every day," Eliza said, rolling her big green eyes. "She's no good."

"She's *fine*," Emily said with a pointed stare. "Nice, even. She's kinder than most of the other inmates, Blues or not. You should give her a chance."

"Why? So's I can go nuts just like her? Have 'er stab me in the neck with that knife you give 'er every day? I seen you do it. Don't get caught by none o' the matrons."

Emily turned off the rusty faucet with an ear-piercing squeak and shook her head. Out of the corner of her eye, she saw Eliza wince.

"What's the matter?" she asked. "Are you all right?"

"Got some bloody pain in my fanny," Eliza said. "Burning, itching."

Emily set the bucket down.

"I've had all the vermin before and none of 'em were near this bad," Eliza continued, unabashed. "Started yesterday. Got bumps and everything. Worse than bedbugs."

"Eliza, have you been to see Dr. Stone?" Emily ventured.

Eliza shook her head. "No. But I'll have to, though, maybe after we're done 'ere."

"No, I mean did you go see her sometime recently? The past couple of weeks or so?"

She nodded. "Yeah. Went in for a stomach ache, was heaving up my guts from some milk that'd gone off, me and three other girls got hit with it, all had it in our tea, we—"

"And what did Dr. Stone do for you?" Emily interrupted.

Eliza made a face. "Gave me some pink stuff to drink, then I ended up on the table with my legs spread open."

"Did you ask why?"

"No!" Eliza said, surprised by Emily's tone. "How many times I gotta tell you, you can't question shit around here! Sure as hell can't question the doc. She'd go nuts on ya."

"I know she would," Emily said darkly as her skin prickled at the memory of that visit. "That's part of the problem."

"Inmates!" Matron Smith barked from the doorway. "To your posts, *now*!" Her red face was a fury.

"Come on," Eliza muttered, scratching at her groin as she heaved up the bucket. "We gotta get going, or we'll be stuck mucking rat shit out of the boiler room for a week straight."

CHAPTER 26

RACHEL

July, 1986

"Ugh, I think my ass is numb," Kimberly groaned from the driver's seat of her mom's '78 Omni. Rachel laughed, shifting her own butt and stretching her legs as the breeze whipped her hair from the open window.

Both girls were home from university for the summer, and were just returning from a long-weekend trip to Toronto. They'd seen Gowan perform at the Forum and eaten their own weight in Korean food—which was difficult to come by in Bayfield. They'd stayed in a cheap twelve-room hotel in Corktown, sharing a double bed with the dresser pushed up against the door, which didn't lock properly. But the price was right.

They headed home on Monday morning, nursing bloated stomachs and mild hangovers but high on that delicious youthful sense of irresponsibility and self-focus. Rachel was once again working at Two Scoops, which wasn't glamorous, but bestowed as many hours as she wanted during the four months she had to save for tuition. She could have stayed in Windsor for the summer, maybe gotten a waitressing job with better tips and cute guys at the bar, but she'd have felt guilty not coming home to Dora. And besides, her grandmother didn't charge her rent, so she could save more than she would have been able to in the city. But the ice cream shop was starting to feel a little juvenile, and she thought next summer she might try for a job at one of the restaurants here. They were flush with tourism cash from June to September when travellers and locals descended on the beaches and the shops along the treed, picturesque Main Street.

They were just outside of town now, and Rachel's bladder was about to burst from the two large takeout coffees they'd each had to sustain them for the drive. Kim finally turned off the highway onto Main, then drove down to Rachel's street, which was lined with tall pines that mostly blocked the view of the houses and cottages.

Rachel's heart sank when she saw the car parked in her driveway, close to the small front porch no one ever used. It was a grey sedan with a rusted back-left wheel well and one door handle that didn't work. Mary's old Falcon was long gone, but she'd had this grey sedan for a few years now.

"Whose car?" Kim asked conversationally.

Rachel exhaled. "I have an idea."

Kim's head snapped over. "Is she back again?"

"I guess," Rachel muttered. She'd still not shared much with her friends about her mother's volatile lifestyle, or her illness, whatever it was. But they knew Mary came home from time to time, saw her in town. And they knew Rachel was always more on edge when Mary was around.

Mary had never shared an actual diagnosis, if she had one, though Rachel didn't know if a label would make things easier or harder. On the one hand, it might help to put a name to the condition, to read up and try to understand it better (something Dora certainly did not exhibit enough patience or interest to do). On the other, she wondered if someone like Mary might just use a diagnosis as an excuse. It was nearly impossible, as Dora had always said, to sort out what Mary *couldn't* do, and what she simply *wouldn't*. How much was genuine illness and how much was just shitty personality? Rachel wanted to have more empathy for her, but it was a struggle.

She hauled her bag out of Kim's back seat and shut the door, then leaned down and said goodbye.

"Let me know if you need anything, eh?" Kim said, eyes narrowed.

"I will," Rachel answered. She knew she wouldn't tell Kim any of what was about to transpire during her mother's visit, but appreciated the support all the same.

"Movies next week?"

"Sure. Sounds good."

Kim drove off, leaving Rachel alone with her resentment, her canvas overnight bag resting against the knee of the acid-wash jeans she'd scored on a clearance rack at Honest Ed's for three bucks after someone sloshed beer on her other ones at the concert. She stood in the laneway for a good five minutes, reluctant to go inside.

It had been a year since Mary's last visit, when they'd had their faceoff near the cliff and Rachel had implored her to explain herself. Mary had left a week later, after giving Rachel the cold shoulder for days, and Rachel concluded that she was only desirable to her mother when she didn't ask anything of her. As soon as she touched on anything meaningful or real, Mary threw up that wall of bricks she was so adept at constructing.

Rachel continued to stand in the front yard until there was no point delaying it any further. She trudged toward the house, shaking her head and wishing, for the thousandth time, that things could be different, her family life more stable. And it was, really, when it was just her and Dora. But then Mary would drop into their peace like a transient grenade and blow it all to shit, leaving Rachel and Dora to clean up the pieces. As she pulled open the screen door into the dim, cool front hall, Rachel understood why Dora sometimes shoved the metaphorical broom back at Mary with a bitter sneer, telling her she could damn well clean it up herself.

———

As the summer wore on, the three Mackenzie women once again navigated the choppy waters of cohabitation. Although she was reluctant to admit it, given the treatment she'd received from Mary during her last stay, Rachel noticed that her mother had in fact retained the more even-keeled nature she'd demonstrated before, when she'd told Rachel she "had her shit together." Rachel assumed that must translate to being medicated, and she was grateful, at least, that this visit didn't require her and Dora to play the role of unqualified psychiatric nurses ill-equipped to handle Mary's extreme depression, her erratic and destructive behaviours.

This time, though, Mary went to church with them every Sunday and stayed afterward to talk to Reverend Holland, who still seemed to express interest in her well-being. Rachel continued to attend every week for Dora's benefit, but she hadn't trusted the reverend since he'd tried to pray Mary's illness away years before. Had she told him she was on medication? What did he make of that? Rachel was sure he thought his prayers were what had finally done the trick. How often religion took the credit for what science had actually accomplished.

As for Mary, Rachel did have to admit that her mother at least mildly contributed to the household now. She'd taken to doing the dishes every night after dinner, standing at the steaming sink in her bare feet, long legs extending down from the cuffs of her tennis shorts. She had a perm now. The bleached curls were piled on top of her head, strangled by a neon-green scrunchie. She'd lost some weight since the last time Rachel had seen her, and her skin was tan and clear. She was into her forties now and looked good, really. Healthy. She'd put on the radio and sing to Def Leppard, Elton John, UB40 as she scrubbed the pots and pans—upbeat, fun stuff she'd never listened to before. And it was all because of her new boyfriend, she said. Kevin, who was (according to Mary) bright and straight-edged and sanguine, had allegedly wrought more improvement in Mary than her own family had been able to in decades of strife and struggle.

"Sometimes it just takes the right person," Mary told Rachel, smiling so genuinely that it almost made Rachel angry. She resented the implication that she and Dora were "wrong" for Mary, despite being the only two people on earth who were willing to give her one more chance again and again and again. They were the place Mary always came back to when everything was falling apart.

Rachel had been skeptical, given Mary's lies last time about a non-existent boyfriend, that "Kevin" was real. But Mary had photographic evidence this time, which she pulled out of her beaten-up brown-leather wallet to show Dora and Rachel on the very first night of her visit.

"A friend of ours took this one when we were all down at the CNE last August," she said. "That wasn't long after we met, while I was waitressing downtown."

"Toronto?"

"Yeah."

"When did you move there?" Dora asked, brow furrowed.

Mary shrugged. "I was living with a friend in Mississauga and taking the train in. Cheaper rent there, bigger tips in Toronto. It worked out."

The photo was of a group of seven people, all middle-aged, with their arms around one another's shoulders. The midway of the enormous annual fair formed the backdrop, a large Ferris wheel visible in the distance. The blue-and-red lights of the Polar Express ride they were waiting in line for glittered behind them.

It was strange for Rachel to see these images of her mother looking normal and happy. These friends were new, too. Kevin's coworkers and their wives, Mary said. "And they've all got legit jobs."

Rachel took in their straight teeth, polo shirts, and expensive sunglasses. Mary always had friends, though not in the way Rachel would have defined them. From the bits and pieces she'd learned over the years, they never stuck around long. Just like Mary. They were all fair-weather and usually connected to some temporary job Mary was working, or they were pals of the dealer who supplied her pot. They provided a couch, or cigarettes, or served as a bank when she needed a place to crash or a spot of cash to make it to payday. They weren't the kind of friends that would drive you to chemo and let you barf in their car, or tend to your paranoid delusions and mop up your tears when your depression was so bad you couldn't be bothered to feed yourself. Rachel didn't know whether Mary was even capable of identifying that sort of friend—not that she could be one herself, either, so maybe it was a fair transaction. Some relationships were just surface-level, after all. The junk-food version of human connection. Colourful and exciting and fun in the moment, but quickly digested and offering no real nourishment.

"So where is Kevin while you're here?" Dora had asked her after Mary returned the photos to her wallet.

"He takes a golf trip down to South Carolina with three of his friends every summer," Mary said, "so I thought I'd come up here for a bit while he's away. I had a fight with my roommate and my rent went up, so I got him to let me move in with him. He's got a nice house just outside the city. He works down on Bay Street. Some finance thing," she said, eyebrows raised conspiratorially. "I'll move in when he gets back."

Rachel and Dora exchanged a look of knowing surprise. Mary had learned the art of gold-digging, and was sharpening her pick.

Two weeks later, Mary still hadn't shown any signs of looking for a job, and Dora was beginning to lose patience.

"Kevin'll be back in a week anyway, Mama, and then I'll head out. No point getting a job here when I'll be leaving soon," Mary said one morning over a breakfast of Dora's signature omelettes: heavy on the ham and peppered with a secret herb blend of Dora's own creation.

"That's what you always say, and then you end up staying for weeks, or months. And you could at least cover the cost of some groceries and the damn phone bill," Dora fired back. "You've spent at least two hours on it long distance to the States, and you *will* pay for it, Mary."

But Mary shrugged, not meeting her mother's eyes. "I'll send you a cheque once I'm back at Kevin's. Relax, Mama."

Dora pressed her tongue to the inside of her cheek and glanced at Rachel, who shrugged with a *There's no point arguing her about this* look. She was sometimes keenly aware of the topsy-turvy dynamic of the house, that she and her grandmother were essentially parenting Mary alongside one another, both rolling their eyes and sighing at the irresponsibility of their charge. The mothers of Rachel's friends acted their age. They contributed to their retirement funds through hard-earned work. They gardened, cleaned, and worried for their daughters, pleaded that they not walk alone at night and call when they got somewhere. As a child, Rachel pined for a mother who would actually parent her. But now that she was grown, she just yearned for a mother who didn't need to be parented by her own child.

"And how do you know Kevin will pay for your phone bill?" Dora pressed, pouring some coffee into her own and Rachel's mugs with precision, though her eyes were still on Mary.

"Because he will. He loves me. *He* takes care of me."

Dora slammed the coffee pot down on the table with a tremulous crash. Rachel stopped chewing, eyes darting between Dora at the head of the table and Mary across from her. Rachel set her fork down carefully, silently composing the tirade she longed to throw at her mother. But Dora got there first, let her have enough vitriol for both of them.

"And we do not take care of you?" Dora snarled. "Has Kevin yet witnessed one of your mental breakdowns? Fielded midnight crisis phone calls? Has he spoon-fed you applesauce when you couldn't feed yourself? Does he *actually* know anything at all about who you are? Does he know about—"

"Mother, *stop it!*" Mary shouted, with a fear-stricken glance at Rachel. It was somehow imploring, as though she wanted or expected Rachel to take her side.

"Don't look at *me* for help!" Rachel scoffed.

"How dare you, Mary? How *dare* you?!" Dora snapped, her rage surging like a geyser. "And besides—" Her mouth contorted suddenly into a sneer, the same one Mary made when she wanted to wound, and for a moment Rachel was both reminded that they were related, and baffled that Dora had produced a woman like her mother. "What would you know about proper *care?*"

"Oh don't start, Mama! No!" Mary shot Rachel a look again, then pushed her chair back from the table with a trumpeting scrape, like an angry elephant. She made for the staircase near the front hall, then stopped and turned, a strange look on her face. The anger was gone. This was curious, calculating, which somehow frightened Rachel more than the anger.

"He'll take care of me because I'm having his baby."

Rachel's mouth fell open. "You can't be serious."

Mary didn't look at her, didn't answer.

Dora let out a little hiss. "You're forty-one years old. You can't be pregnant," she said, her voice low, like a threat.

"I *am*, Mama," Mary said.

Rachel was in a dizzying state of internal conflict. Her mother was a compulsive liar. But Kevin had turned out to be real. She was clearly on her meds. It was possible this wasn't a lie.

"Besides, celebrities are having babies at my age. It's not a big deal."

"Having a child is *always* a big deal, Mary," Dora said, clearly fighting against the anger building again in her chest. She looked at Rachel, who was watching with dismay, like she always did when Dora and Mary descended into this gladiatorial pit together.

"Well, I don't need to care what you think, Mama, because this has nothing to do with you," Mary spat. "Just leave me alone. I'll be gone in a week, and then you and Rachel can both get back to your perfect little life together without me."

"Sounds good to me," Rachel growled.

Tears filled Mary's eyes now, and Rachel didn't think they were forced. Mary turned and pounded upstairs to her bedroom, where the walls were still stubbornly papered with the posters of her teen years, unchanging and immature.

Dora and Rachel both remained seated, staring at their plates, at the half-eaten omelettes that had grown cold during the argument. Finally, Dora spoke.

"I'm so sorry you have to go through this every time, Rachel," she said, sounding defeated and resentful. Like ugly debris swept up onto the beach after a crashing wave, the drama of the fight had receded, leaving weariness in its place. "So often I wish she would just stay away. I feel awful saying it, but I do. She's exhausting."

Rachel watched her grandmother. She always looked older in these moments, her shoulders more stooped, eyes dull with fatigue. "I get it, Gran. I do." She paused. "Do you think she's really pregnant?"

"Well . . . if she actually is, she'll probably have gone off the medication. But I doubt she is."

Rachel saw the lines around her mouth deepen as she bit her lips. She was holding something back, and a chill crept up Rachel's arms despite the warmth of the kitchen, knowing both she and her grandmother were thinking of the miscarriage in the bathroom all those years ago. The one Rachel wasn't supposed to know about. The one Dora might have induced.

Dora shook her head then, not meeting Rachel's eyes. "I suppose it's possible. Though she could just be saying it to spite us." She glanced toward the staircase. "That girl never seems to run out of ways to self-destruct."

It was seven-thirty in the morning, two days after the argument, and Rachel was standing in the dim scullery off the kitchen in her tank top and pyjama bottoms as the kettle rumbled on the stovetop to her left. She'd slept poorly the past couple of nights, her dreams full of darkness, and she needed one of Dora's energizing tisanes, a blend of ginseng, ginger, holy basil, and spearmint. She'd woken to Dora already in the scullery, grinding up her own morning blend. She was now out in the yard, harvesting some herb she'd run out of.

"Something calming for Mary," she'd said. Chamomile or valerian, maybe.

Rachel reached for the jars one at a time, measuring them out with the set of silver spoons Dora kept on the counter. Rachel placed the herbs in the marble mortar and began to grind, pressing and twisting the pestle as her grandmother had taught her years ago. Dora had ground up nearly a year's supply of this particular blend for Rachel to take to school with her. It had come in handy during exam periods and the mornings after inexperienced and regrettable nights at the bar.

"What are you doing?"

Rachel jumped, the pestle knocking against the rim of the bowl with a clunk. Mary was standing in the little pocket doorway, one hand on each side of the frame. She scrutinized her daughter.

"Making tea," Rachel said, as the adrenaline drained from her hands. "I've been tired, and I have to work today. It helps with my energy."

"You shouldn't trust her with any of this shit," Mary said, scowling at the shelves of jars, the bouquets of dried lemon balm and lavender that hung upside down from the ceiling with brown twine.

"It's just tea," Rachel said, looking away from Mary and back to her hands. She finished grinding, the grumble of stone on stone unnaturally loud as Mary stood there silently, watching, like a bird of prey on a wire.

The past two days had been uncomfortable, but Mary had seemed surprisingly upbeat despite having been in tears at the end of the argument. But when Dora asked, she still maintained that she was pregnant, and Rachel had even caught her running her hand over her flat abdomen once or twice while she was watching TV. Rachel didn't really know what to do with this news. Either Mary was pregnant or she wasn't, she was lying or she wasn't, and only time would tell. Rachel was sick of trying to figure her out.

She transferred the herb blend to a small lidded Mason jar and stood awkwardly in front of Mary until she finally stepped aside to let Rachel through. A bubble of tension pressed between them. She wondered how many other girls she knew felt their mother's presence like an existential threat.

She stood at the nearby stove with the tea leaves in her favourite ceramic mug; a handmade, expensive splurge she'd picked up at one of the local summer craft sales a few years ago. It was a little chipped now, but the size and shape were perfect, and she'd bought it with her own money, which always made something feel more valuable. Rachel liked to earn her keep.

Mary was in the scullery now, looking at all the rows of jars, eyes squinted the way Rachel's got when she was working out a math problem.

"What's this?" Mary demanded a moment later, lifting a small open glass jar off the counter.

"Oh, uh, probably Gran's," Rachel said. "She was . . ." She trailed off, losing her voice as the penny dropped.

"Making me *tea?*" Mary snarled, her eyes burning, unblinking. "Did she think I wouldn't recognize this shit from last time?" She shook her head in disgust. "Always trying to 'cure' me. And the joke's on her because I'm not even pregnant! I knew she would try this. I *knew* it. I wanted to hope she wouldn't, but . . ." Her eyes were shining now, and she looked at Rachel intently.

"Mom—" Rachel was frozen in a state of wretched realization.

"She's my own mother, and I can't even trust her," Mary whispered, her eyes imploring Rachel to understand, utterly ignorant to the spectacular irony. "That fucking *witch!*" she screamed, and threw the jar to the floor where it shattered, leaves and shards flying in all directions, narrowly missing Rachel's legs.

"Mom!" Rachel shouted. "That could have cut me!"

But Mary never cared who got caught in her crossfire, didn't concern herself with who might get hurt, or who would clean up the mess afterward. That the shards of her own malevolence could lacerate someone else's skin, settling in for a lifetime of pain.

"Where is she?!" Mary screeched. She looked crazy.

"Don't, just don't!"

But Mary's eyes homed in on Dora's yellow sunhat in the gardens out back.

"Leave her alone!" Rachel begged, but Mary stormed across the kitchen and out the porch door, letting it slam behind her as the metallic rumbling in the glossy red kettle grew louder, steam issuing from the spout in a steady stream of heat that looked harmless enough, but would burn if she got too close. Inside, the water was boiling, bubbling faster and more urgently. Before she bolted after Mary, Rachel quickly lifted it off the element. She'd done this enough times to know exactly when the kettle was about to scream.

CHAPTER 27

EMILY

November–Early December, 1961
Day 140 (43 to go)

"You got the burn, too?" Maria asked quietly, holding Emily's eyes in the mirror. "No one seems able to sit down comfortably right now."

After months of dealing with her perpetually greasy and tangled shoulder-length hair, Emily had finally been called to visit the hair salon for a cut. The hairdresser, Maria, who months ago had doused every inmate's hair in gasoline in an attempt to tame the lice, only worked in the salon twice a week—in lieu of factory duty—so inmates were granted a haircut on a rotation that moved slower than molasses in a snowstorm. The prison salon consisted of one client chair that could be raised and lowered, a sink, a mirror, a comb and scissors, and a single bottle of setting spray.

Emily gnashed her teeth. The lineup outside Dr. Stone's office was getting longer by the day, and more girls were complaining about an infection in lowered tones. "Yes," she said. "I take it you don't?"

Maria shook her head, turning her focus back to Emily's cut, but she glanced at the open doorway.

"I've never seen anything like this. Even in, you know . . . my line of work. It doesn't spread around the house. Mama makes sure her girls are clean. I don't understand how it's—"

"Wait," Emily interrupted, eyes narrowing, "you're one of June Jones's girls?"

Maria nodded. "I am. That's how I got this gig," she said, snipping her scissors demonstratively. "Mama fixed it with the warden. They wouldn't give these to just anybody, you know. And it keeps me out of the factory. I hate the factory."

Emily knew Maria had been a high-end prostitute, a favourite of a few prominent politicians, but she hadn't known she was connected to June. She watched Maria bob and weave around her damp head as she snipped and clipped, considering the best way to prod her for more information. She decided to keep it light.

"I've heard she's been in a few times," Emily said. "June."

Maria nodded. "Yeah. Every time the police need to up their quota, or show somebody in government that they're cracking down on crime and prostitution." She rolled her eyes. "Filthy hypocrites. June's girls have probably bedded half the force over the years, and they always come back for more.

"Mama hates getting cycled back through here," Maria went on, "and having to leave the house to her assistant to manage. But I don't think she'd deny that getting sent here has its advantages. It's a great recruiting ground."

"Oh, wow," Emily said, with an air of benign interest. "So some of the girls in here go to work for her after?"

"Mhm." Maria nodded again, flipping her own dark hair back over her shoulder as she combed out Emily's. "One of the girls I've seen her with lately was in here before, for vagrancy, I think, but she's got a sweet little face and a nice shape. The other one's new, I guess. But they both came in with June, I saw them from here." She waved vaguely at the front doors just outside the hair salon. Emily knew which two girls Maria was talking about—she'd seen June with them almost exclusively at mealtimes. They had their factory shift together, too.

"And it's not a bad gig, you know," Maria went on. "Working in June's house."

Emily met her eyes in the mirror again as Maria reached for the can of setting spray and began to shake it. She must have seen the flash of disbelief in Emily's eyes, because she laughed, shook her head.

"I know what you're thinking," she said, "but really... the way I figure it, no matter what work I'm doing, I'm selling my body, right? Working with my hands and feet doing something like this, or other parts of me, doing... other things." She paused, and Emily thought back to her conversation with Doris about this, how they didn't think any woman would ever choose prostitution. But it sounded as though perhaps Maria had.

"Might as well work three hours a day and have Mama's protection and a room of my own in a safe house than toil in some dark factory with no protection at all, twelve hours a day, and have some foreman take what he wants from me anyway in a storage closet without paying for it."

The colour was high in her cheeks now, and Emily understood. A rush of pity hit her.

"Where did that happen to you?" she asked quietly.

"Leather factory over on Spadina. God, that place stank. I've hated the smell ever since. Can't stand it."

"I'm sorry," Emily said. She was beginning to really like Maria.

"Anyway," Maria said, taking a deep breath and gesturing that she was done with Emily's cut. "You look fab. I like shorter hair on women. Maybe not as short as Bernie's, though," she said with a chuckle.

Emily patted her strands, experienced a rare moment of vain satisfaction in her new look. It was still long enough to pin back, though, which was necessary for cleaning or meal prep. Her eyes met Maria's in the mirror as she thought back to the day Bernie had joined her and Annie at breakfast. "Do you know why Bernie keeps it so short?"

"Yes. She doesn't shy away from telling people. Anyway, if she likes her hair that short, that's fine by me. I give the girls what they want. It's about the only thing they get to choose in this place, and I figure if a woman can't even have a say over her own hair, then what's she got left?" She fluffed Emily's hair a few times with her fingers. "I wish we had a proper hair dryer, but you'll get the general idea once it air-dries, and maybe when you're out of here, you can get it properly styled."

Emily smiled politely. She wasn't one to frequent the beauty parlour for "styling." A wet comb, some pins, and a touch of her mother's spray were more her speed. "Thanks," she said, standing to leave.

"Hey." Maria held her arm, not unkindly. "I'm not sure what exactly your story is, but you seem like a smart girl. A bit plain-looking"—she took in Emily's features—"but you could be pretty enough with your makeup done right, and that new cut."

Emily tried not to feel offended. "Erm, thank you."

"My point is, if you wanted to, I think you could get in with Mama once you're out of here. She'd probably be happy to have you."

Emily suppressed a laugh. June Jones being "happy" about anything to do with her seemed about as likely as a landslide in the middle of downtown. "I don't think I'm her type," she said.

---

1 December
Dear Mom and Dad,

Things have been much the same here since my last letter. We had fresh apples in October, which had me looking forward to Mom's apple tart at Christmastime. I cannot tell you how much I miss her home-cooked meals.

I am very happy to report that after several months of dedicated effort, I have made a few friends who are keen storytellers, and I believe I have learned the lessons we had all hoped this place would impart on me, and which might benefit my future prospects. I look forward to seeing you all for Christmas in a few days' time, and regaling you with tales of my reformation.

Your loving daughter,
Emily

EARLY DECEMBER, 1961

Emily was working alongside Gertrude in the factory, feeding the boring white fabric through the machine as the others around her whirred and thunked in a clamorous mechanical chorus. Under Gert's tutelage, she'd gotten much better, and could now work faster, with fewer finger pricks and muttered curses, producing straight seams. These sheets were all for government institutions, and thus made by prisoner labour with the cheapest material available. Emily had read in the paper a couple of years before about a woman from Alberta who'd filed for a patent on an elasticized sheet that would cling right to the mattress. She didn't like to think how finicky it would be to sew those elastics into the corners, and was grateful for the government's bargain-bin approach to bedding production.

She finished the set she'd been working on, then stood to fold it, embracing the stretch for her back and arms as she walked to the long table at the front of the room, folded the sheet, and set it on the stack.

As she hurried back to her seat, she met eyes with June, two rows behind her, flanked by her two ever-present friends. June's face was impassive. She hadn't yet acted on her information about Emily's identity, and Emily was grateful. June had said she wouldn't do anything unless it gave her an advantage, so evidently, one had not yet presented itself. Emily could only hope that would hold out until her release on the nineteenth.

She was feeling an overwhelming sense of relief that the ordeal was shortly coming to a close, and also excitement. She had plenty of information for the story now, and—she thought with a little shiver of pride—much of it was similar in significance to Nellie Bly's exposition on the Blackwell's Island asylum: reprehensible treatment of inmates, revolting living conditions. The lice, vermin, and dreadful diet. Dr. Stone's barbaric pelvic exams, and the infections. The baking summer heat and lack of any actual "reform" activity. The empty classrooms half-heartedly staged, like some long-forgotten and dusty dollhouse. The one thing she still couldn't figure out, though, was why exactly Stone had infected them to begin with, just to then have to provide treatment. It made no sense.

Like Bly's exposé, this was a good story obtained in a bold way. Emily was a proper "girl stunt reporter" now, and that thought filled her with satisfaction. She smiled to herself. She could hardly wait to get back to normal life, return to the office, where she would make a name for herself and—almost certainly—receive a promotion, maybe even to a junior staff writer.

After the factory, Emily was due for what would hopefully be her last treatment in the infirmary, where Stone would sign off that her infection had cleared. Just before the bell rang to signal the end of the shift, Matron Lockheed swept into the room and over to the desk where the matron on duty sat. After a brief exchange, she stood.

"Matron Lockheed will read out some names. If your name is called, you will accompany her to the infirmary for routine examinations."

Emily's eyes snapped to the clipboard in the matron's hands.

"Irene Fox. Anna Lawrence. Louise Beaumont. With me."

Irene and Anna were June Jones's new compatriots, and Louise was one of the girls who had come over from the St. Agnes maternity home back in the summer, due to give birth any day now. She was built small like Eliza, slim little shoulders and no hips with a huge rounded belly in front. She looked like a child playing house, with a pillow stuffed beneath her shirt. No girl that age should be pregnant, and Emily didn't want to think of how her condition had come about.

"Why them?" June's voice boomed from behind. Emily turned to face her, along with most of the other women. No one else ever talked back or questioned the matrons, but somehow June always got away with it.

"None of your business, Jones," the matron on duty said. The bell rang shrilly near the door. "That's it, clean up and get a move on to your next shift, girls."

Emily swept up the errant white threads on her workstation, set the thimble and measuring tape in the little tray beside the machine, and got in the queue to return her scissors to the matron, who checked off each inmate's name before they were allowed to leave the room.

Outside in the hallway, Emily ducked into the bathroom to pee as she puzzled over June's reaction to her girls getting called to the infirmary. She washed her hands, then made her way quickly upstairs to the second floor. June, Anna, and Irene were right at the front of the line outside the infirmary door.

Emily took her place at the back. The little Louise came up the stairs a moment later, clutching the railing for support. She paused at the top to catch her breath, belly heaving, before falling into line behind Emily, who offered her a small smile. Emily felt she should say something comforting, but she had no idea what.

She turned again to face the front, leaning one shoulder on the brick wall. Noise from the floor below was drifting up the stairwell. A psych prisoner shouted something from down the hall. Emily wondered what serene silence would feel like, and savoured the idea that it was coming.

The infirmary door opened, and Emily straightened, alert. She strained to see around the heads of the women in front of her. June was at the front, saying something to the matron. She went in, and the door shut with a snap.

Not five minutes later, it opened again, and June sidled out, her face inscrutable.

"Lawrence, Fox, out of line," the matron said. "Report to your next shift. The doctor doesn't need to see you."

Emily sidestepped the girl in front of her for a better view. Irene and Anna smirked at June, who winked almost imperceptibly. Without another word, they scurried off together toward the staircase in June's wide wake.

It wasn't until Emily was prone on the infirmary table, preparing herself as Dr. Stone's face disappeared behind the tent of her legs, that the pieces of what she had just witnessed finally fell into place, jolting her like a car crash.

———

All through supper that night, Emily tried to engage in conversation with her friends, but her eyes kept roving over to June Jones, Anna, and Irene.

The three were laughing together as they finished their bland shepherd's pie. The dish was mostly potato—mashed with water instead of butter—with a thin layer of beef along the bottom and a sad measure of canned peas sprinkled throughout. Emily had smothered hers in salt and pepper in an attempt to revive it, thinking longingly of her mother's version.

Not long now, she told herself.

After supper, she found Annie and they headed upstairs together. Emily had lost track of June on the way out of the dining hall, but soon spotted her on the staircase up to the third floor, where the common room was. June liked a good time, and often held court at the card table of an evening, playing rummy and Go Fish. Emily strongly suspected that the madam could hold her own at poker like any male card sharp, but settled for easier games in the absence of other inmates who knew how to play.

"Common room tonight?" Emily asked Annie with a smile. The psychiatric inmates who ate with the general population were also permitted time in the common room on Tuesdays and Fridays. Annie nodded.

June was indeed there, playing solitaire this time as her companions gossiped at a table nearby. She looked up as Emily and Annie passed, but made no comment, turning back to her game as the other two found a pair of chairs near the pitiful little library shelf, just a dozen battered cast-offs from the local library branch and some churches.

Foot jiggling in anticipation, Emily waited until the room filled up more—the collective noise causing everyone to raise their voices to be heard over the din—before she made her move.

"I'll be back in a few," she told Annie, standing. "I just need to go talk to someone for a minute."

"Who?" Annie asked, looking mildly hurt at being abandoned.

"June Jones."

Annie stared. "The . . . *madam*? Why? You're not . . . ?" She gaped a little in horror at Emily.

"No, goodness, no. It's nothing like that," Emily said. "It's for . . . you know. My *project*. I'll be right back."

"Emily—"

But Emily stood, a prickle of guilt tickling her gut as she turned away from Annie and walked casually over to June. She paused, then sat down across from her in the empty chair. June looked up slowly, glowered at her with a defiance laced with something like amusement. "What do you want?"

Emily leaned forward. "Did you pay off Stone to leave your girls alone?"

For the first time, she saw discomfort flash in the madam's face, a crinkle of a frown around her mouth.

"She's infecting inmates with VD," Emily said confidently. "I can't imagine that would be good for your business, if your girls brought it back to the house." She spat out the last bit, watching to see if shock or doubt would cross June's face, but she saw none. There was, however, an icy sheen to her eyes.

"Outside," June said, setting down her cards with a snap and standing. Emily followed her out of the room, down the deserted hall and around a corner, stopping just beside the stairwell. After making sure no one was around, June turned to face her.

"I think you know," Emily accused before June could speak. "You *know* what Stone's doing and you've gotten your girls exempted from the infection. How? And why is Stone doing it?"

"Kid," June said with a sardonic smile. "Sometimes you seem real smart. And then you ask stupid questions like that. Why does anyone do anything? *Money*," she said. "It's always about money."

Emily's eyes widened, mind racing. "So someone's *paying* her? To infect the inmates? But why?" She thought of the endless queues, all the girls who worriedly compared experiences on the lancing and the stinging sprays, the pain.

"And then . . . to *treat* them." Emily's brow crinkled. "Why? And how did you find out?"

June actually rolled her eyes. "I come back here after a summer away, and all of a sudden half the population's got VD? What, these girls are all rubbing up on each other in the breakfast line?" She scoffed. "I knew there was more to it than that."

"So Stone is getting paid to treat us?" Emily pressed.

June looked at Emily as though weary of reprimanding a disobedient puppy. "Well, I've never seen those aerosols she's got now, I'll tell ya that. I know VD, the usual treatments, and I've never seen whatever that stuff is."

Emily recalled the label on the can.

Trichloroacetic acid – trial preparation.

"So it's new?" Emily asked, more to herself than June. "Then . . ." The penny dropped with a clink. "She's *testing* it. A drug trial. Right?"

June licked her lips, but didn't answer.

"For whom?" Emily demanded. "Why is she doing it?"

But June was already backing away. "Jesus, honey," she said. "I've never heard anybody ask that question as much as you do. You're the only one who gives a shit *why*. What did I just tell you?"

Emily watched her as she began to stride slowly backward down the dimly lit hall, big hips swaying beneath her faded brown dress.

"Money," Emily said.

The ghost of a smile flitted across June's face. "Gotta get that money, honey!"

As she backed away, another thought flashed for Emily. "And why is she so vicious? What's going on there?"

June's eyes narrowed and she shook her head. "That one's got nothing to do with money. And I'd advise you not to dig too deep on it, reporter lady. She's dangerous."

Emily took a step toward June. "Will you help me with this?"

June's red eyebrow arced. "I thought I just did."

She disappeared around the corner and for a fleeting moment, Emily wondered why she was being so forthright. But then she remembered that June could expose her at any moment, get her thrown out of the prison—or worse. Emily might have sussed out June's under-the-table accord with the doctor, but if it were to get out, it wouldn't be the madam suffering for the bribe—it would be Dr. Stone. Emily gave a half laugh. June didn't need to care how much Emily knew. She still held the cards, and that was all that mattered to her.

What is going on in that office? Emily wondered, her mind jumping ahead to what lay beyond Stone's door, right beneath her feet on the floor below. There had to be a paper trail of some kind for this drug trial, whatever it was. Or at least enough detail to fit the pieces together with some accuracy. Enough for the story.

A shiver skipped down Emily's body, goosebumps erupted on her bare arms.

The *better* story. The *real* story. The one she'd had no idea was even lurking beneath the surface of all the truths of the whistleblowing inmate's note.

If Eris Stone was not only abusive but actually *corrupt*, that was the real scoop. And—another tingle crept from the back of her neck downward—if the corruption led back to the government's front door, for funding a vermin-infested, dilapidated institution where women were subjected to this kind of horrific abuse for *profit* . . . that was headline, national news.

But this wasn't just about Emily's career anymore. This wasn't about a promotion or an office with a window, her name in the byline. It wasn't even about escaping a marriage she didn't want in favour of the life she did. This was about her existence as a woman, and Annie's and Eliza's and all the girls who were imprisoned here—or could be—because of that law. She'd come to know them now, knew that they had lives and dreams that were constantly overshadowed and ruined by the fear of living in this system where women could be imprisoned and abused and even tortured on the government's dime.

Fire burned in her gut. She needed to break this story. For all of them. It was a moral imperative now.

She needed to see the patient files, Dr. Stone's personal records. Anything concrete she could get her hands on to prove the drug trial, the abuse of power.

She needed to break into Stone's office.

PART THREE

intolerable

(Adj.: unendurable;
insufferable)

I am no longer accepting
the things I cannot change.
I am changing the things
I cannot accept.

ATTRIBUTED TO ANGELA DAVIS

CHAPTER 28

EMILY

December 15, 1961
Day 179 (4 to go)

Emily was feeling the pressure. There were only a few days left in her sentence, and she still had to gain access to Dr. Stone's files, or all of June's claims of bribery and Emily's own deductions about the doctor deliberately infecting the women were nothing but hearsay and suspicion. She needed facts. Her infection had cleared and she was due for release on time. She hoped she wouldn't need more, but if it came down to the wire, her plan was to try to find some way to convince Stone that she felt the warts returning, or had burning of some kind that wasn't visible. If she had to swap another couple of weeks of painful treatments to get everything she needed for this new, bigger story, she would. If she were able to secure the evidence she needed, she could lay bare all of Stone's corruption. The power was about to shift drastically in Emily's favour, and it would feel sweet.

But she needed to get her hands on the evidence before she could indulge that fantasy. She had an idea for how to accomplish that now, and had woken early, keen to get on with it. She was eager for work today, since she would be on shift with Eliza.

Annie wasn't in the dining hall, which made Emily nervous. But perhaps she was ill; seasonal colds and flus were circulating now. Hopefully she would make an appearance at dinner or supper. Emily sat down instead with Gert, Lizzie, and Peggy. As Emily hurriedly ate, Eliza arrived with her tray, and Emily greeted her with a warm smile. Once they were in the narrow corridors and shadowy corners of the basement, she was going to ask Eliza for her help.

"Where's your nutty Blue friend?" Eliza asked, swallowing a huge bite of toast before washing it down with milk. Emily sometimes forgot that she was a teenager, and had the insatiable appetite of one, along with the accompanying underdeveloped sense of empathy. Emily bit her tongue, refraining from any admonishment. She needed Eliza primed to cooperate with her. "I'm not sure, actually," she said. "Perhaps she's feeling unwell."

"Isn't she unwell every day?" Eliza snarked.

"I heard Matron Carnegie talking to her when I was passing the psych wing," Gertrude said quietly, shooting Emily a look. Her eyelids drooped a little in sympathy. "She had electroshock yesterday, and it sounds like she didn't handle it well. Carnegie was trying to soothe her." Gertrude shrugged.

Emily was aghast. Annie hated the electroshock, and it hadn't done her any good. Yet Stone was once again subjecting her to it. But Emily suppressed her outrage for the moment. She had a plan to deal with Stone.

Later that afternoon, she and Eliza were finishing cleaning duty in the basement. Over by the boiler, Eliza did a half squat and wiggled her bum back and forth, discomfort pinching her strawberry-blond brow. "Goddamnit," she muttered.

Emily saw the opportunity, and pounced. "Is that feeling any better yet?" she asked softly, nodding discreetly in the direction of Eliza's lower half.

"Hardly," Eliza said with an aggravated sigh. She ducked her head behind a large hot-water tank to sweep in behind. "Ugh!" she shrieked a heartbeat later, scrambling back toward Emily. "There's a nest!"

As she backed away, Emily couldn't stop the squeal that issued from her mouth as one large and three smaller dark-brown rats darted past their feet and out of the boiler room, silky tails disappearing beyond the rusted metal door frame.

"This place is disgusting," Emily said, revolted. "I can't believe they make us do things like this."

Eliza didn't answer; she just continued to scrunch up her face. Emily gave her a pitying sort of look. "Had a treatment yesterday," Eliza explained. "It's always worse after, then gets a bit better. Was it the same fer you?"

Emily nodded.

"And now yers is gone?"

"Yes. Mostly, anyway. My treatments are done, thank God." She paused, leaned on her broom. This was her moment. "I hate this place, don't you?"

Eliza was silent for a moment, then swallowed. "Yeah. But there's rats everywhere. Had 'em in our shitty little flat in Cabbagetown, too. At least here, they stay in the basement. In that flat they used to come up to the kitchen and get into the pantry in the middle o' the night. There'd be holes in the oatmeal bags and feckin' droppings on the floor. Then Da'd scream at Mam like it was 'er fault."

Emily watched her, feeling her chances of success draining away. Eliza still believed the Mercer was better than being back in her parents' home. And perhaps it truly was. But Emily gathered her determination and pushed on. Their uninterrupted time together was limited—and the noise from the boiler muted their conversation.

"Listen, Eliza," Emily said urgently, "I need to tell you something." She paused, heart hammering. It felt dangerous to expose herself to someone as fickle as Eliza, but at this point, it was worth the risk. She was so close to the end of her sentence, so close to scooping this story, and she needed this girl's help.

"I'm a reporter," she said. "With a magazine."

Eliza blinked at her in the yellowish light of the bare overhead bulb with eyes far older than her years. "What?"

Emily took her in, how small she was, how young. She would need to phrase all of this simply. "I'm a reporter, I work for the news. I got put in here on purpose to get information about how the women are treated. I'm writing an article on it, so people will know how bad things are here."

"What?" Eliza asked again. "Wait, yer not incorrigible?"

She said it so earnestly that Emily nearly smiled. "Well, technically yes. My dad told a judge I was unmanageable so that I could get into the prison."

"But you didn't do anythin' wrong?"

"No. But I think the same can be said for most of the women in here," Emily added gravely.

"So you been lyin' to us all? This whole time?" Her brows knitted in offence.

Emily nodded, surprised by the guilt she felt. "In a way, yes. I couldn't tell anyone what I was doing."

Eliza stepped sideways and squinted, as though trying to see Emily better.

"And why you tellin' me?"

"Because I need your help," Emily said sincerely.

Eliza crossed her arms. "Why?" The boiler hissed behind her.

Emily took a step closer to Eliza, and chose her words simply. "Listen to me: You have VD because Dr. Stone infected you on purpose. She did it to loads of us."

"Why in the hell would she do that?" Eliza exclaimed, looking at Emily like she was crazy.

"Well, that's the question. I think someone was paying her to do it," Emily said, "but I need evidence. Proof." She took a deep breath. "I need you to break into her office and steal any papers that might tell us why she did it."

Eliza's mouth fell open. "Break into Stone's office? You *are* loony. You know what'd happen if I got caught?"

"I didn't think you minded getting caught?" Emily challenged.

"Well, yeah, when I know I'm headed back here for a bed and three meals a day. Not when I think Stone might chuck me down 'ere with the rats fer a month, or give me a beatin' fer nickin' shit from 'er office! Are you mad? Why would you want a mess with that witch?"

"Because, Eliza." Emily took a step toward her again, feeling harried with desperation and urgency. They didn't have much time left. They still had to actually finish the cleaning before the end of their shift, or risk punishment she didn't have time for. "My job as a reporter is to expose the truth. The treatment of the women here is awful, and people need to know about it."

"Who?" Eliza scoffed. "Who needs to know? Who's gonna give a rat's arse what happens to us?"

Emily swallowed, thinking of how June Jones had said nearly the same thing. These women were so used to being ignored and forgotten when they weren't being punished and shamed. They'd internalized it to the point where the idea of anyone in power caring about their quality of life, or whether they lived or died at all, was not only foreign, but ludicrous.

"I told you before, Em—" Eliza paused. "Is that even yer real name?" Emily nodded. "I told you before, I got a better deal here than anywhere. I need to stay til I turn eighteen, then I can skip the province, or go somewhere else entirely. Maybe even back to Ireland, I dunno. Anyway, I can't help you. I won't spill yer secret, but I can't help." She looked away from Emily and made to sidestep toward the boiler room door. "Now let's—"

"What would you do if you went somewhere else?" Emily asked, scrambling for another tack.

Eliza shrugged. "I dunno. Clean? I'm good at cleaning and it's not something rich folks like to do. There's always work."

A flash of an idea occurred. "If you do this, when you get out, you can come live with me for a while," Emily said. "I can teach you things, how to type and read, so you can get a secretary's job."

Eliza rolled her eyes. "Right. And your old man and lady are gonna be right pleased to have a little thief living under their roof, are they?" She smiled bitterly. "Come off it. I inn't that stupid."

"I wouldn't tell them you're—"

"And *typing?* That might be *yer* life, writin' for papers, but it's not mine." Eliza shook her head. "I like you, Em, but you and I inn't the same. You can't offer me any better'n what I got here. I got nobody lookin' out fer me. So I hafta look after meself. And part of that," she said forcefully, "is getting this bloody basement clean before they skin our feckin' hides."

Then she slipped away before Emily could say another word, leaving her standing alone and defeated beneath the bare overhead bulb as the boiler hissed once more.

"You," June Jones barked. "I need to talk to you."

From her usual spot at the isolated breakfast table with Annie, Emily's brow furrowed. June loomed over her, mouth pinched so tight it looked as though she was struggling not to scream aloud.

"Uh," Emily said, wondering what on earth she could have done to aggravate the madam this time. "Sure. All right." She gestured for June to sit beside her, but June shook her head.

"In private," she said, glancing at Annie, who looked exasperated.

"I'll be right back," Emily told her, rising.

"Emily!" Annie protested. "*Why* do you keep—"

"I won't be long," Emily promised. She hated the way Annie looked at her as she followed June out of the dining hall, as though she were being led off to the brothel.

Emily followed June past the matrons—who didn't stop them, Emily noticed—into the currently empty Classroom 2, and June shut the heavy metal door behind them, sealing out the ambient noise from the dining hall and corridors before looking at Emily square on.

"Do you pay off the matrons, too?" Emily asked, only barely sarcastic.

June ignored the comment and exhaled, infusing Emily's lungs with the stale stench of cigarettes. They were contraband, but somehow it didn't surprise her that June had managed to get herself excused from rules the rest of the inmates were bound to.

"Stone's no use to me anymore," June said baldly. "So I've decided it's time to help you with your story."

Emily's heart leapt. She'd been expecting some sort of reprimand or threat, not this. "Are you serious? Why? What's changed?"

June chewed her upper lip and was silent for a moment, regarding

Emily. "I was paying her to leave my girls alone, like you said," she admitted. "The two that came in here with me are promising, the men like 'em a lot. I got to keep 'em clean. And that racket Stone's got going on . . ." She paused. "Anyway, she named a price and I paid it and now she's gone and doubled it, the bitch. I can't pay it, and I'm not one for a shakedown, either way. Doesn't sit well with me, you know what I mean?"

Emily nodded. She'd never been extorted, but could imagine how a woman like June would react to it. She paused, then decided to squeeze more information out of the crack that had just appeared in June's armour. "What happened between you?" she asked. "Why the change in your arrangement?"

June let out something like a growl. "Nothing to do with me. She just needs more money. Trying to fix all her brother's bullshit, the fool."

"What . . . bullshit?" Emily pressed, the unfamiliar curse awkward in her mouth.

"Oh Christ," June swore. "See? That didn't kill you, did it?" She laughed, shoved Emily playfully in the shoulder. "Anyway, Stone's brother's a drunken louse, gambles away the family's money—including her inheritance—even comes into my place every so often. She's been trying to keep the collectors at bay for years, so she's been taking these kickbacks from the drug companies for testing their medicines on the girls here. That's why she was so easy to bribe. Needs the cash. I told you, it's all about the money."

Emily was reeling. "But—how did you find this out?"

June scoffed. "God, you got a lot to learn, kid. You gotta get out there more, understand how things work. How *people* work. You want to get the real measure of a woman, get her drunk on cheap wine and she'll spill her guts like roadkill."

Emily blanched at the imagery.

"Oh don't look so shocked. Anyway, Stone's adamant on her price, thinks she can get away with it because she doesn't know I've got you up my sleeve." Her lips twisted, smug but hostile. Emily had known June Jones was not a woman to cross, but seeing her ire on display was still disquieting. "And the truth is, Stone is a nut. A psycho. Belongs in there with the Blues. So maybe your way *is* the only way to make this all stop." She searched Emily's face. "So what do you need? I can back you up about her taking my bribes to keep my girls out of the trial. But I'm done with her. She's got to go down."

The bell rang shrilly on the wall above their heads, and Emily startled. June didn't.

"The problem is, I'm going to need more than your word on the kickbacks," Emily said. "The bribery is one thing, but that will still be your word against hers, I'm afraid." *The word of a brothel madam.*

June opened her mouth to protest, but Emily cut across her. "I need actual evidence of the kickbacks for this to stick. There must be some kind of paper trail in her office. Patient files, something. I need to get in there to find it." Her pulse was racing. "I approached Eliza about this, told her who I really am." June's eyebrows popped. "She's a thief, a repeat offender. I'm sure she could be of great use if she were willing, but she's not."

"Why not?"

"She claims this place is better than her home, and from what she's told me, she may be right," Emily said with defeat. "She wants to stay in here as long as possible."

"Well, we gotta offer her something better, then. An incentive."

For a woman with no education, Emily was continually impressed by June's vocabulary and cleverness. She was evidently intelligent.

"I tried," Emily said. "I told her she could come stay with me for a while."

June frowned. "Mmm. Didn't work, did it?"

"No."

"That's because you don't know that girl."

Emily was stung. "I've been her friend since—"

"But I think I might," June continued. "I've got an idea. Meet me in the recreation room after supper."

And before Emily could respond, June swept out into the hall.

CHAPTER 29

EMILY

December 15, 1961
Day 179 (4 to go)

Around seven-thirty, Emily and June found Eliza in the noisy recreation room, where she was playing cribbage with another inmate.

Eliza looked up from her game to see Emily and June standing over her. She made a face so irritable that Emily nearly laughed. As much as Eliza's lot in life had forced her to grow up early and fast, sometimes her petulance betrayed her immaturity. Though Emily knew it would infuriate her to know that.

"Need to talk to you for a minute, kid," June said in a tone that left little room for argument. Eliza rolled her eyes, but set down her cards without sparing a glance at her opponent and stood, leading them out of the room. Emily followed June, in awe of her ability to convey her authority like that. It was a brand of confidence Emily could only aspire to, and she wondered whether it was innate or learned; if she herself could ever move through the world the way June and—in an undeniably more collegial way—Doris Anderson did. They both seemed cut from a cloth that was usually reserved for the creation of men, not women. A fabric woven from entitlement and inborn self-assurance on a great loom constructed eons ago, exclusively for Adam's sons.

The sounds of harsh, competitive laughter and rattling Yahtzee dice faded as they entered the cool hallway. The three women turned a corner at the end of the hall, and Eliza pulled up short beside a row of empty cells, entering one that must be hers. Emily glanced around, but they were mostly alone. Nearly everyone would be in the rec room or waiting in the queue for their revolting bath at this hour.

"So this one knows, too?" Eliza directed at Emily the moment they were over the threshold. She flicked her chin at June.

"She does," Emily said.

"Well, yer not gonna strong-arm me," Eliza said to June. "I already told Emily no. It inn't worth gettin' caught. I'm not spendin' a month in the hole when there's nothin' in it fer me 'sides endin' back up in me da's house, or on the bleedin' street."

Emily was growing uncomfortable. She needed Eliza's help, yes, but didn't want to force her, because that would likely backfire anyway. Eliza had to be willing.

"I know that," June told her, and her tone was softer now. "Because I've been there, kid. My mama was a whore. I was on the street as long as I can remember. She got me to school during the day sometimes until I was eight, then . . ." Emily glanced at June, who was blinking rapidly. "She ended up in a bad brothel, and the pimp there took advantage of me." She paused, and Emily's stomach twisted. "I know a girl like you needs protection," she told Eliza. "Grown women do, too. That's why I run my place the way I do. 'Cause whoring is all some women can do to feed themselves in this man's world, and they deserve not to die for doing what they need to do."

Eliza stared at June, and Emily saw a glint of a tear forming in the corner of her eye.

"If you do this for us," June continued, "I'll give you a job. You don't have to go back home, and you don't have to be on the street, either."

"I don't wanna be a—"

"As a *maid*," June clarified. "You're a thorough cleaner, Emily says. You come clean my place, do some cooking and dishes and the like, you can have an attic room to yourself. It's small, but it'll be your own."

Emily watched June with fascination. She did seem to understand Eliza, how to woo her.

Eliza's mouth was tight, eyes still locked on the madam. "I don't want any men comin' at me," she said firmly.

June nodded. "They won't touch you. I'll make sure they know you're off-limits. I promise. Those men pay good money for my girls; they know not to cross Mama, or they'll never be let in my place again, and they'll have to take their chances with the dirty street whores. You'll be safe."

Eliza shifted her feet, exhaled. "But I could get some cleaning job someplace else, there's lotsa—"

"Who's gonna hire a little thief, a jailbird, to clean their nice big house?" June challenged. "Nobody. Sorry, kid. But you come work for me and I'll give you a chance. Don't steal from me, my girls, or clients, and I'll be true to my word. I'll give you a place where you've got some protection until you're grown, then, well . . . what you do then is up to you. But I know at your age, I would have traded my left arm for the deal I'm offering you now."

Eliza's gaze darted between Emily and June. They waited.

"How big's this attic? It have a window?" Eliza demanded.

June let out a snort. "Big enough for a bed and dresser and a bit of room to move. And yes, there's a window. And a lock on the door."

"You got meat in yer icebox?"

"Yes."

"Rats?"

"Only in the alleyway behind."

Eliza scrutinized June, creases of suspicion streaking her forehead. "All right. I'll do it," she said finally, looking at Emily. "When?"

Emily's heart leapt. "As soon as possible."

"Show us what you got, then, kid," June said, her large arms akimbo. Emily might have blanched under the intensity of June's stare, but Eliza seemed to rise to it, like a sunflower trying to prove how high it could stretch its stem.

"Well, what is it exactly that ye need?" she asked, looking skeptical.

Emily filled her in on the details, that they needed to find proof of the drug trial in Stone's personal files.

"All right," Eliza said. She studied the floor for a moment as the distant sounds of the recreation room's chatter floated down the hall. They still had a little time before lights out.

"There's really only a coupla ways to do this," Eliza said thoughtfully. Emily could see the gears turning in that strawberry-blond head of hers. "The first way would be to try to bribe or blackmail one of the infirmary matrons to nick it fer us."

Emily looked at June, who was already shaking her head. "That opens us up to risk even more," Emily said. "Enough people already know who I am and why I'm here. I don't fancy having to pay off a matron to keep quiet about it."

"We came to you because theft is the most straightforward method," June said.

"I know!" Eliza scowled, defensive. "I was gettin' to that. I do think stealing is the way to go."

"How will you do it?" June pressed.

A thought suddenly occurred to Emily and her heart sank. "Eliza," she said, "are you even good at stealing things? You told me you *try* to get caught to get sent back here. Do you even—"

"Yeah! 'Cept tryin' to get caught means I know how to trip those wires! If I know how to trip 'em, I know what they are and how to avoid 'em, too! Jeez, I ain't a total fool."

Emily raised her hands in surrender as June's lip twitched. "Sorry," Emily muttered. "Go ahead."

Eliza appeared even more determined after Emily's doubtful inquiry. "It's gotta be at a time when Stone ain't in the office," she said. "Not worth the risk tryna get 'er outta there. So that's a night after she's left, or a weekend." She looked at Emily, then June, who both nodded in agreement. "We'd either need the keys, or I can pick the lock on 'er office. But we'd need to draw the night matron away. Some sorta distraction or disturbance or some such."

Emily thought for a moment. "Have either of you ever spent the night in the infirmary? Do you know whether the night matron stays awake or sleeps?"

"No, I haven't," June said.

"Me either," Eliza agreed.

"Well, if she sleeps," Emily mused, "maybe we could get admitted to the infirmary overnight, then steal the documents quietly?"

"And what if she doesn't sleep?" June posed.

"Drug 'er?" Eliza suggested.

Emily frowned. "I don't like the idea of having to assault someone in this process."

"I think a diversion's the way to go," June said. She inhaled, her large bosom rising. "I can take care of that. Something in the recreation room, or downstairs. A fight of some kind."

"Big enough to draw *all* the matrons?" Emily asked.

"There are fewer of them after supper, you know that," June said. Emily was silent. In truth, she hadn't noticed that, but hoped June was right. She'd been in and out of the Mercer repeatedly, after all. Few women knew the place so well. "If there's enough of a fuss, they'll set off the alarm, and then they all come as a matter of policy."

"How do you know that?"

"'Cause there's been riots before," Eliza said.

"Really? When?" This was the first time Emily had heard of it.

"Last summer there was one," June told her. "Got so goddamn hot in here we could hardly breathe. Had a big riot in the dining hall til they called the cops so we could show them how hot it was, get 'em to do something about it."

"And did they?"

Eliza scoffed, and June glared at Emily. "What do you think, reporter lady?"

Emily's anger burned. "The police came in here, felt the heat, saw the conditions, and did nothing?"

"You got it."

And Emily finally understood; despite her willingness to help bring down Stone, this was why June doubted Emily's ability to effect any real change. If the police had seen this with their own eyes, and still hadn't done anything about it . . . what chance did some article in a women's magazine have?

"You didn't tell me that," Emily said, trying not to sound accusatory.

"Why would I?" June snarled. "But Stone wasn't testing drugs on us a year ago, so things have changed. If the cops don't give a shit, we gotta make noise some other way, and right now, you're the only noisemaker we've got. God help us."

Eliza was watching them with a keen eye. "Back to the plan, then," she said.

Emily swallowed hard, shoving away the doubt that had crept into her vision.

"She have drawers or somethin' where this stuff's gonna be?"

"Yes," June said. "There's a filing cabinet beside her desk. Patient files and other papers, too, I'm sure."

"How you know that?" Eliza frowned.

"'Cause I've been in there," June answered, one eyebrow raised as though daring Eliza to challenge her again. She didn't.

"How much time do you need to pick two locks?" Emily asked. "And what supplies?"

"Not long," Eliza said, "unless it's somethin' fancy I ain't never seen. And just a paper clip or somethin'." Emily nodded. Those were easily sourced, even at the prison.

"So are we doing this in the evening, or overnight?" June asked. "'Cause I think evening, when the girls are all out of their cells. Creates more chaos in the diversion."

Emily thought for a moment, but Eliza leapt in. "Yeah. You get all the matrons away to the rec room or dining hall or somewhere, and Emily and I can wait down the hall from the infirmary. When the night matron comes out, we go in. Doubt she'll lock the door if she's leavin' in a hurry. If she does, I can get in. It's not even a deadbolt, that one. Easy."

Emily felt a smile forming despite herself. "Could you get yourself out of your own cell, Eliza?" she asked.

Eliza straightened. "'Course I can! But I told ya, I don't want outta here, do I? Nice to know I could get out if I wanted to, though."

June laughed this time, a low rumble of a thing. "You're starting to grow on me, kid."

Emily saw the colour rise in Eliza's cheeks. Something told her Eliza would be happy at June's, and that brought her a surprising sense of comfort.

"Okay." Emily considered the stages of the plan in formation, her mind darting ahead, looking for tripwires. "What if there are girls in the infirmary overnight?" She directed the question at Eliza, their little mastermind. "If we get in when the matron runs out, what do we do about anyone else in there? That's a possibility we can't control."

Eliza ran her tongue over her teeth and shrugged. "Sometimes there's people around ya don't expect. Like you say, can't control it all, even with a good plan."

"So what do we do in that case?" Emily asked.

Eliza cocked her head to the side and surveyed Emily with a frown. "You say you got yerself sent to prison so's you could get a story, eh? What was *yer* plan?"

Emily was speechless, taken aback. Eliza waited, still frowning. June's eyes were on her, too.

"I suppose . . ." She tapped her thigh with a nervous finger. "I knew I needed to get in here. I didn't think much beyond that."

"Why not?"

Emily swallowed. "I didn't know what to expect. I figured I'd just have to take things as they came."

"Right," Eliza said, looking at Emily as though she were simple. "Half a succeedin' in somethin' is just flat believin' ye can do't. We need to get this shit outta Stone's office, so we will."

A wry smile crept across Emily's face as Nellie Bly's refrain echoed in her head once more.

I said I could, and I would.

CHAPTER 30

EMILY

December 17, 1961
Day 181 (2 to go)

Emily's nerves were on edge as she sat in the dining hall with Annie, pushing food around her plate as her stomach swirled. After giving the idea and plan a day to settle, Emily, June, and Eliza had decided to execute their plan that night. Dr. Stone left by six in the evening every day, around the time supper began for the inmates. After that, it was recreation and bath time until nine. The plan was straightforward enough: around eight, June would provoke a fight between two of the most aggressive inmates she could lay eyes on—Thelma at the top of her list—either in the recreation room or the third-floor corridors. Eliza and Emily would lurk in conversation near the stairwell on the second floor and listen for the commotion. June's goal was to create enough of a tussle for the attending matrons to whistle for backup. It was easy enough to goad others into fights, June claimed, especially in a place where no one felt like they had enough. All you had to do was tell someone her neighbour had received special treatment, or stolen something. It wasn't ethical, but Emily had agreed to it, weighing the cost against the ultimate benefit.

"Are you quite all right, Emily?" Annie asked her before lifting her tin cup to her lips. "You've hardly said a word all meal. Unusual for you." She smiled fondly.

Emily forced a smile. "I'm all right," she told her friend. "Just tired, is all. It was a rough cleaning shift today and I didn't sleep well last night." She hated to be disingenuous with Annie, but she didn't have a choice. Because the plot involved June, whom Annie still believed was a terrible influence on any girl who crossed the madam's path, it would be easier to fill Annie in on their exploits once they had actually—hopefully—succeeded.

"I'm sorry to hear that," Annie said.

"How are you?" Emily asked, changing the subject. "You seem bright today."

"Well," Annie said, "I meant to tell you; I've found myself with more energy and a clearer mind than ever since Dr. Stone stopped the electrotherapy a few days ago. And that drug she's got me on now . . . Ip—Iproniazid? I think that's what it's called . . . It's fairly new, she says, but I think it's helping. I really do."

Emily studied Annie. This latest medication *did* seem to be having a positive effect on Annie's nervous debility. Would Stone allow her to stay on it? If it did indeed bear such a positive result in her behaviour, there would be no further justification at all for her continued incarceration. But then, Emily thought with a surge of anger, there was no option or mechanism for Annie to plead her own case for discharge. Annie's life and liberty were utterly at Dr. Stone's mercy.

The end-of-meal bell clanged and the usual deafening scrape of chairs sounded as a hundred and twenty women stood to head off to their pointless pursuits. She and Annie exited the hall with the chattering swarm. They inched forward in the crowd until it began to thin out as the bodies moved off in different directions. Annie was dragging her feet as they approached the psychiatric wing. It was her bath day, something Emily knew she wasn't looking forward to. The psych prisoners had their own bathroom at the end of the wing; it was smaller than the regular prison population's bathrooms, but the experience was even more unpleasant. There was never any warm water, Annie said, even for the first bath of the day. The matrons ran it cold, saying the Blues were too deep in their insanity to even notice water temperature, and couldn't truly appreciate creature comforts of any kind. The more violent psych inmates were wrestled, screaming and sometimes bound, into the large copper tub and scrubbed with a horsehair brush until their skin nearly bled. Annie, at least, was spared the worst of that sort of treatment, as she was able to clean her own skin with a bar of soap without incident.

Inmates weren't supposed to touch one another, so Emily didn't embrace Annie as she left her at the gates of the wing, but she wanted to. There was a chance that Emily would be caught during the course of the burglary that night, and she assumed that would precipitate her immediate unmasking and ejection from the prison. This could possibly be the last time she saw Annie, though she hoped, for several reasons, that that wouldn't be the case. If tonight's mission was successful, she might just have enough evidence against Stone to have the dreadful woman removed from the Mercer entirely. With Stone gone and the administration under review, Annie might stand a better chance for release, and Emily would vouch for her in whatever way she could.

She did her best to focus now on the task ahead. She was excited, in a way, at the thrill of doing something so daring. At any rate, the decision was made, and the thing had to be done.

―

At eight o'clock that night, Emily lingered around the corner from the infirmary in a spot that allowed her to see both the psych-wing gate and the entrance to the inmates' bathroom at the far end of the south corridor. It wasn't busy; most of the inmates were now in a tidy line for the bath or had made their way upstairs to the recreation room. Emily could already hear the noise on the floor above. She soon spotted Eliza coming downstairs from her third-floor cell. The girl skittered up to Emily with those short strides of hers, running her hands along the front of her apron.

"Do you know where June is?" Emily asked her quietly.

Eliza shook her head. "No. S'okay, though. She knows how to handle things."

Emily cocked her head in reluctant agreement. "I just don't like not knowing exactly what she's planning to do, or where the commotion will be."

"Oh, calm yerself, it'll be fine. Now what have ye seen since ye been 'ere?" Eliza nodded to the open infirmary doors, twenty feet away. "Are there any girls in there tonight?"

"Oh," Emily stuttered. "I haven't—"

"Christ alive, you got a lot to learn," Eliza hissed, and without another word, strode confidently toward the infirmary. It looked mostly dark inside, as far as Emily could tell from a distance, just an orange light emanating from somewhere within, casting a bar of gold across the tile floor. Eliza poked her head around the door frame.

"What do you want?" a voice snapped loudly. Matron Jansen, Emily thought. She wasn't as bad as Matron White, but came close.

"Sorry," Eliza said, "I thought Peggy might be in 'ere."

"Not tonight. For once, not complaining of a headache. It's a wonder a rattled brain like hers can even contract one. Now, away with you!"

"Hey, 'er man knocked her mind silly with 'is fists!" Eliza replied. "It's not 'er fault." She withdrew from the infirmary as the matron barked something Emily didn't catch, and began walking back toward Emily.

"Just one girl," Eliza said quietly. There was suddenly a loud shout from the main floor below. "Bed closest to Stone's office, though. She looked asleep, so we'll have to sneak carefully."

Emily nodded. "Eliza," she said then, unable to resist. "Can I ask you . . . you have sympathy for Peggy, how her mind's been affected by her husband's abuse. How is that any different than the psychiatric inmates? The Blues, like my friend Annie?"

Eliza shook her head in a quick snap, pulled a face as though Emily had just offered her salt for her tea. "Dunno. It's different if a girl's got an addled brain 'cause somebody hit 'er, than if 'er brain just did that on its own. My mam gets the headaches, too, 'cause of all the stress Da puts on 'er. You gotta feel sorry for somebody like that. Inn't her fault."

A door slammed on the main floor, raised voices sounded.

"But fer somebody that just goes crazy fer no good reason . . ." Eliza continued. "Look, we got shit to do, Emily, I ain't talkin' about this anymore. Now let's—"

"FIRE!" someone screamed from below, and Emily and Eliza looked at each other, eyes wide. The commotion downstairs was cresting. Another door slammed, women's voices shouted questions. "FIRE!"

"Is that . . . is this June's diversion?" Emily breathed, incredulous. They hadn't discussed a *fire*.

Eliza gaped. "Christ, that woman's insane if it is! This place is a feckin' fire trap, and no mistake! She was supposed to start a *fight*!"

Emily raced over to the stairwell and hung over the railing, trying to see below. At that moment, an alarm sounded that Emily hadn't yet heard at the prison: a deafening klaxon issuing from a large red bell on the wall beside the stairs, just to her left. She clapped her hands over her ears and watched as women ran about downstairs, brown skirts swishing as they circled together, shouting. A thunderous sound from the third floor began, and Emily backed away from the stairs as the footfalls of over fifty, sixty, seventy women and girls pounded above her head, evacuating from the recreation room and third-floor cells. Matrons were calling instructions over the screaming.

What was June thinking, doing something as risky as this? The plan had been to goad some inmates into a brawl. Was the fire just a coincidence? Emily thought of June's newfound contempt for Dr. Stone, her ongoing resentment of the Mercer and her determination to maintain her business, the one thing she had control over.

No, this was not a coincidence. June, as she herself had put it, was here to play the game. And she'd just taken a big damn swing.

Emily ran across the hall to Eliza, and looking left, saw the infirmary door burst open at the end of the corridor as Matron Jansen emerged, her arm around the shoulders of her single patient, ushering her quickly forward. The patient was pale, awkwardly trying to tug a shawl around herself. She was in sock feet. They sped past Emily and Eliza, who both still pressed their hands to their ears, desperate to dampen the terrible, rhythmic clanging that only paused for a few seconds before starting up again. Eliza nodded to her, and without so much as a backward glance at the stampede of panicked inmates and matrons making their way downstairs, Eliza sprinted toward the open infirmary door. Emily followed, a nervous cold sweat breaking out on her back as she ran.

Over the threshold, Emily skidded to a halt to get her bearings as her eyes adjusted to the darkness. Eliza was already across the room, crouching down in front of Dr. Stone's office door.

"Turn on the light, I need to see," she shouted to Emily, who located the switch. The overheads flickered to life and she wove her way through the maze of beds and over to Eliza, trying to catch her breath. She watched, face screwed up against the continued noise as the girl squinted into the keyhole, working with a paper clip in each hand.

The noise from the floor above had ceased, but Emily could still hear the prisoners below. They'd never had a fire drill, and she wondered where they were congregating. The dining hall, perhaps, though the matrons might risk taking them all outside. Surely the fire brigade was on its way. Her pulse pounded as she wondered what would happen when the firemen arrived. Would that extend or cut short the time they had available in Stone's office?

"How much long—"

"It ain't a *key*!" Eliza snapped.

Emily's finger drummed her own thigh in agitation. "Eliza—"

There was a tinny *clink* as something fell to the floor. "Damn it!" Eliza swore. "It broke!" She scrambled to pick up the pieces of the paper clip, then threw them away in anger.

Emily's eyes darted around the infirmary for something small, something metal. Anything they could use to pick the lock . . .

"Wait! Here!" she gasped, reaching up and pulling the hairpins out of her bun.

"Oh thank Jesus," Eliza breathed, snatching them.

A full minute later, she grunted, then gasped and withdrew the pins. They were in.

The room was small, with no window. There was a desk and chair in one corner, a spindly table upon which sat a hot plate, teapot and set of cups, and a coat tree with two of Stone's white jackets hanging a few inches off the floor, hovering like ghosts above an old brass umbrella stand.

And there: the filing cabinet, just where June said it would be.

"Shit," Eliza said, and Emily's heart fell. There were four drawers, each with an individual lock. They were labelled:

A–E
F–L
M–S
T–Z

Emily tugged on each in turn, but of course they didn't budge.

The relentless clang of the fire bell paused in its rhythm, and in the distance, they heard the unmistakable wail of a siren. Panic spiked in Emily's chest, and for a moment she debated abandoning the operation.

"Which one first?" Eliza began. "We don't have time fer all a them."

"Um, M to S," Emily answered quickly. Her own file would at least tell her something of the drug trial in practice. There would be notes about her treatment, and possibly something more incriminating about the trial itself, the date of infection or some such detail.

Eliza dropped down and began to work at the lock as Emily stood behind her, feeling helpless. The sirens had abated, which meant the firemen were at the prison now.

How much time do we have?

Three or four agonizing minutes later, Eliza let out a hiss of satisfaction as she wrenched the door open.

"Yes! Eliza, well done!" Emily nearly shouted to be heard over the bell. "Which one next?"

"F to L. I need Annie's," Emily said.

"Why—?"

"Just do it, please!"

Emily knelt in front of the now-open drawer, a little squashed between the filing cabinet and Stone's desk beside it, as Eliza worked on F–L. Emily ran her fingers through the manila folders to R, snatched up her own file and began to read.

It was mostly what she would have expected, but there, in the margin for each treatment log, was the aerosol drug's name:

Trichloroacetic acid.

She tried to focus on the details as the fire bell hammered her brain. She cursed June; this all would have been so much less stressful with only the distant sounds of a fight to manage instead of this assault to the eardrums.

The second drawer opened faster.

"Always easier once I figure out the first in a set," Eliza said, stepping aside. Emily shut her own file and sought out Annie's. It was over an inch thick. She dropped it, and several of the sheets slid out onto the floor.

"Damn it!" Emily scrambled to stuff them back into the folder. She shook her head at her own rattled nerves, and as her eyes slid to the right, her gut flipped.

"Wait, Eliza, *there!*" She pointed to a thin drawer affixed to the underside of Stone's desk beside her, which was only visible from her vantage. It had a lock on it. Surely a half-hidden, locked drawer would be where the doctor would keep her most personal or highly sensitive documents.

She swept up Annie's mess of a file and scooted aside to give Eliza some space in front of the drawer.

"Yeah, that'll be it, won't it?" Eliza grinned, then bit her lip and, bending her neck awkwardly beneath the desk, began to pick the lock as Emily opened Annie's file. As she read, her face grew hot and her fingers cold.

"Emily, I can smell smoke," Eliza said suddenly, her voice rising on the last word.

"I know. I know," Emily said absently, still horrified by what she was reading in her friend's file.

"Wherever the fire is, it's either getting worse or closer or both!" Eliza screamed.

APPEAL FOR DISCHARGE DENIED 1/23/1960
APPEAL FOR DISCHARGE DENIED 8/16/1958
APPEAL FOR DISCHARGE DENIED 10/4/1955
APPEAL FOR DISCHARGE DENIED 2/10/1952

"EMILY!"

Emily tore her eyes away from Annie's records to look at Eliza, whose hands had begun to shake. She dropped one of the hairpins and swore.

"I'm leavin'!" Eliza bellowed over the fire alarm. "I ain't about to die in a brick oven! This wasn't the deal—"

"Eliza, just wait," Emily begged, "we're almost—"

"No!" Eliza backed away from her, toward the door. "Every window is barred up here, I'm gettin' out. We need to go!"

"I can't!" Emily shouted back. "I'm—"

"God help ye then," Eliza said, and bolted out of the office.

"Eliza!" Emily tried to shout, but her voice cracked. She began to cough. The smoke in the air was undeniable now, more than just a distant odour. And more than smoke. There was something chemical about it that choked her.

Her watering eyes went to the drawer beneath Stone's desk again. It was only a matter of time before Stone realized Emily and Annie's files were missing—it would make no difference at this point if the doctor knew her personal files had also been accessed. Besides, they might go up in flames any minute now, anyway. She had to retrieve any bulletproof evidence that might exist before it was all destroyed.

She needed something sharp or hard or wedge-shaped to force the drawer open. She cast around the small room, fighting her panic. She spotted the umbrella stand beside the door and lunged, withdrawing a long black brolly with a heavy mahogany handle. She bolted back to Stone's desk and stood in front of it, coughing. She hauled the desk away from the wall, then, with a guttural bellow she'd never before produced, overturned it, scattering the stationery, pen cup and other detritus. Emily lifted the umbrella and, with another almighty roar, brought the handle down hard onto the back of the drawer. Panting and coughing, she repeated the assault three more times as sweat dripped into her eyes before the drawer gave way with a *crack* of splintering wood.

Emily threw the umbrella aside and knelt, ripping the pieces of the drawer apart. With a leap in her chest, she gathered up the lone file inside and tucked it under her arm. Then she reached into the drawer and pulled out the limited contents; aside from the folder, there was only some cash, a chequebook, and a few personal sundries.

Seizing her own patient file and Annie's, Emily made for the door, out into the infirmary and the corridor beyond.

Smoke filled the air, and coming from the stairwell, she heard deep male voices: a sound that hadn't reached her ears since the judge sentenced her six months ago. The firemen were headed to the second floor.

Wheezing, Emily took a moment to shove the files down the front of her dress. Annie's was thick, and bulged a little, but she had no other option, and hopefully no one would notice the lumps in her dress amid the chaos.

Emily made toward the stairs, then skidded to a stop.

My notes.

She spun and pounded back toward her open cell, dove to the tap and wiggled her fingers in to retrieve the roll of tightly coiled paper. She tucked it into her brassiere, then fled back out the door.

She was at the top of the stairs when she heard muffled screams coming from the psychiatric ward. The gates were open, but all the cell doors were shut. Emily's insides turned to ice.

Annie!

She ran to the ward and through the iron gates, following the screams, and stopped outside Annie's cell. Her friend's terrified brown eyes were in the window, and bulged when she spotted Emily.

"EMILY, HELP!" she screamed, pounding on the door. "We're locked—"

"Just—just wait!" Emily shouted. "I'm going to get help!" She coughed, and feeling a little sickened, turned away from Annie and her stricken face, back toward the staircase just as the firemen had reached the landing.

"Miss!" one shouted. There were four others on the stairs behind him, all dressed head to toe in their alarming-looking gear: navy-blue coats, hard hats, gloves, and smoke-repellent gas masks. She could hardly see his eyes through the goggles. "What are you doing up here? Get down—"

"There are people!" Emily cried, then doubled over in another coughing fit. "Th—there!" she croaked, pointing toward the psych ward. "They're locked in!"

He began shouting instructions to his fellows, who all rushed forward through the gates. Emily was rooted to the spot, unable to leave until she saw that Annie was safe.

"Sir, my friend—!"

"The fire is *out*, miss," the firefighter shouted over his shoulder. "They aren't in great danger; we'll get them out." Emily's panic came down a notch. "But the smoke is toxic, it'll burn your lungs. For God's sake, get downstairs and outside with the others!"

Emily's eyes flicked back to the ward, where the firemen were now shouting at the patients to stay back from the doors as they hammered their axes at the locks.

"*Go, miss!*" the fireman urged, and Emily scrambled down the stairs. She flung herself around the corner. It was freezing down here. To her right, the front doors of the prison were wide open. With a final burst of adrenaline, she sprinted toward them and out into the frigid December air.

CHAPTER 31

EMILY

December 17, 1961
Day 181 (2 to go)

For the first time in six months, Emily was outside.

Her vision blurred, eyes watering. She blinked several times as she took rasping breaths in the darkness. It was frigid, and she wrapped her arms around herself. There were people all around her, a sea of brown and white, some faces just coming into focus in the golden light of the nearby streetlamps.

"Emily!" someone shrieked, and Eliza came running toward her through a throng of inmates. She pulled up short on the gravel path leading to the front door. "Good God, what were ye thinkin', ye loon!" She sounded angry, but Emily saw that her eyes were glassy.

"I got it," Emily whispered with a shaky smile before buckling into another coughing fit. "I got it."

"Jesus H.," Eliza breathed, the puff of heat fogging the air.

"Radcliffe!"

Emily looked up. It was Matron White.

"What in God's creation took you so long? You—"

Annie's terrified face staring back at her through the glass of the cell door filled Emily's mind, and her rage erupted.

"You just *left them there!*" she shrieked, voice cracking. She stepped toward the matron, whose eyes widened. "What is the matter with you? Have you no—"

"Who?" Matron White demanded, brow contracted. The assembled inmates had gone quiet.

"The psych patients!" Emily shouted. "Why didn't you evacuate them?!"

Matron White scoffed, her meaty hands coming to her hips. "We can't just *let them out!*" she said. "The fire was minor. What if they'd got loose, or tried to murder us all?"

"*What if the fire had been major?*" The pain in Emily's throat was dry and sharp. "Was your plan to just leave them locked in their cells to burn to death?!"

Just then, a baby, wrapped tightly in the arms of her mother, began to cry. Emily hadn't even thought of the nursery, the infants there, who were now spending the night outside in the cold. What had June been thinking?

"You're out of line, Radcliffe," Matron White warned. "Step back! I assure you the isolation cells are still perfectly intact for your immediate reception. I suspect one of these fine officers would be more than happy to assist." She gestured to the two policemen standing off to the side with the warden, who wore a coat over her thick cotton nightdress, hair still rolled in curlers. She had evidently been called or woken from her private residence at the northwest corner of the property. She and the police were all looking sternly at Emily.

After a brief moment of internal debate, Emily stood down. She'd already drawn more than enough attention to herself. She glanced around at the tall wrought-iron fence that surrounded the prison grounds; there would be no escape tonight, not with a swarm of able-bodied firemen and police who could chase her down in a heartbeat. She wanted to say as much about the psych patients' chances of escape, but held her tongue. Satisfied, White turned around and walked over to the other matrons, and the excited inmates began chattering again. Emily fell back into the crowd, in search of June. Eliza was at her heels.

"Do you know what happened?" Emily asked her.

Eliza shivered and wrapped her little arms around herself. Emily stepped forward instinctively and rubbed Eliza's back to create some friction.

"Fire was set in the factory. Firemen're tryin' to sort out what 'appened but Lucy Bothwell says the sheets all caught like a dry feckin' forest and up it all went."

The factory was, at least, about as far as June could have gotten away from the cells—but the basement would have been safer. With the factory's location, there had still been a chance the nursery and chapel wing could have become blocked if the fire had gotten out of control.

In the dim light cast by the moon and streetlamps, she finally found June, who skulked near the back of the crowd of women with her usual two accessories, Anna and Irene, and Maria, the hairdresser. June looked as though she were trying to hide behind Anna, despite the fact that her stature and flaming hair rendered her about the most conspicuous person Emily had ever clapped eyes on, even in the dark of night. Her arms were crossed over her large bust. June mumbled something to Maria and the other two young women, who melted away into the crowd at her evident bidding.

Emily stalked over to confront her. "*What the hell was that?*" Emily spat. "What happened to the fight?"

"I never said I'd start a fight," June said defensively. "I said that was an *idea*. We needed a good diversion. This one presented itself, and I figured it was both easier and more likely to give you the time you needed."

"What did you do? Eliza said—"

"I got Maria to get the gasoline jugs from the hair salon," June said quietly. "Doused some piles of sheets in the factory and lit 'em up with matches from the kitchen. I knew the fire would burn longer with the gas."

That explained the strange smell that tainted the smoke.

"And besides, with the factory destroyed, we can't be forced to make sheets for the government machine," June continued. "Let's see how they like it now that their free labour force has disappeared. It's one of the reasons they keep this place open, isn't it?"

Emily was silent. Though she appreciated June's act of dissent, she knew that if the administration needed the funding provided by the inmates' factory labour, they would find a way around it. She thought of the empty, useless classrooms. Emily would bet new sewing machines would appear and the classrooms would become the factory within a few weeks, at most.

Eliza stood beside them, and Emily suddenly realized how suspicious this might look, since the three of them weren't normally seen together. Although, she thought, perhaps not. Onlookers might just assume she and Eliza were new recruits. Everyone knew June's game.

"So did you get it?" June's eyebrows were raised, not a trace of shame or guilt on her face.

"Yes, I got it," Emily said, patting the bulge beneath her apron, then went into a coughing fit again, doubling over. "Nearly killed me, but I got it."

"She stayed after I bolted," Eliza said, nodding impressively at Emily. "Crazier 'n the Blues, I say."

> It occurred to me, as I stood on the lawn gasping cold air into my seared lungs, that society always calls a woman crazy when she knows she is right about something, or when, like the ill-fated Cassandra of lore, she sees something the others cannot—or will not. And when a woman knows she is right and refuses to give in, well . . . that's when they lock her up.

It was nearly two o'clock in the morning before the fire marshal gave the all-clear and the half-frozen women tramped back inside. The four babies from the nursery were sent over to St. Joe's Hospital for the night, though their mothers were not permitted to go with them. Emily was still hacking, and the pungent smell of smoke hung in the air. She was certain that in any other building or institution, the residents would have been transferred elsewhere until the smoke had entirely cleared and the building was aired out, but there was nowhere to send a hundred and twenty delinquent women in the middle of a frozen December night.

The matrons had opened the barred windows at either end of the long north-south corridor on each floor, but it had to be at least minus five degrees outside and, as had been the case since October, the stone walls of the prison retained the cold. Opening the windows now for fresh air would mean the place remained frigid for days, maybe even weeks afterward, as the old furnaces struggled to remain relevant. These women would pay for June's disastrous—though effective—diversion long after Emily had left the Mercer.

With a glance over her shoulder at the empty corridor, Emily withdrew the files and scroll of notes from inside her dress. She inserted the scroll back into the tap, but the only place she could possibly hide the files was beneath her mattress. It seemed obvious, but there was nothing else for it. As she settled down onto her bed and pulled the thin wool blanket up over her shoulders, her thoughts were still an agitated, uncomfortable battle between outrage and gratitude.

The psychiatric inmates' doors were destroyed by the axes of the firemen, so tonight, because there were no doors to lock, the women of that wing had all been strapped to their beds with restraints. Emily knew this because at least two of them kept screaming about it, bemoaning the pain and pleading for release until their wails eventually seeped into background noise. It nearly brought Emily to tears imaging Annie lying there on her own slim cot, leather-and-chain belts strapped around her torso and limbs as she stared at the ceiling. Emily hoped to be able to see her tomorrow, but had no idea if the prison's daily routine would carry on as usual after such a disruption.

As her brain hummed, Emily realized that after tonight, her ruse might finally collapse. Dr. Stone's office was a disaster, and the matrons had all witnessed Emily emerge from the prison on her own, and well after the rest of the inmates. She'd shouted about the psychiatric prisoners' treatment. It was only a matter of time before they discovered that patient files were missing, including her own. After that, it would be all too easy to put the pieces together as to who had stolen them.

So now, the question became: Would they be able to narrow it down and uncover Emily before her release in forty-eight hours?

Emily couldn't say, and had no control over it. But she had what she needed for the article now, that was certain, and she felt a little shiver of thrill at the knowledge. But she also had something else of value: a bargaining chip to use against Stone to secure Annie's release. She could blackmail the doctor, threaten to expose the details of Annie's file, her treatment, if Stone didn't agree to sign off on her discharge. And she could always expose Stone anyway, after Annie's release was finalized. Emily didn't feel any need to adhere to her side of such an agreement, and Stone certainly didn't deserve Emily's integrity. But regardless, she still had plenty of evidence beneath her mattress about the drug trials, the file proving Stone was deliberately infecting the Mercer women and getting paid by the drug company to test their products. On top of it all, she had June's testimony that Stone was also accepting bribes from inmates on the side in exchange for preferential treatment. Add in Emily's own testimony and experience of the deplorable living conditions and abuse at the hands of the matrons, and the Mercer might just get shut down.

It all tasted of bitter triumph. Nellie Bly had felt similarly, upon exposing the treatment of patients at the Blackwell's Island lunatic asylum in New York. She'd described the guilt she'd felt at leaving, as though she were abandoning those women to whatever fate the State had in store for them. Emily understood that sentiment now, because she knew that the State did not spare much thought for the fate of women. The bottom line was even lower than it was for men in the same situation. Women were always expendable.

Emily rolled over, tugging the blanket as closely around her body as she could, tucking her socked feet up close to her bottom. She stared at the grey wall across from her, stinging eyes a little out of focus. It was all on her, now.

Shivering and coughing, Emily struggled to fall asleep to the distant cries of the psych patients begging for deliverance. She knew they were keeping other inmates on the floor awake, too, because some of the regular population had begun shouting back.

"Shut the hell up, would you!"

"Jesus *Christ*, we're trying to sleep!"

"Couldn't you just drug them?!"

The pleas continued through the night.

Everyone heard.

But no one was listening.

CHAPTER 32

EMILY

December 18, 1961
Day 182 (1 to go)

The day after the fire, the smell of smoke still hung thick on the air despite the circulation from the open windows, which, as Emily had predicted, seemed to have merely frozen the inmates and done nothing whatsoever to curb the stench of the blaze. What had before been a comforting scent that called to Emily's mind memories of summer campfires and Christmas in her parents' cozy living room now stank of adrenaline and the chilblains she'd woken up with on her second and third toes after the frigid night's fitful rest.

She'd risen with the others at the sound of the bell, wondering how many of the prisoners had gotten any sleep at all, with the combined onslaught of the wintry air and the psych inmates' cries. After lining up outside her cell for the morning roll call and Chamber Pot Parade, she'd followed her fellow inmates, all half numb and grumbling, past the psych-wing gate toward the staircase. She peered down the hall and saw the open doors, the splintered wood around the lock and handle area from the firemen's axes. Several of the psych inmates were moaning and talking, one was screaming for a man named Lester.

"Oh would you SHUT THE HELL UP?!" a woman shouted on her way by, then launched herself at the gate, giving it a furious rattle. "SHUT UP!"

The matrons didn't even admonish her, and several women in line cheered their support. Emily's insides clenched. The state of the prison today was all her fault. But, she reminded herself as she descended the stone stairs to the dining room—which felt slightly warmer by virtue of the stoves in the kitchen—this was all for the good of these women, when all was said and done. *If* she could succeed with her article. She simply had to make something of this whole debacle. She must.

When they reached the main floor, there was a flurry of conversation and pointing down the east corridor. Emily saw that the burned-out factory had been blocked off with tape. She didn't have factory duty today, but wondered how the women who did would be re-deployed. They would probably just languish in one of the empty classrooms.

Emily thought back to the two times she'd tried to teach the women typing, and Stone's assault when one of the inmates—Thelma, most certainly—squealed on her. The surge of rage she felt at the woman—or women—who had betrayed her reinforced for her how tired she really was of being held in such a terrible place with these women who often didn't seem to know what was best for them. But then, she knew rationally that she couldn't entirely blame them for it, not when so many of them were coming from situations where they were forced to eat what they killed, always on the lookout for an opportunity to secure some sort of favour or leverage for themselves. They were never handed advantages. They had to scrape and snatch them wherever they could. It was the whole system's fault they behaved the way they did, not the individual women's.

In the dining hall, Emily filled her tray, then made a beeline for Annie's table. The relief she felt at seeing Annie safe and well was profound. She set her tray down and slid into the hard seat.

"Good Lord, Emily," Annie said, setting down her fork and reaching out a hand. "Last night . . . that was *dreadful*. Are you all right? Was anyone hurt? What happened?"

Emily searched her blue eyes. "Everyone's okay. It was uh—" Emily shifted in her seat. "It was part of a plan to get some records out of Stone's office. It didn't exactly go as I thought it would, but . . ."

"*You* started the fire?" Annie blanched.

"No. Well, sort of. I don't have time to explain, I'm sorry." She shoved it all aside. She had to speak to Annie, and had absolutely no idea how much time she had before Stone and the warden came down on her and ejected her from the prison, or had her arrested. Surely, by now, Stone would be informed and seeking answers. She would have seen that her files from the drug trial were deliberately targeted, and the other matrons would tell her that Emily and Eliza had emerged from the prison much later than all the others after the fire broke out. Emily would be at the top of the doctor's suspect list, a place cemented by her clash with Stone over the typing classes. She was already a "problem" inmate. She could come for Emily any time now.

But not if Emily got to her first.

"Emily—"

"Annie, if you got out of here, what would you do?" Emily asked without preamble.

Annie blinked in confusion. "What? I . . . I don't know. It used to be all I thought about, but . . ." She shrugged. "Why do you ask? What's going on?"

"You would want to see your son, surely?" Emily pressed. "Get some custody of him?"

Annie looked at Emily as though she were suggesting Annie might wish to fly to Mars.

"If you were discharged," Emily said, "you'd be a free woman, and unmarried. But you could see your son."

Annie puffed out a long breath, made a soft drum-roll sound. "I mean . . . that's just a dream, isn't it? I've asked Dr. Stone so many times—"

"Annie," Emily's heart thumped with anger at the mere mention of Stone's name. "There's something I need to tell you."

"All right."

"I know you've asked Stone yourself for your release, but Annie, your mother has appealed to get you out of here *four* times in the past ten years. Stone has blocked every one of them because the law is set out so that the prison *physician* has the final say, not the judge."

Annie's mouth opened in shock. "My—my mother has tried to get me out?"

Emily nodded.

"Helen Sharrock?"

"Yes, that's the name on the records."

Annie's hand came to her mouth. "How do you know this?"

Emily heaved a breath. "Because last night, I broke into Stone's office and took both our files."

Annie stared. "Emily, oh my God . . ."

Emily grabbed Annie's hands and held them tightly, not caring at this point if the matrons saw. "I know. I know. But Annie, the point is, you have a place to go. Your mother *wants* you released. *She hasn't abandoned you.* It's Stone that has prevented your release."

"But *why*? Why would—"

"Because Stone is corrupt," Emily said emphatically. "She has a whole business here, running drug trials under the table for kickbacks, taking bribes from inmates and who knows who else. You're a *test subject*, Annie. A lab rat she makes money off of. She controls all the psych patients with drugs and the authority this ludicrous law allows her." Emily was breathing heavily now, hardly able to channel her rage. She couldn't wait to get her fingers on a typewriter a week from now. Her brain was utterly bursting with this story. She released Annie's hands.

"So here's the thing," she continued, as tears began to course down Annie's pale cheeks. "We can use this. We can use this evidence to blackmail her into signing off on your release. I'll tell her I know what she's doing, and that I'll go to the authorities with the evidence if she doesn't release you. It's that simple."

Annie was wringing her hands now, panting. "Oh Emily, I don't know, I told you before, Stone isn't anyone to trifle with—"

"At this point, I don't care," Emily said firmly. She could almost feel the fire burning in her own eyes. "What's she going to do? My family is expecting me tomorrow, and so is my boss. My infection has cleared. She can't keep me here. I think we have her cornered, and I want to use this information to get you out with me." She looked into Annie's eyes. "So you can see your son, Annie. Your *son*."

Annie still looked doubtful, but Emily spied a crack of hope. The thought of her son was powerful motivation. It shone through Annie's fear like a bar of morning light.

"God, I just want to be able to explain everything to him," she said, blinking back tears. "I want to hold him, tell him a day hasn't passed that I haven't dreamed of his little brown eyes." She sniffed, and held Emily's gaze. "All right, say we do this," she began, and Emily almost beamed. Annie was so much stronger than anyone gave her credit for. "Aren't you lying to Stone?" She dropped her voice and glanced around. "Aren't you going to publish this article anyway?"

"Yes."

Annie hesitated.

"I have absolutely no ethical issue with double-crossing Eris Stone," Emily said with conviction. "She doesn't deserve either of our leniency. She sure as hell hasn't shown *us* any, has she?"

"No," Annie said quietly. "She certainly hasn't."

"She's kept you away from Gregory for fifteen years, Annie."

Annie swiped once again at the tears on her cheeks, which even had a little colour in them now.

"So do I have your blessing to do this?" Emily asked, placing her hands on Annie's shoulders. She rubbed a thumb back and forth, felt the rough cotton fabric of Annie's blue dress. How liberating it would surely feel for her to finally change out of it and shed the stigma of her illness, a butterfly emerging from a cocoon. Emily would take her to Eaton's and buy her any dress she liked, in any style or colour—except blue—with pumps to match.

Annie took a deep breath, then leaned forward and embraced Emily with surprising strength. Her dark hair tickled Emily's cheek as they held each another for a long moment, a quiet little island in the middle of the raucous dining hall.

"Yes," Annie whispered. "But please be careful."

"I will. I'm not afraid of her."

They pulled apart, and Annie sniffled. They stared at one another, and Emily suddenly knew she had found a friend for life. She couldn't wait to visit with Annie on the outside. To meet her son, go for a walk through High Park in the spring and talk about anything, everything else.

The bell rang, slicing through the tender moment with obnoxious force.

"Well," Annie said, rolling her shoulders back. "I'll talk to you soon, I guess."

"I'm going to try to confront Stone this afternoon," Emily said as their fellows all stood and headed noisily for the doors. "I don't know what will happen. But if I'm still here at supper, I'll eat with you today, okay?"

"Okay," Annie said, smiling, and for the first time, Emily saw true joy in her face.

As Emily exited the dining hall, making her way toward the chapel for prayer time, a sudden throat-clearing behind her made her whip around.

June was standing several feet away, lurking near the blind corner by the classrooms. "Those sound like some big plans," she said.

Emily frowned at her. "June, how long were you—?"

"What do you expect that woman to do once she's cornered?" June demanded, brows narrowed over unblinking eyes. "She's gonna bite, that's what. Trust me. I know. And Stone's got the sharpest teeth in this place. Bribery's one thing. Theft, another. But you try this, kid, and somebody's gonna get hurt."

Emily scoffed. "That's a bit rich, coming from the woman who set fire to the building," she said, taking no care to file down the edge in her voice. She'd had about enough of June Jones's self-righteousness.

June hissed like an angry goose and stepped toward her. "To help *you*!" Emily was aware a couple of other inmates were watching them.

"To help everyone in here!" Emily fired back. "To get the right people to pay attention! To get this place shut down!"

June pinned Emily with her sharp green-eyed gaze. "The most dangerous people are those with either plenty or nothing to lose, and Stone's got plenty. Her job is everything to her, she needs the money to pay those creditors or she's liable to end up in here with us."

"I *know*," Emily fumed, her anger coming out hot. "And she belongs in the psych ward! That's why—"

"You've pushed far enough, you've got the evidence you need," June said, voice low now. "Wait it out, and if there's an investigation, that friend of yours might get released anyway. But if you try to blackmail Stone, I tell you right now, you'll end up in an unmarked grave, kid."

"I know what I'm doing," Emily said firmly.

"Do you?" June spared her one more appraising glare before she swept past, leaving a trail of doubt in her wake.

CHAPTER 33
RACHEL

Clinton, Ontario—June, 1996

Rachel stands from her desk and faces the corkboard on the wall behind her. She stares at it for a while as one of the old light bulbs in the drop ceiling hums overhead. It started doing that four months ago, and was annoying at first, but as Rachel's request to have it replaced has gotten bumped farther down the maintenance list behind Green's own priorities, she's found it actually provides a welcome sort of white noise right above her as she puzzles over cases.

She fingers the five strips of paper in her hand, on which she's written the names of the women from the Mercer prison who died or were unaccounted for in the records from the mid-fifties until the prison shuttered in 1962. Her eyes slide over to the board beside it, the Stacy Cooper case that she still can't bring herself to dismantle. Because she knows, in her gut, that it isn't over yet. Knows that she'll spend the rest of her career trying to solve it.

She reaches for a box of thumbtacks. She pins the names up, one by one:

JESSICA HAWKINS
ELSIE CHALIFOUX
ANNIE LITTLE

WILMA CARDINAL
EMILY RADCLIFFE

She stands back, eyes narrowed at the list, which currently means nothing to her. But, as always, she knows the connections will emerge, one after another, as the breadcrumbs of the trail get closer and closer together.

She'd gotten back from Toronto two days ago, late in the evening, and took a sick day yesterday, claiming she must have eaten something bad on the road. But the truth was, she'd gone to bed fighting the urge to drink, and battling another monstrous panic attack. She'd called her sponsor around midnight and then her therapist for an emergency appointment at nine in the morning, even though she didn't need her therapist's analysis to understand why this was happening. Stevens asking about her past, having to deal with the Millgate Cemetery, all this talk of women's prisons—it was all as good as a sharp shovel for dredging up the shit she's been trying for years to keep contained.

She's doing better today, though, after a day of talk therapy, sleep, and gardening until her nail beds bled. Because the world doesn't stop for anyone's mental health; all you can really do is push forward until you push through, and if all else fails, fake it. To the extent that there's leeway for any cop to admit they're struggling, there's even less for woman officers. As is always the case, the women are held to a higher standard. Any show of emotional instability can get you put on the desk and ridiculed until you give up and quit. Rachel's seen it before.

At a hard knock on her office door, she turns, and Stevens pokes his head in. He's polite about it, doesn't just barge in like all her other coworkers do. She's starting to really like him.

"Hey Stevens," she says, "Come on in. I've got updates."

She fills him in on her findings in Toronto, what she gathered at Cartwright-Cambridge Co. and the archives. He nods, takes his own notes without her having to suggest it. He's learning fast.

"Okay," he says, brow furrowing at the corkboard. "So where do we start?"

"Where do *you* think we should start?" Rachel prompts him.

He smiles genially. "Death certificates for the three deceased, for sure, and see if we can locate any for the two that are unaccounted for, in case the deaths just weren't recorded properly at the prison."

Rachel nods.

"Then maybe cross-reference to see if there's any connection to Millgate?"

"Very good. As for the other two that are unaccounted for, that gets trickier." She sighs. "My first thought is some sort of administrative gap, if they were in fact discharged but the records weren't updated. Or maybe they were transferred to another prison? Other names on those registers stated when someone was transferred, but . . ." She shrugs. "As we know, records are never perfect, because humans aren't either."

"Yeah," Stevens agrees, shifting in his seat. "But . . . I guess human imperfection is kind of why we have jobs, right?"

Rachel watches him, a little puzzled. "Uh, yeah, that's true."

"Because people make mistakes. Sometimes big ones. Right?"

They meet eyes over the desk, and Stevens blinks first. "Listen, Mackenzie—"

She lets out a little hiss of frustration. "Who have you been talking to?" She asks it directly. There's no point being coy. "Did your uncle actually tell you my story, or have you just been playing me?"

"No, he didn't, I swear." Stevens raises his hands in surrender. "I'm sorry, it's just, one of the guys said—"

"Of *course* 'one of the guys said,'" Rachel snaps, fighting the clutch of anxiety in the centre of her chest. *This* is the problem with staying in this area after everything that happened with her family. Except her work is here, and she can't sell Dora's house for all kinds of reasons, both practical and emotional. She glares at Stevens, but then realizes this isn't his fault. People talk about her and her family. She's known that since she was a kid. But if his uncle Tom truly hasn't spilled the beans on her yet, she'd rather Stevens get the facts from her instead of some butchered or doctored version from one of her colleagues. She doesn't like telling this story, but Stevens is her junior. They need to trust each other if they're going to be partners.

"All right," she says. "Get your keys. I'm not talking about it here."

SUMMER, 1987

It was four hours into their visit, and Rachel still couldn't quite figure out why Mary and her new fiancé had come.

They were too old for any traditional foolishness like Kevin asking Dora for Mary's hand in marriage. This would be his second, and he had two kids from the previous one. They were younger, Mary said, twelve and fifteen. If Rachel had much patience or empathy left, she would have felt glad for her mother. But Mary's behaviour—some chosen, some a result of her illness—made it difficult to feel much joy on her behalf when she'd stolen so much from Rachel and Dora over the years.

Kevin and Mary had arrived in Bayfield a little after three in the afternoon, this time with advance warning—an actual *plan*. They rolled up behind Rachel's dusty red Dodge in some sleek, black, expensive-looking foreign car that screamed *money*. It was bizarre, and more than a little suspicious, to see Mary step out of it looking clean and preppy in khaki shorts and a pink polo shirt, her usually brassy locks dyed a salon-quality sandy brown. She looked unrecognizable, like she was on her way to a golf course.

Mary had offered to help Dora with dinner, and told Rachel to give Kevin a tour of the yard.

Hesitant in her cloud of confusion, Rachel gave him a cursory walk-about of Dora's gardens before he asked her if they could go talk on the old iron bench beneath the big maple beside the house. He sat, pulled a pack of cigarettes out of his pocket. He offered her one, which Rachel declined.

"Thanks for showing me around," he said politely, flicking open a monogrammed silver Zippo lighter with a soft *clink*. Mary usually got the colourful plastic ones they sold at the corner store. "The truth is,

Rachel, I told your mother I wanted to talk to you for a minute. I hope you don't mind."

Rachel watched him. He was handsome, tall and blond-haired, and he smelled like expensive cologne. Not at all her mother's usual type.

"I'll get right to the point," he said. "I know things haven't always been easy between you and your mom."

Rachel had been wondering how much he knew. Dora had already pressed Mary on that, during her last visit two years ago when they had learned of his existence. Frankly, Rachel was amazed he'd stuck around this long. Though knowing Mary, she'd probably kept plenty from him, partly because she was a compulsive liar, and because she really did seem to want a fresh start. She was always searching for them in the wrong places, but Rachel wondered if this time she might have actually found a real opportunity for a clean slate.

Rachel swallowed, looked straight ahead, out over the cliff. "Yeah. It's been tough sometimes." She hesitated as all the realities and omissions flashed through her mind. It wasn't tough, it was a fucking disaster. "Can I ask what she's told you?"

He blew the smoke out through his nose, just like Mary did, every time. "Enough," he said.

She turned to look at him now. "What's 'enough'?"

He sighed, tapped the filter on the armrest. "Well . . . I know she had a hard time when you were little. With her, you know . . . mental health, right? She told me that's why you lived mostly with your grandmother. And I think she hooked up with some bad guys over the years, eh?"

Rachel nodded. Mary had clearly scratched the surface with him, at any rate.

"I know things are a bit strained between her and Dora," he continued. "I don't know the details, but she says she's trying to make it right. That's why she's in there with her right now. I know there was some big fight years ago, when she was a teenager." He dragged on the cigarette again, then let out a breathy chuckle. "I know I should quit. But it's about my only bad habit, honestly."

Rachel almost believed him.

"I'd like you to meet my kids at some point," he said earnestly. "Before the wedding, I mean. Justin and Dawn." He smiled at her. "Dawn's twelve, and I think she's excited to have a big stepsister. Mary's told her all about you."

Rachel tried to meet his smile. *Told her what?* she thought. *I doubt Mary even knows my favourite colour.*

"Yeah," she found herself saying. "That'd be nice." She swallowed. His eyes were blue to Mary's brown, light to her dark, and in them, Rachel thought she saw something genuine. She could tell right away that he wasn't like the other guys Mary had hooked up with, the ones who were completely interchangeable in their looks and failures, threats and vices. Kevin might actually be different. He might actually be good. And maybe even good for Mary.

But would she be good for him? Did it matter?

"Can I ask, though . . . why are you here?" Rachel posed. "Mary—my mom—only comes here sometimes, for visits. Then usually she and Gran have an argument, and she leaves again. No offence"—she shrugged—"but to be honest with you, I don't get why she'd bother bringing you here to meet us. Why not just get married?"

Kevin put the cigarette back to his mouth, but found it spent. He just held it then, instead of stubbing it out on the rocks like Mary did before flicking it into Dora's garden.

"Well, she did try to do that," he said. "When I first asked her, she just wanted to elope to Niagara Falls, or Vegas or something. But this is important to me. I'd like my kids there, and I'd like you and Dora there. We're all going to be a family, and family's important to me. My ex-wife and I messed that up, and I'm trying to do better this time. So . . . I told Mary I wanted to meet you both before we got married."

Rachel wondered what he saw in Mary that Dora and Rachel didn't, wondered whether he knew the whole story. If Mary hadn't yet told him the ugliest details about her history, did he have a right to know? Perhaps. But Rachel had already taken on enough age-inappropriate responsibility for her mother. It wasn't on her to force full disclosure on Mary's soon-to-be-husband. That was between the two of them. She shouldn't get involved. And besides, she didn't really know much about Mary and Dora's relationship, either. Only that they'd always been at each other's throats, particularly when Mary was a teenager, and in the years after, when Rachel's grandfather Walter died. But so much of it stemmed from the way Mary was. She was a difficult person to love.

"The point is, I love her," Kevin said, and Rachel smiled painfully at the irony. She hadn't ever heard those words from Mary. *I love you.* She wondered how often Mary said them to Kevin.

"I can take care of her," he said. "And I'd like you and Dora to be a part of our lives."

She studied his face, the flecks of grey at his temples that were conveniently camouflaged by his light-blond hair. Mary's words to her the previous summer resounded in her mind.

Sometimes it just takes the right person.

Rachel had been offended at the time, that Mary was somehow insinuating she and Dora weren't "the right" people to steady her ship, that they were lacking in some way, despite being the only ones in the world who would put up with Mary at her worst. But maybe she'd actually found someone who—for whatever reason—could elevate her to her best.

The breeze from the lake caressed Rachel's bare shoulders as she let her thoughts roll over one another in time to the waves below. Maybe this was the start of a new chapter for her mother, or even Rachel's relationship with her. Maybe Kevin would be a calming influence on her mother's waywardness. Or maybe she'd manage to fuck it all up within a year. But the fact of the matter was that Mary would have a keeper—and not just anyone. Kevin was a guy with means and money, and he said that he loved her. Mary would be his responsibility, and there was relief in that fact. There would be no more crisis calls, no more disruptive visits when Mary's cash or meds ran out.

Maybe this was all, truly, a good thing for everyone.

"So, have you set a date, then?" Dora asked from the head of the table later that evening. Her eyes were fixed on Mary as she chewed the lemon roasted potatoes that Rachel loved so much.

Mary cleared her throat and looked at Kevin, who shrugged. "Not exactly," he said. "We wanted to talk to all our family first, then decide. But I think we're agreed it won't be anything big. Maybe not City Hall, but we were wondering about just the families on a cruise or something."

"A destination wedding," Mary said, beaming. "They're becoming quite popular, apparently."

"I think my kids would love it," Kevin added, "and I was telling Rachel, my daughter's so excited to meet her, she loves the idea of a big sister. A cruise might be a good chance for us to all really get to know each other and have some fun."

Rachel nodded politely, smiled at Kevin. It sounded idyllic. It didn't sound like Mary.

"A nice family gathering," Dora said, setting her fork down.

"Yeah," Kevin said, taking a sip of wine. Rachel could see the smallest beads of sweat breaking out at his hairline. He was nervous about Dora, who, Rachel had to admit, had so far been less than hospitable to him. She hadn't had a chance to speak to her grandmother without Mary and Kevin there, so she had no idea what her current thoughts were on the matter. Though she knew she would get them later tonight, once she and Dora had a moment to themselves. All she knew was that she had come back in from her walk with Kevin to find Dora and Mary in aggrieved silence at either ends of the kitchen, the heat of a recent argument hanging over the room like cigarette smoke.

"I know Mary's had some, uh, some tough times in her past," Kevin went on, reaching out and covering one of Mary's hands with his own. He gave it a squeeze. "But I know she's come so far, and we both feel like this marriage would be such a fresh start for everyone." Mary beamed at him, and she looked like a stranger. Rachel had never seen her smile like that.

"Oh, so she's been very open with you, has she?" Dora asked him. "About her past? These 'tough times' you speak of?"

"Gran . . ." Rachel began. Dora shot her a scathing look she wasn't used to, and she was struck dumb.

"Well, yes," Kevin said, stuttering. "She—"

"Mama, *please*," Mary begged, eyes round with fear, like prey. "Don't do this."

Rachel watched her mother, could see the carefully curated preppy veneer beginning to crack. The train wreck was still there, and Dora had poked her enough that the old Mary was showing through.

"*Gran*—" Rachel found her voice, louder this time, her pulse quickening as she looked from Dora to Mary to Kevin, who was watching Dora now with uncomfortable curiosity. "We're celebrating tonight, right?" Rachel said, raising her eyebrows at her grandmother.

She's almost off our hands, Gran. But he won't want her anymore if you fuck this up.

"I don't think now's the time to—"

But Dora just kept on going, ignoring Rachel, which she never did. She only had eyes for Mary now, and they were blazing a painful hatred Rachel had never seen in them before.

"Mary is an absolute disaster, Kevin," Dora snapped, her voice a leather strap. "I can assure you your affections would be better directed to someone more stable."

Mary was on her feet now. "No! Do NOT mess this up for me!" she cried, pointing at Dora. Rachel silently agreed. "You have *hated* the idea of me being happy ever since Walter died. Admit it! I'm sick and tired of this shit! Kevin, don't listen to her."

"What does Grandpa have to do with this?" Rachel asked. Only then did Mary look at her.

"Not Grandpa," Mary said. "My brother. Walter Jr."

"Oh, so you're finally going to tell her the truth, are you?" Dora shouted. She never yelled.

"What truth?" Rachel demanded of her mother. "Wait, *what brother?*"

Dora found Rachel's eyes now. They were bright and hard and brimming with grief. "Mary had a brother. She killed him when he was ten."

"What?!" Kevin and Rachel both shouted together. Mary was sobbing now. Kevin had risen from his seat. Rachel's mouth hung open, dry. Her body was cold.

"I didn't—don't—" Mary stuttered, eyes darting wildly from Kevin to Dora to Rachel.

Dora threw her napkin on the table and shook her head, eyes on her daughter. "I've kept this from Rachel for you, Mary, but my God, I have reached the end of my generosity and I will not allow you to lead this perfectly honest man down your thorny garden path. You've ruined enough lives already."

"What is this?" Kevin whispered, his eyes searching Mary as tears poured down her red face.

"Mama, STOP!" Mary screamed.

"She decided to get stoned while she was babysitting her brother," Dora told him, her tone caustic but so, so brittle. "And she *says* he fell off the cliff edge." Dora gasped a little as the words hit the ground, sharp as shattered glass. "You should probably know that, Kevin, if you intend to marry her and let her care for your children."

"Mary?" Kevin breathed.

"Gran?" Rachel was the only one still sitting, and she felt like a child then, looking up at the adults around her, uncomprehending. Except as her grandmother's words hung in the air above the table, Rachel's stomach turned acrid, because she knew it was true. The Christmas stocking. Dora's obsessive fear of the cliff edge. Her resentment of Mary that sometimes veered into hatred. The induced miscarriages and her insistence that Mary was unfit to care for anything at all . . .

"Mom," Rachel pleaded, standing now on unsteady legs. The light above the table shone like an interrogation lamp over them. "It's true. Isn't it?"

"It wasn't my fault," Mary whispered.

Rachel stared at her, sickened. "Because nothing ever is, is it?"

"Then tell me what happened!" Kevin this time, his voice rising to the ceiling, harsher than Rachel thought him capable of.

"He got too close to the edge," Mary gasped. "It was an accident!" She clutched at Kevin, but he pulled away.

"Oh, come off it," Dora shrieked. Rachel had never heard her sound so unhinged. She realized then that this fight had been coming for years. Decades. She had just been in the dark about it. "You always thought he was the favourite, you hated—"

"Well, wasn't he?!" Mary cried. "Your *golden boy*, the—"

Kevin threw up his hands and left the table.

"Kevin, wait!" Mary begged, hurrying after him.

Rachel looked at her grandmother. The fan above their heads grumbled its low *whump-whump-whump* as it tried to dispel the heat of the argument. Condensation dripped off Rachel's wine glass like tears. They could hear Mary screaming pleas at Kevin in the driveway.

"Gran—" Rachel began, her own throat closing on emotion.

Dora looked right at her, eyes unusually cold, and Rachel saw now the grief that she'd been so adept at hiding. She'd always thought her grandmother had been in perpetual mourning for her lost husband. But all along, she'd been grieving the loss of her entire family.

"It was time, Rachel," she said. "I'm sorry."

"You had a son."

Dora's eyes glistened with tears. "Yes."

The ringing in Rachel's ears drowned out the thrum of the fan. "And what about Grandpa?" she asked. "You said he died of heart failure."

"And I didn't lie to you about that. His heart did kill him. But his insane daughter killed his son. Walter Jr. was everything to him. So he drank himself to death and his heart failed. And who could blame him?"

Tears were pouring down Rachel's face now. She mopped them off her chin as a sickening thought occurred to her.

"Gran," she said. "Your walks around the cemetery." She could hardly get the words out. "Your son is buried there, too. Isn't he?"

Dora's face crumpled. "Yes, little one. He is."

"And you fought with Mom this afternoon. When I came in, I could tell."

"Yes. She wasn't going to tell Kevin. I believed he needed to know."

Car doors slammed in the distance. Mary's voice echoed, unintelligible.

"I need some air," Dora mumbled. "Excuse me." She turned and walked toward the door to the back porch, let it slam shut with the clap Rachel had heard a thousand times, but which now made her flinch as though it were a gunshot.

Head reeling, she swiped the tears from her hot cheeks and made to follow her grandmother outside, where they might all be able to cool down.

Rachel had no idea what would happen, what came next. She needed time to think this all over, to ask her mother if there was any more to the story. But Mary hadn't really tried to defend herself just now, not beyond denial of responsibility—her lifelong modus operandi. She surely would leave, try to patch things up with Kevin. It might be for the best. Then Rachel and Dora could actually talk about all of this. Help Rachel make sense of it all.

But really, doesn't this explain so much?

She stared out at Dora's silhouette, standing in the middle of the yard between the two bordering gardens, her greying hair illuminated in the moonlight. Rachel had just reached out for the wooden handle when a figure came barrelling around the side of the house toward Dora.

Mary ran at Dora and gave her an almighty shove. Dora staggered. Mary pushed her again, shouted something.

"Hey!" Rachel cried, wrenching open the door and launching herself onto the porch. She ran for the lawn. "Get off her, Mary! What's wrong with you?!"

But Mary didn't even seem to notice her. She lunged at Dora again, screaming like a fire alarm.

" . . . You just go be with Walt, then!" She gestured to the lake, arms wide and teetering, like a plane that couldn't right itself. "That's what you want, isn't it?"

"Get away from me!" Dora cried.

The cool wind hit Rachel's face, stinging the tear tracks. "Mary, calm down!" she shouted, reaching the pair of them just in time to intercept Mary's outstretched arm as she tried to strike Dora. "Just—"

"Don't you *dare*, Mary," Dora growled. She stepped in front of Rachel, facing down her daughter. Rachel's breath was coming hard and fast, heart beating an allegro against her ribs as she stood on the sidelines.

"Both of you, just stop it!" she cried, but she was invisible to them. All they could see and hear was each other. This showdown had been predetermined long before Rachel was born. She was irrelevant to this inevitable battle, and the way they were looking at one another, dry eyes burning with unrestrained hatred, was frightening. Rachel felt helpless. Unarmed.

"You've been like this your whole life," Dora shouted. "Utterly—"

"Mom. *Please*," Rachel begged. "Just leave. Leave. Let's just give it—"

"And did you expect Walt's death to not fuck me up, Mama?" Mary shot back. Her hair was tangled from the wind. She looked more deranged than Rachel had ever seen her. The veneer she'd put on for Kevin's sake had worn away in the skirmish, the polish sanded with abrasives to reveal the damage beneath. Rachel had been delusional to think that Kevin's influence could solve their problems, that maybe Mary was fixable.

"You have no one to blame but yourself, Mary!" Dora cried. "And you were a disgrace long before you killed Walter. Don't you *dare* try to hang your failures on—"

Mary pounced at Dora before she could finish, landing a punch to her jaw.

Rachel cried out and instinctively moved in front of her grandmother, began to grapple with Mary.

The neighbours' dog, roused by the commotion and the women's cries, was barking incessantly now. Their porch light flicked on.

"HELP!" Rachel screamed in their direction. "Someone!"

There were voices, a shout. Dora was clutching her mouth.

"Get *off* me, Rachel!" Mary shrieked. She slapped Rachel across the face, then her leg came up and she kicked her—hard—in the stomach. Rachel doubled over in pain and shock, gasped on a surge of nausea. Her face stung, burned. She fell to her knees, and it was from there that she watched, horrified, as Mary kicked Dora, too, and in the second in which

Dora was recovering from her second blow just feet from the bluff, unbalanced, Mary ran at her again and pushed her with both hands.

Rachel's scream tore through the night air like a scythe as her grandmother's body disappeared over the weedy cliff.

"NO! *Noooo!*" Rachel rose and stumbled toward the edge, unbelieving. She felt separated from her body, as though she were watching it all from a distance. Waves crashed against the shore far below as she screamed for her grandmother, her voice carrying on the wind.

No response came.

Panting, Rachel inched closer to the bluff, then gasped as she felt Mary's hands on her shoulders, rough and pinching.

Rachel screamed again. But Mary didn't push. She grabbed her, wrenched her away from the cliff edge, then held her face hard.

"Rachel!" Mary cried, inches from her nose. Rachel felt her mother's breath, could smell it, and tore her gaze from where Dora had gone over.

Mary looked wild, eyes glinting in the moonlight as her hair whipped around her face in the wind. There was shouting nearby.

"What did you do?!" Rachel sobbed, nearly falling to her knees as her legs gave way. "What did you do?!"

Mary shook her head. "Nothing. She tripped. She *tripped*, Rachel. Right? You saw her trip."

Rachel pulled out of her grasp, recoiled. "You're insane. You're CRAZY!"

"We were arguing and she tripped. That's all!"

Rachel gaped, staggered away from her toward the house. "Like your brother did?"

Mary stood still, a grey statue in the glow of the moon overhead. She stared down her daughter with eyes that were cold and dry, and said nothing.

CHAPTER 34

RACHEL

Rachel takes a deep breath, finally meeting Stevens's eyes across the table at the little coffee shop as she finishes the story. The real one. Not the scattered rumours and inaccuracies he'll have heard from the other guys.

"I remember sitting on the steps of our front porch," she says. "We always sat in the back, facing the lake, so it felt bizarre to sit there. I never sit out there at night now—ever—because all I see are the red-and-blue cruiser lights flashing off the trees, and the tape going up around the whole place. I always make someone else do that, put up the tape. Don't know if you've noticed," Rachel says, mouth twisted. "The neighbours were all out along the road, watching. And then your uncle came up and sat down beside me. Didn't loom over me. He just sat, like he'd been waiting to have some heavy conversation with me, and said 'I'm sorry, Rachel.' Then he gave me some water to rinse the taste of vomit out of my mouth. No one else thought to do that."

Stevens watches her beneath his furrowed brow, but says nothing. Rachel takes a deep breath and another sip of coffee. It's bitter, but she doesn't mind.

"He took my statement like it was a heart-to-heart. He just let me tell it, didn't push or pry. I *wanted* to tell him, like he was a therapist or something. I've never seen anything like that since I've been on the force.

I've tried to emulate it, but I don't know if it's a skill you can acquire. Maybe you'll inherit it," she added, eyebrow raised. "But we just sat there as I held that scratchy grey emergency blanket around my shoulders even though it was a hot night. I told him everything that happened while my mother watched from the back of the squad car."

"I was going to ask," Stevens says. "She didn't try to bolt?"

Rachel shakes her head. "No. And I've wondered sometimes why not. I guess that in such a small town, there's just not really anywhere to go. You can't exactly slip into the underworld, disappear into a crowd. She tried to get me to lie, though."

Stevens's hands are clenched tightly on the table. Rachel watches him flex the fingers, loosen them. He's on edge with the conversation, and a pang of guilt hits her, tempered with curiosity about why. "And you didn't, did you?" he asks.

She pauses. "Have you pulled the case file?"

"No. I wouldn't do that."

She nods approvingly. "I told your uncle everything. He interviewed the neighbours, too. Ron saw it all from his porch next door, he was out having a smoke when the fight broke out. It was his wife who called the police, right before my mother pushed my grandmother. So it was pretty clear what had happened, plus our stories corroborated. They called poor Kevin into court, too. He was just stunned by the whole thing. I really do think he knew a completely different version of Mary than we did. She'd crafted it well. But she tried to plead not guilty, said Dora had emotionally abused her her whole life, and it was some form of self-defence." She chews on her tongue. "Of course that all fell apart with the prosecution's witnesses. We saw what happened. She wasn't in any danger of my grandmother killing her. She deliberately murdered her own mother in a moment of impulsivity fuelled by mental illness and years of pent-up hatred. Self-loathing. That was her MO. That was just *her*." She shrugs. "Impulsive and sick and unable or unwilling to control *anything* to do with her choices. It would almost be poetic if it weren't so fucked up.

"And they called in John Holland, the reverend at Millgate Methodist." She lets the name dangle, distaste stinging her tongue.

"Oh! Shit," Stevens says. "But . . . wait—"

"Senior," Rachel clarifies. "The current reverend's dad. He fancied himself my mother's counsellor, except I was always advocating that she get real medical help, and he maintained that all she needed was God. Just pray the cray away, right? Because that's how it works. Anyway—" She took a deep breath, tried to gather herself. "He turned on her. In court he testified that he tried to counsel her religiously, but realized she was beyond that and needed medical attention that she didn't seek. He said he should have pushed her harder to get it. Which was total bullshit. And that's the thing I hate him for, honestly. That's it."

She runs a thumb around the rim of her mug now, worried she's overshared. Just thinking about John Holland sends her nervous system into flight mode, and her verbal filter disappears. She'll need to talk to her therapist and sponsor again tonight. But Stevens doesn't seem fazed.

"Did you have to testify?" he inquires gently.

Rachel rolls her shoulders. "Yeah. I wanted to, though, to be honest. After everything she'd put me through, and taking my grandmother away from me." She swallows. "I couldn't let Mary sit there and disparage Dora, for one thing." A deep breath as she regains her composure, pushes down the rage. "She didn't have much to go on, though. There was no evidence of emotional abuse, and plenty of evidence of her own neglect and mistreatment of me. But I think the clincher was the death of Walter Jr., my uncle. They now had this woman on the stand accused of murdering her mother by pushing her off the same cliff her own brother mysteriously fell off twenty-seven years before."

They're quiet for a while, and Rachel takes the opportunity to ground herself, finding five things she can hear, five she can see, five she can smell. The job is well-suited to her for many reasons, not least because she's forced to touch down with her own senses as part of an investigation, to notice everything; the same skill she uses to quell panic attacks and her chronic anxiety. Stevens watches her silently.

The espresso machine. That woman's weird laugh. The pager buzzing on that table . . .

Coffee. Cinnamon. That guy's cologne . . .

"I wondered if your uncle was going to re-open Walter Jr.'s case," Rachel says once the spinning has stopped. "But he didn't. And Green hasn't. But Mary's in prison. No point spending the resources, I guess. She's serving time."

Stevens is quiet a moment, nods. "So you'll just never know if she deliberately killed her brother?"

Rachel presses her tongue to the inside of her mouth, feels the ridge on her cheek where her mouthguard digs in every night. She's clenched and ground her teeth since she was nine years old. She cracked right through a guard while the trial was going on, woke up with it in three pieces, panicking that she'd shattered her teeth.

"The last I heard, she still maintains that he tripped. The same word she used when she tried to gaslight me into lying for her. Make of that what you will."

Stevens exhales, takes a sip of his tepid coffee. "She went away, I assume?"

Rachel nods. "Yeah. Second-degree. She's in max security at Grand Valley."

"Have you ever visited her?"

"No. She writes me letters sporadically, but I never open them. There's nothing she could say at this point that would make me forgive her. I decided to find my own closure elsewhere."

Stevens watches her. "Where?"

"Well, first it was vodka." She pulls her eyes away from his. "Then expensive rehab and therapy paid for with my grandmother's life insurance."

He runs a thumb up the handle of his empty mug. "And now?"

"Oh, Stevens," Rachel says, exhaling half a nervous laugh. "That's uh . . . that's a question. Right now, it's my job. Helping find answers, solve mysteries." Her eyes widen and she smiles with bitter sarcasm. "Because I've got enough of my own unanswered questions and cold cases that I know will just never be resolved. So I pay it forward and try to help other people not have to live with the unknowns. Because those unknowns can eat your fucking brain."

She hails their server and asks for some ice water, mentally checks herself as she feels her nervous system go into overdrive again. If she isn't careful, the eye twitch is going to make an early reappearance. It happens every July, near the anniversary. She sips the water gratefully when it arrives a minute later.

"It's been a long time since I've talked about this," she tells the rookie, who is now leaning a little on the table, arms crossed. She didn't even like to talk about it with Lynn in rehab, but she had to.

"Well . . . thanks for telling me," he says.

She nods. "Good cops need to understand where people are coming from," she says. "Especially, you know . . ." She hesitates, rubs a shoulder absently. "When it comes to mental health. This job affects most of us, but we don't talk about it, do we? And you and I both know a lot of us got into policing because of shit from our pasts. Let's be real."

They share a faint, knowing smile, then both sit back, relaxing a little. Rachel feels the tension drain from her shoulders. The café has gotten busier as they inch closer to the lunch hour. Conversation swells around them as mugs clatter. A milk frother hisses from over near the counter.

"So we have to thread this needle of allowing our experiences to help us be good police, without letting them totally colour our view of people." Rachel clears her throat. "I have trouble with the parent-and-kid cases, the Children's Aid calls. They're the worst for me. Worse than a murder. Every time. But fortunately, we don't get too many around here. It's one of the reasons I stay rural. In a city, there'd be too much of that." She inhales the scent of coffee and sugar, the bitter and the sweet. "And yet . . . in some ways they're the most satisfying. Helping to make sure some kid gets out of a bad situation."

Laughter breaks out at a table ten feet away, two young women with heavily made-up faces and non-fat lattes. Both of them have hair styled just like Jennifer Aniston's on *Friends*. They're probably imagining they're at Central Perk, and who could blame them for wanting a sitcom life, scripted and polished to a prime-time shine. But there's always darkness and mess behind the walls of a brightly coloured set. Clutter and chaos you don't see on screen.

"You're a good listener, Stevens," Rachel says. "Maybe you did inherit some of your uncle's skill after all."

He inclines his head modestly. "We'll see." He's quiet for a moment. "Do you mind if I ask, why didn't your grandmother ever tell you what your mom had done?"

"I've had a lot of time to think about that one," Rachel says. "And I honestly believe she thought I already had enough to think badly of my mother for, the pain she'd caused me personally." She pauses. "I think, on a level, Dora was trying to spare my mom some shame. But mostly it was for me. Because, unlike my mom, she was always thinking of me. She always wanted to do what was best for me."

Stevens nods. "So, what happened with your mom . . . that's why you became a cop?" He lifts his mug and looks surprised to find it empty.

"No." Rachel eyes him. "Well . . . yes and no, I guess. I studied forensics in school, before the academy. It didn't take my shrink at rehab analyzing my experiences for me to know that I was always drawn to science for answers."

"And detecting is the same."

"Yes." She presses her lips together. "Since your uncle told you to follow my lead, pick my brain . . . something tells me you can relate."

They meet eyes for a long moment, and Rachel searches them. He's quiet, clearly struggling. But he's not ready yet, to tell her whatever it is. She bails him out.

"If not for your uncle's . . . intervention, I guess I'd call it, well . . . I'm not sure where I would have ended up."

Stevens tilts his head a little to the side, frowns. "What intervention?"

FALL, 1987

Leaves and gravel crunched beneath the wheels of Dora's old car as Rachel drove up the laneway and parked behind the house. She stared out at the lake for a moment. The water was choppy in the autumn wind, the whitecaps cascading over one another in their rush to crash against the cliff edge below.

She'd thought about selling the place and moving to Toronto, or even back to Windsor. Being there might at least have encouraged her to re-enroll in school. She knew Dora would have wanted her to complete her program, proud as she'd been about Rachel being the first university-educated person in the family. But Rachel didn't really see why that sort of thing mattered anymore.

The problem was, nothing at all mattered much to her anymore.

She'd gone to live with Kim's family while the police took over the property for the investigation, and moved back in the week before she was due to return to school. But instead of packing her bags, getting a fresh haircut and hitting the road with her tuition savings, she'd crawled beneath the quilt Dora had sewn her when she was eight and slept for nearly a week. The first week of September came and went, and then they began to slip by in a miasma of alcohol, debilitating depression and valerian-root sleep aids ground in Dora's mortar. Rachel didn't know where to go, and she didn't know how to leave. Kim called long distance from her sorority house in Waterloo to check up on her every few days, but Rachel didn't say much. And sometimes she just let the phone ring, the shrill metallic whirr echoing through the empty house as she pulled the quilt up over her ears, tried to catch up on sleep that was often elusive to her at night, when intrusive thoughts and memories washed over her in rhythm with the tide outside the window.

She didn't leave the house anymore, except for necessities. She had no social life—her friends were back at their respective schools now—and no family. No goals for a future she hadn't even considered since the day Mary pushed Dora to her death. And Rachel didn't suppose she'd even be able to sell the place if she wanted to. Who wanted to buy a house where not one but *two* people had fallen to their death? And so she stayed, rattling pointlessly around a house that felt dead and hollow without Dora, just like Rachel did.

But it was mid-October now, and the past two months were a blur, each day the same as the ones that came before and after. Rachel had just come back from the grocery store, paper bags weighed down with frozen dinners and ketchup chips. She unloaded the bags from the car and was thinking of the Irish coffee she'd make once she got inside when a police car turned into the driveway.

Her adrenaline flared at the sight of it, and her mind began to race. Had something happened to Mary in custody? Or worse, was she being released? She swallowed as the car's engine cut and the officer stepped out. She recognized him immediately.

"Detective Stevens?"

"Hi Rachel," he said, coming slowly around the side of his squad car and stopping five feet from her. He was tall, somewhere around fifty, with a deeply receded hairline. "Can I take one of those?" He indicated the bags.

"Uh, sure. Yeah. Thanks." He relieved her of one, and she clutched the other tighter, as though holding a toddler who might try to squirm out of her grip. "Has something happened with the case? I thought we were still waiting on a trial date?"

"We are," he said, looking grim. "But I wanted to come check up on you. I know you're on your own now, and uh, I was in the neighbourhood."

He wasn't, though. The "neighbourhood" was just one long street of houses that backed onto the lake, surrounded by trees. And no one other than the Mackenzies had ever had reason for the cops to visit their house. Rachel averted her eyes from him. She wasn't entirely surprised by the visit.

The day before, she'd been down at the little LCBO just off the highway to refill the liquor supply that was rapidly dwindling as empty bottles piled up against the far wall of the scullery. She'd seen Detective

Stevens there, off-duty, and she knew he'd seen her, too. She'd tried to move her body to block his view of her purchases as she dug in her wallet for her ID. She was getting used to the array of curious, pitying, and judgmental looks she got from people in town whenever she did venture out. But for some reason, she didn't want Detective Stevens to know how much she was drinking, didn't want to disappoint him.

"How about we bring these in, and I'll make some coffee?" he said now.

"Uh." Rachel was taken aback, but felt a distinct pressure to agree. "Sure. Yeah."

She led him toward the back of house and through the wooden screen door into the kitchen. She set her grocery bag down on the table and he followed suit, cleared his throat.

"Go ahead and make yourself comfortable. I can make the coffee," she said, turning away and busying herself with the coffee maker. She was suddenly very aware of the state of the place. Dishes were stacked in the sink and beginning to smell. Mail and flyers were piled on the table amid a clutter of general detritus, and she hadn't washed her hair in at least three days. She couldn't recall the last time she'd swept and mopped. Possibly before everything went to hell. The air was stagnant, and she wrenched opened the kitchen window to tempt in a breeze.

She watched him look around a little at the photos on the walls. His eyes swept over the mail on the table, then stopped on one of the envelopes. He picked it up and studied it.

"When did you get this?" he asked gently.

Rachel's stomach squirmed. "A few weeks ago, I think."

"She isn't supposed to be in contact with you."

"No?"

"No. Not while the trial is pending. You're a witness." He scoffed. "Jesus. I'll report that. She's left your name off, I guess that's why it got missed. But they need to monitor her outgoing mail. I can't believe this." He paused, ran a finger over the back of the envelope, which was still sealed. "You haven't opened it?"

Rachel shook her head. She'd meant to toss Mary's unopened letter right into the recycling bin, but for some reason, she hadn't yet. Detective Stevens watched her, waited, and just as she had on the porch the night of the murder, she found herself compelled to talk to him. Other than Kim's occasional calls, and brief "thank-you"s to cashiers, she hadn't spoken to another human being in two months.

"I . . ." Her eyes pricked and she blinked hard as the coffee maker began to drip behind her. "I don't think there's anything she could say that I would want to hear. It'll just be lies, like always. I don't think she even knows how to tell the truth."

Detective Stevens nodded slowly, didn't press for more. His mouth stretched into a small, kind smile. The sort you give to a skittish stray. The smell of coffee filled the kitchen, which felt warmer with him here. When it was ready, Rachel poured two mugs and handed him one.

"How about we take these out to the porch," he said, gesturing to the back door. "A bit of fresh air."

Rachel nodded and followed him. They settled down in the creaky Muskoka chairs, a foot apart. The breeze blew softly. It was a cool fall day, but the sun was still warm. Crispy leaves swished in the trees overhead. They sat in silence again, sipping.

"You saw my cart at the liquor store, didn't you?" Rachel finally asked, blowing across the surface of her drink, watching it ripple.

"Yup."

"And that's why you're here?"

"Yup."

She glanced at him, but he was staring out at the water. She drank her coffee, felt the warmth trickle down through her core. He chewed on his lip a bit, then seemed to come to a decision about something.

"Between you, me, and the lake . . . I had a problem once, too. Had to take a long leave from the job and everything. My chief at the time insisted, or he woulda had my badge."

Her eyebrows raise.

"I won't uh . . . I won't get into why, but I went down fast. No one ever talks about how steep the slope is, eh? The dependency can come on real quick." Rachel felt a swell in her throat at the words. It had only taken about three weeks for her to wake up in the morning wanting a drink. To need one to get to sleep at night, and most of the time in between. She'd begun mixing the booze with a high dose of the antidepressants she'd been on since she was sixteen. When she'd poured this coffee, she had to remember not to spike it out of habit.

"It's the desperation that gets us," the detective said. "You just want to smother the pain, and aside from actually killing yourself, this is the quickest route to numb."

She squinted her eyes against the threatening tears, the accuracy of what he'd said. He understood.

"You need to put up a fence over there," he said then, matter-of-fact.

"I know." Rachel watched the weeds on the cliff edge bend over, flutter in the wind. With what she knew now, she couldn't figure out why Dora never had one installed. That was just one of the many riddles and mysteries she was now stuck with. "But I don't think it would have stopped Mary from killing her. It was clear she wanted my grandmother dead."

"You could be right," he said. "But still. You should get it done."

"I will."

They were quiet, both draining the last of their drinks.

"So how did you pull yourself out of it?" Rachel finally asked.

He sighed, set his mug down on the arm of the chair. "There's a rehab place called Pineview, just outside of Guelph. They had good therapists, too. Helped me get through a lot, figure some stuff out."

"And have you been sober since?" she asked.

"Yup. The rehab was even harder than the addiction and depression. But worth every fucking minute of effort."

She swallowed. "Can I ask why you're helping me?"

He meets her eyes square on. "Because I don't know where I'd be if my chief hadn't pushed me to get help. He saved my life. I see you stranded in the same boat, and you're too young to let your life get derailed." He paused. "And if I may, I'm sure your grandmother would never have wanted to see you like this."

Rachel broke down then, gasped at the cool air through the sobs. Sometimes all it takes to pull us back from the brink is for a good person to just give a shit. To see you struggling from the shore, and throw out a life preserver, to offer a bit of thankless, genuine compassion, make sure you don't drown.

Detective Stevens reached out a hand. Without hesitation, Rachel grasped it, felt the unfamiliar sensation of fatherly support course through her as she gripped the rough skin, calloused with experience. Those hands had helped people, she knew. And maybe they could help her, too.

CHAPTER 35

EMILY

December 18, 1961
Day 182 (1 to go)

Emily's heart pounded on her collarbone like a judge's gavel as she stood in the interminable queue outside the infirmary.

It was the morning before she was due for release. She'd had a poor sleep the night before, spent most of it preparing the speech she was about to give Stone and considering what the doctor's response would be. She was sure to be angry, and unhappy. Emily had no delusions that she would snivel and cry and beg. But she might be savvy enough to actually strike the bargain: Emily's silence on the drug trial in exchange for Annie's release. As she'd told Annie and June, Emily had no qualms about reneging on the agreement. Neither she, nor any of the other inmates, owed Eris Stone a damn thing, least of all their honour. They'd all been tricked to benefit the doctor's own financial needs; now it was Emily's turn to do the tricking. She'd had enough. She was exhausted and resentful, full of rage at Stone and the entire institution, at the laws that made it all possible, that gave Stone all the power.

When it was finally her turn, Emily took a deep breath and entered the bright white room, as she had so many times over the past several months. It felt empowering to have the upper hand for once while visiting the infirmary, instead of lying spread-eagled on the dirty sheets while the doctor assaulted her in the name of medicine.

"What's the gripe, Radcliffe?" Matron Smith asked dispassionately.

Emily steeled, stood up straight. "Nothing. I just need to speak to Dr. Stone."

The matron blinked. "Radcliffe, we've got a lineup outside. If nothing's—"

"She'll want to speak to me. I have information I'm sure she'd like to be aware of."

Matron Smith sighed. "What sort of information? About another inmate or—"

"Please just let me speak to her. I—"

At that moment, Dr. Stone emerged from her office, crisp white lab coat billowing overtop her usual black skirt and blouse. She took Emily in with a piercing stare.

"Radcliffe has something to say to you, apparently," Matron Smith said, rolling her eyes.

"Yes, I'm sure she does. Come over here then, Radcliffe," the doctor said, beckoning. She disappeared back into her office and Emily followed as Matron Smith looked on, curious.

Emily entered and shut the door behind her. Stone surveyed her, leaning back against the broken desk, hands clutching the edge of it, nails painted crimson as blood. Emily had already decided there was no point in preamble, so she took a breath and launched right in.

"I'm a journalist, Dr. Stone."

She watched for the doctor's reaction. Stone's eyes narrowed, scrutinizing her. "Am I really supposed to believe that?"

"Yes. You are." Emily let the claim settle on her.

Stone shifted her feet. "Prove it."

Emily's gut squirmed with a self-consciousness that she quickly dismissed. Stone could believe her or not, but if Emily could convince her, she could secure Annie's release sooner. But either way, her friend was getting out. Emily would make sure of that.

"I can't," Emily said. "Not right now. But I work for a magazine. We received a note from an inmate here alleging all manner of poor treatment, so I set out to confirm the story. As you can imagine, I've discovered it's all entirely true."

Stone bit down on the inside of her cheeks, making her face look more hollow and unsettling than ever. "*If* what you say is true, which I highly doubt—"

"Why do you doubt it?" Emily challenged. "I'm sure Warden Barrow told you a journalist called, back in the spring. That's why the outdoor time was suspended."

Stone was very still. "Who do you work for?"

"I'm not going to tell you that. But rest assured, it's a big enough publication that you should have cause for concern if I publish." Emily's mouth had gone a little dry, but she steeled herself and pressed on. She could do this. "It's come to my attention that in addition to using your psychiatric patients as lab mice, you've been deliberately infecting the inmates with VD in order to treat them with the trial drug Trichlorovir."

A long pause. "And why would I do such a thing?" Stone crossed her arms over her chest now, protective yet confrontational.

Emily smirked, just for the sheer pleasure of antagonizing her. "Because you're getting paid to by the drug company that developed it."

Stone was pallid, and Emily saw her throat twitch as she swallowed. "So you *are* the little rat who stole my files," she said, realization dawning on her. Her eyes flicked to the closed door beyond which Emily could only hope the infirmary matron was eavesdropping. That might come in useful later on. "White thought it was you."

"Yes," Emily said. "I did." She was proud to hear her voice was steady. She hadn't had much reason to stand up to authority before. It felt simultaneously terrifying and exhilarating. She and Stone stared each other down.

"What do you want?" the doctor finally demanded, taking a step toward Emily, whose heart fluttered, but she held her ground.

"I want you to discharge Annie Little immediately. Tomorrow, when I get out. Do that, and I'll write about the atrocious conditions in this place, but leave out mention of your personal little scheme with the drug trial. The administration, the warden, and the government will be implicated, but not you."

Stone's lips pressed again into a thin line. She straightened. "You do realize this is blackmail."

Emily shrugged. "Is that what you'd call it?"

"That's what the authorities will call it."

"Yes. And they'll call *your* behaviour aggravated assault and corruption, I think."

The clock on the wall ticked away the seconds, and in the silence, Emily felt the trickle of sweat down the back of her dress.

"Don't think for a moment that you've won, Radcliffe." Stone's voice was black ice, the treacherous kind that's difficult to spot until you've suddenly lost control.

"Except I have, Stone," Emily assured her with a mirthless grin. "You don't have power over me anymore. You don't get to decide. The choice *you* get to make is whether you want to release Annie Little and save your career, or go down with this place when I expose the whole thing. It's up to you. But I suggest you decide—"

She gasped as Stone rushed to her, and instinctively shot up an arm. She backed toward the door, eyes wide, and found that she was cornered.

"Ohh, not so brave as you act, eh?" Stone whispered an inch from her face. "Not so brave. Not so smart. You don't seem to understand, Radcliffe, that these women are a *pestilence*." She hissed the c, drawing it out as she held Emily's eyes with her own. Emily dodged, tried to look away, but Stone followed her gaze, bobbing her head around like a charmed snake.

"Get *away from me*!" Emily finally shouted, giving her an actual shove. She didn't care if Matron Smith heard. If she could eventually testify Emily had been threatened by Stone, so much the better.

"What is *wrong* with you?" she demanded finally. Her hand was on the doorknob now, and something began to tingle. Something ominous and disturbing that reverberated inside her alongside June's words:

She belongs in there with the Blues . . .

Stone simply stood there, feet from Emily, and watched her open the door.

"Just release Annie Little with me tomorrow," Emily told her firmly, struggling now with a sudden fear she didn't want Stone to see. She also knew she didn't want to be alone with this woman a moment longer.

Matron Smith was indeed right outside the door, listening. She looked from Emily to the doctor and back again, eyes wide, as Emily pushed past her and out of the infirmary.

"You're not eating much," Emily said to Annie that evening at supper, stuffing a bit of unbuttered, stale bread into her own mouth. She was still riding the wave of adrenaline from her encounter with Stone. She didn't know yet what would happen tomorrow when she was released, whether Annie would be with her or not. Hopefully Stone would consider it overnight and determine Annie's release was in her own best interest.

"No, I don't have much appetite, I'm afraid," Annie said, grimacing. "Dr. Stone gave me some kind of medication this afternoon, and it hasn't agreed with my stomach."

"Well, soon enough, she won't be able to push anything else on you," Emily said. "Whether she responds to my demand or not, I'm getting released tomorrow. And getting you out of here will be my first priority while I write the article. I promise. You won't have to wait much longer, Annie." She smiled and reached out, covered Annie's hand with her own. It was cool to the touch. "She was angry that I would dare to challenge her, of course, but she's got to be scared, too. She might approve your release to leave at the same time as me, if we're lucky. Then I could help you get in touch with your mother, get yourself settled just in time for Christmas next week."

"It's hard to even believe I'll get to see Gregory," Annie said, blinking fast. "He'll be so grown up. I have so many questions to ask him, so much to talk about." She inhaled shakily. "I'm nervous, though, about what he'll think of me. It's a lot to explain, and none of it casts his father in a . . . in a good light."

"No, I shouldn't think so," Emily said darkly. She watched Annie for a moment as chatter continued around them. She couldn't wait to eat a good meal in her parents' quiet dining room— *the next night*. It wasn't anything when compared to Annie's eagerness to see her son, but Emily still felt it keenly. "I suspect it will take some time," she continued. "To explain everything to him and have him understand. I'm certain he'll be just as glad as you are that you've been released." She smiled and downed the last of her tea, took another bite of bread.

Annie bobbed her head in acknowledgment, but her eyes were a little strange—out of focus, the pupils small. "I, uh, I really don't feel well at all," she said.

"What's the matter?" Emily asked, ceasing chewing as she watched her friend's face with growing alarm. She was breathing heavily through her mouth now, as though each inhale was a struggle.

"Annie?" Emily asked, louder. Annie's face had suddenly paled to the colour of soured cream, her eyes half-closed. Her forehead and temples were sweaty, and she continued to pant. Something was wrong, very wrong.

"Matron!" Emily shouted, rising from her seat just as Annie slumped onto the table. "Help! We need help!"

She was aware of a sudden silence in the room, then it erupted again in alarmed voices, other women calling for help on her behalf. Panicking, Emily acted on instinct, wrapping her arms around Annie and lowering her to the floor, supporting Annie's head in her lap.

"HELP! For God's sake!" she screamed, tearing her eyes away from Annie's, which had slid out of focus. She was heavy in Emily's arms.

A crowd of inmates had formed around them, all asking what was happening. Gertrude and Lizzie were screaming at a pair of matrons near the doors. Gert tried to grab at one of them to come, but the woman withdrew. The other followed Lizzie over to where Emily and Annie were heaped on the floor beside their table.

"Gertrude, get Matron Carnegie!" Emily bellowed across the room. Gert nodded and sprinted out the door. If these matrons were too stupid or stubborn to respond, they needed Carnegie. She knew Annie better than any of the others.

"What's happened?" Matron White was there now, demanding answers from a standing position, hands on her hips.

Emily gaped. "She's ill, terribly ill, can't you see? She's nearly unconscious, something's wrong!" She hated to say it, but did anyway. "She needs the doctor!"

"The doctor is gone for the evening," White said dismissively. "It's after six."

"Well, *you* come help, then!" Emily shouted. Other inmates were goading White now, too, shrieking at her to do something.

"She's probably just having a fit, she has them all the time, she's a lunatic!" White snapped back. "Just leave her, she'll be fine."

"She doesn't have fits like *this*," Emily heard Bernie say from somewhere in the crowd. "Just look at her!"

"Emily!" Gertrude shouted, and Emily watched her shove the other girls aside as she led Matron Carnegie over. Relief at the kind matron's arrival crashed over Emily in a wave that broke the dam of her shock, and then the tears came.

"Please," she begged. "Help her!"

"Leave her!" White snarled.

"What happened?" Carnegie asked, ignoring White's protests entirely as she knelt.

"We were talking and she said she didn't feel well," Emily recounted, "then she got all pale and clammy and collapsed." Her own breath was coming in sharp stabs now. Tears fell from her eyes. "Please help her!"

Carnegie fingered Annie's throat. "Her pulse is dangerously slow," she muttered. "Matron White!" she snapped, "go fetch some adrenaline and a large syringe from the infirmary."

Above them, White blustered, "I don't take orders from you! I'm the head—"

"Just do it!" Carnegie barked, and White's mouth fell open, but she pushed her way out of the room anyway. Emily frantically watched her leave. Was she going to get what Carnegie needed? Or had she just abandoned them?

"Stone's gone," Carnegie said. "We're on our own. Here, let me try, there's something I can try, I read about it. Set her head down on the floor, but keep your hands under it for support, just gently. And the rest of you, back up!" she called to the surrounding women, who did as they were told. All was quiet now.

"Okay," Emily sniffed, complying, feeling as though she might be sick. "What are you going to do?"

Matron Carnegie didn't answer, but lowered her mouth to Annie's and blew air into it. Emily watched, fascinated and terrified, as the matron pressed her fists into Annie's chest with all her might, counting under her breath, then leaned forward and blew more air into Annie's mouth. She repeated the process several times before exclamations from around the room signalled the return of Matron White, along with two other matrons who now flanked her like security guards.

"Move aside!" she sniped, making her way through the throng. "I don't know why you're bothering, but here it is." She shoved a syringe and vial toward Carnegie, who was still occupied with this treatment she was attempting. She looked up at White and snatched the supplies from her hands.

"Radcliffe, keep doing what I was doing," she said. "While I prepare the adrenaline."

"What? Um—" Emily panicked.

"Just do it."

Emily took a deep breath and followed Carnegie's lead, placing her mouth over Annie's with renewed sobs. Her friend's lips were blue. "Oh my God," Emily said as she pressed down on her chest in repeated thrusts. "Annie, no . . ."

"Stop," Carnegie said. "Open her dress, right to the skin."

Emily pulled at the fabric, but it wouldn't give. Her eyes darted to the table next to them and she lunged forward, seizing her dull dinner knife. Several inmates gasped or shrieked as she held Annie's dress with one hand and, after three attempts, sliced it with the other to reveal her brassiere.

"Wait," Emily said. "What are you going to—" But she watched in horror as Carnegie plunged the syringe into Annie's breastbone.

Emily cried out as several of the onlooking inmates screamed.

Carnegie watched Annie's chest, then lowered her ear to her face, frowning, before starting up the chest pressure again. The dining hall was silent but for Carnegie's panting breath as she pressed in that horrible rhythm. Tears streamed down Emily's face. To her left, Gert and Lizzie looked aghast as Lizzie cradled a sobbing Peggy to her chest.

After what felt like an age, Matron Carnegie stopped, and sat back on her heels, swiping her brow. "She's uh—" She sighed. She looked at Emily sadly. "She's dead. I'm sorry. She's dead."

Everyone froze.

Emily's sobs became louder as reality began to cut through the layers of shock. She continued to cradle Annie's head in her hands, ran her thumbs over the soft hair at her temples. Tears dripped onto the floor and Annie's forehead. Annie had endured so much in this hellhole, and she had come so far in her sense of self-worth and hope for her future since Emily first met her six months ago. After a long moment, she removed her hands and used them to pull the blue fabric back over Annie's exposed chest, a small dignity at the end of a life that was mostly devoid of it.

They had been so close to getting Annie out of here.

So close.

. . . Too close.

A chill lowered down then, trickling from the tips of her ears to the soles of her feet, the creeping frost of realization.

"Stone did this," she said aloud, looking up now at the crowd of distraught faces all turned toward her and Annie. But her eyes sought Matron White. "This was Stone."

"Steady there, Radcliffe," Matron White said, eyes blazing with warning. "You are clearly hysterical, you—"

"*No*," Emily said, standing up on unsteady legs. "This was Stone! It must have been!"

"You are speaking nonsense," White snapped. The room was deathly quiet.

"Annie told me, at the start of supper, that Stone had given her a new medication today, something she didn't recognize!" She fought a wave of nausea at the thought that Annie had been alive and breathing and talking mere minutes ago.

"Dr. Stone is frequently altering the psychiatric inmates' courses of medication. Inmate Little always had—"

"No! Stone gave her something bad, something that did this!" Emily gestured to Annie's body and felt every eye in the room drawn there, too.

"That's enough, Radcliffe!" Matron White said, taking a step toward Emily now. "This is your final warning!" She turned and said something to Matron Jansen, beside her, who darted away into the crowd.

But the rage and exhaustion and grief were driving Emily's body and mind now. She was beyond caring who knew about her.

"I'm a journalist!" she screamed to the room at large. "I'm a journalist and I came here to see everything that's been happening, how you've all been treated in this horrible place!" She looked around at the surrounding women. All eyes were on her now, some full of confusion, others excitement or disbelief. Matron White's eyes were narrowed, but Emily didn't care.

"Stone's been infecting you all with VD!" she bellowed as loudly as she could, her voice filling the crowded space. There was a general outcry, and she heard Eliza moan. Her eyes sought June now, visible at the back of the room. Her mouth was twisted to the side, either in a sneer or appreciative smirk, Emily couldn't tell. "That's why you can't figure out how you got it! And she's getting paid to do it by a drug company! I have the proof!" she cried.

"That's enough, Radcliffe!" White said, and she and Matron Grimes lunged toward Emily, who was still at the centre of this ring of witnesses, the eye of the storm.

"Get off me!" She struggled against White and the two other matrons who shoved her, face down, to the ground. She cried out as White pressed her knee into Emily's spine and her fellows wrenched Emily's arms around behind her back.

"Stop that! What are you doing?" Carnegie shouted.

Emily felt restraints being pulled tight around her wrists. One side of her face was pressed painfully into the gritty dining hall floor. The inmates were chattering now, the noise swelling. At least now they all knew. There were witnesses to Annie's death, witnesses to her own abusive takedown, witnesses to her claims against Eris Stone. Awkwardly, she met eyes with several of the inmates now, imploring someone to help her. Thelma just sneered.

"These are the ravings of a madwoman!" Matron White shouted. "And they will be treated accordingly! Radcliffe is clearly insane!" With a dawning sense of horror, Emily realized it was a performance. A justification for what they were about to do.

"White, no!" Carnegie cried.

Matron Jansen was back. She handed a package of something to Matron White and Emily strained with her one available eye to see what it was. The sea of brown-clad women watched, and several began to exclaim and gasp as White leaned over Emily, whose panic crested.

"NO!" Emily screamed. "No! No! Get off me! Get off me! June! Eliza! Help! *Please*!"

But no help came. She should have known her "friends" couldn't be real. Not in this place. Annie had been the only one. And now, because of Emily, she was dead.

The last thing Emily heard was one final protest from Matron Carnegie before the sting of a needle pierced her neck.

The iron bedsprings were digging into her back.

She was cold, uncovered. The air smelled different—musty and humid. She gasped a breath and, eventually, her eyes fluttered open. Her body felt heavy, her mind and reactions slow. She blinked several times, noted the dark stone wall across from her. She winced, and shifted her weight with a little grunt. She sat up, ran a hand over her face.

She was in the basement, she realized. She looked around. In one of the isolation cells. She took a deep breath, massaged a particularly painful spot near her right kidney. She glanced down and saw, through the dark, that the mattress had been removed from the bed, leaving only the springs for her to sleep on. Her eyes flicked to the corridor beyond her cell door. The only light came from the sconce on the wall opposite. She couldn't tell, from here, whether it was night or day. Perhaps whatever White had drugged her with had knocked her out all night. Perhaps it was already her discharge day.

She stood then, shaking her head once more to try to clear the fog that was only just beginning to lift. She staggered to the cell door and clutched at the bars. A cold fear gripped her as she saw the woman sitting on the old wooden chair across from her cell.

Eris Stone stood and slowly stepped forward, just out of Emily's reach. Her glasses flashed, white coat glowing eerily yellow in the light of the sconce on the wall. Emily swayed a little, knees feeling as though they might buckle.

"Stone—"

"No one threatens me, Radcliffe."

Emily's mind was slow, struggled to respond.

"So you may as well get comfortable," Stone said with a terrifying grin that didn't meet her eyes. She turned and disappeared down the corridor, her footsteps growing quieter.

Emily stood at the cell door, her breath coming shallow. And in the dim light, her gaze finally landed on the skirt of her dress.

Emily's scream tore from her lungs and echoed down the barren corridor as she stared in horror at her brand-new, unmistakably blue dress.

PART FOUR

indomitable

(Adj.: that which cannot
be subdued or overcome;
unconquerable)

The older I get, the more I see
how women are described as having
gone mad, when what they've actually
become is knowledgeable and powerful
and fucking furious.

SOPHIE HEAWOOD

CHAPTER 36

EMILY

December 21, 1961
Day 3 in isolation

By my count, it was the winter solstice; the darkest night of the year, when this little corner of the earth turns as far away as it will ever be from the light of the sun, crouching into itself in protection from the bitter cold. It is the lowest point of the valley we descend into each year, beginning in October, as the light starts to retreat from us to go warm others on the opposite side of this great, swirling globe. It's only fair that they have their turn with the sun's attentions. But how lonely and dark it becomes at the bottom of that vast wintry canyon. And all we can do is forge on, one day at a time, ascending back up the hill as the light grows slowly brighter, until we finally feel the heat of the sun on our skin again and are reminded that this is the cycle, the ebb and flow of light and dark that conducts the rhythm of our lives.

But that day, I could only see the darkness. I kept blinking my eyes to adjust, but they would not. I could only assume, at that point, that it would always be black.

Emily shifted her weight a little to tuck one of her cold feet beneath her. She was huddled in the loosely knitted blanket on the springs of the bed frame; she couldn't even lean her weight against the stone wall, because it was too cold. One or two degrees colder, and she would see her breath in front of her face.

She listened to the sounds on the floor above her, the distant hum of chatter from the dining hall. It was suppertime, and her stomach ached. She was starving, her head throbbing from dehydration, but she'd been declining the food and drink Matron Grimes brought her over the past two days. After what happened to Annie, she couldn't trust that it wasn't poisoned.

She swiped at a tear, warm against her cool cheek. She could hardly believe that after witnessing the murder of one of their own, right there in the dining hall, these women could carry on like they were, chattering and eating as though it didn't matter. Emily scoffed in disgust, for the hundredth time. It was every woman for herself in here. She should have known that. Everyone was just greedily scrambling for their piece of the very limited pie, the small sliver they felt they were entitled to as they were fed through the meat grinder that was the Mercer Women's Prison.

Over the past two days, Emily had had plenty of time to reflect, with nothing at all to occupy her time besides her own tormenting thoughts. In hindsight, she couldn't believe she thought she could just waltz into a prison and take some notes and bring it all down from the inside. Nellie Bly might have done it, but that didn't mean just anyone could. Emily had vastly overestimated herself, as had Doris, her parents. She felt ashamed that she'd failed at what she'd come here to do, failed as a journalist. And she'd also failed these women, and all the women who would come after them, funnelled into the prison system by laws that sought to punish them for things men were never punished for, solely because they were women. There was no law that could put teenage boys in prison for sneaking in after curfew, or impregnating a girl of another race. Emily had come in here to try to make a name for herself, and that need had morphed into wanting to make a *difference* for others. But she'd failed at both.

White—and by extension, Eris Stone—had declared her insane and forced her into this blue dress. Her file would now be marked with a "P," for "Psychiatric." Would she be left here in isolation interminably, she wondered, or would Stone ever release her up into the psychiatric wing? Emily wasn't even sure she wanted that. It might be warmer up there, but she'd then be in the company of truly insane women like Rose, who probably wanted to harm her even more than she had before, since Annie was dead.

And it was all Emily's fault.

She buried her face in the tent of her knees.

None of it mattered. The system was rigged to beat them at every turn. They never could win.

She thought of June's words, so long ago now.

That's been women's lot since the beginning of time. There ain't no changing it, and the sooner you get that through your head, the better off you'll be.

But the rules had been written by men, for the benefit of men. Could any woman ever rewrite them? What a fool Emily had been to think that she—from her cozy, privileged corner of the world—could undo that kind of systemic injustice with a few of her own words. Perhaps June was right. There just was no changing it. But how devastating it was to admit defeat.

She probably should have believed the madam from the start, trusted that she—and Eliza, and Annie—might know a little more about the real world than she did, might have some knowledge and experience with the true villains and monsters that Emily had only read about in stories. She should have believed them when they tried to warn her about Stone's power. But she'd thought she knew better, and now Annie was dead, and Emily could be kept here as long as Stone wanted. She'd come into this place so green and naive and bursting at the seams with idealism. She'd thought her experiences had filed that down a bit, had weathered and wizened her, but she'd gotten too carried away, so caught up in her goals and story that she didn't stop to listen to the women who truly knew this system.

At some point, she knew, her parents and Doris together would make some sort of effort to secure her release. She wondered how long they would let it go before they started to make inquiries, contact a lawyer. But they would need to expose her and the fact that they'd lied to the court, and Emily's gut churned at the consequences that might come out of that, particularly for her father. What a disaster this had all turned out to be. She longed for her parents now, but could hardly stand the thought of having to face them after this debacle.

The sound of a door opening at the end of the hall interrupted Emily's thoughts and she straightened, but stayed where she was on the bed. Standing would release all the heat she'd worked so hard to contain under that blanket.

"Supper, Radcliffe," Matron Grimes said in her deep voice, which echoed a little down the empty hall. There were no other inmates in isolation right now. Grimes appeared in the door frame a moment later, holding a tray. She took in Emily's appearance and sighed with irritation. "Look, you need to eat something."

"I won't trust it unless Carnegie brings it," Emily told her for the seventh time.

Previously, Grimes had just scoffed when Emily said this, but this time she hesitated. "Carnegie's been sacked," she admitted, a little quieter.

"What?" Emily's insides swooped. Her only remaining ally was gone now.

"Warden fired her yesterday, because she kept insisting . . ." Grimes shook her head. "Anyway, she's gone. But I got this food off the supper line myself, and I tell you, it isn't poisoned, so just eat it. You're starving."

"What about Stone?" Emily asked. The doctor's name was bitter in her mouth. "What's—"

"Stone's not even here, it's the bloody Christmas holiday now, isn't it?"

She unlocked the little gate in Emily's cell door and passed the tray through. After a moment of hesitation, Emily stood and took it, sat on the cold floor and shovelled mashed potato and ham into her mouth with her hands. They didn't give you utensils in solitary—not even a spoon. Emily looked up at Grimes, who was lingering uncharacteristically with a funny sort of look on her face.

"Look," she said, dropping her voice and glancing over her shoulder before squatting down close to the door. "If you are who they say you are, keep my name out of it all, and I'll keep bringing you decent food."

Emily swallowed. "None of the food here has ever been decent."

Grimes actually laughed, full-bellied. "You got an attitude on you, I'll give you that, reporter. But you can at least *trust* the food if it comes from me, anyway. I can't say any of this is right, but it's not my place to have an opinion if I want to stay employed."

"Can you help me get a letter out?" Emily asked, heart lifting, but Grimes shook her head.

"I can't do that, but I won't let you starve, either. That's as much of a deal as I'm fit to make."

Emily nodded. "All right. Thank you."

For once in her life, Emily didn't know the next step, the next question to ask. After Grimes left and her meal was done, she buried her face in her knees again as a fresh wave of tears erupted, and the darkness descended once more.

CHAPTER 37

RACHEL

June, 1996

JESSICA HAWKINS
ELSIE CHALIFOUX
ANNIE LITTLE
WILMA CARDINAL
EMILY RADCLIFFE

Standing in front of the Jane Doe board in her office, Rachel stuffs a half-stale blueberry muffin into her mouth, a leftover from a Tim Hortons box someone brought in yesterday. But she's too absorbed in the case to duck out for lunch.

Earlier in the week, she'd contacted the chief coroner's office with the five names on the corkboard. She figured she'd try the coroner's office first to see if there were any suspicious deaths for any of these names— given the strange way in which the remains were buried. There would be fewer hits on those names than in the Registrar General's records.

She was right. The coroner's office confirmed that Jessica Hawkins, Elsie Chalifoux and Wilma Cardinal were dead and accounted for, with causes of death listed as "old age," "heart failure," and the maddeningly vague "natural." It had two Annie Littles in its system, but no Emily Radcliffes. Stevens had swept into Rachel's office two days before with the news, as soon as the fax had come through.

"What have you got?" Rachel had asked him, sitting down and leaning back in her chair. The overhead lights cast his hair a little fairer than it usually looked, and something about that, combined with the way he furrowed his brow, reminded her so much of his uncle Tom in that moment that she'd grinned.

Stevens had shuffled the short stack of pages in his hands. "One of these reports," he said, sliding it across the desk to Rachel, "has an Annie Little with place of death listed as the Mercer Women's Prison. December 1961."

Rachel's eyebrows shot up, and she nodded with satisfaction. "Excellent." Her eyes slid down the page, and she felt a little twinge of pity.

```
Cause of death: Suicide
```

"Okay." She'd handed the sheet back to Stevens, who looked on eagerly. "What's the next step, then?" she said, testing him.

"Uh . . . Registrar General, I think?"

"You got it. Request all five of the names, then we can cross-reference birth and death certificates and see what we get. We'll need marriage certificates, too." Name changes for women were always a nightmare—it made everything harder to track. "We're looking for any connection one of these women might have had to Millgate, or Huron County at all."

Stevens had sent over the request that afternoon, but Rachel knew that, as always, it would take a few days for the registrar to come back with the records. In the meantime, they were still stumped on this unaccounted-for Emily Radcliffe. Was she dead? Or alive with a poorly managed prison record? Rachel hoped she might still be alive, as that would narrow the possible Jane Doe ID pool down to four.

Her next thought had been to get a warrant for tax records from the CRA, to see if any of that information might align with a woman who was alive and imprisoned in Toronto leading up to the early sixties. After waiting impatiently for the warrant to come through, Rachel was able to request information from the CRA: specifically, last known address and last employer of Emily Radcliffes born between 1915 and 1945. But if the Emily Radcliffe from the Mercer prison hadn't been born a Radcliffe, then they'd have to go back through marriage records to try to isolate new possible women.

"Rachel?" Crystal asks now from the doorway.

"Detective Mackenzie. Yes?"

"This came through for you. From the CRA." Crystal walks in, hands her a large stack of paper.

"Thanks," Rachel says after she's already left, her attention turning immediately to the documents. She sifts through the pages. There are multiple hits from across the county, but two of the Emily Radcliffes are currently near Toronto.

She washes down the muffin with a swig of coffee and sits down. She runs a finger over the first record to locate the phone number, then dials.

"Hi there," she says, introducing herself and her credentials. "I'm trying to track down an Emily Radcliffe who served time at the Mercer Women's Prison in Toronto in the late fif—"

"I'm sorry, the *what?*" the woman exclaims.

"The Mercer Women's Prison. In Toronto. Were you ever incarcerated there, ma'am?"

"I'm sorry," she says, "I haven't any clue what you're talking about. I think you're looking for someone else."

She sounds genuine, so Rachel believes her. If she's lying, Rachel has all her information now and can easily follow up. "All right, thank you for your time," she says.

She takes a deep breath as sounds from the outer office drift through. She pulls out the record from the CRA for the second Emily Radcliffe and finds the number, but a harsh beeping sound fills her ear as a cold woman's voice tells her it's out of service. Frowning, Rachel hangs up and tries it again, with the same result.

"Okay," she mutters. "Let's see . . ."

She sifts through, scanning this woman's information. She's had a pretty stable life; just three addresses listed, the most recent of which is in the north end of Toronto. And one place of employment: Maclean-Hunter Ltd.

Rachel picks up the phone again, dials 411 and requests to be connected to Maclean-Hunter. A woman answers after one ring. Rachel identifies herself and explains the situation, and is promptly transferred to the human resources department, where she waits on hold for nearly ten minutes, doodling on the corner of her notepad as her mind wanders. When the HR rep finally picks up, Rachel gives her whole spiel and is put back on hold again while the woman checks their records. She comes back two minutes later. Rachel poises her pen over the page now, ready to write. She listens, her shoulders drooping as the woman speaks.

"Oh, okay," Rachel says. "And when did that happen?"

CHAPTER 38

EMILY

December 24, 1961
Day 6 in isolation

The noise began after suppertime.

Emily had just forced down the last of her tasteless shepherd's pie when the sounds of shouts, bangs, and scraping began to seep through the floor above her. She sat on the exposed springs of her cot and listened, straining her ears to catch any snippet of information that might explain what was going on.

Ten minutes in, the noise had grown louder, and Emily reckoned it was concentrated in the dining hall and the main corridor. What could be happening? Had a fight gotten out of hand? She thought of Eliza and June telling her about the summertime riot a couple of years before, when the women had risen up in protest of the oppressive heat of the place. Were they doing the same now, about the extreme cold? Emily herself had been shivering for days, like the beggars she'd sometimes passed on her way to work. They huddled in alleyways, unseen by most passersby, who averted their eyes and pulled their expensive wool collars higher against the wintry wind. It was so much easier for the average John and Jane to not have to witness struggle that wasn't their own. And that was the point of dreadful institutions like the Mercer. To pack away the undesirables behind locked gates and tall stone walls so they didn't besmirch the otherwise pristine landscape of the city.

CRASH.

It took a second for her to identify the specific sound, which she took to be something large being overturned, followed by bellows and cheers of delight. Emily stood now, though she wasn't quite sure why. Instinct had her on alert. She paced her tiny cell, padding back and forth in the worn-out slippers inherited from some previous miserable inmate, her nerves beginning to jangle. Her tapping finger drummed.

A few minutes later, there was a sound from down the hall, a door creaking open near the stairs that led to the main floor.

She ran to her door. "Hello?"

There was no reply, but soft, shuffling footsteps grew closer.

"Who's there?" she demanded, suddenly on edge. "Grimes?" Another resounding crash from above, as a small woman came into view. Emily's heart stopped.

Rose.

She stood before Emily's cell door, hair dishevelled around a gaunt face with eyes black and piercing as a shark's, the pupils dilated. Her blue dress was smeared with something dark, something . . . red. Emily gasped, and Rose grinned. Her sinister smile was devoid of two front teeth, giving her the disturbing appearance of a deranged child.

Emily scrambled backward to the wall farthest from the door, heart hammering in her throat now as she pressed her back and palms into the rough, cold brick. "What do you want?" she asked, trying not to sound frightened. "What's going on upstairs?"

But the woman didn't answer. She was bent over a little now, her blond hair hanging like dirty tentacles in front of her face. A flash of silver in the glow of the corridor lights. A knife.

Emily felt the blood drain from her face. "I didn't kill Annie!" she shouted, but her voice cracked with the terrified conviction that she had. Rose ignored her, started trying to pick the lock with the blade . . .

"MATRON!" Emily screamed as her brain whirred wildly, casting around for a way to defend herself. But there was nothing in the isolation cell. There wasn't even a sheet to strangle someone with, because an inmate could hang themselves with it. "HELP!"

"They ain't comin'," Rose said with a low chuckle.

Emily's breath suspended.

"Rose," Emily appealed through her fear. "What have you done?" No response. "Have the psych patients escaped? Is anyone hurt?"

This is it, Emily thought. After everything that had happened, she was going to be stabbed to death by a Blue in a basement isolation cell.

A crash and a scream issued from upstairs, somewhere directly above them.

She was still grappling with how to defend herself when she heard a voice down the corridor. "Hey!" it called. "I said I'd feckin' do that!"

"ELIZA! HELP!" Emily bellowed. "Get help! She has a knife!"

"Jesus H.," Eliza said, coming into view. She nudged Rose on the shoulder. "You'll feck up the lock real good doin' that! And cut yerself. Let me do it!"

Confusion gripped Emily. "Eliza, what—?" she began, but then June Jones stepped into the frame of her cell door. *"June?"*

June smirked, shook her head. "You look like hell, kid. What did I tell you about trying to blackmail Stone? Get back for a sec, and Eliza'll have this open."

Emily obeyed, now eyeing Rose. "Isn't she . . ." She nodded at the woman's dress, reluctant to say it. "Crazy?" She met Rose's eyes. "Aren't you crazy?"

Rose stared at Emily a moment with her wide eyes. "No. Are you?" She pointed at Emily's blue uniform.

Emily's shook her head, speechless.

"None of us up there are half as crazy as they say we are. It's all the goddamn cages they shove us into that drive us mad." Rose paused, then wiped away a drip from her nose. "Annie was my friend, too. And Stone killed her. We all know that now."

Emily's eyes welled with tears.

"We're getting you out," June said, and Emily faced her now. "Right now. Tonight. We have a plan."

"What in the hell is going on upstairs?" Emily asked, composing herself. Her mind was reeling.

June raised an eyebrow. "The plan. Quick now, put this on."

Through the bars, she passed Emily a piece of white cloth that Emily didn't recognize until she held it up to view it in the dim light.

"Stone's coat?" she asked incredulously. "What are—"

"Just put it on," June told her. Dizzy with questions, Emily complied.

"Got it," Eliza said triumphantly, and Emily's cell door suddenly swung open with a creak. She darted over the threshold with relief.

"Ugh, you smell like 'er now, don't ya?" Eliza said, screwing up her face. "Well, come on. Let's get back to the stairs before the cops come down."

"The police are here?" Emily gasped.

"Yes," June confirmed. "The matrons called them when the riot started."

"Riot? So that's what I've been hearing?"

"You ain't as clever as they said you were," Rose muttered.

"Well, we needed a diversion, and I couldn't very well set the place on fire again," June said with a shrug. "Let's go."

She started down the hall and the others followed, Emily hurrying to keep up. When they reached the bottom of the stairs, the sounds from above became louder.

"We told the girls you were telling the truth," June informed Emily. "That you're a reporter here to break the story of this place, and hopefully get us all out. Fortunately, I've got cred, and after what happened with Annie, well . . ." She shook her head darkly. "It didn't take much to convince them to do this. Besides, I think—" Another series of bangs overhead. Women jeered and shrieked as male voices tried and failed to bellow over them. "I think they needed to blow off some steam, anyway."

"So what happens now?" Emily asked. She looked down at her disguise and worriedly up the stairs.

"Well, we've snagged one of Stone's coats for you for a reason—"

"She added two more bleedin' locks to 'er door since the fire," Eliza said, "but she can't keep *me* out." She beamed smugly.

Emily looked at her small friend and nearly laughed, despite the situation.

"You have to pose as a doctor," June continued. "Most of these cops won't have met Stone, they usually talk with the warden when they come. Last time they were here was for the riot in the summer of '59. So they won't know the difference as long as you act convincing. And here, we got to fix your hair." June pulled the pins from her own bun and smoothed Emily's down, then twisted it and pinned it back. It was a surprisingly intimate gesture that made Emily feel somehow taken care of.

But she hesitated, watching them all. "Can't I just tell them who I am? To let me out?"

June withdrew her hands from Emily's head and gaped. "This is the *cops*, kid. They aren't gonna believe you. You're wearing a blue dress, in case you forgot. I knew a Blue once who said she was Queen Victoria!"

Emily opened her mouth to protest, but held her tongue this time. She'd dismissed June and Eliza and their knowledge before, with deadly consequences. They were here now, trying to break her out. She had to trust that they might know something she didn't. "So what happened at the last riot?" she asked instead. "What can we expect?"

She glanced at Rose, who was standing still, staring up the stairs, knife in hand. Had she already attacked one of the police with it?

"Well, they didn't take anyone down to the station," June said as another crash sounded upstairs. "'Cause they're just gonna get charged and sent back here anyway. So they contained the prison, wrestled everyone back into their cells. But some of the girls aren't rioting, they're just in their cells staying safe. Your friend, Penny?"

"Peggy?"

"Yeah. Lizzie said she's terrified of cops, so the two of them stayed out of this, but Lizzie said good luck and she's rooting for you."

Emily smiled in wonder. They'd all finally come together—for her. For each other.

"So . . . we need to get you out that door somehow," June was saying. "It's Christmas Eve. Not sure if you knew that. I figured the cops would have a skeleton staff tonight, and the matrons, too. Even Warden'll probably be off somewhere with her family. I hope," she added. "The police may not know you're not a doctor, but Warden's another story, and the matrons. We might have to improvise, kid."

Emily nodded. "Okay." Then a thought flashed to mind. "The files!" She said, "Annie's records and the drug trial, the documents—"

But June shook her head. "Gone. Stone tossed your cell the morning after Annie died and found them under the mattress. Lizzie was listening, watching from her cell door. And before she got sacked, Carnegie told me Stone burned them."

Emily's heart fell, but there was nothing to be done. Maybe they could find some other way to prove Stone's actions, but the important thing now was getting the hell out of this prison.

"What about *my* notes?" she asked suddenly.

Silence. "What notes?"

"I've been taking notes almost since I arrived, writing them on toilet paper and hiding them in the tap in my cell."

June and Eliza's mouths fell open. Rose cackled.

"Lizzie didn't say anything about that," June answered.

"I have to check," Emily insisted, as her mind finally zoomed in on the situation. This was it. This was her escape. It was happening. "I need those notes, if they're still there."

June took a deep breath but nodded. "All right. Let's see if we can get up to the second floor first, then out the back door. Eliza, stick with us, but let Emily do the talking, because we got to convince these cops she's the prison doctor."

"Yer still gonna hold up yer bargain, right?" Eliza demanded. "That I can come work at yer place?"

"Yes," June said. "As soon as you're out. You have my word."

Eliza nodded, visibly relieved. "But how are we gonna get you out with 'er?" she asked, indicating Emily. There was a moment's pause as all four women looked from one to the other, then June's eyes landed on Rose. On her knife.

"Can I have that?" she asked Rose, who hesitated, but handed it over.

A policeman shouted at some unseeable inmate at the top of the staircase as June held her left hand out flat. Emily sucked her breath in through her teeth as she watched June slice into her own palm.

"June—!"

"Yer feckin' crazy," Eliza said, matter of fact. Rose chuckled darkly and accepted the knife back. June grimaced, then palmed the side of her face, her temple, up into the freckles on her flaming hairline, then brought it down her neck for good measure.

"There," she said, meeting Emily's eyes. "I got hit in the head, bleeding like hell. Tell them you need to get me to the hospital, and say it with authority. *Convince* them. I know you can do this, kid.'

Emily swallowed the lump in her throat and fought to latch on to the bead of excitement in her belly instead as she ascended the stairs beside June, Stone's starchy white coat billowing out from her hips. After months of this drudgery, days in the hole, June Jones, of all people, had orchestrated her escape.

They emerged into the main corridor upstairs, right at the X-junction, and Emily struggled to take in all that she was seeing and hearing. It was the same prison, but it was as though someone had let a pack of wild animals loose in the corridors. Pieces of furniture littered the floor, a battlefield of splintered wooden legs. There were smears and muck on the walls—remnants of the shepherd's pie, she thought. Women were running to and fro, blue and brown dresses alike, some cackling with glee and frenzy and others with pinched, angry faces. One of the pregnant girls from the shuttered maternity home hurled a dining chair at a raging policeman, and Emily's jaw fell open. Nearly all of the women turned to look at June and Emily—who suddenly felt very conspicuous, both because she was sporting Stone's white coat, and because she knew these women were all aware now of her true identity.

She swallowed hard, and she and June stepped forward. She was vaguely aware of Eliza behind them, though, rather ominously, Rose seemed to have melted into the ether along with her knife.

Suddenly, another woman was in front of them. Thelma. She paused, chest heaving, then smirked at Emily, raised an eyebrow, and bolted away. Emily watched, her senses overloaded by the chaos unfolding in all directions, as Thelma darted across the hall toward the fire alarm. It was a pull-rod that ran a thin red pole all the way up the wall to the alarm several feet above their heads.

"You better get us the hell out of here, *Doctor!*" Thelma shouted, then yanked on the rod.

The bell began to peal its deafening rhythm. Thelma grinned maliciously and ran off into the fray, pursued by a policeman, leaving Emily, Eliza, and June covering their ears. The noise was twice as loud down here as it had been in Stone's office the last time it went off. It added significantly to the distraction they were all working to create for Emily's escape, but it also meant the fire brigade would be there soon.

June was clearly thinking along the same lines. "Go! Upstairs! Now!"

They ran as fast as they could, and found the second floor nearly deserted. It had been recreation hour, so the cell doors were open. Emily hurried to her cell and found it in a state of disarray; the mattress was on the floor, the chamber pot on its side, lid beside it. Just as she had the night of the fire, Emily darted to the tap and, with a surge of relief, found the roll of paper notes. It had not been discovered. Shoving it into her brassiere, she returned to June, who was speaking with Lizzie in the cell next door. Emily looked in to find Lizzie sitting on her bed, holding Peggy to her with her hands over her ears as tears poured down Peggy's face.

"I'm so sorry," Emily shouted over the bell, shaking her head. She felt wretched about what they were putting Peggy through. "I'm sorry."

But Lizzie's calm brown eyes met Emily's, and in them she found the forgiveness she needed. "Just get us all out of here, Emily. Please. Go. *Go!*" she urged, and Emily, June, and Eliza made for the stairs.

"We need to find the cop in charge!" June said loudly in her ear as they reached the landing of the main floor.

Emily nodded, then picked a direction, turning toward the dining hall. They looked in as they passed, and Emily's guess was confirmed. The riot had clearly begun as some sort of food fight, combined with furniture destruction. Several of the women and police were clustered in here, engaged in too many stand-offs and battles for Emily to fully process it all. But she gasped at the vision of Gertrude, who was standing on one of the remaining dining tables, taunting a police officer below and dancing out of his reach as he took a swing at her ankles with his rod. She looked up at Emily with surprised triumph on her face, and the cop turned, too. His brow furrowed at June.

"Hey!" he shouted. "Jones! What—"

"Hey, copper!" Gert bellowed. She leapt down from the table with impressive agility and tapped him on the behind. He spun back around to face her, enraged. "How fast can you run, pig?" And she sprinted away toward the kitchen door, the officer hot on her heels.

"Go. Go," June pressed, shoving Emily forward as the incessant fire alarm tore their eardrums. "Over there, that's the chief. It's all you now, kid."

Then she threw a heavy arm around Emily's shoulders and went half limp, eyes closed. Emily staggered a little, adjusting to her weight and the sudden feeling of being left alone, then lurched toward the man in uniform at the end of the hall. She'd never had cause to speak to a policeman before, and a knot of nerves tightened. He squinted at her coat as they approached.

"Hello, uh . . . doctor?"

"Stone, yes. This woman needs the hospital. She has a bad head injury."

He took in the blood on June's face. "Jones, eh? Serves her right, pulling some bull like this on bloody Christmas Eve. Little shits."

"Has the warden been called?" Emily demanded in her best authoritative voice.

He nodded. "She's not answering her phone, or the door. It's all dark over there. Do you have an emergency number for her?" he shouted. "One of the matrons was trying to reach her at some relative's in Scarborough . . ."

"No, I don't, I'm sorry," Emily said, relieved, though she knew that they could reach Barrow soon. Their time was limited. "Where are all the matrons?" she asked.

"Most of 'em locked themselves in the chapel down that hall a few minutes ago," he shouted, indicating the south corridor. "With three infants."

Emily nodded. "Well, uh, I'm glad they're all safe. We'll get this nonsense sorted out shortly. But this woman, she needs the hospital immediately. How can I get her there?"

He looked June over with distaste, but nodded. "This way. Not her, though," he added, indicating Eliza. Emily's brain buzzed, but she couldn't find a plausible reason for Eliza to come with them, and if she tried to press the matter, that could draw unwanted questioning. Emily met the girl's eyes, and hoped Eliza would see the honesty in them.

"Get on back to your cell, inmate," she said. "We'll call for you later."

Eliza glowered at her, but there was something else beneath the anger, something pitiful, like a wounded animal who has been kicked one too many times. Like she should have known better than to trust this time, either. But she stayed back, jaw set.

Emily's heart ached with disquiet as she followed the policeman to the south doors of the prison that emptied out onto the unused courtyard and the loading dock. The empty nursery was on their right; on the left, the chapel where most of the matrons had apparently barricaded themselves, praying for God to save them while leaving Toronto's finest to carry out His will.

Most of the noise was now coming from the dining hall, and began to wane as they made their way down the corridor. Emily ducked her head a little behind June's as they passed the chapel, not wanting to be spotted through the small windows on the doors. She had one arm around June, whose eyes were half closed as she faked semi-consciousness. And then they were at the exit. The officer explained what was happening to the policeman guarding it.

"Tremblay, run the doctor and this inmate over to St. Joe's," he shouted, "then come right back."

The back doors were heavily bolted on a normal day, but he unlocked them all with one of the massive key rings he'd evidently gotten off a matron, and they stepped out into the freezing night.

This is it.

Emily's insides flooded with relief at her deliverance.

The wind stirred up a little cyclone in the open courtyard, swirling snow around her and June's thin skirts. She shivered, but kept her eyes on the three police cars parked in a line beyond the fence. There must be others surrounding the place, more on King Street at the front doors.

June continued to walk as though requiring Emily's support, and as Emily guided her across the courtyard and through the gate, she felt an eerie warmth, a sense of her life coming full circle. She could hardly believe that six months ago she'd met June right there, at that very spot, and now they were escaping together.

June got in the back seat of the police car, and Emily walked around the trunk to the other side, slipping a little on the slushy curb and splashing water up onto her ankles. Stone's coat was flapping in the wind, exposing the front of her blue dress. She glanced back at the prison to see three matrons with their faces pressed against the glass of the Protestant chapel's back window, pointing and gesticulating wildly, mouths open in alarm or shouts, she couldn't tell. All she knew was that she had absolutely been recognized. Two of the matrons disappeared from the window. There was no time to spare.

Emily slipped into the back of the car. It was hardly any warmer in there, though at least they were protected from the wind. She felt as though she'd left her insides back in the isolation cell.

But the car wasn't moving. Emily glanced at June and saw, through the window beside her, two matrons and the chief of police standing at the now-open back door, a bar of yellow light flooding the courtyard. Matron White was pointing at the car and shouting.

"Officer," Emily snapped at the man in the front seat, her voice rising. He was looking down at something in his lap. "We need to go *now*, right now, this woman is in serious condition."

Emily heard a faint shriek. Something else was happening at the back doors now. Another woman had appeared, a tiny woman—a girl—in a brown dress, her strawberry-blond hair illuminated in the backlight from the door.

Eliza.

For a fleeting, horrid moment, Emily feared Eliza was trying to chase them, perhaps afraid now of being left behind, afraid that June wouldn't come through on her promise. But then she screamed again, and threw something toward White and the police chief. It shattered at their feet and she jumped up and down, hands in the air.

"Come and get me then!" Emily heard her cry as she bolted back into the prison, drawing the aggrieved chief away from the door and Matron White, who stood powerless, watching June and Emily's flight . . .

With a rush of gratitude for Eliza, Emily tore her eyes away from the prison to find their driver peering out the window, too.

"Hey," he said, "what's—"

"She's losing consciousness, Officer!" Emily snapped, diverting his attention. "The hospital, please! *Now!*"

"Okay, okay, Doctor," he said, tossing a notepad down onto the console without looking at it. "I'm just making a log. Been a hell of a night. We're tryin' to get backup from Port Credit, but they aren't here yet. Fire brigade can help when they arrive, I guess. Lucky them."

The car peeled away from the curb, slowed briefly, then blew through the stop sign at the corner of Fraser Ave. It was Christmas Eve, so there was no traffic. Still looking out June's window as they sped past, Emily glimpsed the sign for Liberty Street on the post high above them, glowing like a flare in the flashing red lights of the cruiser.

———

They sped down King Street West, past the low-rise apartments and churches that defined the neighbourhood. The policeman drove in silence and Emily wondered briefly if a real doctor would have engaged him in conversation during the ride. But no matter; he didn't seem to suspect anything, had no reason to. June sat with her head leaning back on the vinyl bench seat. Emily caught glimpses of her in the streetlights as they flashed by the window in a slow rhythm, like a lighthouse beacon swinging past every few seconds. The blood was crusted and darkening around June's temple where she'd smeared it, but Emily was worried about the cut on her hand, which might legitimately need medical attention. Looking down, she saw June was cradling it in her lap. Silently, Emily reached over and lifted her wrist, trying to see. June flinched, and her eyes snapped to Emily, brow furrowed with inquiry. But she allowed Emily to take a look. It was a short cut, right at the fleshy base of her thumb, but looked a little too deep. Emily pulled down the sleeve of Stone's clean white coat and pressed the fabric onto the wound. June winced, but said nothing.

As they continued on toward the Queensway, the shoreline of the lake dark and frigid on their left, Emily felt June's fingers close tightly around her own. They stayed like that, grasping one another in silent victory until the car pulled up in front of the brightly lit hospital a few minutes later.

Emily had been so lost in thought about all that had just happened, June's surprising show of emotion, and the shock of their current situation that she hadn't considered what they would do once they finally arrived at the hospital. She caught June's eyes as the car wound its way to the entrance, trying to silently communicate, but June shook her head and closed her eyes, feigning unconsciousness again.

Emily recalled her words of not even an hour ago: *We might have to improvise, kid.* She took a deep breath. They'd managed well enough so far . . .

"All right," the policeman said, shifting the car into park with a sigh. He turned in his seat to face her. "How—"

"I need you to go inside and ask for Dr. Anderson," Emily said, inventing recklessly with the first name that came to mind. Her mouth was dry. "He's a brain specialist. This woman has a bad head injury. And hurry, please!"

"It's Christmas Eve, ma'am. What if he's not here?"

Emily faltered. "He'll have a resident, or someone covering for him. Please, go now!"

The officer nodded once, and hopped out of the car. He darted into the hospital with an inconveniently admirable haste to save a criminal's life. There probably was no Dr. Anderson, and if there was, odds were excellent he wasn't the brain specialist. The ruse would collapse within minutes, and then the officer would start asking questions.

"A cab," June said suddenly, snapping out of her hoax. "There." She pointed at three taxis lined up twenty feet away in the drop-off loop.

They leapt out of the cruiser and scurried through the snow toward the closest black-and-orange taxi, which was running, staying warm for the next hire. Without knocking, they opened the back doors and threw themselves in. The surprised driver, who hadn't seen them approach, turned around.

"Evening, ladies," he said, then saw Emily's coat. "Doctor? A lady doctor?" He smiled, though not maliciously. "Never had one of you before. Where you need to go?"

Emily cleared her throat and looked at June. "My friend's, uh . . ."

"Mansfield Ave., in Little Italy," June supplied.

"You got it." The driver shifted the car into gear.

Snow continued to fall as they looped back down King Street West. Emily sat back, staring out the windshield in a state of disbelief. Slush whirred in the wheel wells but otherwise the journey was quiet, the streets nearly deserted. At this very moment, Emily thought, people were sitting down to family meals, attending Christmas Eve services in warm, candle-lit churches, carrying on as though there weren't a riot happening at the Mercer Women's Prison a few blocks away. But after the chaos of the escape—*escape!*—the silence was a bit disorienting. Unnerving, even. Emily's throat tightened thinking of Eliza, Rose, Gertrude, Lizzie, Peggy, and even Thelma. All the women who had banded together to help get her out. She owed them everything now.

June rode silently beside her until, fifteen or twenty minutes later, she finally spoke, her voice a little hoarse.

"Number sixty-one," she told the driver, who slowed and then stopped against the curb. Emily looked up at the narrow, red-brick row house sandwiched between a nearly identical building and a large Catholic church, its windows glowing gold from within. She raised her eyebrows and, had she had any mirth to spare, would have laughed at June's daring. A nondescript house of ill-repute snuggled up against a house of the Lord in a middle-class neighbourhood. One-stop shopping for the sinful and subsequently repentant.

"The precinct is down the street," June muttered, and Emily turned to see the madam watching her inspect the church. "I'll be right back," she said louder, to the driver. "Cash is inside."

"Alrighty," he drawled, tapping a finger on the steering wheel.

Emily sat, trying to calm her heart rate as June knocked hard on her own door, which was finally opened by a tiny woman Emily recognized. She squinted, trying to recall her name through the buzzing in her head. Lola. Lila. June returned two minutes later with a tidy roll of bills from which she peeled a few, handing them to the driver through the open passenger window. She leaned her head in then, resting her large bosom on the window frame.

"There's enough to take my friend to her destination, and extra in there for you," she told him. "'Cause it's Christmas and all, and I think you're going to forget where you picked us up and dropped us off. Aren't you?"

The driver counted the bills, then nodded. "Merry Christmas, ma'am."

"Whatever's next, you know where to find me," June directed at Emily, meeting her eyes, unblinking. "I'll need to lie low for a bit. But I'll corroborate anything you need. You have my word."

Emily nodded once. For some reason, she was next to tears. "And Eliza—"

"If you get her to me, she has a place. I gave my word on that, too."

"Okay," Emily croaked. "I'll uh . . . I'll be in touch soon, then."

June paused, then reached in to grasp Emily's hand with her good one, squeezing it remarkably hard. "Thanks, kid," she said, and her eyes were shining. "Get home to your folks, now. You've got work to do."

CHAPTER 39

EMILY

January 11, 1962

The Christmas decorations were still up.

Emily was seated at her father's desk in the living room. Winter light filtered through the sheer, lacy curtains that hung on all three sides of the bay window as Emily stared, gaze out of focus, at the unlit Christmas tree to her left.

Christmas trees always looked so strange when they were unlit, so cold and incomplete. She rose suddenly, her father's chair scraping the floorboards, and strode to it. She located the cord for the lights and plugged it into the wall, then looked up at the tree, taking in the starched crochet snowflakes and shiny baubles that now reflected the multicoloured lights. The tinsel. Emily smiled. Always so much tinsel. Her mother couldn't get enough of the stuff, and Eleanor's children were only too happy to add their own heavy-handed touch to the decorating. It was a wonder Emily could see the ornaments at all through the thicket of shimmery lead-foil strands. She breathed deeply—she could still just discern the faintest whiff of fir.

She'd arrived home under cover of pitch darkness, nearing midnight on Christmas Eve. The night of her escape from the Mercer was still, in many ways, a blur of chaos and confusion. She'd hammered on the door of her parents' house, oblivious to any concern for the neighbours at such a late hour, on such a significant night. Her hot breath had puffed in the air in front of her, though her body was half frozen. She'd fled the Mercer wearing only her blue dress and Stone's thin white physician's coat.

After a minute or two, lights had appeared in the window of the front door, and she heard someone approaching. Her nerves had nearly given way in those few breathless moments as she leaned against the door jamb, waited for it to open, to see the shock and pain on her father's face. To fall, sobbing, into his chest as he wrapped his arm around her, rested his cheek on top of her head like he had when she was a girl and sat in his lap while he read her stories.

After that, it was a flurry of questions, of the best answers she could give, of piles of blankets and soft furniture and hot tea thrust into her hands by her mother's shaking ones as she hurried off to heat up some leftovers. She learned that her dad had gone down to the prison on her release day at the appointed time, but no one had come to the back door, and the gates at the front on King Street were locked. He'd also tried telephoning, but got no answer. The courts were closing for the Christmas break, and they'd begun to panic that something had indeed gone wrong before Emily turned up on the doorstep.

Emily had gone to bed for a while then, and awoke in the early afternoon on Christmas Day, utterly disoriented. Her mother had called Eleanor to put off her family's visit until at least Boxing Day. In the most bizarre Christmas Emily had ever experienced, no turkey was stuffed and cooked, no gifts exchanged. Just words. Words upon words as Emily recounted her story to her rapt and emotional parents. She ate and drank continually, regaining some lost strength and comfort with every mouthful.

But it had all felt sort of mechanical, and it was only now, in the process of actually writing the article over the past several days, that Emily had come to fully appreciate all that she had gone through, all the trials the other women continued to go through, and would, indefinitely, if she didn't get this thing written and blow the lid off the Mercer's corrupt and leaking roof.

And now she was putting those words to paper, threading together her scribbled notes and memories. She'd gotten to work as soon as she was able to convince her parents to let her cease resting and just *do* it. They'd wanted her to take some time, and she understood that. But what had the ordeal been for, if she didn't get it down as quickly as possible? Every minute she spent not writing in the comfort of her warm home, the women at the Mercer—her friends—were enduring God only knew what treatment at the hands of Dr. Stone, or even the warden and the more punitive matrons like White. Thoughts of what those women might be going through dominated her mind every moment Emily took a break from writing.

She'd phoned Doris at home the day after Boxing Day. The *Chatelaine* staff had her telephone number, though it was with the understanding that it only be used in an emergency. Doris had gasped when Emily announced herself on the line, twisting the phone cord around her bitten-down fingernail as she leaned against the kitchen wall, her free hand tapping her stress into the floral wallpaper.

"It's bigger than we thought, Doris," she said, watching her mother's back as she washed dishes at the sink. "There's corruption, too, not just maltreatment. And someone died." She swallowed the lump of grief. "A friend of mine." She outlined the main points for Doris as Bess glanced back over her shoulder, dark curls bouncing, and gave Emily a smile of encouragement. Of pride. But it was thin. Her distress for her daughter lay thick underneath.

"Good Lord, Emily," Doris had said, sounding uncharacteristically breathless. "I should never have let you do this. I am very sorry, I—"

"No, Doris," Emily said through the lump that persisted in her throat. "I'm grateful you did. It'll be good, in the end. I think." She let out a shaky chuckle, aware of her mother's eyes on her. "These women . . . well . . . what I've got, it just might get this place shut down for good. Truly, it might."

There was a long pause.

"Well," Doris finally said, "take the time you need to rest, then write it. As quickly as you can." She heaved a sigh. "I'm immensely proud of you, Emily. We'll talk soon. Come into the office when the piece is ready."

Now, Emily tilted her head side to side to loosen the tension in her neck that felt almost permanent, then took a sip of cold tea, the rhythmic *clack-clack-clack-ding* of the typewriter filling the living room.

"I thought you might need a fresh pot."

Emily turned to see her mother walking toward her, red apron on, as always, carrying a tray with a Brown Betty under a knitted tea cozy. Emily stood and stepped aside as her mother set the tray down on William's desk.

"Good timing. Thanks, Mom."

"It's funny," Bess said, the corner of her mouth curling into a soft smile as she stared down at the tray. "I couldn't tell you how many times I've brought your father this teapot, here, to this desk. And now . . ." She looked at Emily, who met her gaze with tired eyes, then stepped forward suddenly, seized with an urge to embrace her mother.

Bess let out a little "*oh!*" of delighted surprise that made Emily want to cry, made her think that perhaps she needed to hug her mother more often.

"Well," Bess said after a moment. "I've made you those chocolate almond cookies, there with the tea." They were Emily's favourite, but labour-intensive, and usually reserved for birthdays and special occasions. "We need to get some weight back on you, or you'll need to buy all new dresses. Goodness." Her eyes shone.

"Thank you," Emily said. "I'm just uh, just getting to the part about Annie. It's very difficult."

"I'm so sorry about your friend," Bess said, patting Emily's cheek. "What she went through, it's just awful. The 'baby blues,' we like to call it. But sometimes it's far more black than blue, I think." She hesitated a moment. "I don't know that she would want me to tell you this—people hardly speak of such things, and I suppose that's part of the problem, isn't it?—but when Eleanor was in that terrible state after she had Charlie . . . Not quite like your friend, mind you." Bess shook her head. "But I thought she had lost the will to go on, at one point. Truly I did. She spoke of such terrible things, of not wanting to live anymore. It was terrifying."

"*What?* Mom," Emily began, aghast. "Why did—"

"She didn't want to tell anyone," Bess said. "Not even Harry. She was afraid she'd be sent away, just like these poor women you knew. She was terrified of what was happening to her. Absolutely terrified. She knew it was wrong, wrong enough that she should tell someone. So she told me. We got her through it, it went away eventually. But my God . . ."

Emily was nearly speechless. She knew Eleanor had had a hard time, was depressed. But Emily had just figured all new mothers were exhausted, that was just how it was.

"You hear these things whispered about, you know," Bess said.

Emily didn't know. Not really.

"Among women, mothers. In church group, at the school bake sales. Sometimes someone will mention something, hint at how they felt after they had their babies. It's so common, but no one talks about it for exactly this reason, Emily. Because it doesn't take much for a woman to be called insane, or hysterical. And all it takes is the wrong doctor, one who thinks sending her away will solve the problem." She was clearly still haunted by Eleanor's experience. Emily felt hollow. She should have had some inkling her sister was struggling so badly.

Bess reached forward and held her shoulders.

"But this thing you've done, Emily, you've gone and you've listened to these women. You've *heard* them. And now you're going to shout about it with everything you've got, because they can't shout for themselves. I'm so wonderfully proud of you."

"But you were so against it at the start. You were so—"

"Frightened, yes! And now you understand why, don't you?"

The tears slipped down Emily's cheeks. "But will people read a story about convicts and lunatics and prostitutes? Will they even care?"

"Of course they will care. Because your friend Annie, and even these other women . . . they're all of us, in a way, and we're all them. If your article can get this horrid place shut down, or at least change some of the laws, well . . . maybe other women won't have to feel so afraid to ask for help when they need it." She swiped at a tear and smiled. "I just can't believe . . . well . . . those poor girls. I just keep thinking, they're each someone's daughter, aren't they? Just like Eleanor. Being starved and abused and all the rest of it. Someone's baby girl."

Emily nodded. "Though many of their parents are responsible for them ending up there in the first place. Dad told you how easy it was to convince that judge a prison sentence was proportionate punishment for my obstinance. He'd practically decided before we even got there."

Bess sighed. "Girls never are valued as highly as boys. Even by some parents. That's the ugly truth of it. I hope things will be different one day. And I'm sorry the change hasn't come quick enough for you, my dear."

"Dad told me back in the spring that things would have been easier for me if I'd been a boy."

"Well," Bess said, "that may be true. But we need girls—women—like you, to carve these paths, don't we? Because the men sure aren't going to do it for us."

Emily's eyes stung. "'Carving the paths,'" she echoed. "Sometimes it feels like I'm out in the woods alone, Mom. In the dark, with nothing but a damn butter knife to clear the way. It's very . . . isolating. Not wanting what Eleanor wants, or what other girls my age want. Having dreams that are a man's dreams."

She thought then of Bernie, and true understanding settled on her. How singularly isolating it would be to feel as though you were born in the wrong body. That you were, in fact, a man. The heartache of it nearly took her breath away.

Bess watched her, thoughtful. "Of course it feels that way. But what *courage*, Emily, to take that on. And remember," she added, "there are women on the path ahead of you, who set out with even fewer tools, in even darker woods. Women like Doris, or your idol, Nellie Bly. Keep your eyes on them when you feel alone. Call out to them. They'll wait for you, give you a hand when you need it, show you their scars and the hurdles to watch out for, guide you over the ground they've already worked so hard to clear."

She brushed back a wild strand of Emily's hair.

"The brambles might close in again from time to time, or grow over the path. But it's still there, beneath. Stay on it, my dear. Push the thorns back, even if you bleed. And be sure to look over your shoulder, from time to time, to see who's on the path behind you, or who might have fallen along the way. Reach down, and help her back up again. Because she's following *you* now, my dear. She's following *you*."

Emily let out a sob and embraced her mother again. "Thank you, Mom."

They clung to one another in the silence of the room, the grey winter light beaming in on them. Finally, Emily pulled away, and Bess ran her thumbs over Emily's cheeks, brushing away the tears as she had so many times before. The tenderness of Bess's words sank into Emily's skin like a healing balm.

"Now, then," Bess said, her own eyes glistening. "That typewriter is your scythe. Go clear the path."

———

Three days later, Emily rose from the desk she'd hardly left for ten days, other than to eat and sleep and use the bathroom. She exhaled, deliberately long and heavy. She felt as though she'd just been cleansed of something toxic.

She was consumed by competing feelings of relief and anxiety about the stack of papers in her hand, her final draft of the Mercer article. Or at least, her final draft before the copyeditors got their hands on it. But she had a feeling Doris wouldn't cut much, that she would run it longform, to make sure the whole story was told, the full truth finally known and acknowledged in print.

Doris had told her to come into the office when it was ready, but first, Emily wanted her father's professional opinion. She also felt that with all the emotional turmoil she had put her parents through by taking on this story in the first place, they deserved to be the first to see it.

She walked into the dining room, then into the kitchen, finally spotting her parents out on the back patio, wrapped in thick winter coats in the two slatted lawn chairs beneath the awning, protected, somewhat, from the soft snow that fell outside in the late-evening darkness. She smiled, watching them both from the kitchen window, the light illuminating their backs. They were in muffled conversation, and smoke curled, then dissipated in the air beside her father as he nursed his after-dinner cigarillo.

She walked to the back door and stepped outside. They both turned at the sound.

"If you're finished for the day, your dinner's still in the oven keeping warm, dear," Bess said. "You must be hungry. It's nearly eight o'clock."

Emily had declined dinner and worked through, unable to stop as her mind and fingers stumbled over one another. That was her favourite part of writing, when what was in her mind and heart felt unstoppable, connected and fluid, the thoughts and words pouring out of her fingertips onto the page of their own volition, when she was more medium than scrivener, when she felt unable to think or type fast enough. There was nothing else like it.

"I'm finished," she said, approaching them now. "Not just for the day. I mean I'm done. It's written."

Her mother's mouth was open a little, pencilled brows pressing against her hairline. A smile played at her dad's lips as they puckered around the cigarillo.

"I'd like you both to read it first," Emily said, walking forward and pulling her burgundy cardigan closer around her. It fit like a tent on her now, but wouldn't for long, at the rate Bess was pressing second helpings on her at every meal.

William leapt up, Bess right beside him.

"Let's get comfortable in front of the fire, then," he said with an excited smile Emily couldn't help but return. "It's bloody freezing out here."

Emily coughed in the dry winter air as she made her way down Augusta Avenue through Kensington Market, chin tucked into the collar of her peacoat, her satchel containing the article slung over her shoulder. She always preferred this route to work, avoiding the traffic, streetcars, and diesel-fuelled hustle of Spadina for the side street lined with walk-up coffee windows and market stalls.

She passed the poultry shop with its butchered chickens hanging in the window, the live ones cooing in cages just off the narrow sidewalk, and breathed in the smell of fresh-baked bread from the bakery next door. She'd had a full breakfast, but still her mouth watered. Although she had been imprisoned under false pretences, the experience of the incarceration was real, and her newfound freedom still felt strange and wondrous. It was as though she had been squashed into some cramped case for six months and was only now able to stretch her legs, to remember that she in fact had them, could use them to live and explore. Like she had somehow escaped death, a death of the soul.

She kept up her pace as she made her way onto Dundas and through Chinatown, mulling over what she would say to Doris and her colleagues. It occurred to her, as she passed the sprawling art gallery, that she didn't know who at *Chatelaine* knew about her undercover project at the Mercer besides Doris and the staff writers. Doris wasn't the type to share information with anyone she didn't believe had rightful claim to it, so it was possible she simply told anyone inquiring that it wasn't their business. Emily smiled then, thinking of her old officemate Betty, and what she would have had to say about Emily's foray into a women's prison. But perhaps she hadn't stuck around for more than a few days after her engagement was announced. She would be married by now. Emily wondered who had taken her place at that desk in the Closet.

A light turned green, and Emily stepped forward onto the crosswalk with a small crowd of other office workers headed toward the banks and legal offices that lined Bay Street to the east. Heart racing a little from the brisk walk and her nerves, she heaved on the heavy door and entered the familiar lobby of the grand building. She pressed the elevator button and stood back.

She remembered how she'd waited in this same spot for the elevator on the afternoon she got back from scoping out the Mercer and meeting

June Jones, when she went to Doris with the seed of this story in her little green hand. She'd felt exhilarated then, bold and excited, to do what she thought was "real journalism," to get her hands dirty. But those hands were worn and older now, and she would be scrubbing at that grime for a long time to come. Because she was indelibly altered by her time at the Mercer, just like every woman who walked through the creaking, aged front doors that had, for nearly a hundred years, swallowed the women society didn't like, didn't want, or didn't know what to do with. Locking women up was the default reaction of the men in charge who neither understood nor respected them. Who viewed the white, mentally healthy women as second-class, and the others a step farther below that, something subhuman.

In some ways, Emily felt as though she now had more in common with the Mercer girls than she did her colleagues at *Chatelaine*. There would, in many ways, be no going back. She wasn't even yet able to truly face the changes she'd already seen in herself, afraid of what they meant. The night sweats, nail-biting, the rotting sense of dread in the pit of her stomach. The surge of panic that rose, sometimes out of nowhere, and made her feel like she was about to die. The permanent lump in her throat. She worried that being forced into that blue uniform had done something to her that she might not be able to reverse.

The version of herself that had rushed here to ask Doris if she could pursue the story felt young and naive now. But all the same, look at what she'd accomplished. She wondered whether, if she had been older and more experienced, she would have had the daring to do what she'd done. As her father had said, youth was the perfect time for such exploits and recklessness. The naivety of what she was undertaking might have been a strength, really. If she'd truly known how it was going to be, would she have had the courage to do it? Perhaps opportunities did come to people at just the right time.

The elevator arrived at the main floor and the doors slid open with a rattling *whoosh*. Fortunately, there was no one inside, and Emily stepped in, relieved that she wouldn't have to make small talk with any of the

Maclean's executives. Her heart rate quickened again as the elevator began to rise. She glanced at her watch; she was due for her meeting with Doris in three minutes.

She hadn't planned anything beyond handing Doris the article and seeing what she said. She'd taken on this project to advance her career, but even now that the ordeal was over, that she was back at the office where it all began, that desire was secondary. She wasn't particularly concerned with what sort of impact the article might have on her career, so long as it made a real difference to the lives of the women and girls at the Mercer—or better yet, ensured that there would be no more imprisonment there: an end to the reign of terror on Liberty Street.

The elevator arrived at the fourth floor and Emily looked down, straightened her outfit. It had been strange to get back into her old clothes, as elated as she was to be out of that blue dress, which was now folded in the bottom drawer of her dresser, her roll of toilet paper notes tucked into the breast pocket. She'd thought to throw the dress out, but the complicated truth was, it reminded her of Annie, and she wasn't ready to part with it just yet.

The doors slid open to reveal Doris standing in front of the reception desk, arms crossed over the front of her cream blouse, lips a thin line.

"Emily," she said, opening her arms as though to embrace her. Emily couldn't help but smile at the sight of her boss waiting.

"Hi Doris," she said, glancing furtively over Doris's shoulder. There was a new receptionist there, someone Emily didn't know, wearing a curious expression. Perhaps Constance had left to get married, too.

Doris swept an arm through the air, her hand landing on Emily's shoulder, guiding her forward. "Come on."

As they made their way down the long, noisy hallway to Doris's office, several of Emily's colleagues noted her as she passed. Mouths opened, a couple outright pointed and she saw her name on their lips.

It hadn't occurred to her what she would say to them, and after a fleeting moment of stress, she understood: Doris had come to escort her to the corner office so she wouldn't be accosted with inquiries on the way there.

Emily entered Doris's office and her boss followed, shut the door. The noise of the ringing phones and feminine twittering muted, and Emily relaxed a little.

"Who knows where I've been?" she asked.

"Just the staff writers and Clara," Doris said, taking the seat behind her desk and indicating Emily should sit in front. "I told everyone else it was none of their concern, that you were taking a leave of absence."

Emily smirked, though it was mirthless. "I'm sure they're all going to think it was something scandalous. That I've *gone to an aunt's* or something." She swallowed then, thinking of Vera and the St. Agnes girls, the prison nursery for babies of the girls who didn't have parents decent enough to send them *to an aunt's*. The parents who wanted to punish their daughters more than society already would for the crime of motherhood outside of marriage.

"Well, if they do, they'll know soon enough where you were. Any scandalous rumour will be full and truly quashed."

Emily bobbed her head. "True."

"So," Doris began with a heavy air, "do you want to tell me about it first, or shall I just read?"

Emily retrieved the article from her satchel, set it down in front of her boss. "Yes, maybe just read it. And then we can talk."

Doris leaned back in her chair as Emily sat and waited, fighting the nervousness swirling in her chest as her boss's eyes glided over each page. She set them face down on the desk, one after another. A few minutes later, she finished and cleared her throat. She tapped the sheets back into a tidy stack and attached them together with a bulldog clip. She stared at the title for a moment:

MURDER AT THE MERCER:
Abuse and Torture Rampant at Liberty Village Women's Prison

Doris looked up, watched Emily with her sharp eyes over the top of those black horn-rimmed spectacles for so long that Emily began to wonder if her boss was waiting for her to say something. But then, suddenly, she pulled open her desk drawer and withdrew the same bottle of brandy and two glasses she'd presented when Emily had first come to her with the story. Red mouth pursed, Doris poured with a heavy hand, and Emily laughed. It was only nine-thirty in the morning, after all. What would her mother say?

As though reading Emily's mind, Doris said, "Never mind propriety at a time like this. I need a drink after just reading what you went through. I can imagine you need one after living it."

"Well . . ." Emily hesitated, then took it, but didn't drink.

There was a long silence in which Doris sipped and Emily sat, watching her mentor, unsure of what to say. She was rarely at a loss for words, but at this point it felt as though she had been drained of them, a bloodletting that would hopefully—in the long run—prove therapeutic.

"You're alleging murder. This Annie L., whom you befriended?"

"Yes. She was murdered."

"Can you prove it?"

Emily licked her dry lips, then took a swig of the brandy just to wet them. It burned. "I don't know. They would need to find her . . ."—she breathed deep—"her body, first, I suppose. I don't know where she was taken. Her parents might have claimed her? Maybe . . ." She thought of Annie's father having disowned her, her mother trying in vain to get her released. Surely they would have been informed of her death.

"But there must be ways of testing what was in her system," Emily continued. "An autopsy. The drugs . . ." She knew she sounded desperate. Her voice was cracking. "If there were too many drugs in her system, if that caused her heart to fail?" She shuddered, then tried to pull herself together, sat forward in her seat. "It's medical malpractice at the very least, Doris. But that, combined with my and the other inmates' testimonies about the infections, the gynecological torture . . ." She angled her thighs together instinctively.

"It's all right," Doris said, pressing one large hand down on the article as though trying to calm Emily's agitation through its pages. "Let's uh . . ."

She glanced at the title again. A long moment passed. "'Murder' is strong. I wonder about changing it to 'corruption' or 'malpractice.' Though I suppose you're already alleging abuse and torture, aren't you?"

"Yes. Because it all happened," Emily said urgently.

"I believe you," Doris said firmly, homing in on Emily's agitation. "So I suppose . . ." She sighed, fingered the pearls at her throat. "Yes. Hell. We'll keep 'murder.'"

"Thank you." Emily paused. "Legal's going to have a fit," she added wryly.

Doris nodded. "Yes. Though as we know, it'll take them a while to even hear that the allegations were published. We'll deal with it then. You know I'd always rather ask for forgiveness than permission," she said, swivelling her chair back and forth a few times. She looked up and met Emily's gaze over the desk. "But my hope would be some sort of formal investigation gets opened on this place, and then I don't think the administrators, or this Dr. *Stone*"—Doris said her name with the revulsion one might muster to describe a slug—"would dare try to sue us if the police end up charging them with the same allegations we're putting up."

Emily struggled for a breath, shifted in her seat. "She needs to be brought to justice," she said, louder than intended.

"I agree."

Another silence stretched across the desk. A lighthearted laugh was just audible on the other side of the door, over near the kitchen. Emily glanced at the clock; it was morning teatime. The girls would all be gathering for cake or biscuits now. Perhaps a test version of an Easter tart.

"Are you okay?" Doris asked quietly.

Emily had mostly held it together for her parents during the three weeks she'd been home, and, really, for herself. For the sake of the article. She'd relived the horror through her writing, recounted it to her parents. But she hadn't had an opportunity to really sit with it all, to weigh it in her hands and feel it on her shoulders and try to figure out just how heavy it was going to be for her to carry, now and into the future. She blinked hard, fighting tears that caught her by surprise. She kept eye contact with

Doris, though, who looked on with a forced neutral expression that didn't quite hide the maternal concern beneath.

"I don't know," Emily whispered.

A tinkling laugh sounded again outside the door. Life in the office was carrying on. How would Emily be able to join them again? How could she ever talk about frivolous things when there were so many more critical topics to discuss, problems to fix?

She thought of the men with shell shock from the wars, her mother's father. People had no other word for what happened to those soldiers, but wasn't it similar to what she was going through? How could anyone expect her to go on living a normal life as though she hadn't witnessed—and been subjected to—systematic suffering for months on end? Her own father hadn't held a gun, hadn't fought, but he'd witnessed it all as though he had. He'd been injured as though he had. Just like Emily.

The floodgates opened then, under Doris's sympathetic stare, and Emily broke down. Doris rose from her seat and came to her, a handkerchief held aloft. Emily buried her face in it, equal parts embarrassed and relieved at the release.

Doris said nothing, but stood by Emily's side, one arm around her shoulder, pulling her close like the mother swan that she was. Through her anguish, Emily felt a visceral awareness that she never wanted to work for anyone but Doris Anderson for the rest of her career. There would never be another place like this.

Once Emily had regained her composure, Doris stepped away and lifted the article from the desk. She strode to the door, opened it and called for Clara, who appeared a moment later.

"Get this to copyedit," Doris said, her tone clipped. "And it'll be Emily's name in the byline, as a staff writer." She breathed deeply and looked back at Emily, whose red eyes brimmed once again with tears. "We're running it."

CHAPTER 40

RACHEL

June, 1996

Rachel takes a deep breath and looks down at the phone number she's been given by the HR rep at Maclean-Hunter. Emily Radcliffe retired from *Chatelaine* three years ago, and they don't have a new phone number for her. Instead, they've provided the contact for the magazine's former editor-in-chief, Doris Anderson, who's apparently still friends with Radcliffe. Her name rings a bell, but Rachel can't quite place it. Something to do with politics, she thinks. She'll have to look it up later. But for now, she dials.

"Hi, Ms. Anderson," she begins. "My name is Rachel Mackenzie, I'm a detective with the OPP in Huron County."

A pause. "How can I help you, Detective?"

"I was given your phone number by someone in the HR department at Maclean-Hunter. I've been trying to track down one of your former employees. The person at Maclean-Hunter said she worked under you at *Chatelaine* in the early sixties until your departure. Emily Radcliffe: Do you know how I might be able to reach her?"

"Is she in some kind of trouble?"

"No," Rachel says. "But I very much need to speak with her about a current investigation. She may have some detail that's essential to the case."

"Well," Doris Anderson says, her voice age-crackled but strong. "Emily was my protege. One of my best journalists and employees. Yes,

I can give you her phone number. We still have lunch once or twice a year." She gives a little cough.

"And can I confirm her address with you?" Rachel reads off the one in Rosedale.

"Yes, that's correct. Now, might I inquire as to the nature of your investigation, Detective?"

"It's regarding the time she spent at the Mercer Women's Prison in Liberty Village. We're investigating the ID of a Jane Doe that was found in a cemetery up here in Huron County recently. We had five possible IDs, but we've been able to rule out three, leaving Emily Radcliffe and another inmate who was there around the same time, an Annie Little. I'm trying to figure out whether Radcliffe might have known Little while she was there."

There's a long sigh on the other end of the line.

"Ms. Anderson?"

"Yes," Doris says softly. "Emily knew Annie Little. They were friends. And Annie died in Emily's arms, right there in the middle of the prison mess hall with the other women looking on. Dreadful thing. Just dreadful."

Rachel's gut gives a little lurch of excitement, the same one she gets every time she feels that tug at the end of a good lead. If Annie Little is dead and Emily Radcliffe is alive, she might finally have the identity of her Jane Doe. Though how Annie Little ended up in Millgate remains the big question. Except . . .

"How . . . how does Radcliffe say Annie Little died?"

Doris clears her throat. "Emily vehemently maintains that Annie Little was murdered by the prison doctor, but it could never be proved. That horrid woman went down for corruption and abuse, but not for the murder. She claimed one of the matrons must have been careless, allowed Annie Little access to an overdose of medication, and that she deliberately took her own life after years of psychosis. But Emily believes to this day that Annie was well in the mind, and was murdered."

"The coroner's report deemed it suicide," Rachel tells her.

"Mm. Is that so?"

"Yes."

"Mm," Doris grunts again. "Seems a rather unlikely cause of death for a woman who perished in front of a hundred witnesses, all of whom said the only matron who took any action was the one later accused of recklessly allowing access to the drugs. It seems rather odd, does it not, that that particularly inept matron would be the one to care so much about Annie Little's fate, and attempt to save her life. That seems rather inconsistent to me.

"But, I suppose, the hundred and twenty witnesses *were* all criminals," Doris goes on. "Prostitutes. The mentally ill. And all women. Not populations that are typically given the benefit of the doubt by society, now are they?"

"Ma'am," Rachel says, "it's not my place to comment on that. I'm sure you understand."

"I wonder if coroners are corruptible," the older woman says, her voice a little louder now. "Whether they have greater fortitude against bribery or blackmail than, say, politicians? Or judges? Police officers?" Rachel shifts in her seat, and unwittingly, her eyes seek Green, just visible through her glass door in his own office across the hall. "But I suppose that's for you to find out."

Rachel is eager to bring this interview to an end. She's used to being able to command a conversation, especially if her interviewee is a woman. But something about Doris Anderson makes her shrink as though she's being challenged by a stern and intelligent schoolteacher.

"Could I have Emily Radcliffe's number, please?" Rachel asks pointedly.

"Yes. But Detective." Doris pauses, and her bristly demeanor suddenly falls away to softness. "Please be . . . *gentle* with her. I'm afraid the scars she acquired in the line of duty have never fully healed."

"Well, she's not in any trouble," Rachel assures her. "I think, actually, we might be able to provide her with a bit of closure. There's just one piece missing from this case that I'm hoping she can help us solve."

"Which piece?"

"How and why Annie Little's body got from the Mercer prison dining hall to an unmarked grave in Huron County."

"Yes, why indeed?" Doris muses.

"And do you know why Radcliffe ended up in the prison?" Rachel asks. "Was that before her time with you at the magazine, or . . . ?"

Doris lets out a low sigh. "Emily was at the Mercer prison *because* of her time at *Chatelaine*."

"I'm sorry?"

"By her own request," Doris says. "I allowed her to go undercover at the Mercer in 1961, to help uncover the truth of the deplorable conditions of the place."

Rachel's brows pop up. "Really. How long was she there?"

"Over six months. Longer than she was meant to, but that's a whole other story. At any rate, we published her piece in early '62, and it led to a grand jury investigation that shut the place down. There were court cases, lawsuits, all sorts. Total scandal. And it was all down to Emily and the women who helped her. Including poor Annie Little, God rest her soul."

Rachel scribbles her notes hastily. "There's a grand jury report?"

"Yes. And I can send you a copy of Emily's article, too, if you'd care to see it."

Rachel nods to herself, makes another note. "Yes, please. And Ms. Anderson, what did you mean when you said it's a 'whole other story' why Radcliffe was at the Mercer for so long?"

Another long pause. "That's Emily's story," Doris finally says, her voice softer now. "It's always been Emily's story. You shall have to hear it from her."

TORONTO—JULY, 1996

"Good morning, Detectives." Emily Radcliffe stands on the porch of her large brown Tudor-style home on Whitehall Road in Rosedale. Rachel and Stevens shut the car doors and walk up the handsome flagstone path.

She's an average-sized woman with mid-length greying hair pulled back in a low ponytail. Her lips are painted, but she wears no other makeup, and is dressed in a neat beige sweater-set and slacks. Her hands are on her hips, giving the strange impression that they're late, though in actual fact, they've arrived six minutes ahead of their promised time.

"I hope you both like coffee," she says, and turns toward the front door, leading them into a large tiled foyer with a tasteful chandelier overhead. It's so clean and tidy that Rachel fights the urge to remove her shoes, and shakes her head at Stevens when he looks as though he's about to. They're police. Not guests.

"Come on through into the sitting room," Emily says, settling herself on a large rose-coloured wing chair and gesturing Rachel and Stevens to the sofa across from her. Her handshake is strong, especially for a woman her age. But Rachel recognizes the signs in her ragged fingernails, the sweat around her hairline. The pristine surroundings are a coping mechanism for what lies beneath.

"Now then," Emily says. "Doris told me everything you talked to her about." She clears her throat. "That this maybe has to do with Annie. That you might have, uh, found her body. I didn't know she was missing. Anyway, I'm happy to assist where I can." She leans forward, pouring them each a coffee from a French press. The liquid agitates a little in the carafe as her hands tremble.

Rachel accepts the drink, then gets straight to the point.

"Yes. We're investigating a woman's body that was uncovered in an unmarked grave in a cemetery up in Huron County. Through forensics and some cross-referencing, we narrowed it down to five possible women. Including you."

"Not me," Emily says, with the ghost of a smile.

"No, ma'am."

She breathes deeply. "But you think it's Annie."

"Yes, ma'am."

Rachel watches Emily's hands, one balled into a fist as she massages the knuckles with the other. There's a plain gold band on her ring finger. She blinks several times. "How, uh—" She clears the rasp from her throat. "What happened?"

Rachel glances at Stevens, gestures that he should take the lead on this one. She wants to focus on Emily's body language. He sits forward on the couch.

"By process of elimination, Annie Little is the only possible ID for this Jane Doe. But we're still trying to figure out how she ended up there."

"Huron County, you said?" Emily asks him.

"Yes. Did you know that she was born in Goderich? That's the city listed on her birth certificate."

Emily shakes her head. "I didn't know that. She told me she was from a small town, but I never knew the name. She talked about strawberry fields nearby, and growing up there with her parents." She blinks hard again, glances at the end table, and plucks a pre-emptive tissue from a box.

"Did she ever mention a town called Millgate?" Stevens asks.

"No," Emily says. "Not that I recall."

"Hm. Okay." Stevens taps his pen on the pad. "The coroner's report listed her hometown as Toronto, but you're sure she didn't grow up there?"

"I'm sure," Emily says, frowning. "She said she grew up in a small town."

Rachel's mind is whirring. There are two large strawberry farms around Millgate, but that's true of plenty of southwestern Ontario towns. Still, the evidence is mounting.

Stevens presses for the next question. "Do you happen to know whether her parents are still alive? Still there? Or if they were, at the time of her death?"

With a heavy sigh, Emily recounts a conversation she'd had with Annie Little about her parents' move to Ottawa, how her father had disowned her when she became ill, but that her mother had continually tried to appeal for her release.

Rachel's brow is furrowed. "None of that was in the grand jury investigation. Why not?"

"You read it?"

"Yes, ma'am. And your article in *Chatelaine*. Doris Anderson sent me a copy by courier."

Emily swallows, her eyes growing dark. "Well, I was told it was an investigation into the overall conditions and management of the Mercer, and that they weren't focusing on individual inmates' experiences. I tried to tell them everything I'd put in my article, about Annie, and her murder. But all the matrons except for the one who tried to save Annie corroborated with the warden and doctor," she says, her voice louder, stronger now. "It was appalling. Eris Stone had already thrown Matron Carnegie under the bus, so the others were all happy to have her take the blame, and they went on to other jobs. You're police officers," she says, her mouth twisting into a wry pucker. "I'm sure you know that when push comes to shove, most people will do anything they can to save their own skins. Morals and ethics tend to go out the window in the face of threat."

Rachel is quiet for a moment, refrains from agreement with difficulty. She can't count the number of times she's seen exactly that in her line of work. She has no doubt Emily Radcliffe is right.

Emily takes a long sip of coffee, staring at her lap. Rachel and Stevens exchange a glance, silently trying to decide how to proceed.

"Okay, uh . . . what was Annie Little's mother's name?" Rachel asks. They need to confirm whether Millgate was the family's hometown. That might help explain at least why the deceased was brought to the cemetery there, if not the reason for the grave to go unmarked.

"Helen," Emily says. "Helen Sharrock. It was on the records I saw in Stone's office. It was unusual enough that I never forgot it. Not that I would have anyway," she mutters.

"Did you ever try to contact Helen after you got out of the Mercer? Or for the article?" Stevens asks.

Emily wrinkles her nose, continuing to fight tears. "Uh, no. No, I didn't. I uh, I couldn't."

Rachel watches the guilt settle into the creases of Emily's face. "Why not?"

Emily is quiet for a long moment, staring down at the tissue twisted in her hands. "Because I blamed myself for Annie's death for a long time. I couldn't face her mother."

"But do you have any idea where Helen Sharrock is? If she's still alive?" Rachel presses.

"With respect, Detective, I don't see how that's relevant to the investigation, and I don't want to talk about it," Emily says firmly. She takes a deep breath. Rachel wants to challenge her on that—it *is* relevant—but gives her a pass for the moment. "But I have always wondered what happened to her body," Emily adds. "There was a lot of chaos, and it wasn't until after I had been home for a while and wrote the article that I actually stopped to think about it, and by then, I sort of didn't want to."

"Do you think Helen Sharrock would have claimed her daughter's body?" Rachel asks.

Emily nods. "Yes. Of course. She'd tried to get Annie released several times, but Eris Stone blocked it. That was what . . ." She lets her breath out slowly. "That was what finally galvanized Annie to let me try to use the information I had about Stone as leverage to secure her release."

"Blackmail?" Stevens asks.

Emily raises one eyebrow, shrugs. "If you like."

"You say Eris Stone killed Annie Little," Rachel begins.

Emily nodded emphatically. "She did."

"And you're saying that was because you tried to blackmail her?"

Emily licks her lips. "Yes. But I also believe she was a eugenicist, and a psychopath. I think she used her position of power over those women as an outlet for her psychopathy. We know now that psychopaths and sociopaths do that. It's documented. And Eris Stone deserved that blue dress far more than most of the psych inmates did. That I know for certain."

Stevens shifts uncomfortably in the chair beside Rachel, who merely nods. "And can you tell us what happened after the article ran?"

"Sure," Emily says, though she sounds a little reluctant. "It ran in the February edition, and it might have been the first time one of the articles in *Chatelaine* really picked up national attention. From other media, I mean. We made sure copies got sent to everyone in a position of importance, within the government, the chief of police, all of it. And it did what I hoped it would, it triggered an investigation. The grand jury came in, did their inspections—without advance warning this time. And as you can imagine, their findings were somewhat different than they were when the warden and Stone had time to set the stage for the scheduled yearly inspection."

"And what happened to Eris Stone?" Stevens asks.

"She was stripped of her licence," Emily says. "She said Matron Carnegie must have been negligent and allowed Annie access to an overdose. But Carnegie was one of the few matrons who ever challenged Stone, and showed compassion to Annie and some of the other psych inmates. And the coroner's report said it was suicide, so . . ." She releases a shaky breath. "They couldn't prove the murder, but they could prove the rest. The investigators contacted the drug company, who said all *they* knew was that Stone had a pool of participants for the trial, so they sent her the drugs and her payment. But they turned on her fast when they learned what she had been doing, and cooperated fully with the authorities. My friend June Jones, and several of the other inmates, corroborated on the gynecological abuse and torture, of being deliberately infected and enduring the drug trial treatment. That all checked out." Emily pauses, plays with the ring on her left hand. "Stone went to prison for a time, and that felt good. I liked picturing her in a uniform, taking orders. Even if it was only for a few months."

Rachel waits a moment, lets Emily settle a bit. "Do you have any thoughts on why she would kill Annie Little and not you, if you were the one threatening to expose her?" she asks.

Emily meets her eyes square on, a first for the conversation. "I've thought a lot about that," she says, "and I did when I was in isolation, too. But I think . . ." She clenches her hands into fists again, staring into the middle distance of her living room. "It removed Annie from the equation, and sent a message to me about who was in control. That was always Stone's obsession, having the inmates know that she was the one in control, not us. If she'd killed me outright, the message wouldn't have stuck, would it? And I think also, really, she might have been a bit scared. Or at least, I think she made a calculation."

"How so?"

"Well, once all the other inmates knew who I was, and what had happened to Annie . . . if I'd turned up dead, that would have triggered an investigation itself, and it would have all become pretty obvious that I'd been murdered. But I think she figured she could keep me in there as long as she wanted to, and she was right. She had the authority to, despite any appeals that would have come from my family, or my boss, who would have hired a lawyer to get me out. I had advocates on the outside more powerful than Helen Sharrock was. But the legislation gave Stone all the power, regardless. In black and white." She shakes her head and barrels on, talking faster now as Stevens struggles to keep up with his notes.

"I think, by shoving me into that blue uniform, she thought she was buying herself an infinite amount of time. In her twisted mind, when I *was* finally released—God only knew when—I might not have even had the job at *Chatelaine* anymore, and who would believe the story of a woman who had been locked up as a lunatic for years on end? I know I would have gone mad in that place, stuck in isolation. I would have come out of the Mercer even crazier than I did."

"What do you mean?" Rachel frowns.

Emily takes a sip of her coffee and a deep breath. She taps her knee with her free hand as she speaks, surveying Rachel with a keen eye.

"Three of my toes twitched constantly, day and night, for two years after I came home. I had night sweats worse than my menopause. Had to change the sheets every morning. I had migraines I'd never had before in my life. That sense of dread and doom that crouches down right here," she said, pointing to her sternum.

Rachel knows the one.

"I had the sensation of a lump in my throat for several months at one point, worried it was cancer. I had all the unpleasant tests, and they found nothing. And strange things that cropped up with no other explanation, like hives, vertigo." Emily exhales through a little O in her lips. "All the average person really heard about back then were things like housewives with "delicate nerves," the veterans' shell shock and the behaviours they still sometimes called "hysteria." Now, of course, even a layperson knows those as anxiety, traumatic stress, and panic attacks. All of which I still grapple with from time to time." She takes another sip of coffee. "I can only drink decaf now. The caffeine exacerbates it all. I learned that the hard way. At any rate," she continues, blinking a few times, "I was afraid to tell anyone besides my parents what was going on, for fear they'd lock me up for real this time, send me over to 999 Queen or some such place."

Her eyes drift off for a moment, and Rachel watches her. *Where has she gone?*

Emily shakes her head, breaking the trance. "Fortunately, I had wonderful, understanding parents. But you coming here now, Detective, and bringing up Annie Little . . . well . . . I knew then, and I know now, how easily I could have been her. How easily those women were incarcerated. They needed *help*, and care. Not punishment. We don't punish people for having broken legs or cancer, do we? We don't blame them and abuse them for it."

Rachel thinks of Mary and shoves the image aside. "I'm sorry you've gone through all that," she says.

"Annie had postpartum psychosis, they call it now," Emily says. "I think my sister might have, too, though more mildly than Annie. But women recover after a while, with medications and other help. Not shock therapy and sedatives and restraints." A tear slides down her cheek now. "Annie got better, and they just . . . kept her anyway. Because they could."

They're all quiet for a moment, the only sound the soft crackle of paper under Stevens's hand as he completes his notes. Rachel is still connecting the dots in her head as Emily finishes her drink, eyes unfocused. She stands suddenly.

"Here, let me refill your drinks."

"Sure. Thank you." Rachel watches her leave with the tray, knowing it's an excuse to compose herself.

"What do you think?" Stevens asks quietly.

Rachel runs her tongue over her teeth. "I think our Jane Doe is almost certainly Annie Little. Cause of death is overdose, per the coroner's report, with no way to prove foul play. That allegation will be a question mark, probably forever." Her shoulders fall a little. "But we need to confirm whether Millgate was in fact the Sharrocks' hometown.

"Ms. Radcliffe," she calls to Emily, who returns from the kitchen a moment later with the tray of mugs. "Do you happen to know how old Annie Little was when she died? Approximately, even?"

Emily sets the tray down. "Mid-thirties, I think."

Rachel does some quick math. It's likely the elder Sharrocks are dead. A little flare rises in her gut. They need to go back to the Millgate Cemetery office and search for Helen Sharrock's name. If she's buried in the same cemetery, odds are excellent this case is nearly solved; she brought her daughter's body back to her hometown cemetery. But why, she still wonders, was there no headstone, and no record? She doesn't want to doubt Julie, and she'd thought they had thoroughly eliminated the question of an administrative error. But maybe they missed something.

"Well," Rachel says, rising a moment before Stevens does, hastily shoving his notebook back into his pocket, "I think we should get back. Thank you for your time, Ms. Radcliffe. I'll be in touch if we need anything more."

"You're welcome," Emily says, standing along with them now. "But wait," she adds, focusing on Rachel. "Why is Annie a Jane Doe? Why don't you know whose body it is?"

"Because it was in a casket, but the grave was unmarked."

"Why? If you think Millgate was Annie's hometown, why wouldn't she have a headstone? That just seems so . . . inadequate. After all she'd been through, for her resting place to not be marked. *Why?*"

Rachel gives Emily a regretful sort of look. "That's exactly what we're trying to figure out, Ms. Radcliffe."

CHAPTER 41

RACHEL

Millgate, Ontario—July, 1996

"Hey, Julie," Rachel says as her old classmate opens the door to the cemetery office, mug in hand. Stevens and Rachel headed to Millgate immediately after touching down at headquarters and updating Green on the case. Rachel doesn't want to waste any more time waiting on the final piece of this bizarre puzzle. She tries to keep her emotions out of her work—the job would be nearly impossible if she didn't—but her curiosity is burning by the end of any case. And she cuts herself a little slack on that score, because it's the curiosity that drove her to detective work to begin with. It's her fuel and fire.

"What can I do for you, Rachel?" Julie asks, blinking in the morning sun. "Uh, come on in."

Rachel and Stevens scale the small metal steps and enter.

"Thanks, Julie. I'll get straight to the point," Rachel says. "We've nearly got an ID for the Jane Doe, but we need to cross-reference with a family that might be buried here. The name is Helen Sharrock."

After the briefest beat, Julie's eyes light up. "Yes, Helen Sharrock is here! And her husband, Richard. Same plot, same stone."

"You're sure?" Rachel's heart leaps.

"Yes. I know it because I always think it's *Sham*rock. It's in the northwest quad, actually, not . . ." Her mouth opens a little in realization.

"What's this about Helen Sharrock?"

A flash of irritation rises in Rachel's chest as Reverend Holland pokes his head around the corner. "We have it in hand, Reverend, thank you. We just need Julie's assistance with another piece of the investigation." She looks away from him and back to Julie. "Let me guess: The Sharrock plot isn't far from the unmarked grave?"

Julie nods enthusiastically. "That's right! Come on, I'll show you."

They follow Julie back out of the office, and Rachel has to increase her pace to keep up. She glances behind her, but the reverend hasn't followed, evidently taking the hint.

The headstone is in the second last row of this section, right on the end. The Jane Doe excavation site is still taped off, not twenty feet away. She reads the tall grey headstone:

SHARROCK
RICHARD BERNARD
Mar 1, 1902 – Dec 12, 1956
Beloved husband of
HELEN ANNE
June 16, 1904 – Sept 2, 1978

Rachel takes out her notepad to record the names and dates, and does some quick math. This is the same Helen Sharrock—it *has* to be.

"So that's her, then?" Stevens asks.

She nods. "Yes. But—"

"Detectives?" Rachel is interrupted by Reverend Holland hurrying across the grass toward them in his khakis and golf shirt.

What in the fuck does he want now?

He stops next to Julie.

"What is it?" Rachel huffs. "We're in the middle of—"

"You need to talk to my father."

Rachel frowns. Is this some kind of joke? "Excuse me?" she says.

"I just called him, and we can go over there now, he's—"

"What are you talking about?" Rachel snaps. "What does your father have to do with any of this?" She notices Stevens's eyes on her, and clamps her mouth shut, willing herself to calm down and be professional.

"Because he was the reverend at the time Annie Little's body was buried here."

It takes Rachel half a second to realize what he's just said. No one around here but she, Stevens, and Green know the suspected name of their Jane Doe.

A chill runs through her despite the warmth of the morning. "How do you know that name?"

"Rachel, please," he says, extending his hands out, imploring, as he would during a sermon. "I know you and my father have never seen eye to eye, but . . ." He looks at her as though she's about to order his execution. "He was watching the news at his care home and saw that a body had been discovered here, and that it wasn't Stacy Cooper's. He called me two days ago, said I needed to come down there to talk to him, wouldn't give me details over the phone." He drops his hands. "He knows who Annie Little is, and why she was buried here without a headstone."

Reverend John Holland Sr. has been living at the local nursing home for six years. His room is small, with a window overlooking a corn field and the adjoining parking lot. Rachel hasn't seen him since her mother's trial, but he hasn't changed much. He still has the same thin build, just with more papery, wrinkled skin now, the whites of his eyes yellowing, a little bloodshot.

"All right, Reverend," Rachel says once she, Stevens, and the junior reverend are all clustered around the old man's bed. "Your son says you have information for us about Annie Little." She'd been irritated enough that this investigation had involved the Millgate Cemetery, and now can't quite believe how luck would punish her even more by having Reverend Holland Sr. emerge as a possible witness. This is what she gets for continuing to live in a small town.

She pulls out her notepad. She's taking the notes for the interview this time so she won't have to look at their subject much. She can hang it on the need to train Stevens, who volunteered to take point on this one without her having to ask. They're on their way to a solid partnership.

"Well, she was born Annie Sharrock, but became Little, yes," the senior reverend says, trying to make eye contact with Rachel, who keeps hers trained on the page in front of her. Eventually he gives up, and addresses Stevens.

"The Sharrock family were my parishioners, you see. I knew them from before they even had Annie, up until they moved to Ottawa when Dick got elected to Parliament. Everyone who knew the family was very proud, but none more than Dick himself. He had big dreams, that one. Never seemed to fit here. But Helen would have been happy to stay forever." He reached out a slightly shaking hand and sipped some water before continuing. His voice was hoarse, and slow, but full of confidence. He never had any shortage of that, Rachel thought snidely.

"She was a devout woman, Helen, involved with the church. But after she had Annie, she became very depressed. Very depressed indeed. And I guided her through it, with prayer, and reminders that all dark clouds eventually pass. She confided in me, and I gave her counsel a couple of times a week. It took time, but Helen's cloud dissipated after, oh, I don't know. A year, perhaps. Maybe less."

Rachel gnashes her teeth but says nothing, thinking of all the damn useless "counsel" he gave Mary over the years when she needed a doctor. *Real* help.

"And she came alive again," he continues. "Nothing gave her more joy than being a mother to Annie. They never had another, though. Could have been they just weren't blessed, or perhaps she—or Dick—didn't think she should go through all that again. But the years passed, and then Annie got married to that chap who took her to Toronto. There was pressure from Dick, I think, for that match, and it broke Helen's heart. One heartbreak of many." He took a deep, slightly wheezy breath. "Annie got in the family way not long after, and Helen was delighted at the idea of a grandchild, but she worried that Annie might face the same sort of depression she had after the birth. But then, oh, dear . . . Helen showed up at my office door, absolutely frantic. She'd spoken to Annie the day after the child was born, and she'd said she was feeling low, and not quite herself. Helen tried telephoning back every day for at least a week, with no answer, and was trying to get Dick to drive her into Toronto when Annie's good-for-nothing husband called." He swallowed, his Adam's apple clearly outlined in the thin, age-speckled skin of his throat. "He told her he'd admitted Annie to a lunatic asylum."

Rachel looks up from her pad now, pen hovering.

"Said she'd been hysterical, seeing things that weren't there. Voices, and the like. She thought he and his mother were trying to poison her and the baby, just dreadful stuff." He pauses. "I told Helen I was sure it wouldn't last long, like hers hadn't. But Annie's was darker, different, and I guess it did. Annie was in that place for ages. Helen kept trying to get her out, but got denied every time. And Dick wouldn't help, even with his influence. *Because* of his position, he told Helen. Wanted nothing to do with Annie because no one wanted to elect a politician with a lunatic daughter. His dirty little secret, Annie was."

Rachel's chest feels heavy, thinking of Emily's article, her recollections of Annie and her insistence that she had been cured of her postpartum psychosis long before her death.

"The Sharrocks kept their home in Millgate to stay at in the summers, when Parliament wasn't sitting, so Dick could be in the constituency he served. When he died, Helen moved back permanently, and Dick was buried there, in the Millgate. They'd bought the plot years before, for the both of them."

Rachel scribbles furiously as the reverend continues his testimony.

"Helen told me Annie's husband divorced her while she was in the prison and married someone else, had a family and all. He would let Helen see the child from time to time, but goodness, she was heartbroken, being cut off like that from Annie. Just a no-good man, that one. But then Annie died and they said she'd killed herself, poor soul. Annie's mother was informed of her death by her ex-husband. In a *letter!* Wouldn't even pick up the bleeding phone. He wouldn't claim Annie's body, and Helen wanted her back in Millgate, anyway. But there was a problem."

"What's that?" Stevens asks.

"Well." The elder reverend grunts and shifts his shoulders uncomfortably. He looks up at his son, who closes his eyes, nods at him to continue. Rachel sets her pen to the paper again.

"Helen wanted her buried in the Millgate, but I knew we would run into trouble. Word had gotten around by then that poor Annie was in an asylum, and the congregation was even more conservative than it is now. Times were different then. I knew if anyone found out she'd taken her own life, well . . . they wouldn't have wanted her buried there. Not with any sort of ceremony, anyway."

Rachel exhales a long breath of realization as the old man reaches out and hands her the last piece of the puzzle.

She looks up, though reluctantly, and finds his eyes on her.

"You understand now, don't you, Rachel?" he asks.

"Detective. And yes, but I need to hear it from you."

He keeps his eyes on her a moment, then nods. "I didn't think I could convince folks to allow a lunatic suicide to be buried there, even if she was—or had been—one of their own. So Helen and I had her brought back here and buried in secret, as close as we could to Dick's plot without a headstone, at the base of that big maple. And then no one would have to know, or be offended. I didn't want to upset anyone, but Helen needed her daughter home, needed the family to all have the same final resting place. I was glad to give her what she needed, after so much struggle for so long." He blinks hard. "I knew Annie. And I just never could really believe that she would take her own life. But if she did, I knew she must have had a good reason. One that God would understand."

He's visibly upset now.

"I never meant to cause any harm," he says, looking at them each in turn, eyes red. "We picked a spot so far off from the other headstones, I believed it would be ages before anyone wanted that plot, if we ever spread out that far at all." He shrugs his stooped shoulders. "I am sorry, Detectives. For the hubbub and confusion. But not for what I did. That girl deserved some peace beneath the shade of that tree. I know when Helen was in her decline, it soothed her to know they would all be together."

Everyone is quiet.

"Do you know the address?" Rachel asks him finally. "Where the Sharrocks lived?" They'll need it to cross-reference a birth certificate for Annie Sharrock, if there is one, and sort out all the paperwork for the case.

"Of course," the reverend says. "Even with this rattled old brain." He attempts a weak chuckle. "It's 1879 Garden Street. Just a five-minute walk from the cemetery."

Rachel jots down the address, then nods, folds up her writing pad. "Thank you for the information, Reverend, " she says mechanically. "We'll be in touch if we require any follow-up."

She looks to Stevens, and he follows her out of the room. When they get into the car, they both stare straight ahead out the windshield.

"How do you want to handle this?" Stevens finally asks.

Rachel shakes her head. She hates corrupt cops and those who skirt the lines, like Green, but his choices are often more to do with lazy police work than outright corruption. But she's been drilling into Stevens the importance of going by the book, checking your lists, covering your ass and dotting your i's.

"Well," she says. "We *should* be looking to charge him with indignity to a human body, for an improper burial."

Stevens bobs his head until she meets his eyes. "I think intent needs to count for something, here, Mackenzie," he says. "There was no foul play, just misplaced good intentions. And it's hard to blame people for those."

Even the reverend, Rachel thinks, with reluctance. She nods. "I agree. A charge feels extreme for a man whose only real offence—in *this* case—was to help a grieving mother repatriate her daughter's remains." She pauses. "'Indignity' to a body doesn't fit here. It's the opposite. Annie Little's burial near her parents in her hometown cemetery was far more dignified than a mass pauper's grave somewhere on the outskirts of Toronto. Right?"

"Yup." They sit for a while longer as Rachel's mind wanders back to that winter with Mary and the reverend. She knows she'll have to dig it up now in therapy, reconsider her perceptions of it at the time, and since. But the prospect is exhausting. She's not ready yet.

"What's next, then?" Stevens asks.

Rachel thuds her skull back against the headrest, feeling drained. All she wants right now is to go home, get into her sweatpants and eat pasta until *Friends* comes on at eight-thirty.

"It's already late afternoon," she says. "Let's head back to the office, then tomorrow we can figure out what we need to do to tie this all up. I'd like to sleep on it."

Stevens agrees, turns over the ignition and tosses the car into gear. They head northeast, away from the care home and back toward Clinton. After ten minutes, they pass the sign for Millgate, and Rachel somehow knows what Stevens is going to say before he even opens his mouth.

"Want to drive by it?" he asks quietly.

"Yeah. It's just off the main road."

He finds Garden Street, scans for the address, and eventually slows, rolling down his window. It's a small ranch-style home, red brick with an off-white door and matching shutters on the front windows. Resilient peonies are in bloom in a slightly neglected-looking and overgrown front garden. As they watch, a woman comes out to check the mailbox. Her brow knits as she reaches in, eyes on their car.

Rachel almost smiles. No one can ever ignore a police car on their street.

"Can I help you?" the woman calls, absently withdrawing the newspaper and a pile of flyers that cascade out of her hands onto the porch.

"Just having a look at the street, ma'am," Stevens replies.

She continues to look suspicious, and Rachel wonders if she'll relax a little if she sees a woman officer. She gets out of the car. The woman stands with the flyers still littered at her feet as she watches Rachel approach.

"Is this your home, ma'am?" Rachel asks.

"Uh, ye—well, no, actually," she stutters, stooping to gather the flyers. "We rent it."

She stands again, some messy blond hair falling in her face. "Is everything okay? Is—"

"It's fine," Rachel says. "You have a good day, ma'am." She's turning to leave as the thought occurs to her. "Ma'am," she calls to the woman, who throws a foot out to stop the screen door from shutting.

"Yeah?"

"Can I ask who your landlord is?"

"Why, is he in trouble or something?"

"No," Rachel says, wishing the woman would just calm down. But she's long since learned you never know what sort of experiences people have had with the police in the past that colours their interactions in the moment. For better or worse.

"Well, that's good," the woman says, though her shoulders relax a little. "'Cause he seems like an okay guy."

Rachel's instincts tingle. "What's his name?"

"Greg," the woman says. "Gregory Little."

CHAPTER 42

RACHEL

"It's just off the highway, I think," Stevens says, a map of southwestern Ontario spread out on his lap in the passenger seat. It's so well-worn that it hardly even crackles anymore; it's closer to fabric than paper at this point.

Their upcoming interview with Gregory Little should be the last one of the investigation before they compile their report for Green and put this case—and Annie Little's remains—to rest. They reach Cambridge around ten-thirty after a quick stop for coffee in Stratford.

They pull up at the curb of the treed suburban street and get out. Rachel scans the road and spots the black Volkswagen parked across from them. A young girl is down on her knees on the sidewalk near the car, a plastic bucket of chalk beside her. Her friend or sibling dangles from a tire swing on the lawn ten feet away. Both girls look up at the police, mouths hanging open a little. They have a half-hearted lemonade stand at the bottom of the driveway, currently unmanned.

Rachel squints at the driver of the black Volkswagen, gives a wave, then leads Stevens up the path to Gregory Little's house.

He answers the door immediately; he's clearly been waiting on the other side. He looks like your average fifty-year-old guy; clean-shaven in faded jeans and a nondescript dark-grey golf tee.

"Officers," he says. "Come on in."

"I'm Detective Mackenzie, this is Officer Stevens," Rachel says, pulling out her notebook as they step over the threshold. "Thank you for taking the time, Mr. Little."

"Of course."

They settle on the sofa across from him in the comfortable living room. Rachel can tell there's a Mrs. Little somewhere. The room isn't dissimilar to Emily Radcliffe's, and a stack of *Chatelaine* magazines rests on the glass coffee table beside the TV Guide. Despite the gravity of this interview, Rachel has to push down a smile.

"So," Gregory Little says. "I have to say, this was a bit of a surprise phone call."

"I can imagine it's difficult for you," Rachel agrees. "As Stevens told you on the phone, we're just tying up an investigation into the discovery of Annie Little's body in the Millgate Cemetery. We know there was no foul play—in terms of the body's location, at least," she adds. "No one is in trouble here. We mostly just need your statement about what you knew of your mother's life, death, and, most importantly, her body's removal to the cemetery by your maternal grandmother, Helen Sharrock."

"Yeah," Gregory says. "Sure. Uh, well . . ." He looks from one of them to the other.

"Begin at the beginning, if that makes it easier," Rachel prompts him. "We'll just take what we need for our notes."

He nods. "Well . . . when she was alive, my grandmother told me all about my mother, from her childhood until she was married. And then everything she knew about what happened when, uh, when I was born. And after." He takes a deep breath. "It was really difficult to hear it all, to realize that my father basically had her locked up for being sick. I didn't want to believe my grandmother. She was just a woman I'd seen from time to time in my childhood, like one of those distant aunts you see at someone's Christmas get-together every few years, you know? I didn't really appreciate that she was my real mother's mother until my teens sometime. But I guess kids don't . . . I don't know." He shifts his legs, staring at his jeans.

"I grew up with my stepmother as the only mother I knew, and she loved me. She wasn't, you know, *warm*, but she loved me, and her own kids, my two sisters. I thought when I was younger that she preferred the girls just because I was a boy, and she was more interested in girly things. But the pieces started to fit together as I grew up." He clears his throat. "My father never really sat me down to explain it all, I just kind of figured it all out on my own, that my stepmother wasn't the woman who had given birth to me, that there was some other person who had done that. No one talked to kids about that kind of stuff back then." He grunts. "Anyway, when I grew up, I guess I started asking my grandmother more questions when I'd see her, and she told me my mother was unwell after she had me, and that my father had her committed to an institution. I could tell she resented him for it, but I figured things must have been bad for him to do something like that, right?"

He waits for Rachel to answer. She nods. "I think your mother *was* in bad shape, Mr. Little, yes. From what I understand. At first, anyway."

"Well, that's just it!" he says, voice rising now. His hands pop up from his lap for a moment, then quickly curl back into fists. "My grandmother told me she got better, but my father wouldn't ask for her release because he'd divorced her. That's all he ever said to me when I'd ask, just 'she wasn't my wife anymore, she wasn't my concern.' He pauses. "So my grandmother kept asking a judge to let my mother out, but the prison doctor kept denying it." He shakes his head and shifts again, agitation building. "I knew from my grandmother that she uh, she died. Killed herself, not long before that place shut down. I kept in touch with my grandmother for a long time after that, until she died, actually. And then she left me their house in Millgate."

Rachel makes a note. "And did she tell you where your mother was buried?" She watches him closely.

He looks up at her now, sorrow and guilt in his eyes. After a moment, he nods. "Yes. I knew she was buried in an unmarked grave there. And why."

Rachel waits for him to say more.

"I never moved into the house my grandmother left me, but I also didn't want to sell it." Gregory shrugs. "I'd heard stories about my mother as a kid, and having the house let me sort of . . . walk through those memories a bit. But my wife and I live here with our kids, we didn't want to move to Millgate." Another shrug. "I've been able to rent it out most of the time. We usually get tenants for the summer. Cheap rent fifteen minutes from the lake isn't bad, right? I go every once in a while, to check in on the place, do some landscaping or whatever. I visit my grandparents' grave while I'm there, tend to the weeds and stuff. And I visit my mother's, too. Such as it is," he adds. He's quiet a moment before he continues. "You know why she was buried unmarked, right?"

"Yes, sir."

He nods. "Makes sense for the time, I guess. Things were different. And maybe things were bad enough at that jail that it made sense she'd kill herself. I can't really know. I try not to judge it. But I wonder what she would have been like, if she'd just been able to hold on for a few more months. That place got shut down in, like, the early sixties or something, right?"

"Yes, it did."

"I guess she couldn't have known it was going to get shut down, though," he says, looking to Rachel imploringly. "Otherwise I'd hope she would have held on, to be able to see me. I was almost grown by then, we could have . . ." He shakes his head.

"I don't have all the answers about what happened to your mother at the Mercer prison," Rachel says gently, wishing she could tell him to seek therapy, if he hasn't already. "I only know as much as you do, about how and why she ended up there." She pauses. "But off the record, I don't think she killed herself."

He clears his throat, nose twitching. "They uh, they said she did, though. The coroner's report and everything said she did. And that's why—"

"I know," Rachel says. "But there's someone I think you should talk to, who might know more about this than even the coroner did, or your grandmother."

Gregory's brow furrows. He swallows. "Okay. Sure. Yeah."

"Stevens will go get her."

"Now?"

"Yes. She's waiting outside."

"Oh," Gregory says, sitting up straighter. "Uh, okay. Sure."

Stevens returns a moment later with Emily, who has been waiting in her Volkswagen across the street. She looks like a nervous job interviewee, dressed in a smart grey pantsuit, clutching a white handbag in a tightened fist. Stevens gestures her over to the sofa, then falls back out of the way. Rachel offers Emily her seat, and she accepts, licking her lips as she finally meets Gregory's eyes.

"Gregory Little, this is Emily Radcliffe," Rachel says.

"Hi." Emily extends a hand. It's a little shaky, but she manages to still it before it's grasped by Annie's son. "I'm uh . . ." Her eyes land on the pile of magazines, and she falters, exhales something between a sigh and a laugh. "I was a reporter who went undercover at the Mercer prison in 1961."

Gregory exhales hard. "The year my mother died."

"Yes."

"And you were there . . . sorry, why?"

"To break the story about the conditions, about the way they were treating people like your mother."

He takes in her features. "Can you tell me something nice about her? Something good that she did, or how she was? My grandmother obviously couldn't tell me those details. From my mother's adult life, anyway. There's this huge gap where I know nothing about her."

Emily considers a moment, then smiles. "She loved strawberries," she says, and he lets out a watery chuckle.

"Me too."

Emily sighs. "She was unhappy, for obvious reasons," she says gently, "but the happiest I saw her was when she told me about Millgate, and her childhood. About the strawberry fields around there. And when she spoke about you, Gregory." Her voice breaks. "She was a good friend to me."

"How did you meet?" he asks, wiping away a tear.

"Well, they wouldn't let her have a knife to cut her meat, so I let her have mine. And then we ate together almost every breakfast for six months."

Emily tells him about her time there, and her interactions with his mother, about playing cribbage and reading terrible cast-off library books in the recreation room.

"And what about the bad stuff?" he asks after a few moments.

Emily glances at Rachel, then runs her hands over the knees of her suit.

"I can handle it," he assures her.

She nods, then talks about Annie's struggles, the conditions that her investigation hoped to draw attention to. And then, finally, she tells him about Annie's death in her arms in the middle of the dining hall on that cold December night. He resolutely dries his eyes with the back of his hand several times before excusing himself to retrieve a tissue box.

"But your mother's death inspired the other women," Emily tells him when he sits back down. "I think it's important that you know that. The psych and regular inmates all came together once they knew who I was, and why I was there. And they witnessed your mother's death. Her *murder*," she corrects herself. "I think if that hadn't happened, they might not have been so motivated to help me get out. And getting me out is what led to the Mercer being shut down, which brought an end to the abuse of so many women. Her death should never have happened, but it did end up meaning something."

Gregory clenches his fists in his lap, over and over again, for several minutes. Stevens clears his throat. She's feeling the gravity of this one weighing on her, too. And she's glad the case has been able to provide closure to both Emily and Gregory, in a roundabout way. So often the resolution of her investigations is just pure tragedy. It's a relief to see something good come out of it.

"Did uh," Gregory begins, "did my mother—"

"Hey Dad!" A teenage girl comes whipping around the corner from the hall, and all four of them are jarred from the conversation. "Do you know where my—oh, sorry," she says, a little quieter now as her big blue eyes look down at the three unfamiliar adults. "Are you in trouble? Did Tyler crash the car?" she asks, eyeing Rachel and Stevens in their uniforms.

Gregory smiles tightly. "No, Annie, we're not in trouble."

Something warm clutches at Rachel's heart as she looks at the young woman, all brown hair and innocence.

"Annie?" Emily asks, eyes glassing over.

The girl and her father both nod, and she moves to sit next to him. He runs a large hand over her shoulders.

Emily smiles widely, almost a laugh, as tears slip from her eyes. "She looks just like her," she says.

CHAPTER 43

RACHEL

Rachel pulls up outside the Grand Valley Institution for Women and turns off the ignition. Stevens has been her constant travel companion over the six weeks of this investigation, but she's alone today. He'd offered to come with her, to drive her home after, but Rachel declined. It was nice of him, and he seemed to genuinely care when she confided in him about Mary. But this is something she needs to do alone. As for driving home, well . . . she's been through worse. She can handle this.

She makes her way across the parking lot to the visitor entrance, feels the heat from the afternoon sun baking up at her from the asphalt. She hikes her purse up her shoulder in a determined sort of way and heads for the front doors as though she's visited a thousand times.

But she hasn't. Not once.

It doesn't take long to get through security, and soon she's shown into a large white-walled room scattered with round tables, chairs bolted to the floor. Rachel wills her hands to still in her lap. She's only ever been inside jails and prisons in uniform, armed, and the sense of vulnerability she feels in her floral midi skirt and tee is doing nothing to help the anxiety raging up from her gut into her throat. She starts to question why she's come at all, and is just wrestling a panic-induced urged to leave when the guard appears at the door with a line of inmates.

Heart pounding, Rachel stands up, knowing she doesn't want Mary to approach her sitting down. She needs to be at eye level.

And there she is, fourth in line with all the other women, equalized by their dark-teal prison uniforms. Rachel inhales sharply when she gets a full look at her mother.

Time and incarceration have not been kind to Mary. Her skin is sagging a little beneath her chin and her mouth is lined with wrinkles. She's pale, and her natural dark-brown hair colour is all grown out, but heavily grey at the temples and hairline now. She's gained weight.

The guard guides Mary to the table, and she's visibly surprised to see Rachel standing there. She saunters over, not in any kind of rush, and faces her daughter for the first time in ten years.

"Didn't think you'd ever show up," she says. Her voice is lower than Rachel remembered, a little gravelly. Damage from years of smoking and drinking, or lack of use in prison, Rachel isn't sure. Maybe both. But the tone is the same—indignant judgment laced with self-destruction and hurt.

Mary lowers herself into the hard plastic chair with a little grunt, and Rachel's feet itch to leave, but she gets a hold of herself and sits down again. They stare at one another for a long moment.

"Well," Mary says. "How you been?"

Rachel opens, then shuts her mouth. She hasn't really considered how much to tell her mother about her life now. She's wondered how Mary would respond to her being here, given that Rachel had testified so strongly against her. But then, she's the one who's been writing to Rachel all these years. Rachel has never opened any of the letters, but it must have indicated some desire to talk.

"You married?" Mary asks.

"No."

"Huh. You do anything for work?"

Rachel swallows, unsure of how her mother will react, but she reminds herself that Mary can't hurt her here. If she's ever going to have the upper hand, this is it. "I'm a cop," she says. "A detective."

Mary's eyes narrow, but then she throws her head back and laughs.

"Sounds about right," Mary says, crossing her arms over her chest now, protective. Maybe a little angry. "You still in the house?"

Rachel doesn't answer. She doesn't really want Mary to have confirmation of where to reach her. For all Mary knows, those unanswered letters were tossed out by the new owners before Rachel even saw them.

"Well, good you finished school, anyway," Mary says with a shrug. "Beats scooping ice cream for the rest of your life."

Rachel watches her mother, curious about the comment. Mary still sees her as a child, still pictures her in that paper hat behind the counter on Main Street. She can't even conceptualize Rachel as the adult she is now. Her mother never understood her, and never will. Because she doesn't want to. And if Mary doesn't want to do something, it isn't going to happen.

Rachel decides to dispense with the small talk, and get right to it. "I want to ask you something. Between you and me, here, today, tell me the truth. Did you push your brother off that cliff?" she asks, watching Mary closely.

Mary runs her tongue over her teeth. Slowly. "You don't actually want to know the answer to that."

A chill runs through Rachel. "So you *did* kill him?"

"That's not what I said. I said you don't actually want to know."

"Don't speak to me in fucking riddles, Mary, or I'm leaving."

"No you won't," Mary scoffs.

"Excuse me?"

"You won't leave, because you came here for an answer. But what I'm saying is, I don't think you want it."

Mary locks eyes with her, and it takes everything Rachel's got to meet her gaze and hold it. "You want to keep thinking I killed Walt," Mary says, "because then this all makes sense to you, and you get to keep hating me and loving Dora and then we get a nice black-and-white picture, don't we? Nice sharp edges." She pauses. "You don't want the grey. Especially not now that you're a damn cop. You want a yes or no and you can't live with a maybe. You've always been like that."

"You wouldn't even know what I've always been like," Rachel fires back. "You were in and out of my life for twenty years and you've been in here for the remainder."

"Well, you heard my defence, didn't you? He was always the golden boy, couldn't do anything wrong. And that was all stacked up next to my little fucked-up self, so that's one hell of an idyllic backdrop to have to live in front of. Dora was abusive, and so was my dad. Emotionally abusive, psychologically. They didn't give a shit about me once Walt was born, and even before that, I know Dora didn't think I was good enough. Nothing I ever did was good enough because I wasn't a boy, and she wanted a boy. They both did."

"None of that sounds like her. You're a liar, and always have been. Pathological. I don't even know why I—"

"It might not sound like the version of her *you* knew, Rachel, because you were both always united against me, like I was some kind of curse you'd both been hit with. She tried to abort my fucking fetus, she—"

Rachel holds up a hand. "Enough. You always hang everything on that, but do you not hear that you sound crazy? Calling your mother a witch and talking about curses?"

"Well, that was my whole defence, wasn't it?" Mary says, flashing Rachel a sarcastic smile with intent to wound. "That I'm just too crazy to be responsible for myself."

"Right. And that defence failed, didn't it? Has it not occurred to you that you were sick enough for her to maybe know what might be best? That she was actually trying to *help* you by terminating—"

"Just stop it," Mary says, and now her eyes are shining. "Stop it."

They're silent for a minute as the conversations of the other inmates and visitors swell in the large white space.

"You won't just tell me, will you?" Rachel says finally. "About Walter Jr.?"

"My parents didn't have me charged, did they?" Mary says. "So what does that say?"

The lump forming in Rachel's throat threatens to choke her, but she manages a shuddering breath. "I think that says they were loving parents who didn't want to lose *both* of their children. I think that says they were trying to protect you."

Mary is quiet, but only for a moment. "Except they still just acted like they hated me. *Hated* me. Is it even possible to love your kid and hate them at the same time?" She shakes her head, scoffs.

Rachel sighs deeply, knowing the conversation is at an end, and that this will probably be the last one she ever has with her mother. And she's okay with that. As has been the case her entire life, she's never going to get what she wants or needs from Mary. Her mother is too sick. Too selfish. Too much of a run-of-the-mill asshole. Too complicated, yet too narrow-minded. Too everything. But Rachel will still spend the rest of her life wishing things weren't such a mess, and trying, day in and day out at her job, to tidy up the messes for other people.

"I wouldn't know," Rachel answers. "But I think *you* do."

CHAPTER 44

EMILY

Huron County—August, 1996

Emily sits on the edge of the bed at her hotel, a lovely little historic inn in Bayfield, with creaky, uneven floorboards and tall, bright windows looking out onto the leafy main street. She runs her hand over the quilted bedspread, takes a moment to ground herself as she feels the stitching beneath her fingers. It would be an inconvenient time for the panic attack she can feel building. It's just simmering, but at least, after so many years of therapy, Emily has the tools now to prevent it from overtaking her.

"It's going to be all right, Em," her husband, Howard, says. She looks up to find him standing near the full-length mirror on the back of the door, hands frozen midway through fastening a tie beneath his grey, grizzled, and slightly paunchy chin. He watches her through glasses that have gotten thicker every year. He had them when they met, back in 1970 at Doris's annual Christmas at-home. He was a photographer working freelance for various papers and magazines, including Maclean-Hunter. They were married three years later in a small ceremony at the new City Hall. They both enjoyed travel and adventurous dining, agreed on their politics, and neither wanted children. Despite the usual conflicts from time to time, they were a good match, and the absence of children meant that they had space in their comfortable home for both an office for Emily and Howard's darkroom in the basement. Howard knew the entire story of what had happened to Emily during the Mercer assignment, and his understanding for both her drive to do it as well as its lasting impact on her is one of the things she loves most about him. He always knows when she's struggling without her having to say anything at all.

"Thank you," she says. She takes three deep breaths in succession, then stands and moves into the bathroom to finish getting ready for Annie's reburial.

Rachel Mackenzie had called her a few weeks ago to let her know that the case was now considered closed, and that she'd spoken with Annie's son, Gregory, about his wishes for the remains. He requested they be cremated and buried in the plot with Helen and Richard Sharrock. Emily thought that plan not only made the most sense, but was certainly what Annie—and Helen—would have wanted. Gregory had called Emily the following day to ask if she would please attend. She wants to, but the experience isn't without its emotional hurdles. She's had twice-weekly therapy sessions in the interim to deal with the mess of emotion and trauma this business with the police has churned up. But her therapist has assured her this is a huge step for getting the necessary closure on Annie's death, that the reburial is an opportunity to put it all to bed.

She's struggled for decades with guilt that she caused it. No one else seems to see it that way, though—not Doris, Howard, her family, not even Gregory. They'd had another chat when he called a few weeks ago. He had some follow-up questions from their conversation with the detectives, and Emily was happy to give him whatever she could. But he refused to hear any sense of responsibility on Emily's part.

"That place had been trying to kill her for fifteen years before you arrived, Ms. Radcliffe," he'd said. "You were doing what you could to get her released so she could come be my mother again. There's no shame in that."

Emily slicks on a muted dark-pink lipstick—the only makeup she ever wears—and gives her hair one final spray to help ward off the humidity. She steps out of the bathroom to find Howard whisking the sleeve of his jacket with a lint brush.

"You're going to bake in that, I'm afraid," Emily says with a frown. She herself is wearing a green floral dress with a light cardigan over top. She's never been a particularly vain person, but she can't do sleeveless anymore, not since the skin on her upper arms decided to give up clinging to the muscles beneath, preferring instead to sag. She lets the few varicose veins in her legs have their moment in the sun, though. She liberated herself from pantyhose in 1982 and never looked back.

"I know," Howard says quietly, "but it's like a funeral, isn't it? Closest thing to one. It doesn't feel right to just go in shirtsleeves."

Emily nods. "That's very honourable of you." She offers the best smile she can manage while feeling as though she might vomit. "Thanks for coming, sweetheart."

"Of course." He embraces her, and she homes in on his heartbeat, the scent of his aftershave, the prickles of the suit jacket under her fingers, the warmth of his body beneath the fabric. "Do you have the magazine?" he asks as they pull apart. Gregory had asked her for a copy of it. Fortunately, Emily's kept an entire box of them since 1962.

"Yes, in my bag here."

They drive the ten minutes into Millgate with directions provided by the hotel receptionist. Halfway there, Emily spots a market stall at the side of the road near a long country laneway.

"Oh! Honey, can you pull over there?"

He obliges, and Emily seizes her purse from the floor and gets out, returning a few minutes later with two quarts of fresh strawberries.

They arrive in Millgate and find the cemetery; easy, as the town is so small and the park-like cemetery appears to be the centre of it. Howard drives into a gravel lot beside the church and parks next to a police car, leaving their sedan running for the air conditioning. He turns to face her, searching her eyes.

"I'm ready," she says, already blinking fast. "I am. This is good."

Emily loops her arm through his as they walk over to the small crowd of people clustered around a headstone on the northwest corner of the cemetery. She's holding one of the quarts of strawberries in one hand as her purse dangles from the other arm. The smell of the fruit fills Emily's nostrils and a bee lands on top of the juicy red pile, investigates, then flies off to tell its friends.

As they approach, she spots Detective Mackenzie and her junior, both with their arms crossed over their chests. Mackenzie is in conversation with a man wearing a minister's stole. He says something and she responds, smiling genially. It might be the first time Emily's seen her smile. It's a good one, it reaches her eyes, but Emily gets the sense she doesn't exercise it much.

Off to the side, nearer the headstone, are Gregory Little and his daughter, Annie, along with a rather surly-looking, stooped teenage boy and a curvy woman who must be Gregory's son and wife. They're all dressed in shades of purple, even the boy, who tugs uncomfortably at the collar of his eggplant-coloured dress shirt. Gregory looks up at Emily's approach and smiles a little sadly.

"Emily." He greets her with an enthusiastic embrace that nearly triggers her tears, then introduces his wife and son.

"And this is my husband, Howard," Emily says. They shake, then she holds up the strawberries. "I spied them at a stall on the way here. For all I know, maybe that was the same farm stand your grandmother used to get them from, for her jam. I'd like to think so, anyway." She pauses. "May I ask why all the purple?"

"It was her favourite colour, my grandmother said," Gregory tells her. "Did you know that?"

She shakes her head. "No. But now I do. Thank you."

Without a word, they all move into a semicircle around the stone. A hole has been dug in the earth there. A pewter urn rests beside it, and Emily's breath catches at the sight, her heart suddenly tight. She kneels to set the quart of strawberries next to the stone where Annie's parents' names and dates are etched, and below them, a recent addition:

ANNIE SHARROCK LITTLE

Apr 15, 1926 – Dec 18, 1961

Mother, daughter & friend

Emily kisses her fingers and touches them to Annie's name, then rises and takes her place again beside Howard, who reaches for her hand. She watches through shining eyes as Annie's son and granddaughter lower the urn into the grave, then place their bouquet of purple irises at the base of the stone.

Emily wipes away a tear as Gregory makes his way over to her.

"Thank you, Emily. For coming today. And for being her friend when she had no one else."

Emily nods, but can't speak. Howard squeezes her hand, and she steadies herself on the grounding pressure.

"I know this is what my grandmother wanted," Gregory says. "I think she'd be happy. And my mom, too."

The leaves sigh in the warm summer breeze as birds twitter from the branches above. The sparrows sing to their newborn babies songs of the wide and never-ending world, of the liberty that is their birthright, in all its complexity, its joys and sorrows and horrific dangers. And they only wish what all good mothers do: that their babies' wings should grow strong, their sense of direction true, and that any suffering be minimal.

And in that moment, Emily knows they are posthumously fulfilling Helen Sharrock's greatest wish: to have her baby fly back home to the warm and protective wings of her mother.

"All Annie wanted was to be free again," Emily says, finally able to get the words out. "To be free, and reunited with you, Greg. To be back in this place that she loved so much."

"So I guess, in a way, she has all of those things now," Gregory says. He's quiet for a moment. "Do you think she's looking down on us?"

His eyes reflect the same complicated peace that Emily feels within herself now that Annie is at rest. But there's a desperation there, too. A longing to believe that some part of his mother might still be watching over him.

Emily reaches for his hand now, clasps it firmly. Her eyes move to Gregory's daughter, who so resembles Annie that it still takes Emily's breath away to see her. And she remembers that Annie *is* alive in Gregory, and his children. She lives on in them.

As for her spirit? Emily doesn't know. But she finds she's all right with that, because the uncertainty at least allows room for a comforting wish.

She smiles at Gregory. "I hope," she tells him. "With all of my heart, I hope."

AUTHOR'S NOTE

Dear Reader,

Liberty Street lived rent-free in my head for nearly five years before it finally made it into your hands.

Authors have a myriad of answers to the question "Where do you get your inspiration?," but most of them will remember where they were and what they were doing when The Idea clicked into place. For me, when I know it's an idea worth pursuing, I get a sort of electric jolt at the crown of my head, and I have to drop everything I'm doing to write it all down, everything that's in my mind at that moment, because I know I've landed on something my heart and soul need to write.

This story came to me when I was driving down a quiet country highway, and I had to pull over and put my flashers on while I furiously thumb-typed the sketchy outline for *Liberty Street* on my phone's note app while my baby slept in the back seat. I think of that moment every time I pass that spot on the highway.

Sometimes we find the idea, and sometimes the idea finds us.

THE MERCER

The Mercer Women's Prison, as I named it in the book, is primarily inspired by the Andrew Mercer Reformatory for Females, which actually had several different names over the course of its existence from 1880 through 1969. It took up an entire city block at 1155 King Street West in Toronto's Liberty Village, bordered by Fraser Avenue, Liberty Street, and Jefferson Avenue. Liberty Street got its name because it was the main street the prisoners at the Mercer (and its neighbour, the Central Prison for Men) would walk down upon their release, headed toward the amenities in Liberty Village, which was their first point of contact with the outside world at the end of their sentence. I knew this novel's title from the moment the idea first hit me on that quiet county highway.

The Andrew Mercer Reformatory was originally intended as a "female refuge," where women with addictions or who were leading so-called "lives of vice" would be sent for a period of, on average, about six months to a year. Staff sought to instill the valued feminine virtues of the era—namely subjugation and docility—in the name of reform. In the decades that followed, the Mercer eventually evolved to house a broader spectrum of prisoners, including women who were considered violent criminals, those suffering from psychiatric conditions, and those deemed "incorrigible" under the Female Refuges Act, an eye-wateringly misogynist piece of legislation.

The Female Refuges Act came into effect in Ontario in 1927, and did indeed, precisely per Emily's research, allow for women and girls to be incarcerated at the Mercer and other reform institutions (sometimes called "industrial refuges") for such trivialities as repeatedly breaking curfew. There was also a clause stipulating that if a woman was found to have venereal disease (an STI) or was mentally ill, she could be held at a reform institution *indefinitely* until she was cured and her medical condition deemed acceptable by the prison physician. I think my jaw might have actually hit the floor when I read that, and I'm sure you can see how I thought this mind-boggling clause was ripe for use as a significant plot device in both Emily's and Annie's storylines. The Female Refuges Act was finally repealed in 1964, though the Andrew Mercer Reformatory remained open for several years beyond that. If you're interested, you can view the entirety of the Female Refuges Act on my website.

Although I exercised artistic licence in having *Chatelaine* magazine break the story of the Mercer (lots more on that decision below!), it was actually broken by the *Toronto Star* after a grand jury investigation in the mid-1960s uncovered the deplorable conditions of the place, many of which are depicted in the novel. After a series of exposés in the *Star*, the entire prison was razed in 1969 and the Allan A. Lamport Stadium built in its place. Today, there is nothing to denote the tragic history of the site aside from an historical plaque outside the stadium, at the corner of Liberty St. and Jefferson Ave. The only building remaining from the Mercer's era is a home at the corner of King and Fraser, formerly the superintendent's (warden's) residence.

THE RESEARCH

I was able to track down and access pre-construction blueprints that provided information on the physical layout of the Mercer prison and grounds, but accessing detail about the experiences of the inmates in the 1950s and '60s became a bureaucratic maze. There are many records related to the Mercer inmates, including prisoner registers, medical records, and punishment records. I tried to gain access to these through a Freedom of Information request, but because so many of the inmates at the Mercer were minors, the documents were nearly all protected not only by the Freedom of Information and Protection of Privacy Act (FIPPA), but also retroactively by the Youth Criminal Justice Act. As such, I was told I would only have been granted access to these records with a court order from a youth court justice, which wasn't going to happen, and the fact that I wasn't a descendent of any of the inmates meant I was pretty much shut out of those records. So, I had to rely heavily on the few existing first-hand accounts from women who experienced incarceration at the Mercer, as well as older, partially redacted inmate records that provided insight into the reasons for women's incarceration and their experiences at the Mercer prior to the 1920s (since the records are sealed from public access for 100 years).

But in those earlier records, I found my inspiration for June Jones: a woman whose crime was listed as repeatedly "running a house of ill repute," and who was held at the Mercer on at least three occasions. I also turned to coroner's reports, records that were available from other women's prisons that existed around the same time (namely the Kingston Prison for Women), and details from the grand jury investigation that triggered the closure of the Mercer, which were readily available in the *Toronto Star*'s archives.

Special thanks go out to the member of staff in the FOI office at the Ontario Archives for his bureaucratic acrobatics in trying to get me access to as many of these records as possible within the strict confines of the privacy laws. He wished to remain unnamed in my acknowledgments, but he truly went above and beyond to help me with this difficult research process. Thanks also to Aziza, who provided research assistance on-site.

THE SUBVERSIVELY FEMINIST HISTORY OF *CHATELAINE* MAGAZINE

I could have written an entire novel just about *Chatelaine* magazine in the 1960s. Doris Anderson was a real person, and an original #girlboss. For those who don't know, you mostly have her to thank for securing sex-based discrimination protections in the Canadian Charter of Rights and Freedoms when she was head of the Canadian Advisory Council on the Status of Women. This is Section 28, which states simply that men and women are equal before and under the law. It is the most basic of equality guarantees, and one that women in countries around the world—including America—are *still fighting for*.

Anderson was the editor-in-chief of *Chatelaine* throughout the 1950s, '60s, and into the '70s. In the late '50s and '60s, she added a distinctly feminist tone to the magazine, and has been hailed for having a large impact on the burgeoning 1970s feminist movement in Canada. But *Chatelaine* was never considered a threatening publication by those in power, because it was "just" a women's magazine. It was lumped in with its glossy American counterparts, but in addition to the usual recipes and beauty tips, *Chatelaine* contained articles on oral contraceptives, abortion, politics, woman and child abuse, divorce laws, and equal pay. But it could sit with magazines like *Glamour* and *Ladies' Home Journal* on the table at the doctor's office and no one thought twice about it. I imagine many a controlling husband was entirely unaware of the outspokenly feminist text sitting beside a pair of reading glasses on his wife's bedside table. In it, she was reading about how to prevent pregnancy and what her rights would be if they were ever to divorce. On the cover? The best swimsuits for summer, a pineapple upside-down cake recipe, and how to save on back-to-school clothes for your kids.

Nothing to see here, boys.

Chatelaine magazine was a lifeline for many women, particularly the socially isolated suburban housewives of the '50s and '60s. The conversation between Emily and Doris where Doris explains how the magazine had to meet women where they were at, to "coax them into the tent," was paraphrased from Doris Anderson's memoir *Rebel Daughter*. She knew that if *Chatelaine* could reach women on practical and emotional levels, gain their trust and loyalty, they might then have a better chance of reaching their readers on a *political* level to show them how their lives could be improved if they dared to demand more from society and government. Interestingly, the letters-to-the-editor section at the back of the magazine became a place of exuberant discourse between Canadian women about the pressing issues of the day at a time when "housewives" had very few outlets or opportunities for this sort of philosophical stimulation or political debate.

Under Doris Anderson's leadership, *Chatelaine* became the most successful magazine of any kind in Canadian history, and continued to fly under the radar of its parent company Maclean-Hunter who, as Doris said, was only ever looking at the revenue lines, not the table of contents.

THE "GIRL STUNT REPORTERS"

In the early 1900s, there was a trend that saw young female reporters take astonishing risks, putting themselves in physical peril to secure news stories and make names for themselves in the male-dominated field of investigative journalism. Collectively, they came to be known as the Girl Stunt Reporters. I could lecture for a good two hours on the fact that women so often have to do a series of backflips and then stand on their heads just to accomplish what men have been able to do from a seated, relaxed position of privilege. But I think, for better or worse, this fact makes these women's accomplishments all the more impressive.

When I created the character of Emily Radcliffe and knew she was going to go underground to scoop the story at the Mercer Women's Prison, I also knew she had to work for *Chatelaine*; that her character would have been drawn to work there in the first place, and that an editor like Doris Anderson would have championed her suggestion to get the Mercer story in such a bold way.

Emily's character was inspired by two journalists: Canadian Lotta

Dempsey—who also worked for *Chatelaine* and in fact wrote several of the *Toronto Star* articles about the Mercer Reformatory grand jury report—and American journalist Nellie Bly, who spent ten days in the psychiatric institution on Blackwell's Island in New York to break the story of the horrifying conditions there. I learned about Nellie Bly at least a decade ago, and had been trying to find a way to fictionalize her incredible story. When the idea for the Mercer hit, I knew immediately that I had found a place to plug it in.

Incidentally, breaking the story at Blackwell's Island is not Bly's only claim to fame: she also trained as a pilot and flew around the world in seventy-two days. You can read about her exploits at the psychiatric institution in her series of articles, which have been compiled into a short memoir titled *Ten Days in a Mad-House*. I highly recommend the audiobook version.

HISTORICAL INSPIRATION FOR OTHER CHARACTERS

Velma Demerson

Many of my descriptions of the Mercer and the conditions there were informed by the series of articles that made up the *Toronto Star* exposé, the text of the grand jury investigation, and also the memoir *Incorrigible* by a woman named Velma Demerson (the inspiration for Vera's character).

Demerson was arrested in 1939—at her parents' encouragement—for being in a relationship with and becoming pregnant by a Chinese man. Her memoir details the horrific treatment she experienced at the Mercer (including emotional abuse and gynecological torture), giving birth to her son while incarcerated, and the long road to her eventual release. I pulled a lot of my description of the prison and cells from Demerson's memoir, including her mention of the water tap in the cell wall.

Generally, women weren't included in medical trials until the 1980s (the jaw-dropping reality of which is probably a whole novel unto itself . . .

hmm . . .), but that doesn't mean ad hoc and even underhanded experimentation wasn't occurring, because it certainly was at the Mercer. After Demerson's release, through her own research about what had happened to her, it became clear that the prison doctor was infecting the women with venereal disease in order to experiment with VD treatments on them. Some records claim that the doctor who served at the Mercer Reformatory during Demerson's incarceration was also a eugenicist who abused her position to experiment on the prisoners in an effort to determine what made these particular women so "unfit" and "deficient" compared to the rest of the population. Accusations of forced sterilization—with or without the patient's knowledge—were also rampant, and often racialized.

To date, Velma Demerson is the only former inmate of the Andrew Mercer Reformatory to receive an apology and financial settlement from the Ontario government for the abuses she and her baby suffered at the prison. You can learn more about her by reading her memoir, or check out the recent documentary on her life. The links for both are available on my website.

Annie Little and Frances C.

When I decided to write this novel, I knew I wanted a big theme in both timelines to be women's mental health, and I was particularly intrigued by references I found in my research to the psychiatric "treatment" (a word I will use *very* loosely and reluctantly here, for lack of a better one) elements of the Mercer's appalling history. In digging a little deeper into the approaches to psychiatric treatment in the Mercer's era, my research quickly directed me to the prison's neighbour institution: the psychiatric hospital a few streets to the north at 999 Queen Street West, which at the time was called the Provincial Lunatic Asylum. Like the Mercer, the Lunatic Asylum may have had idealistic beginnings, but the hospital at 999 Queen quickly became overcrowded and descended into an atrocious prison of its own, where residents were subjected to reprehensible treatment. I uncovered a lot of shocking detail when I began to dig into this institution's history, but the case that shook me to my core and was a driving force behind writing this novel was a thirty-one-year-old patient named Frances C., the character that inspired Annie Little.

Frances's case file describes her admission to the hospital in 1880, two weeks after giving birth. She was diagnosed with "puerperal insanity," which is loosely translated in present-day terms to a postpartum mental health issue. She had tried to harm herself and others, and threatened her newborn baby. She was also convinced people were trying to poison her. I immediately knew, reading through my modern lens, that Frances was almost certainly suffering from postpartum psychosis, a rare but temporary postpartum condition. Its symptoms are severe, and often involve paranoia and delusion, but typically resolve in a matter of weeks, or a year at most. But Frances was kept at the asylum for fifty-one years. She died there in 1931 at age eighty-two.

Let that sink in for a moment.

I'll admit, reading this case brought tears to my eyes, and I could not stop thinking about Frances. Of course we can only draw assumptions, but based on what we now know of the trajectory of postpartum psychosis, it would have abated not too long after she was admitted. The major question for me then became: What happened next? I assumed Frances descended into a deep depression at being held in captivity indefinitely, and in such horrid conditions, torn from her family and newborn child. Perhaps she appeared "mad," raging at staff about why she was incarcerated at all, demanding she be released. What was their response to that? Did her family ever try to secure her release? If not, why not? The character of Annie Little is my answer to these questions. I crafted her to honour Frances C. and all the other women who we can presume suffered similar treatment and stigmatization for their postpartum mental health in the Victorian and subsequent eras, because it's only in the past couple of decades that we have truly started to properly address and de-stigmatize postpartum mental health.

So . . . this story and others out of the psychiatric hospital's patient records solidified my decision to fold in some of the 999 Queen history and include a psychiatric wing at my prison based on the Mercer. I felt a deep-seated need to immortalize Frances C., whose only "offence," like so many women before her, was that she was a woman, and therefore not granted any control over her own life or body.

Rose

Rose's situation is loosely inspired by the criminal case *R. v. Lavallee* but she remains a fictional character. Angelique Lavallee was a Canadian woman charged with murdering her abusive partner in 1986. The subsequent trial was the first time "battered woman syndrome" (as it was then called) was introduced as a specific facet of a self-defence argument. Lavallee claimed that on the night of the murder, her partner assaulted her during a furious fight, then handed her a gun and told her if she didn't kill him, he would "get her." She argued that based on all prior experience of his abusive nature, she fully believed that he would follow through and kill her, so she fired the gun and killed him first.

In 1990, the case made its way to the Supreme Court of Canada, which upheld Lavallee's acquittal in a unanimous decision. The Criminal Code was then updated to include "the nature, duration and history of any relationship between the parties to the incident, including any prior use or threat of force and the nature of that force or threat" in the assessment of self-defence claims (translated into lay terms: the history of abuse matters to how a woman responds in self-defence). The case has also been applied to criminal sentencing for abused women convicted of killing their partners, the idea being that the history of abuse should be taken into context when determining an appropriate sentence.

THE MATERNITY HOME CONNECTION AND THE "MERCER BABIES"

For those who have read my debut, *Looking for Jane*, you may have noticed the reference to St. Agnes's Home for Unwed Mothers, the fictional maternity home in *Jane*.

When Velma Demerson's maternity home unexpectedly closed, she and several other pregnant girls were transferred to the Mercer. When I read that in her memoir, I immediately knew that in my story they were going to come from St. Agnes's, which shuttered in June of 1961 after a scandal I won't spoil here. *Liberty Street* isn't a sequel to *Looking for Jane*, but they exist in the same universe, and I must admit, as the author I myself was curious about what would have happened to the St. Agnes girls after their home closed. I wasn't quite ready to leave them behind just yet, so I brought them with me to *Liberty Street*.

Because so many of the young women who were sent to the Andrew Mercer Reformatory were incarcerated there *because* they had gotten pregnant out of wedlock, countless babies were born during their mothers' incarceration over the course of the prison's existence (a precise number is difficult to determine due to the record-keeping standards of the era). There was an on-site nursery, though the women were usually sent to a local hospital to give birth before returning to the prison with their newborn to complete their sentence. Sources—including Velma Demerson—describe the malicious or outright abusive treatment of the babies by prison matrons, inmates having very limited access to their babies, and the administration using the infants as leverage, threatening that they would be apprehended by Child Services if the mothers acted out or were in any way non-compliant.

Since I had already explored the heartbreaking theme of the historic treatment of unwed mothers in *Looking for Jane*, I couldn't focus specifically on the Mercer babies in *Liberty Street*. But I do want to draw attention to this significant piece of the reformatory's dark history here in the author's note. These mothers endured inhumane treatment, and justice is still outstanding for them and their babies.

VOCABULARY

Authors of historical fiction often have to stop writing to open a new tab and google "When was thing X invented?" or "When was the term 'such-and-such' first used?" Often, common items and words have been around a lot longer than most of us might think. During this writing process, I had to find out when the word "stigma" was first used, and the answer is interesting, so I thought I'd share it with you.

It's of ancient Greek origin, and spawned "stigmata," the word given to the alleged wounds of Christ. It came to be used referentially to describe something that had left a mark, even a physical scar. It was eventually shortened to "stigma," and only in 1963 was it really used in relation to mental health by sociologist Erving Goffman, who defined it as a "deeply discrediting" attribute. I was actually surprised at how long the term had been in use. In recent years, of course, the word has thoroughly ingrained itself into our cultural lexicon, particularly in reference to mental health, prostitution, and addiction.

Here I need to applaud my highly skilled copyeditor, Melanie Little, who caught the fact that I had Bess taking Emily's grandmother for a walk through High Park to see the cherry blossoms in the spring of 1961. The first of those cherry trees weren't planted until 1959, and typically take at least three—sometimes five—years to reach their full bloom, so these women couldn't have seen the blossoms in their glory in 1961. But I left this detail in, regardless, as Emily's grandmother had such a difficult life that I honestly just loved the idea of her strolling through those blossoms as one of the few pleasures still available to her in her advanced age.

THANKS

As always, first thanks go to my agent Hayley Steed, who guides the reins of my career with a calm and confident hand, and who possesses such fierce commitment to me and the stories I want to tell. It is a friendship and partnership that I hope will last a lifetime.

Enormous thanks to my editor Bhavna Chauhan and the team at Doubleday Canada, as well as Natalie Hallak and Ballantine Books. I am so grateful for your overwhelming enthusiasm for getting this story into the hands of readers across North America, and for your skill in helping me hone *Liberty Street* into its final form.

Special thanks to the inimitable Canadian feminist legends that are journalist Michele Landsberg and former Governor General of Canada the Right Honourable Adrienne Clarkson, for so enthusiastically taking my calls and recounting Doris Anderson's initiatives, voice, physicality, fashion sense, and courage, the Canadian political landscape of the 1960s, and your experiences writing for *Chatelaine*. Thank you both for the groundwork you laid for my and future generations of Canadian women, and for helping breathe life into Emily's beloved workplace.

I also need to send particular thanks to my friend and former professor Stephanie Bangarth (who, it recently horrified us both to learn, was younger than I am now when we first met nineteen years ago). During my last year of undergrad, I did a one-on-one independent study course with her, and two of the texts she set for me were memoirs: *Incorrigible* by Velma Demerson and *Rebel Daughter* by Doris Anderson. Little did I know that both those texts would return to me as inspiration for a future novel.

And on the note of life's quirky tendency to fold over on itself, here I must also thank Constable Mackenzie Hartung for providing invaluable information and guidance on police procedure. Mackenzie and I scooped ice cream side by side for nine hours a day every summer of my undergrad, and fifteen years later she was instrumental to my research process for my third published novel. Go figure. (Also, any perceived errors or omissions in Rachel's police work are entirely on me.)

Thank you to my ad hoc research assistants Jim, Denise, Kim, Sarah, Amy, and Lisa.

And boundless gratitude to my family for their ongoing support for my writing, particularly everything they do behind the scenes—both the profound and the profoundly mundane—to enable me on this journey. When both my professional and parenting careers took off simultaneously, it was a tremendous blessing, but not without significant challenges, demands, and conflicts. I wouldn't be able to do all of this without my family by my side. I love you so much.

LIBERTY STREET

Discussion
Questions

DISCUSSION QUESTIONS

1. The "Incorrigible Law" meant women could be sent to prison for subjective reasons, like being "unmanageable" or leading an "idle or dissolute life." What kind of message did laws like this send about how society viewed and controlled women in the 1960s?

2. Who do you think wrote the note that was delivered to Emily at the *Chatelaine* office?

3. Emily's editor, Doris Anderson, explained that she wrapped articles about big issues—like domestic abuse and birth control—in "fluff" like fashion tips, so "the men upstairs" wouldn't notice *Chatelaine*'s "radical" agenda. Do you think this was a necessary way for the magazine to push for women's rights in the 1960s, or did the focus on fashion and decorating undermine the serious topics?

4. How would you describe *Liberty Street* to a friend? What are the novel's major themes?

5. If you were Emily and expected to marry Jem and quit your job, how would you have felt? Do you think you would've chosen to do what she did?

6. If you were creating a soundtrack or playlist for *Liberty Street*, what songs would you include?

7. Dr. Eris Stone engaged in massive corruption and abuse towards the women imprisoned at Mercer. What allowed Dr. Stone to get away with this level of crime and sadism within a government institution?

8. Who would you cast in the screen adaptation of *Liberty Street*?

9. How would you describe the character of Emily? What about the character of Rachel? How are these two women, separated by decades, similar to each other? How are they different?

10. What did you think of the character of Doris Anderson?

11. The truth of what happened to Walter Jr., Mary's brother, is never made clear. What do you think really happened to him?

12. Heather Marshall has written a historical novel with two timelines, one set in the 1960s and the other in the late 1990s. Does this book feel relevant in our current day? Do you think it will feel relevant 30 years from now?

13. Which of the women incarcerated at Mercer were you most drawn to? Who were you least drawn to?

14. What is the significance of the title of this novel?

15. There are many turning points in *Liberty Street*. What do you think was the climax of the story?

16. Who did you relate to more, Emily or Rachel?

17. How does *Liberty Street* fit into its author's body of work?

18. What do you think happened to Rachel after the book ends?